BRENNA'S HEART WAS POUNDING WITH FEAR.

"Get back!" she said sharply. "Are you a fool to brave my blade?"

A smile curled his mouth but didn't reach his eyes. "And would you stab me before the wedding?"

"Aye. I would slit you from navel to chin with no less haste," she hissed at him.

"Then do it, *demoiselle*." This time the smile reached his eyes, and he moved closer.

He was tall, very tall, and his shoulders were broad, filling out the fine velvet of his tunic. A broadsword hung from a wide leather belt at his side, seeming out of place with the elegant clothes, yet fitting for a man with such a hard face. Brenna felt a thrum of apprehension.

There was an unholy beauty about him, a silent promise of ruthless determination and masculine appeal that made Brenna's throat tighten. She stared at him without blinking, fascinated.

"Do you approve, my lady?" came the slightly mocking question.

Brenna straightened immediately. "What do you want with me?" By this time, every nerve in her body screamed at her to flee, but she refused to have anyone think she was a coward.

Ignoring her first question, his reply was short. "I want you, *demoiselle*. . . ."

LYON'S PRIZE

LYON'S PRIZE

Virginia Lynn

BANTAM BOOKS | NEW YORK
TORONTO · LONDON · SYDNEY
AUCKLAND

LYON'S PRIZE

A Bantam Fanfare Book/October 1992

ISBN 0-553-29691-4

Published simultaneously in the United States and Canada

To Ducci Mastro,
a loyal fan, and newfound friend.
I cherish your support and friendship—
and your love of romance!

LYON'S PRIZE

PROLOGUE

England, 1066

OCTOBER WINDS WERE cold. Ten year old Brenna of Marwald shivered as she tugged her cloak more tightly around her body and tried to stay out of the way. The stockade teemed with activity. After being gone for over a fortnight, her father had returned late the night before. Now he made ready to ride again.

Dunstan was mounted on a fresh horse, and he looked weary. Behind him, her brothers Rannulf and Whitley stepped into their saddles. Ridgely and Corbet led fresh mounts, while Myles sulked because he was too young to ride with the rest of his brothers.

Brenna ran up to Rannulf and tugged at his boot. "Why are you leaving again so soon? You've only just come back from fighting the Norsemen! Where are you going?"

Rannulf reined in his horse and looked down impatiently. "Hawking, little goose. Where do you think we go? With William in Pevensey, and half our men still traveling from Stamford Bridge in York, we have time aplenty on our hands." Brenna flushed with anger at his derisive snort.

"Leave her be, Rannulf," Dunstan ordered; his eyes

were troubled when he gazed at his only daughter. "We go hawking, child. Stay with your mother."

"But why can't you—"

"Stay with her," Dunstan replied shortly, then nudged his mount through the open wooden gates of the stockade. Rannulf and her other brothers followed, leaving Brenna to stare after them.

Her steps were slow when she went back inside. It seemed empty without her father and brothers; most of the soldiers had gone with them two weeks before. Only a handful of servants were left, and those spoke in quiet tones about the bastard Duke of Normandy who had landed on English shores. Brenna shivered again, but not from the cold.

Change was in the air, and she was frightened. Her mother lay in childbed upstairs, and her father was hawking. Their faithful maidservant Gytha was with Lady Clarice, but no one would tell Brenna anything. She'd heard her mother's soft voice laced with pain, and that made her frantic. Even Brenna's friend Hlynn was nowhere to be found, and she was quite alone with her fears.

She huddled against the door of her mother's bed-chamber and wished once again that someone would tell her what was happening inside. No one seemed to have the time for a small girl, not when Lady Clarice's time had come. The midwife set everyone to tasks, and servants scurried back and forth.

Brenna bent her legs and rested her chin on her knees. She wished her father were here. Though usually gruff and frightening, he might serve as protection against her nameless fears.

A shudder pranced down her spine when she heard her mother cry out hoarsely, and Brenna squeezed her eyes closed to hold back ready tears. She would not cry. Her mother had said she must not, so she would not give in to tears. When there was another cry, louder and shriller this time, Brenna put her hands over her ears to block it out.

Where is Father?

She surged to her feet at another cry, then hesitated. After a moment to gather her courage, she pushed open the heavy oak door and stepped inside. Oil lamps cast smoky light, and the central fire in a huge brass brazier smelled of herbs that the midwife was burning. Brenna stepped closer to the wide bed and caught a glimpse of her mother's writhing form.

Mistress Maisie was at the foot of the bed Lady Clarice had brought from Normandy as part of her dowry, and no one noticed the child in their midst. Brenna's gaze fastened on her mother.

Clarice's face was deathly pale, and her lip was bleeding where she'd chewed it. Beads of sweat dotted her forehead despite the room's chill.

"The babe's turned," Mistress Maisie said, and she glanced up at Gytha with a worried frown. "If we cannot turn it . . ."

"We must." Gytha grasped her mistress's hands. "Do your best to save her."

Brenna, unnoticed in the peril of the moment, hid behind the bed curtains at the head of the bed. As Mistress Maisie bent to her work, Lady Clarice's body arched. An agonized scream cut into the air and Brenna's heart. She closed her eyes, choking back a sob, listening to her mother's cries for what seemed like an eternity.

Finally it grew quiet, and she heard the midwife mutter that the child was a boy. "A big one, as are all of Dunstan's get," she added grimly. "Fair tore her in two, I fear."

A thin wail cut into the air, and Maisie held up the ruddy child. "Healthy as an ox, for all that he's killed his mam."

Gytha was weeping. "She bleeds, mistress. See how the bed is soaked? We must stop it."

"We've given her the gall of an oak," Mistress Maisie replied. " 'Tis all that can be done for now. Have her drink the potion every hour. P'raps 'twill save her."

Lady Clarice lay quietly. Her face was so pale, so colorless. Brenna crept forward to stare at her mother.

At last Gytha noticed the small girl. "Brenna! Dear God, lambkin—what do you here?"

"Do not make me leave, Gytha. I want to see my mother."

The old woman hesitated, then said kindly and sadly, "Stay, child. Hold her hand and tuck the furs round her to keep her warm."

Brenna sat on a small stool and held Lady Clarice's hand and tucked furs around her shivering body. She stroked back the dark hair from her forehead and crooned soft words.

"Don't leave me, Mother. You're all I have. . . ." She choked on the words, fear rising dark and sharp inside her. Her mother could not die, could not leave. She'd seen death and knew it was irrevocable. No one ever returned once they'd died.

"Mother . . . Mother, can you hear me?"

An answering squeeze of her hand made Brenna lean close, her gold eyes misted with grateful tears when her mother opened her eyes.

"Brenna . . . sweet child . . . do not weep for me."

Lady Clarice's voice drifted into an indistinct mutter that made Brenna edge nearer to hear the faint whispers from her pale, bloodless lips. Her mother's hand was cold, so cold, the fingers like slim, delicate icicles in her palm. She held her hand with a tight grip, trying to give her some of her own warmth.

"Mother, you'll be well soon," Brenna said with desperate conviction. "I know you will be. Rest, and when Father returns from hawking, he can carry you downstairs to your chair by the fire."

Lady Clarice laughed hollowly, the sound eerie and bitter as it emerged from that pale, waxen face.

"*Non, ma pauvre petite.* I will not go downstairs again."

"But you will, Mother, you *must*." Brenna looked to Gytha, seeking further assurances, but the old woman was weeping into her hands, her bent shoulders shaking. A frown creased the child's brow, and she turned her gaze back to her mother. "Mother?" she said tentatively, but Lady Clarice had lapsed back into a faint.

She was still holding her mother's hand when she died.

Gytha sobbed loudly. Brenna, remembering that her mother had said not to weep, stared dry-eyed as the maidservants tenderly cared for their lady.

After Mistress Maisie had wrapped the infant in clean cloths and given him to a nursemaid to suckle, she came to Brenna and knelt beside her. With an awkward hand, she touched a loose strand of Brenna's red-gold hair, letting it slip through her work-worn fingers. Her voice was sad and helpless.

"I did all I could for your mother, child. I'm sorry."

"It wasn't you who killed her," Gytha interrupted bitterly. " 'Twas that great uncaring ox of a husband! Dunstan, aye, he has slain her as surely as if he smote her with his sword, I vow. I hope the devil takes him for this work."

"Not in front of the child," Maisie said sharply. "I know ye're overwrought, Gytha, but have a care as to the child."

Weeping, Gytha said in a barely recognizable voice, "I have been with my lady since she was a babe, and now she's gone. This is too great a burden for me."

No one tried to stop Brenna when she left her mother's chamber. She went to stand outside in the cold wind and stared into the gathering shadows of dusk.

As she stood there, she swore silently that no man would ever do to her what her father had done to her mother.

"Nay," she said aloud, clenching her hands into tight fists at her sides, "I will never die like that!"

CHAPTER 1

England, Winter 1076

" 'TIS NO MATTER to me if the king lays waste to these lands, or all of England." Brenna shrugged; long coppery ribbons of unbound hair shimmered in the light from the fire. She kept her amber eyes riveted on her father's face, as willing to face him with her defiance as she was willing to voice it. "I will not marry a Norman cur. I will not bed the enemy, as you seem wont to do."

The hall grew quiet. Servants slunk silently away, and minstrels left with their lutes tucked under their arms. A few dogs whined, and feet scraped uneasily over rushes strewn on the dirt and stone floor.

Lord Dunstan rose slowly from his carved wooden chair. His face was red, his bulky body intimidating to most of his servants. They all feared their lord's wrath and his heavy hand, and watched as he approached his daughter.

Brenna kept her chin lifted and her face composed. He did not frighten her. She knew him too well to allow him to frighten her. What were a few bruises to her?

"You defy me?" he thundered, his voice booming even in the cavernous hall.

It seemed to echo; Brenna's eyes narrowed slightly,

7

and she idly fingered the hilt of the small dagger hanging from the links of the girdle around her slender hips.

"Aye," she said quietly, "I defy you."

Her father's hand tightened around the riding whip he carried, and he lifted it threateningly. Brenna did not flinch away or even blink. She met his furious stare with a steady gaze that gave him pause.

"Ye're a shrewish wench," Lord Dunstan snarled finally, and lowered the whip with a frustrated jerk. "But ye'll wed whom I tell ye to wed. And ye'll wed *when* I tell ye to wed, by all the saints, or so help me—I'll see ye whipped to shreds!"

"I tremble with fear," Brenna mocked. She was fiercely glad to see the slow flush suffuse her father's face, and she took a step closer. "Nay, Dunstan of Marwald, you won't frighten me with a few blows or bruises. You know I'm right, and you know I'll kill any man you choose for me before I meekly submit to him."

Her throat worked for a moment, but her voice was still cool when she paused only a foot away from her father and said softly, "I'll not die bearing brat after brat for some overlord too cruel to care about me. I'm not one of those soft women who'll allow a man to tear the life from them. Nay, if I die, 'twill be of my own choosing, and 'twill not be in childbed while my lord is off hawking or wenching."

"Brenna—"

"Nay!" The single word was torn from her. "I saw what you did to my mother. I'll not suffer the same."

Lord Dunstan put a heavy hand on her shoulder, holding her when she would have left; his pale gaze pierced her calm, but she did not allow him to see it.

" 'Twas not my will what happened to my lady, and I'll not be chastised for it by ye." His blunt, thick fingers dug painfully into her tender skin, and his eyes narrowed. "We have a stark king now, a harsh man who has decreed that ye will wed one of his men to bind Saxon and Norman together. In this I agree with William. Ye will wed, Brenna, whether ye wish it or not. I'll not risk the lands I've regained because ye fear the touch of a man."

"Damn you!"

"Nay, listen—ye're well past marriageable age, but we have been given three months to choose a husband, or one shall be chosen for ye." His mouth curled slightly. "If *I* choose, daughter, I will see to it that ye have a man strong enough to discipline ye as I have been unwilling to do."

Her head tilted back, her hair flowing like silken fire over her shoulders. Tawny eyes blazed at him. "Unwilling to do? Or too cowardly?"

It was a deliberate taunt.

Dunstan's broad palm caught her across one cheek. The blow sent her to her knees. "Aye, ye're a shrew sure enough, and I pity the man who weds ye," he growled. Brenna grabbed a wooden bench and pushed the hair from her eyes to face him. "Get to your chamber, Brenna," Dunstan ordered, "and pray for proper humility."

"I'll never be humble, nor will I ever cower before you or any other man," she replied in a half snarl that made Dunstan's eyes narrow. His anger faded into baffled uncertainty at her continued defiance. Sensing victory, Brenna slowly rose, thrusting out her chin. Her father gave a muffled oath.

Brenna laughed. "I'll kill any man you choose, so beware you do not bestow my hand on a powerful man with vengeful relatives."

She whirled away from him, ignoring the gaping, terrified faces that gazed at her as she walked from the hall with her head held high. Fools. Let them stare. Let them whisper that she was a shrew, a termagant, devil possessed. She didn't care. She didn't care what anyone thought. And she would not wed.

Her feet scuffed across the rush-strewn floor as she left the hall behind her, glad to be quit of the huge room with its brawling men and dogs. She hated most of them; she'd hated almost everything since her mother's death.

Brenna steeled herself against the pain of her mother's memory as she mounted the new stone stairs to her second-floor chamber. Since her mother's death, Brenna had never been the same. Dunstan and her brothers had changed, too, hardened into bitter men of few principles. The years they had all spent as hostages in Normandy had taken their toll.

Brenna shut the chamber door and crossed to the high window slit. Her hatred and defiance had earned her the name of shrew; it was well deserved. Yea, she admitted it freely. It kept suitors at bay, mewling, weak men who could not meet her scornful gaze nor fend off her scathing words. They shrank from it, cowered under the sharp lash of her tongue.

Her fingers dug into the stone window ledge, and her throat grew tight as she gazed past the bailey of the new keep to the distant, rolling hills. It was still winter. In the spring they would come, men to seek her hand, to take the generous dowry King William offered for his hostage's hand in marriage.

She would be ready for them.

Noise filled the great hall; smoke from the central fire billowed up. Spurs jangled and swords clanked against wooden benches as knights, soldiers, and lords supped. Platters of meat disappeared as fast as they were brought to the long trestle tables, along with platters of fish pasties, dumplings, and frumenty. Dogs yapped and snarled underfoot for the scraps.

At the high table on the raised dais, Lord Dunstan sat with several of William's knights—and his daughter. Her gaze was fixed on a distant point, and she ignored the men at both sides of her. Minstrels sang praises to her beauty as she sat stiff and silent.

Halfway down the first table, sitting well above the salt, sat two of King William's men. They had arrived late and lingered to break bread. Capons, eels, roast pig, oxen, and goose graced the long table; men shared trenchers of meat and bowls of pudding. Jugs of mead, ale, and wine were quickly emptied.

Raoul de Beaumont grinned and nudged his companion and overlord with an elbow. "You were wise to choose to sit at a lower table, seigneur. I don't hear any songs about the sweet temper of this Saxon lord's daughter."

Rye de Lyon shrugged his broad shoulders. "I have not listened."

Beaumont speared a strip of meat with his poniard. "It's said she's a shrew, and that she has vowed to kill the man who weds her." He chewed his meat with relish. "Which might explain the lack of suitors, save yon foolish knight."

Lyon's gaze drifted to the long table on the dais, where the old lord sat with his daughter. A troublesome woman held no interest for him. He gave a grunt of dissatisfaction.

"Who is the knight?" With a faint frown of concentration, he eyed the man. "He looks familiar."

"Saher St. Maur. He lusts after the girl almost as much as he lusts after her dowry and William's favor." Beaumont grinned. "If he weds her, it may be the last wench he ever tumbles."

Lyon, one dark brow lifting skeptically, glanced at his companion. "Do you truly think a mere woman could best a seasoned knight?"

"This is no mere woman. Look at her." Beaumont gestured to the table. "She's tall, and it's said that she wields a dagger like a man. She even rides her stallion astride like a man. No doubt, her husband may find it most difficult to ride her, though 'twould be a challenge to sit that fine a mare. . . ."

Lyon's attention drifted from Beaumont's laughing, bawdy comments back to the girl. She was lovely. It was the sulky expression on her face that made her less than beautiful. Her unbound hair streamed over her shoulders in a fiery river of light, and softly rounded breasts thrust out the gunna and kirtle she wore. A golden girdle of finely woven links circled slender hips, and a jewel-encrusted dagger caught the light from the fire and threw it back in sharp splinters of colored flame.

He shifted, frowning. It was at William's suggestion he was here, though he'd not divulged that information to young Beaumont. This was, after all, his own choice to make, and he didn't want any unwanted advice in either direction. William had already made it plain that the final decision was up to him, that it was meant to be an honor. Other than the slimmest of details, he knew almost nothing about this Brenna of Marwald.

Except that she was beautiful and angry.

"Tell me more about her," Lyon said, interrupting Beaumont's obscene monologue. "What is said of her?"

"Seigneur, I thought everyone in England had heard of this Brenna of Marwald and her vow to kill the man who dares wed her."

"Nay, Raoul." Lyon shook his dark head. "I was told only that she must wed William's man."

"Aye," Beaumont said then, "I'd forgotten that you were in Normandy so long battling d'Esteray for your father's lands. You are the victor, I presume?"

Flicking him a sardonic glance, Lyon murmured, "Of course. D'Esteray is as big a fool as was his father. That was not what delayed me, Raoul, but a skirmish for William in Anjou."

"Aye, and he will reward you well for that last." Beaumont looked at his friend speculatively. "So why the surly temper?"

"I'm always ill-tempered." Rye shrugged. "Tell me more about this foolish Saxon wench who insults our barons."

Faintly surprised, Beaumont flicked an uneasy glance from his companion to the girl. "She is not for you," he began, then flushed at Lyon's quick, hard stare. "What I meant was that you'd want to kill her before the cock crowed. She has a sharp tongue, and she's not afraid to say what she wishes."

"Are you hinting that she might throw my parentage —or lack of it—in my face?"

"Aye, my lord. She would, and not think twice about

it." He couldn't quite meet Lyon's narrowed gaze. "She told Periault that he was fat and riddled with the pox. Gervaise heard that his mother was a sow and his father a wastrel." Shrugging, Beaumont said, "Scarcely a man in England has escaped her barbed tongue."

A faint smile tugged at the corners of Lyon's hard mouth. "She would not say such things to me but once."

"P'raps not, my lord, but say them she would."

Lyon stretched lazily, dragging a thumb across the stem of his wine goblet in an idle motion. "Tell me what you know about her dowry, Raoul. I have heard some, but would hear what others say."

Beaumont spoke reluctantly. " 'Tis said that William will return to her two keeps, one newly rebuilt of stone and one a small dirt donjon common to the Saxons. Both are located at strategic points on heavily traveled roads and collect a great deal in tolls. They once belonged to her mother, a Norman. After Hastings and her mother's death, she was sent to Normandy as hostage, along with her father and three brothers. The girl was given to her mother's people to raise and has only recently returned to England at William's command. Ten wagonloads of goods are to go with her, as well as three chests of gold and jewels. At Moorleah William has begun fortifying the stone keep as a bridal gift."

"She's fortunate to be a wealthy Saxon in these times," Lyon murmured. His heavy-lashed eyes widened slightly, and he examined Raoul de Beaumont's troubled expression. "So you do not think I should offer for the lady, *mon ami*?"

"Nay." Beaumont softened his blunt reply with another shrug. "I think it would displease William to have you kill her. Dunstan was once a powerful Saxon baron, who has now sworn liege-homage to William. Our king has said that her alliance with a Norman will help bind the two countries together."

Lyon snorted. "I've seen evidence of *binding* all over England. There are a sight too many dark-haired bastards in every keep we've visited."

"Aye, I'll grant you that. But William's intent is to mix Saxon with Norman until the powerful barons would hesitate to war against their own families."

"As in Normandy?" came the mocking question. His companion smiled when Rye added, "I'm still fighting those 'family' battles in Maine and Anjou. William has big dreams."

"Aye."

Lyon drank his wine and let his gaze shift once more to the fiery-haired woman. He rubbed absently at a thin scar curving from his left eyebrow to the angle of his cheekbone. " 'Tis what got William all of England at his feet," he murmured to himself, "those dreams."

Duke William of Normandy, bastard son of Duke Robert the Magnificent, had taken England from the Saxons and ground it beneath his heel. But he had yet to grind all the English barons down, and must slowly ally them to his side, putting down rebellion after rebellion. It had been ten years since he'd been crowned king in Westminster Abbey, and in that time bands of defiant Saxons had risen against him again and again.

This warring baron, Lord Dunstan, had been made hostage and forced to swear liege-homage to William. Though he could count himself fortunate to still be alive, it was humiliating to be stripped of sword and spurs and forced to bend a knee to William with uncovered head, putting his hands between William's and vowing to be the king's man from that day hence, to serve with life and limb and all due honor. Lord Dunstan was now William's vassal, and if called upon to war for him, would be required to provide men and arms and himself.

In the years since William had been crowned, England had suffered greatly. At first the Saxons were stripped of all property. Gradually those Saxons with high connections that William considered suitable for his purposes were being allowed to live on their own lands, or on others he granted them. So far, only a scant few had been able to do so. And of those few, all had offered aid to William or been bound to him by lieu of sons in his service.

Lord Dunstan of Marwald had been fortunate in keeping his life after Hastings, if not his freedom. Four of his sons had escaped capture and drifted from place to place like common vagabonds since William's conquest. Six years passed until Dunstan finally swore fealty and William freed him, sending him back to Marwald with Brenna to build a new keep. Because of his Norman wife and her connections, Dunstan had not been cast out completely. Most Saxon nobles were now largely indistinguishable from the peasantry. But now—now, it seemed as if Dunstan might be able to rise to power again, through the marriage of his daughter to a man of William's choosing.

Aye, Lyon thought, William was wise to require more than just a simple oath from these Saxon barons. Hostages ensured that the rebels would heed their oaths. William had cleverly wrung a reluctant agreement from Dunstan to wed his daughter to a Norman in exchange for reclaiming some of his former lands—and keeping his hostage sons alive and well in Normandy. Yet his unruly daughter seemed determined to flout his authority. It appeared her years as a hostage in Normandy had not tempered her hatred of Normans.

"Why does her father not beat her into submission?" Lyon wondered aloud.

Beaumont laughed. " 'Tis said he saves that pleasure for her husband."

"It seems that St. Maur has decided to forgo that pleasure," Rye observed. Beaumont's eyes followed his gaze.

St. Maur had shot to his feet, his face red with fury, his eyes blazing and one hand resting on the hilt of his sword. The object of his wrath gazed up at him with open contempt. When he said something to her in a low, fierce voice, she looked deliberately away from him and yawned. St. Maur wheeled and stalked from the hall, ignoring the faint titters that followed him.

Rye de Lyon watched closely as the girl listened with

lifted brows to her father's harsh words; before he'd finished speaking, she rose and walked gracefully from the hall, leaving her father sitting with his mouth still open.

She was tall and slender. Her unbound hair caught the light and threw it back in fiery rays, and the delicate structure of her face seemed much too fragile to belong to a woman with such a strong will. Lyon smiled.

"Yea, I'll wed her," he said softly, and when Beaumont drew back in horror as if he'd just said he intended to wed a witch, he added, "And I'll tame her."

Crossing himself, Beaumont muttered, "You'll be drawn and quartered for murdering William's pawn is what you'll be, Rye de Lyon. You're either mad or a fool."

"And which do you think, *mon ami*?"

Beaumont, taken aback by the question, took a moment to respond. "Mad, mayhap. Fool, never. But brave you'll have to be. That woman is a she-cat, seigneur."

"And who better to tame a mere cat than a lion?"

"She won't have you."

"Oh, she'll have me." Drumming his fingers against the scarred wood of the table, Lyon repeated softly, "She'll have me."

He pushed away from the table and strode from the hall, his steps following Dunstan's daughter.

Brenna was quivering with fury and humiliation. To be auctioned off like a cow was humiliating. No matter that the custom was commonplace, nor that William had placed a high value on her. She was not like other women. She would never be like other women.

The years after her mother's death had been harsh ones, growing into a nightmare. She still dreamed about those horrible times, when Lady Clarice was scarcely buried and the Normans came to Marwald to loot, burn, and rape. Shudders racked her when she remembered it. All tenderness for her mother's countrymen had been banished by the cruelty of the invaders. From then onward she had despised the Normans, vowing never to surrender to them. Not like her father, who had bowed to the Norman invaders like the coward he was, she thought contemptuously. But she never would. She would show him how Saxons were supposed to live.

She sneered as she thought of St. Maur. He had been one of the easiest to unman. A few references to his lack of prowess on the field of battle, his questionable ancestry, and the paunch beneath his tunic, and he'd fled like a scalded cat.

Oh, she had done her work well in the past months and was grateful to Ballard for having helped her. Fair, witty Ballard. If not for the minstrel, she would not have had such an arsenal of weapons at her command. With the information he'd given her, she had managed to compose an impressive list of insults for every eligible suitor in William's court.

A faint smile eased the sting of humiliation that had been with her since her father's announcement that she would wed one of William's knights. To see those high-born Norman knights and barons reduced to quivering fury was worth it all.

Brenna began to mount the stairs leading to her chamber, one hand spreading over the smooth yellow velvet of her kirtle. The noise from the hall faded as she walked, though she could still hear the ridiculous ballads being sung in her honor.

William had set Dunstan back at Marwald with orders to fortify it well with stone. Workmen labored daily to erect high walls and dig an outer ditch, rebuilding the simple motte and bailey to an impressive fortress with two moats and impregnable stone buttresses. It seemed that the Norman king knew well how his subjects felt about him.

A burst of laughter erupted below, and Brenna's lip curled. Damn them. Damn them all.

When she reached the small square landing at the angle of the stairs, Brenna caught a glimpse of movement behind her. She turned quickly, her hand moving to the small poniard at her hip.

"Do not pull your weapon," the man said softly in the

Norman tongue, which Brenna understood as well as she did her own.

Brenna sucked in a sharp breath. A Norman, and he looked much too dangerous. And close. Her fingers closed around the hilt of her dagger, and she pulled it from the jeweled sheath in a smooth, graceful motion.

"Stay where you are," she commanded sharply in French. "I have no intention of allowing you within a foot of me. Stay, I said, or I'll shout for my father's guard."

"From what I saw of your father's anger at you, he would not lift a finger to stay me," the man replied with a sardonic twist of his mouth.

Brenna felt a spasm of fear shoot through her and was annoyed by it. Afraid? Of this man? Of *any* man? She jabbed the dagger in his direction.

"Stay away, or I'll slit you from gullet to gut!"

"Such sweet words, milady," the man mocked. He was only two stairs away now, and Brenna felt with her foot for the next stair up.

She looked at him closely. She did not recognize him and would have known if he'd been to Marwald before. No one could fail to remember this man.

He was tall, very tall, and his shoulders were broad, filling out the fine velvet of his tunic. A worked gold brooch held his mantle on one shoulder, and the hem swirled around lean, muscled legs. A broadsword hung from a wide leather belt at his side, seeming out of place with the elegant clothes, yet fitting for a man with such a hard face. Brenna felt a thrum of apprehension. A scar raked his face from eyebrow to cheekbone, slender and curved, giving his dark countenance an even more dangerous appearance. Beneath winged black brows, eyes of a startling blue pierced the air between them, thick-lashed and assessing.

There was an unholy beauty about him, a silent promise of ruthless determination and masculine appeal that made her throat tighten. She stared at him without blinking, fascinated in spite of herself.

"Do you approve, milady?" came the slightly mocking question, delivered in a husky voice.

Brenna straightened immediately. "Whoreson," she muttered in English before demanding in the French language he would understand, "Who are you? What do you want with me?"

By this time the man had reached the step where she stood, and she felt his proximity like a blow. Every nerve in her body screamed at her to flee, but she refused to act a coward. Particularly not before this mocking coxcomb with his fine clothes and neatly cropped hair.

"I want you, *demoiselle*."

Brenna stared at him. Her throat tightened as if a hand had closed around it. For a moment she thought she might actually faint. No. Not this man. He looked too hard, too savage. He did not look at all like a man who would be turned away with a few scornful words. It would take a great deal to turn this Norman knight from his purpose, she realized.

For the first time in years, Brenna was truly afraid of a man. She steeled herself. She could not let him know it. It would be fatal.

Her laugh rippled through the air, and she clutched her dagger tightly at the slight narrowing of his eyes. "Do you want me, sir? How very unfortunate for you." Edging up a step at a time, Brenna put some distance between them. She was not deceived by the man's seeming indolence. There was something about his pose that suggested a coiled spring. He was likely to leap on her without warning.

She reached the top step and flung back her head in defiance. "You won't have me, Sir Knight."

"I always get what I want."

It lay between them, that softly spoken statement, as certain and confident as sunrise. Brenna's mouth felt suddenly dry, and her heart slammed against her ribs. Yea, she'd been right. This man was dangerous.

"I'm afraid, sir, that you are doomed to disappointment this time." Her smile flashed briefly and falsely. "I do not wish to wed."

"That is of no importance to me." He moved at last, his powerful body shifting gracefully up the next stair. "Your king and your father have decreed that you will wed."

"And I do not obey lightly, sir." Brenna felt the last step at her heel, and took it. When she saw him move toward her again, she lashed out with the dagger, catching the velvet sleeve of his tunic and slashing it. Her heart was pounding with fear, and she hoped her legs did not give way beneath her. This man had not moved to avoid the blade, nor to catch her arm. He seemed completely indifferent to the threat she posed, and that was as infuriating as it was frightening.

"Get back!" she said sharply. She was no novice with a dagger; to amuse themselves her brothers had taught her to fight. Now the lessons stood her in good stead, and she balanced on the balls of her feet as she faced this bold-eyed Norman. "Are you a fool to brave my blade?"

A smile curled his mouth, but didn't reach his eyes. "You toy with a dagger. When you think to become serious, I will take it from you."

None of her disquiet showed in her voice when she spat, "I am serious now."

"And would you stab me before the wedding?"

"Yea. I would slit you from navel to chin with no less haste," she hissed at him.

"Then do it, *demoiselle*." This time the smile reached his eyes, and he moved closer.

Brenna stared at him uncertainly. Perhaps he didn't believe that she really would use the dagger on him. He wouldn't be the first to feel the bite of her steel. There had been the overeager suitor who'd thought to dishonor her, thus forcing her into a marriage. He'd worn bandages on his arm for a month after. Now this bold man *dared* her to do it.

"I will," she said softly, and felt the hilt of her poniard slide reassuringly against her palm. "I've no love for Normans. Nay, I've no love for any man. 'Twould give me great pleasure to do what you seem to think I won't."

"Not won't." Amusement glittered in cold blue eyes, the exotic eyes of the devil. "Can't."

Stung, Brenna swung the dagger up, intending to slash his other sleeve and maybe draw a bit of blood along with it, just to show him.

To her astonishment the dagger was sent skittering down the steps in a clatter of metal and bone, and the Norman was gripping her wrist so tightly she gasped with the pain of it.

"Let go of me. . . ."

"Aye, lady." He dragged her slowly to him. "When I'm through with you."

His face was only inches from hers, and she had no warning of what he intended until his dark head bent and he grazed her lips with his mouth. Stunned into immobile fury, Brenna couldn't think for a moment. He dared kiss her without asking permission! Few had done that and gone away unmarked, and neither would this Norman.

When she tried to turn away, his hand folded over her jaw and held her tightly, forcing her lips apart. Before she could snarl a curse at him, he'd invaded her open mouth with his tongue, pillaging with a fiery heat that paralyzed her.

He seemed to take her shock for acquiescence and put a broad hand at the nape of her neck to hold her head still while he plundered her mouth. To Brenna's bewilderment, an odd, curling fire shot through her body. She gave an involuntary moan. When he lifted his head, the triumphant gleam in his eyes shamed her.

With her free hand curled into a fist, Brenna struck out at him. Jerking his head back, the Norman swore softly and grabbed this wrist as well.

"Release me, you lop-eared ass!" she snarled in English, but he only eyed her warily without lessening his grip. She bucked and heaved against him, but he remained as stolid as rock, balanced on the narrow stone step of the curving flight of stairs.

He pushed her back against the stone wall, pinning her against it, and she felt its chill through her clothes.

Her arms were trapped between them. His smile was lazy.

" 'Twill do you little good to fight me. Save yourself the trouble of it, *demoiselle*."

At his light, mocking words, Brenna redoubled her effort to push him away. She shoved the heels of her hands against his broad chest. It was like pushing at a mountain. He merely gazed down at her with one brow lifted in an inquiring slant.

Then she felt it, the proof of his desire, nudging at her belly as he held her to him. It shocked her into immobility for a moment, and her lashes flew up so that she gazed into his eyes. He returned her gaze coolly, though the deep blue color was hot and shimmering with enough fire to warm an entire village. To Brenna's shame, he seemed to sense her sudden fear and was cruel enough to lean even closer, pressing his hips against her stomach.

His movement snapped her out of her momentary shock.

"You cod's head," she blurted between gasps of air. She kicked at him, and had the brief satisfaction of seeing him wince when her foot stabbed into his shin. He shifted his legs, but her unerring aim caught him again, and this time he gave an audible grunt of pain.

"Have it your way," he growled an instant later, and Brenna felt the muscles in his arms flex.

He moved gracefully for so large a man, stepping back to sweep her from her feet in a smooth, effortless motion. Brenna gasped, but the sound was muffled by his mantle as he slung her over his shoulder. She kicked, feeling foolish and terrified and humiliated. Her feet struck his hard-muscled thighs, and one foot grazed his sheathed sword. She heard him grunt as her knee found his hard, muscled belly.

Without warning a broad palm descended upon her rump in a stinging slap that shocked her more than it hurt her. Brenna's loose hair obscured her vision, and she tried to lever herself up with her hands against his back, but failed. She had a disjointed view of gray stone steps as she was helplessly carried like a sack of grain over the shoulder of this enraging Norman.

"Put me down!" she shrieked, hitting at him wherever she could.

Again his hand descended, sending shooting splinters of pain down to her toes. She snatched at the hilt of his sword, but he knocked her hand away. Every move she made, he managed to counter until she was almost sobbing with frustrated fury. Stone walls careened past, and she had brief glimpses of the sputtering wall torches that lit the stairwell.

Slowly Brenna became aware of the increase of noise, of the sound of music and laughter, and then a sudden, startled silence. She closed her eyes and forced herself not to struggle as she realized he'd returned her to the hall. She could almost feel the incredulous stares of the guests and servants.

Curse him, whoever he was!

Brenna had a dizzying view of rushes, spilled food, elegantly shod feet, and then felt the sickening blur of being placed back on her feet. She half stumbled and felt a heavy hand steady her. Shrugging it angrily away, she took a step away from her tormentor.

"Don't touch me." She turned blindly, her father's astounded face swimming into focus. Brenna shook back her hair and would have moved to her father if not for the quick, steely grip on her shoulder that held her in place.

"Lord Dunstan," her tormentor's voice said coolly, "I come to press my suit with your daughter."

For a moment the old lord was speechless. He looked from his daughter's flushed, furious face to the man who had his hand on her so firmly.

"Your name, sir," he managed to say after a moment. He shot a wary glance at Brenna, who stood rigidly beneath the man's hand. "And an explanation, if ye please."

Switching from French to excellent English, the man said, "I am Rye de Lyon, Earl of Lyonfield."

Quiet greeted his reply. No one spoke until Brenna

gave an angry gasp. She was furious that he hadn't been courteous enough to use her language or indicate that he understood it, and even more furious that the man known as the Black Lion would dare come to court her. Her chin jutted up defiantly, and her eyes found his.

"I don't care who you are. You're the king's man."

Lyon made her a brief half bow, not releasing her. "As are we all, milady."

"Nay," she spat. "Not so!"

"Hold your tongue, daughter," Dunstan snarled at her with an air of quiet desperation. "He is a guest at Marwald, and the king's man. Ye'll show respect."

Brenna stared at her father with contempt. "I will show him my back, as any good Saxon should do."

"I do not think so," Lyon said quietly. His grip tightened on her arm. "Gently, *demoiselle*. I mean you no harm."

"Do you not? Then you are unlike any Norman knight I've ever known," she taunted. "You are rough, cruel beasts, with thoughts of nothing save your own pleasure."

"I'm not like any man you've ever known," he replied with an amused lift of his brow. "Do not think it for an instant."

Breaking into the tension between them, Dunstan asked in a curt tone, "D'ye mean to court my daughter, my lord?"

"Nay, I meant no such thing." Lyon seemed amused. "I mean to wed her, not court her."

Brenna trembled with anger. "I'll not mix my blood with a Norman knight of William's! You're all alike, rogues, murderers and worse, and—"

"Do not say it." His hand clamped down cruelly on her wrist, threatening to snap the fragile bones. " 'Tis a waste of breath and my patience."

Brenna saw the warning in his cold blue eyes and surprised herself and everyone else by lapsing into silence.

She stood mute while her father hesitated, then accepted the marriage proposal on his daughter's behalf. He sounded relieved. Only then did Brenna speak, and her gaze shifted from Lyon to Dunstan. Her voice shook slightly, and she spoke in slow, measured English to be certain her father understood.

"I told you what I would do. So be it. It's on your head if you force me to wed."

Dunstan shifted nervously, scowling at her. He wet his lips and glanced at Lyon. "My lord, I feel I must warn ye—"

"I've heard about her promise." Lyon's grip eased a bit on Brenna's wrists, and he smiled slightly. "Some promises are more easily made than kept."

Brenna met his gaze steadily. Her tawny eyes sparkled with golden glints as she said, "I've no doubt I can keep that promise, my lord."

CHAPTER 2

"D'YE KNOW WHO he is?" Dunstan roared, staring at his daughter's implacable face with a baffled, frustrated glare. "The man holds so much power in the palm of his hand, 'tis said that even Odo courts his favor."

"Power is not the same thing as courage." Brenna kept her cool gaze on the courtyard below the window. "And the king's brother is a spineless fool. All know that."

Dunstan snorted. "It matters not if the man has courage. He is an earl—"

"A bastard earl!" Brenna flashed. " 'Tis not the same thing."

"It is if William decrees it, and ye need not forget that he was born of a tanner's daughter himself. He would not take lightly your refusal on those grounds, daughter, so do not think it." He frowned. "Who tells ye such tales? Ballard? The coxcomb. He should stick to singing of lost love and battles instead of whispering sly tales in your ear. Listen well, Brenna. Lyon means to have ye, and William will not say him nay. Though why the earl wants ye escapes me. He must not have heard what a shrew ye are, or how ye torment those who would be kind to ye."

"Kind?" Brenna turned slowly to face her father. "What would you know of kindness? Do not prate of kindness to me as if I should be shamed for not leaping at the chance to wed a man who has handled me roughly —yet still not so roughly as my own father."

"Ye've deserved every blow I've given ye, and if I've not used the buckle end of my belt on ye as ye deserve at times, I've lived to regret it!"

"I pray you live so long," Brenna said softly. Her throat ached with pent-up anger and emotion, and she turned away again so he would not see how he affected her. Damn him. She stared out the slitted window without seeing the activity in the courtyard below.

"Fool!" Dunstan's fist slammed against the table between them. "Ye will wed the man, by all the saints, or I'll see ye wrapped in chains!"

"Chains, Father? You'd put your own blood in chains to wed the enemy?"

"Aye, that I would," he growled. "I'll not let ye destroy my chance to regain all that was lost to me. A man is nothing without land and power."

As she turned toward him, her lips drew back from small white teeth in a feral snarl that took Dunstan by surprise. He watched her warily as she took a step closer, her hand resting on the hilt of her poniard. "Your lands, power, your stupid, petty wars that have cost us everything! What say you now, Father, when William the Bastard decrees that you war for him instead of your own gain?" She laughed bitterly. " 'Tis not the same, is it?"

"Nay, but it still furthers my cause." Dunstan's reply was a low growl, and it was obvious he smarted under William's heavy hand. But it would be futile to fight the Norman king. Dunstan had not lived this long by being foolish, and he knew that the Normans would crush him if he resisted, as they had crushed so many of the other Saxon barons.

He balled his hand into a fist and dragged in a deep, calming breath. "Brenna, ye've not yet learned an important lesson. Yielding is not always the coward's way out. Ofttimes a gentle yielding is a victory of sorts."

She tossed her proud head. "I saw the way my mother yielded. A babe in her belly every year, until she died of it. Nay, not for me, that bitter end."

Dunstan dragged a hand over his face and shook his head. "If ye anger this lord, he will not suffer it well. Ye endanger yourself needlessly, and my cause with it. Ye could win much with honeyed words, instead of venom."

"I'll not bow to him."

" 'Tis said he could have any woman, Norman or Saxon, yet he came and chose ye to wed. 'Tis an honor."

"An honor?" Brenna began to tremble. Her wide amber eyes took on the sheen of tears, though she would not allow them to fall. "You'd deem it an honor for your daughter to lie with the enemy? With a man who's called bastard?"

"Do not be so foolish as to bring that up in front of him, Brenna," Dunstan growled. "I will not take responsibility for your idiocy if ye do." He caught her by the wrist and held her fast. " 'Tis said the king lopped off men's hands and feet for daring to mention his heritage. D'ye think that this man would be as kind?"

"This man is not king."

"Nay, but he has the king's ear. He doesn't need to be brave or strong or powerful, not as long as he has William at his side. God's blood, but I do not know why he wishes to saddle himself with such a vile-tempered shrew, but if ye were the sweetest-natured wench in the world and he wanted ye, I'd not be able to say him nay."

"Coward!" The word was flung at him bitterly, and he released her with an angry shove.

"Ye've none of yer mother's sweet temper in ye, I vow, yet ye're a comely wench and could gain much by curbing your vile nature." Dunstan sighed heavily. " 'Tis up to ye how your life goes, Brenna. Court this lord with sweet words, and he may respond in kind. Give him the sharp side of your tongue, and any man would treat ye cruelly."

"Excellent advice, Father. I shall remember it when I stick my dagger between his ribs."

Waving a weary hand, Dunstan sank into his chair and dismissed her. Brenna fled the hall gladly. She was so near angry, frustrated tears that she could think of little other than escaping to her chambers. Damn this Rye de Lyon! Why had he come to Marwald? And why had he offered for her? He was already wealthy. What did he hope to gain?

Rye de Lyon knew the answer to that question. He knelt before his king and looked up with a rueful grin when William asked how it went with his intended bride.

"Beau sire, she is everything you said. And more. She has the most vicious tongue ever heard, and is over-proud."

William laughed. "I chose her master well, I think. Do you wish advice, Lyon?"

"From you, beau sire, I would take it."

"Brook no insults from the lady. Be fair, but stern. She will yield to you, as did my Maud to me."

Thinking of William's queen, the coolly regal Matilda of Flanders, Lyon recalled how William had taken a whip to her for her insulting refusal to wed him, hurling the taunting epithet of *bastard*. He could well understand the emotions behind such a harsh retaliation to a woman. He'd been called bastard too many times to count them, yet still fought his temper when it happened.

"My thanks for the advice, sire," Lyon said, rising from his knees to take an offered cup of wine. "Once we are wed, she will yield quickly enough."

William flashed him an amused smile. "Do you think so, Lyon?"

"Aye. No woman will gainsay me."

" 'Tis what I ofttimes thought. Before I wed." William took a deep swallow of his wine. "Now I would have you wed her soon. Her mother's sister has pressed hard for her niece to make a good marriage. If nothing else, to save her from her father's heritage." A faint smile touched his stern mouth, and Lyon had a brief impression of a meditating statue before William continued, "It seems that the fair Lady Brenna has not relented in her hatred of Normans at all, despite living in Normandy for seven years. Though well past the marriageable age, she has been trained to be a dutiful wife. She may have . . . ah . . . rough edges."

Rye's brow lifted sardonically. "Rough edges? From what I've seen, the lady would make a decent foot soldier. She wields a weapon most deftly."

"Lyon, if you do not wish to wed the woman, I will bind her to another. Your loyalty is true, and I would not cause you unnecessary misery."

Rye was silent for a moment. Then he said, "Nay, she'll suit me. Ofttimes a firm hand is all that's needed, and no heedless cruelty." He lapsed into silence again, then added with a twist of his lips, "Besides—I like the feel of her. I admit that my brief taste of her prickly charms left me wanting more."

The faint smile on William's face broadened into a grin. "Many a man has been caught in that perfumed trap."

"No woman has ever led me by a chain," Rye muttered with a scowl. "Brenna of Marwald will not do what others have not managed, no matter how fair. 'Tis only a passing fancy, but welcome since I am to wed her."

"Aye," William agreed in a thoughtful tone, eyeing his loyal vassal.

Lyon kept his face impassive, not wanting the king to see the desire he had for Brenna. Damn the wench, her frenzied struggle against him had aroused more than just rampant lust—he'd felt an unwilling admiration for her battle against greater odds. Hadn't he battled against greater forces since infancy? Aye, and he knew well what the maid felt. She would have to learn, as he had, that it would garner her much trouble in the process.

William cleared his throat. "The Lady Brenna has oft wavered on open rebellion. She was known to prefer the company of Saxon hostages to the more gentle conversation of her Norman aunt's ladies. Lady Bertrice has plagued me for some years to do something, but until recently I wasn't certain it would be wise."

"Because of her father and brothers."

William smiled slightly. "Aye. Dunstan was a powerful baron, and I would not like to have him forget his oath. He is not a stupid man, but he has seven sons. One was hostage with him but is yet a lad. Four are yet free. Those I do not trust and would like to have in chains. I still have the two youngest boys in my custody to keep Lord Dunstan's loyalty strong."

"'Tis the wisest course, I would think. Do you believe his free sons have the mettle of their sire?"

"They have not sworn fealty and have evaded capture. With their sister wed to you, they will surely see the advantage in allying with me. If not, we will put them down."

Lyon felt no compunction against crushing his future wife's brothers should they be foolish enough to rebel. Only in unity could England survive against Norway, Wales, France, and all those who sought to tear her from William's grasp. Still, his smile was rueful.

"I could wish the maid had a sweeter nature, beau sire. I do not think her family would take it well if I were to give her the treatment she deserves. She has unmanned so many of your knights and barons, that your army is in danger of being depleted."

"'Tis why I sent you to her," William replied with a comfortable smile. "You're in need of a Saxon wife, and I am in need of a loyal earl in that section of the country. Of late, bandits have taken to preying on villages and men, killing serfs and livestock and trampling crops. I suspect it to be displaced barons who are responsible but am not certain. At any rate, I want more strongholds built, better keeps than some of those dirt stockades. Moorleah is strategic. It guards the coast. I've seen to its strength with stones. You see that it is well fortified after you're wed."

They talked for a while of outlaws to be exterminated, of military plans, of battles fought and to be fought, and spoils gained for those already won. When Rye left the king, he better understood William's desire to wed one of his most loyal men to a Saxon termagant.

Like William, Rye was a bastard, but born of a Norman earl and a highborn noblewoman. And like William, Rye had fought his way up from infancy. Though the king had the stigma of being son to a tanner's daughter, there was no less stigma attached to being the bastard son of a noblewoman. So Rye had taken what he could from life, crushing those who opposed him. He'd chosen to follow William and offer his loyalty and arms, admiring the Wolf of Normandy and his persistence in the face of such overwhelming odds. Now, at almost thirty, Rye de Lyon had won lands to add to the title he'd inherited and fought to keep. And he was to have a wife for his troubles. A mirthless smile curved his hard mouth.

He'd little use for a woman, beyond a casual tumble. It had taken all his energies to follow William. It would still require a great deal from him to hold the lands he'd been bidden hold. And the wife he was to take demanded some thought. His business was war; though he came from a stark school where kindness was equated with weakness, he was not a cruel man. But neither was he a fool. Nay, Brenna of Marwald would find no kindness in him if she chose to be rash.

Rye scowled as the sudden memory of her soft curves against him made his body tighten unexpectedly. Lunacy, to allow his body's unschooled urges to rule his head. 'Twas indicative of the power of her charms that he even thought of her at all. But then, he'd never offered marriage before, so perhaps that was what caused his uneasiness.

Knotting his hand into a fist, Rye grazed it along the walls of the keep, paying no attention to the skin scraped from his knuckles. He had much to do yet. There were plans to be made, betrothals to swear, banns to be posted, keeps to fortify. Then he would settle the woman at Moorleah. She would stay there while he went about his business as always.

* * *

Trembling, Brenna walked the stone corridor to the hall with slow steps. She knew why she had been summoned. She was to make a formal acceptance of this Rye de Lyon's suit. She would not. She could not. Her brief encounter with him had been enough to prophesy her future should she be fool enough to accept. He would devour her, like the lion he was said to be. Nay, she would better go to a nunnery than give herself to that black knight!

She paused outside the doors to the hall. She could see the Normans waiting on her, the envoys sent with documents to seal their betrothal. In the past month she had thought—no, *prayed*—that the fierce knight had changed his mind. Now she knew he had not.

Her knees felt suddenly too weak to hold her, and she grasped the door to hold herself up. It would not do to let anyone know her fear. Not even her maids suspected that she was terrified of the man. He would kill her, for certain, but she would seek that death before she would yield.

Straightening her spine, Brenna entered the hall with her head held high. Her long coppery hair brushed against her hips as she walked, and folds of blue velvet flowed in a graceful rhythm around her long legs. She was tall, taller than some men, and had never tried to hide her height. She certainly didn't try now, not with the interested gazes of the Norman envoys observing her. Rye de Lyon would soon know her mettle, by the Holy Rood, he would!

"Daughter," Dunstan murmured with a nervous glance at her as Brenna took her seat beside him. "These men have come with the written contracts of marriage in their possession." He paused, and his look was meaningful. "Do you the honor of signing them, as I just have, and this will be a done matter."

Brenna sat stiff and silent. Her hands were folded meekly in her lap, and if not for the quick, fierce flare in her tawny eyes, one would have thought her merely pensive. Lifting long lashes to reveal the hot glitter in her eyes, she happened to meet the gaze of Raoul de Beaumont. She remembered him. He had been with Lyon before, a young man with a pleasant countenance, rather gentle.

She smiled softly at him and saw a wellspring of relief in his eyes. It was short-lived.

Turning to her father, Brenna rose from her stool in a graceful swish of velvet. Clasping her hands in front of her, she said in a voice loud enough to be heard throughout the quiet hall, "I shall not sign of my free will. I beg of you, my father and lord, do not ask me to wed with a man who is bastard."

There was a quick gasp, then a hush fell over the hall. As Brenna seated herself again on the low stool near her father's chair, the silence was broken.

"God's blood!" a Norman baron sputtered in French, stepping forward to glare at Dunstan, "do you dare?"

" 'Tis not my folly, but my daughter's," Dunstan said in a low growl, flashing her a furious glance. "She can sign her own name, and she will. I will see to it."

"I will not."

They stared at Brenna, at the hot splotches of color on her high cheekbones, and the tight set of her mouth. Her amber eyes flashed with stubborn fury. Raoul de Beaumont gave a shake of his head.

"My lady," he said softly, "I dare not take your answer back to my lord. Do you think a moment—'tis done, and does not need your signature to be completed. 'Tis a courtesy he is offering you. The king has decreed that you shall wed his man."

"I care no more for the king's wishes than I do your lord's," she said coldly. A fine fury burned in her. Lyon wanted her no more than she wanted him. He was merely obeying his king. Well, let him wed some goosehearted chit who'd stand for it. She would not!

Standing uncertainly below the dais, where Dunstan sat in cold rage and indecision, Beaumont looked up at him. "My lord Dunstan? What bid you tell my lord?"

"That his wife will be given to him as planned," the

old lord said after a moment. "Even if she be delivered to him in chains."

Obviously appalled, Beaumont wavered for a moment. "He will not be pleased," he murmured.

"Nay, no more than I am," Dunstan said heavily, "but the maid has a will of her own and will not listen. If I had another more sweet-tempered daughter, I would bid him wed her, but I do not. He has asked for Brenna of Marwald, and that, I am afraid, is whom he will get."

Rising shakily to her feet, Brenna faced Beaumont. Her voice quavered slightly, and she steadied it. "Do tell your lord that my dagger will find his heart or mine, it makes little difference to me. I will not wed him."

Beaumont's honest face paled. His dark eyes sought hers in earnest as he pleaded, "Fair lady, do not bid me tell my lord such as that. You ask for your own fate to be sealed, and I fear for you."

"Fear for me?" Her smile was cold. "Nay, Sir de Beaumont, fear for your lord. 'Tis his safety that is in jeopardy, not mine. I prefer harsh death to his touch."

Dryly Beaumont answered, "That may very well be what you receive, my lady. I will tell him of what you said this morn, though I am certain you will regret saying it."

It wasn't until she was once more back in her private chambers with her women that Brenna began to wonder what devil had prompted her to speak out so boldly. A simple, dignified refusal would have sufficed. Yet she had chosen to tweak the lion's nose and would surely suffer for it.

But there was something about Rye de Lyon that brought out the worst in her. Perhaps it had to do with his blatant masculine appeal, that devil's brow and the handsome face that had haunted her dreams since he'd kissed her on the stairwell. She'd felt his desire against her, knew that he wanted her, and this terrified her.

"Woe is me," she murmured softly. Her maid heard it and knelt in front of her.

"My lady? You are gravely troubled?"

Brenna bit her bottom lip. Her maid, a knight's

daughter who had come with her from Normandy, was one of the few people in whom Brenna sometimes confided.

"Aye, Rachel. I am afraid of this Norman bastard who would take me for his wife."

"What will he say when your message reaches him, my lady?" Rachel asked after a moment, and Brenna stared at the bright tapestry on the far wall.

"I am glad not to know," she murmured. " 'Tis best he is so far away."

By the time Beaumont reached London and Rye, he had decided to couch his statements in tactful terms that would defuse Lyon's anger. He hoped. Brenna of Marwald could not begin to know the tempest that would be stirred by her words if they reached the earl intact.

His hopes were for naught.

Entering the audience chamber where Rye sat deep in discussion with William over the placement of troops near the Scottish border, Beaumont waited silently. He was still dusty and covered with mud from his ride and considered cleaning up and coming back. But too soon for him, Rye was pushing aside his business and striding toward him.

Aware of the king in the background, Beaumont bent his knee and said, "It is a bad time, my lord. I shall come again when you are not occupied."

"Nay, Raoul. This is as good a time as any." His smile was brief. " 'Tis the king's wish to have this done quickly, too."

Beaumont drew a deep breath. "Messire, I do not bring signed documents."

"Dunstan did not sign?"

"Aye, lord, *he* signed."

"Well? Few women can read or write their names, Raoul. The Lady Brenna's mark will suffice."

"Aye, lord, but the Lady Brenna is well schooled in reading and writing."

Lyon absorbed this for a moment. His chiseled features hardened slightly. "Tell me what honeyed words the fair Brenna sent me."

Bending his head, Beaumont struggled between truth and tact. "She does not wish to wed you and asked that her sire not force her."

"That is not all she said, Beaumont. Do you think me a fool?"

Beaumont's head snapped up. "Nay, lord, but there is no need for you to hear all her unwise words."

From behind Lyon came a soft chuckle, and the murmured comment from William, "History repeats itself."

Lyon ignored his liege for the moment. His blue eyes stabbed at Beaumont, and his black brows gathered ominously. "I would hear her words exactly as she said them."

Indignation grew in Beaumont that he should be the bearer of such words, and anger sparked his retelling.

"She said, my lord, that her dagger would find your heart or hers ere she wed you, and that it made little difference. She does not intend to wed you."

"And that is all?"

"Nay." Steeling himself, he added stiffly, "She asked her father not to wed her to a man who is a bastard."

His eyes flicked nervously from Lyon to William, who bore the same aversion to that word. Neither man moved nor spoke for a moment, and Beaumont began to sweat. His tunic clung to him, and a drop ran down the side of his dusty face, turning dirt into mud.

"Do not kill the messenger, Lyon," King William chided when Rye's hand closed on the hilt of his sword. His voice was dry and faintly amused. " 'Tis best to berate your lady. I know this from experience."

Half turning, Rye forced himself to speak softly. "I had no intention of drawing my sword on poor Raoul. He looks like to die as it is." He flicked a glance at Beaumont. "Go, my weary friend. I bear you no ill will."

After a swift glance at Lyon, Beaumont backed from the room. He'd tried to warn the lady. Let her reap what reward she had earned.

"What do you plan, Lyon?" the king asked when they were alone.

"To bring the bitch to heel," was the swift, savage reply. William smiled.

"Do you think 'twill be easy? Brenna of Marwald seems a bit high-spirited."

Shoving one fist into the other, Rye paced the large chamber for a moment; his dark face was creased with fury. "Aye, she is spirited, but not stupid. She will yield or die."

"So she has said."

Swinging his startled glance toward William, Lyon let his muscles relax slowly. Fury rode him hard, but he would not let it rule him.

"It is said, beau sire, that when your queen was as insolent as this lady, you rode all night to reach Lille."

"Aye, Lyon, I did. And when I found her, I used my whip on her." A faint smile curved William's mouth. "She said later that I dared much to come into her father's palace and beat her."

"Did you consider that before you acted?"

"Nay. Not at all. I had something else on my mind." His smile was cold, and Rye understood.

"I would ask a favor, sire."

"Speak."

"A special license. To wed without wait. Do I have it?"

William grinned. "Aye, Lyon, you have it. But bring me the document, and I will sign."

A scribe was summoned, and the documents Beaumont had brought were signed and sealed, along with a special license for marriage.

Lyon bowed before his king. "With your leave, beau sire, I ride for Marwald."

Having received the king's permission, Rye de Lyon strode from the hall and into the bailey, shouting for his horse and men. He turned to find Raoul de Beaumont at his side.

"I will ride with you, seigneur," the young man said.

"If you desire it. I ride to Marwald."

"Yea, I thought as much."

There was a thoughtful light in Beaumont's eyes that made Lyon smile. "You do not approve, Raoul?"

"I fear for the outcome, my lord."

"There is only one outcome. She will wed me, and she will cease her insults." He tapped his riding crop across his palm and found Beaumont's gaze on it. "Aye, Raoul, 'tis what she deserves, don't you think?"

"Yea, lord, but I'm not one to whip a woman."

Lyon smiled faintly. "Neither am I, Raoul. But a she-devil—ah, that is another matter entirely."

It was dark, and the drawbridge had been pulled up for the night. Brenna heard a commotion below her window. Tossing her needlework carelessly aside, she rose from her place by the fire and peered out into the bailey. Men scurried about and there was the creak of chains as the drawbridge was lowered.

A thump of dread made her chest ache. She turned to find Rachel watching her with wide eyes.

"Visitors at this hour, my lady?" the girl whispered. She ran to Brenna. "Hide! You must! You know it will be the Lion, and he will be angry. . . ."

"No. I'll not hide from any man." Brenna's lip curled in scorn, but she could not steady the slight quiver in her voice. "What will he do to me in my father's house?"

"Milady, he is a fierce Norman knight. . . ."

"Aye, and cowardly Dunstan swore fealty to William!" Brenna folded her arms over her chest to still the quaking of her hands. "He will not dare harm me. His king is my king, and I am a ward of William's by his own word."

Still, when Rye de Lyon crashed into her chamber, she could not help a skittering of fear along her spine. She met his hard gaze steadily, her chin lifted to deny the weakness inside. Had he looked thus the last time she had seen him? So fierce and dangerous? Yea, she recalled that he had, yet she still challenged him.

Lyon stood in the open doorway; he wore chain mail

and was dusty. His mantle swirled around his heels, the bright scarlet edged with gold, proclaiming him a man of consequence. He was bareheaded, his crisp black hair lying over his forehead and barely covering his ears. The trace of a beard shadowed his square jaw, and his mouth was set and hard, the blue eyes glaring at her with hot lights. A well-favored man; not even the scar could ruin his countenance.

"So, my dunghill cock," she said more bravely than she felt, "what do you mean trespassing in a lady's chambers of a night?"

Lyon took several steps into the room, his stride long and purposeful. He smelled of horse and leather and dust. Brenna forced herself not to back away. She saw the fine white lines that bracketed his hard mouth, the opaque glitter in his narrowed eyes, and knew that she braved much with her taunts.

"I received your message, my lady," he said in a flat, hard voice that betrayed nothing. "I came as quickly as I could to answer you."

She shifted uneasily. "I did not require an answer."

"Nay, but I intend to give you one." His voice was soft and menacing. Brenna felt a flutter of fear.

Several of the maids whimpered with fear, and Brenna saw Rachel sidle along a tapestry-covered wall toward the door. Coward. Not that she could blame her. Only pride kept Brenna from following Rachel—pride and an unwillingness to see contempt replace the fury in his eyes.

"I will hear you tomorrow," Brenna said, stepping away as if she had dismissed him. Lyon's hand was hard on her wrists, crushing them as he dragged her back.

It was then she saw the riding whip in his right hand. Her startled gaze flew to his face as he shook the lash loose with a deft twist of his wrist.

"Nay, sweet lady. You will hear me tonight. And every night hereafter that I desire." The whip hissed through the air and cracked loudly, making her jump in spite of her determination not to. "First, you will sign the marriage documents."

"I will not!"

A sibilant sound swept through the air, followed by a slight tug on her skirt, and she knew that the lash had cut through the draped material, much too close to her tender flesh. Another bite of fear raked her.

"Aye, lady, you will. And then we will be wed. Tonight. By a priest."

She gaped at him. "Impossible!" she said at last, her trembling noticeable now. "A priest . . . the banns . . ."

"Have been read once. That will be enough." His mouth thinned. "I have a special license; and a priest. It will be tonight."

"Nay!" A wave of panic swept through her. She pulled hard at the hand curled around her wrists, but the steely grip did not budge.

"You have misread me, my lady," Rye de Lyon said in a harsh voice. "To your sorrow. I made a bargain with your father and your king, and your *nay* is as useless as the bleating of a sheep."

Brenna lifted her golden gaze slowly to his face, breathing deeply to calm herself. "Do you wish to die so soon then, my lord? I have vowed to kill the man who would dare wed me."

"I am not so easily killed."

He seemed impatient, and slightly amused by her words. Brenna grew rigid with a rising fury that drowned out her fear. And caution.

"I have said I will not wed a bastard, and I will not!"

All amusement faded from his eyes. Slowly Lyon pulled her to him until her thighs almost touched his. His metal mail dug into her tender flesh, scraping against her arms. She could see the spiky points of his thick lashes, the glint in his blue eyes, and the flare of his nostrils.

There was something in his face that warned her here was a knight unlike any other she had known. Even her rough, crude brothers did not have the same deadly set to their features as did this man.

Holding her hard by the wrists, Lyon lifted his whip.

"Twice you have tossed that insult at my head," he grated between clenched teeth, "but by God, *demoiselle*, you shall not do so again."

Again the whip cracked, and Brenna felt it cut through the velvet and hiss close to her skin. She writhed, biting her lower lip, her eyes flashing fear and defiance at him.

Pushing her away from him yet keeping his grip on her, Lyon said, "You will sign now, *demoiselle*. And there will be no more of these foolish plays between us."

Brenna fought the urge to sob aloud. She was truly terrified now and hated him for reducing her to such a state. He watched her coldly, no mercy in his eyes.

"Aye," she said, bitterly, "I will wed you, Rye de Lyon. But you shall regret it, that I promise you."

CHAPTER 3

Lord Dunstan heaved an audible sigh of relief. It was over. Brenna was wed to the Norman earl, and no longer his responsibility. Whatever folly she committed now would be laid at Lyon's door, not his.

He glanced across the noisy hall at his daughter, and his mouth tightened into a bitter slash. "She's full of hatred and resentment," he muttered to the man at his side, "but I do not feel I deserve it. I loved my wife as a man should. 'Twas not my fault she died, but Brenna would never listen."

"My lord?" a new voice said at his elbow, and Dunstan turned from his steward to see Lyon's escort waiting to speak to him.

"Beaumont, is it not? Sir Raoul de Beaumont?"

"Aye. The seigneur requests that you make ready a clean chamber for the bridal night," Beaumont said with a polite bow.

Startled, Dunstan said, "Will not my daughter's cham—"

"Nay." Beaumont shook his head. He seemed faintly embarrassed. "He thinks 'twould be better if the lady were in—unfamiliar—surroundings this night."

"Ah." Dunstan nodded his understanding. "I suppose he has already taken her dagger from her."

"Aye." Beaumont looked away, his gaze moving toward the table where Brenna sat staring straight ahead. She sat quietly in the midst of the chaos around her, the minstrels and soldiers and noisy servants. Her back was pressed rigidly to the chair, her arms drawn over her chest and her hands clenched tightly in front of her. Rye de Lyon sprawled beside her, seemingly lazy and bored, but not a man there believed him less than alert. His eyes followed every movement, and there was a suggestion of wary waiting in his powerful frame.

Beaumont shifted uneasily. "The lady is beautiful, my lord."

"Aye," Dunstan agreed gloomily, "but not as sweet as her mother was, God rest her. Would to God I had wed her off long ago and spared myself these past years of her sharp tongue."

He leaned forward, fixing Beaumont with an intent gaze. "Tell your lord to 'ware of her temper, sir. If she is in a rage, there will be no hot supper, nay, nor decent wine. A man is more likely to find sand in his bowl, and sour ale in his cup."

"I think, Lord Dunstan," Beaumont replied politely, "that Lord Lyon will be able to convince her 'twould be most unwise to commit such folly."

Dunstan sat back with a derisive snort. "Aye, so I once thought. She taunts a man with her sharp tongue, then makes him wish he could crawl to his pallet of an eve. I never thought mere words could prick me so, but . . ." He lapsed into a brooding silence.

"Do you think she would listen to words of advice from you?" Beaumont asked after a moment, and smiled faintly when Dunstan threw him an incredulous stare.

"By God's Holy Rood! Have you not been paying attention to matters these past weeks, Beaumont? She would not listen to St. Peter himself if he were to come down to speak to her." He shook his head. "Nay, I've learned to save my breath. Unless I'm so afraid I have to speak or die. Beaumont, I tell you that most troubles are caused by women, and that is the God's truth.''

"So I've heard men say, my lord." Beaumont hesitated. "Is there anyone she confides in, p'raps?"

"What is it, Beaumont?" Dunstan stared at him with suspicious eyes. His gaze narrowed when Beaumont colored and looked down at his dusty boots. "Is there aught amiss?"

"Nay, lord, just that the seigneur has requested that she have someone speak to her of . . . of the wedding night. In place of her mother, you understand."

Dunstan dismissed this request with an impatient wave of his hand. "Brenna is well aware of a woman's duties. She's not ignorant, my lord, just because she is innocent. Why, there have been many times here in the hall she has seen couplings. After a celebration or a feast, when the men grow rowdy—well, you must know how soldiers do. Nay, she is not ignorant of what goes on between a man and a woman."

Beaumont frowned. Was there no one in this dirt-and-stone keep who could speak to a gently bred if not gently reared girl on her wedding night? No wonder Brenna of Marwald was as hostile and rebellious as she was, having lived in a keep full of crude, uncouth men who swore and fornicated in front of her. 'Twas small wonder she did not spit on the floor and scratch her backside.

Beaumont went to report his failure to Lyon and found that man not at all surprised.

Rye flicked Brenna a thoughtful glance. She still sat rigidly, her back straight and her chin lifted. Her women had combed her long hair until it gleamed like firelight, lying in wispy filaments over her shoulders and draping over her arms. A glittering coronet encircled her head, and a mesh net of finely spun gold covered her crown. She wore a deep green kirtle of silk, with long sleeves and a fitted bodice that showed the tempting thrust of her breasts. A delicate golden girdle around her slender hips carried no dagger, and there was ice in the gaze that looked past him.

Standing abruptly, he held out his hand to her. "Come, wife."

Brenna stared at his hand, at the broad palm and long, blunt fingers. Slowly, silently, she put her small hand in his, and it was dwarfed as he closed his fingers around it. He drew her up with him, and they paused to accept the toasts drunk in their honor.

It was not a night of gaiety as was usual at a wedding. Everyone seemed more confused than merry, though the ale and wine flowed freely enough. Dunstan's men-at-arms were not quite certain of this new lord, and some stared at him with surly faces. No matter. They knew he was their liege, as surely as was William. As surely as Brenna would come to know.

"There is to be no bedding ceremony?" she asked in a tight voice. She was relieved when he shook his head.

"Nay," Rye said softly, then held Brenna when she would have taken the stairs leading to her bedchamber. "This way, madam. We use another chamber this night."

Startled, she looked at him with a hint of defiance in her eyes. Then she bowed her head and went with him meekly enough to arouse his wildest suspicions. She had plans, he was certain of it.

Her maid was waiting on them in the small room he had chosen. Rachel dropped Lyon a brief curtsy. "Who gave you permission to come here?" Lyon demanded.

"My lord," she said with a slight stammer, "I am used to tending my lady."

Brenna lifted her head, her hand still held tightly by Lyon. " 'Tis well, Rachel. I do not need a maid this night."

Feeling slightly churlish, Lyon relented. "Tend your mistress, then leave us."

He released Brenna's hand, then stood watching while the two women stepped behind a painted screen. Only their faint silhouettes showed, and he could see nothing amiss as Rachel helped Brenna out of her green silk kirtle and the soft gunna.

Rye moved across the chamber toward the bed. It was

high and piled with furs and feather-stuffed pillows. Woven spreads lay over it, some he knew must be Brenna's. Her maid had obviously readied the chamber for her mistress. A faint unease shot through him. Turning back, he watched with narrowed eyes as Brenna stepped out from behind the painted screen, her chin lifted and her gaze aloof.

His mouth tightened. God's Holy Rood, but she was a fine wench! Her curves were only hinted at by the thin wool robe that swept from neck to ankle, but when she moved toward him, he felt a contracting of the muscles in his belly. Her long legs were slender and shapely, her waist tiny enough to be spanned by his two hands put together finger end to finger end. Hips curved gently, and her breasts . . . he swallowed the urge to move to her and test their weight in his palms. Delicate nipples beaded as he watched, pushing at the soft wool over them, seeming to beg for his touch.

Rye lifted his eyes to Brenna's face and saw the glitter of mockery in her eyes. She flaunted herself before him, daring him to take her. He'd never left a challenge unanswered.

"Leave us," Rye said to the maid.

After Rachel had withdrawn, Brenna obviously decided to press an attack. She moved toward a small table near the fire, her step light and as graceful as a deer.

"Wine, my lord husband?"

"If you like."

While she poured wine from a flagon into a cup, he began to unbuckle his sword belt. He folded the leather in a loop and laid his sword near the bed. He was still wearing chain mail. Shrugging out of his hauberk, he pulled it over his head and draped it on a chair. Though aware of Brenna's veiled gaze on him, he ignored her as he untied the thongs holding on his leather tunic, then untied the straps at his waist that held up his chausses. He saw her lashes droop, then lift slightly when he stood in his wool shirt, and linen breeches and stockings.

Brenna's tongue flicked out to wet her lips, and she

gave a visible start when he turned toward her and began to untie the strings at the neck of his shirt.

"My lord," she said quickly, "your wine." She thrust a cup toward him.

His hand curled around her wrist. "I want you to drink with me."

"Drink with you, my lord?" Again the tongue flicked out to wet her lips. "Wine sickens me if I drink overmuch."

"You've hardly touched wine all night. Drink with me, or I shall begin to think you've poisoned my wine."

She paled, and her chin flung up. "I would not poison you."

"Would you not?" He bent a dark head toward her cup. "Then drink, fair lady."

Brenna lifted the flagon and poured wine with a shaking hand. She turned back to face him, and Rye saw the quick decision in her eyes. As she lifted the cup to her lips, her gaze not leaving his face, he reached out to take it from her.

When she gave him a startled glance, he said, "I think it best we have your woman come to taste our wine for us."

She sucked in a deep breath. "Nay, my lord. That is not necessary."

"I say it is."

Her lips twisted. "I meant, lord, that we shall not drink it."

Though he had expected such perfidious tricks, Rye was angry. He slammed his cup to the table. "What do you think of, to try such a thing? Do you not know how harshly William would deal with you and yours?"

Her head flung up. "I care nothing for that."

"Nothing for yourself, nothing for your family. You are a wench of few loyalties," Rye muttered. He raked a hand through his hair.

He was beginning to regret his agreement to wed this wench with the amber eyes filled with hate. It was only when he looked at her, at the gleaming skin of her neck and shoulders, and remembered the feel of her body next to him, that he renewed his determination.

He led her toward the bed. She did not struggle as he'd expected but allowed him to push her to the mattress with a firm hand. She sat stiffly on the edge. Rye stepped back and untied the straps at his waist belt, releasing his linen stockings, then shrugged out of his shirt and tossed it to a low stool. He turned back to look at his new wife.

Brenna sat with her hands folded in her lap, her gaze fixed on the floor. Odd, that he found himself intrigued by this angry girl with gold cat-eyes, and little else to commend her but fierce courage. He wanted more from her than just her yielding, yet he wasn't certain exactly what. Garbed only in the brief breeches, Rye moved to the bed and put a hand on Brenna's shoulder.

At the touch of his hand, Brenna leapt at him, like a cat, with a short dagger in her hand. Only his quick reflexes saved him from taking its length.

As it was, the dagger raked along his forearm, leaving a trail of blood. He bent her arm up and back until she gasped with the pain.

"Let go of it," he snarled at her. When she held on to it defiantly, he increased the pressure until she paled and abruptly released the dagger. It fell among the furs. He picked it up and flung it far away from the bed.

Blood dripped steadily down his arm, but he paid no attention to it as he hooked his fingers into the neck of her robe to pull it from her. She flinched slightly, but made no move to stop him, and he didn't pause until she was naked.

"We'll see how well you bear the thrust of a different blade, my fine lady," Rye muttered through his teeth, and bore her back into the furs with the weight of his body. She lay stiffly beneath him, staring up at the ceiling, her eyes wide open and her body tense. But when he pushed her thighs apart with his knees, she began to fight him.

Twisting, turning, slashing at him with her fists and nails and teeth, Brenna fought as if against the devil himself. Rye held her with almost contemptuous ease, letting her wear herself out with her struggles. Long strands of coppery hair whipped across his face, and her stream of abuse grew hoarse and breathless as she raged at him.

Rye de Lyon had been reared in a stark school, indeed, where defeat meant death. But in spite of her methods, which left much to be desired, there was something touching about the struggle waged by this one woman against her father, her king, and now her husband. She did not yield. She must be vanquished to be defeated. It aroused unwilling admiration in him.

"Are you finished?" he asked when she finally grew quiet under him. He saw the bitterness of her defeat in her eyes. Rye knew how he must appear to her, cool and composed and completely unruffled by her frantic struggle. "I believe, my lady, that I have the advantage of strength and position at this time," he said with a faint smile. "I bid you yield the day."

"Never!" She heaved beneath him, a poor effort at best. "I will never yield to you."

"Then I will force your surrender." He bent his head and kissed her, and when she turned her head away, he put both her wrists in one of his strong hands and held her jaw with the other. The enticing slide of her bare skin against his aroused him, and his breathing was ragged. He moved his mouth over hers and felt her body quiver beneath him.

Shifting so that his arousal was pressed hard against her, he let his palm move from her jaw down over the arch of her throat, smoothing over velvety skin in a heated glide. When his palm cupped her breast, he heard the wild moan in the back of her throat. Then there wasn't time to move quickly enough before her teeth sunk viciously into his bottom lip.

Instinctively Rye's hand moved to force her jaws apart and release him, and he jerked his head back.

"You vicious little viper!" he choked out, and stared at her. Her eyes were glazed with fury and something more. Was she waiting to be slapped? Raped?

Neither one appealed to him. He'd already felt the bite of his lash through her skirts, and it had left him feeling as brutal as he was certain she thought him. Well, he was brutal, and he was harsh, but not usually to women.

Drawing back from her, Rye sat up and looked at Brenna for several long moments.

"I'll give you some time to adjust, my lady," he said at last, startling both of them. His gaze narrowed. "I will not force you now, but you must give me your word that you will not try to poison me or anyone else again, nor draw a weapon."

Brenna didn't answer for a moment. She returned his stare with one of her own.

"The wine wasn't poisoned; it was a sleeping draught so that you would not force me," she said sullenly. "And I make no guarantees not to take up a weapon."

" 'Twas your choice, my lady." Shrugging, Rye stood and untied the strings to his breeches and rolled them away. He turned to her, and she saw his intent in his eyes and his arrogant male body.

Brenna swallowed heavily and averted her gaze. "Yet I will give you my promise for now, lord," she said quickly.

The bed dipped beneath his weight, and her startled eyes flew to Lyon's harsh face. "Nay lady, you will give me your word not to ever take up another weapon against me."

" 'Tis given!" she cried out when he moved over her, his muscled thighs on each side of her body; he gave a grunt of satisfaction.

"You're a foolish wench, Brenna of Marwald," he said in her ear, "but at least you're not stupid."

Flushing, she gave him a quick push, but he only laughed and pulled her against him. The dagger slice on his arm still oozed blood, but neither of them paid any attention to it. Rye tossed a fur over them and twisted a long strand of her hair in his fist. His heavy arm moved to lie across her waist.

"Tomorrow," he said after a moment, "you will talk

with a woman whose wisdom you respect about how it is between a man and a woman. There will be no more of this. I give you only this night."

"Aye, lord," Brenna said in an oddly muffled voice, and he saw that she'd pressed her face into the pillow.

The long night stretched before him; even with her dagger across the room and his tight hold on her, he dared not sleep. Not with this bloodthirsty vixen next to him waiting for a mistake. Rye wondered with a trace of sardonic mockery if William had known of the maid's inordinate fear before sending him to her. It would most likely appeal to his sense of humor, and he would be waiting to hear how his knight had fared.

Rye bent an arm behind his head and stared into the dark. He recalled the stark terror in Brenna's eyes and frowned. That had cut him deeply. She should not fear him so, not this maid with more courage than most grown men.

CHAPTER 4

SUNLIGHT FILTERED THROUGH the wall slit in a smoky haze that played across Brenna's face. Familiar smells teased her awake, the acrid bite of woodsmoke mingling with the delicious fragrance of hot bread baking in the kitchens behind the keep. There was the distant jangle of metal bits and horses stomping, and she could hear the increasingly familiar bang and scrape of construction. *William's walls.*

She stirred slightly and tried to roll to one side. Sore muscles protested her sudden movement, and her eyes snapped open when she came to an abrupt halt. She couldn't move. Her hair was caught and a heavy weight held her, and for an instant she was startled by it. Then her memory returned. She swept a cautious glance at the man beside her.

Long strands of her hair were wrapped around his fist. She recalled with a surge of bitter rage how he had deliberately coiled it in his hand the night before to hold her. Now his big body lay nestled close to her, as if he had a right to be there, to be in England, much less her home.

Brenna fumed for an instant but lay as still as she could. She wanted to think, to plan without waking Rye. Her gaze flicked over him again. The fur coverlet had slipped from his body. She saw that his hard-muscled frame was marked with scars, some old, some new. In his profession a man bore many scars from battle.

She sucked in a deep breath. The taut, muscled body of the Norman was entirely nude, and she remembered with a hot sense of chagrin how he had made her yield to his demands. She hoped the Norman would forget her cowardly surrender.

The Norman. Her husband now, bound to her by church and law. A sick feeling began in the pit of her stomach. Brenna shot a wistful glance at the door, then flicked the sleeping man another glance. Her throat tightened.

He was awake, his thick-lashed eyes boring into her. A moment passed in taut silence, then he said softly, "I would not even consider an attempt at escape if I were you, *chérie.* 'Twould not be wise."

"But you're not me."

A faint smile touched the corners of his lips. His gaze drifted downward, to where the covers had slipped from her breasts. Flushing hotly at his slow appraisal of her bared body, she scrabbled for a fur to cover herself. Her chin lifted defiantly above the pelt at her throat.

"Let me up."

His mouth quirked with amusement at her haughty command, and a black brow lifted. "Anxious to begin your life as my bride, *demoiselle?* Don't you care to linger in our bed?"

Brenna glared at him and shoved at the arm draped over her waist. "Nay. I'd rather sleep with pigs."

"That can be arranged if your temper doesn't sweeten." He lifted his arm from where it lay across her middle and bent it behind his head, but kept his grip on her hair. "Is this better?" The movement tightened the band of muscles across his bare chest, and she couldn't keep her willful eyes from flicking over the roped muscles of his stomach and lower. She jerked her gaze away and sat up abruptly, wincing when his grip pulled at her scalp. Meeting his eyes with a defiant glare, she pulled her hair from his hand.

"Much better," she said when he did not try to capture her again. But when she tried to get up, he caught her and held her. His large hand grasped her arm above the elbow; his fingers deliberately grazed the sensitive skin of her rib cage as she held the fur against her like a shield.

"Nay, milady. I won't hold you, but you must lie here with me a while."

Tiny pricks of apprehension pranced along her spine, and Brenna met his wary blue gaze with a guarded, "Why?"

"To accustom you to having me in your bed. I gave you last night, but no other."

At the reminder Brenna fought the wave of panic and kept her voice steady. "I do recall that, my lord, but does that mean I must suffer your touch in the light of day?"

"You must suffer it anytime I choose to touch you."

As if to prove his point, Rye ran his hand up over her arm to her throat, curling his fingers into the edge of the fur she clutched and drawing it slowly down. Cold air washed over her. Her skin prickled with gooseflesh, and she couldn't help a slight shiver. He didn't seem to notice as he caressed her with a touch much lighter than she had expected from him after the night before.

Swallowing her outrage, Brenna kept her chin high and her gaze distant, as if his touch were no more than a minor annoyance. It didn't help that she tingled where he touched her, and a slow, curling fire sparked in the middle of her belly, puzzling and unnerving her.

His hand was large and brown against her pale skin, the finger pads rough and callused. The caress sent small waves along the nerve endings of her body. When his palm slid under one breast and he held it, she closed her eyes. For some reason, instead of feeling revulsed as she had half expected, she felt a strange excitement. His caresses over her naked body ignited a warm wash of sensation that was as confusing as it was unfamiliar.

Brenna sat stiffly, her eyes closed, her breathing soft and shallow. She felt him shift on the mattress, felt the scrape of his leg against her thigh as he sat up, then felt his other hand on her. Rye's fingers traced the molding of her collarbone before curling around the peak of her breast and teasing it. Brenna couldn't hold back a gasp of surprise. Her eyes flew open, and she met his hot blue gaze with a start.

"What are you doing?"

"Touching you."

She drew back, but he adjusted so that his hands still cupped her breasts. "I know that," she snapped. "Stop it."

"Nay, milady. You are mine. I have a right to touch you like this"—he drew a finger in a circle around the taut peak of her breast—"and like this—" Bending quickly, he covered her nipple with his mouth. Brenna cried out and arched her back in shock.

Before she could recover enough to attempt to push him away, he slid an arm around her waist and pulled her down and under him as he bent over to press her back into the mattress. She kicked, but her long legs were tangled in the jumble of furs and woolen coverlets, and she only succeeded in tangling them more. Rye quickly slid over her, his weight holding her down, one hand circling her wrists to keep her from striking him.

The abrasive scrape of his naked body over hers startled her into immobility for a moment, and she felt the hard nudge of his growing erection against her thigh. That gave her the incentive to increase her struggles with renewed vigor, and a hint of hysteria crept into her frantic movements.

"Get off me, you big oaf," she managed to say between panting breaths for air. Rye laughed softly; ignoring the curses that followed, he slid his frame along the curves of her body to capture her wet, aching nipple in his mouth again. Brenna moaned, angry tears stinging her eyes at the indignity of his action and her position.

The rough scrape of his morning beard against her skin was painful and oddly stimulating at the same time, and she twisted to escape his searching mouth. It was humiliating that he held her so easily, that her most frantic efforts to elude his touch availed her nothing. Even more horrible was the fact that her treacherous body was responding to the wet tugging of his mouth on her breast. Brenna tried to heave him from her without success. For some reason the spark in the center of her abdomen grew hotter and higher, made her thighs ache and her skin tingle. And Rye seemed to know it.

When he lifted his head at last and looked up at her face, he regarded her thoughtfully for a long moment. Brenna's breath came in tortured gasps, and she couldn't help the writhing motions of her body. Finally Rye's mouth curled in a slight smile.

"You deny your own nature, milady. 'Twill not be as bad as you fear, I promise you that."

"Promise! Do you think I want a Norman's promise?" Hot tears threatened, but Brenna blinked them back. She would not cry, would not let this man see her weakness. Perhaps her body had somehow betrayed her, but she would never yield to him, *never*.

Releasing her wrists, Rye levered his body to a sitting position and looked at her. "It doesn't matter what you want. You must accept it."

Brenna swallowed the hasty retort trembling on the tip of her tongue. Perhaps her father was right. Perhaps she should use honey instead of vinegar to gain her freedom.

Bending her head, Brenna said softly, "Aye, milord."

She could feel Rye's suspicious stare but remained with her head bent down, and her eyes downcast, until he gave an irritated snort and rose from the bed.

"I trust your meekness less than I do your hatred, Brenna of Marwald," he said as he reached for his linen breeches.

Keeping her head bent, she watched him through the screen of her loose hair as he pulled on the undergarment. A tight feeling closed her throat. He was magnificently made, long of limb and thick-muscled, as sleek and lithe as a panther. It was small wonder that he was one of William's best champions. He probably had little trouble in besting his foes.

When snug linen stockings covered Rye's long legs and were tied with tapes to the cloth belt at his waist, he crossed back to the bed where she waited.

"Come and tend the wound on my arm. Then we will go below to break our fast."

Though she had to bite her lower lip to keep from giving him a sharp reply, Brenna managed to give a fair imitation of a docile wife as she shrugged into a loose gunna to tend the wound she had inflicted on him.

" 'Tis just a scratch," she commented as she wrapped a strip of linen around his forearm and tied it so tightly he gave her a sharp glance. "I don't know why you want to make a fuss about it." She took several steps away from him.

"Such a tender little wife," he muttered wryly. "I've no intention of getting poisoning from your dagger, my sweet. What good would a one-armed man be in battle?"

"Ask my older brother, who came away from battle with only a stump for a right arm. A one-armed Saxon warrior can wage war against able-bodied Normans any day."

"So they showed us at Hastings," Rye commented with a faint smile. "It's been over ten years, Brenna. Could you not admit defeat at last? 'Twould certainly save a lot of trouble and lives if some of your hotheaded barons would acknowledge defeat."

She glared at him. "Ten years is nothing."

Reaching for the woolen shirt he wore under his leather tunic, Rye shook his head. " 'Tis a belief apparently shared by many Saxons. William is king, Brenna, and he does not intend to leave England."

"Not willingly, I am certain."

Rye frowned. "Enough. I will not have it said that my wife speaks treason with every breath. You'd best learn restraint."

Brenna clenched her teeth together to keep her unruly tongue from digging a deeper hole for her.

To keep from answering, she concentrated on dressing. It was unnerving to have him watch her every move.

When he insisted that she allow him to help her, she ground her teeth together with frustration. He was only doing it to humiliate her, to show her she must obey him even in this small matter. She wished she had her dagger to slide between his ribs.

"Do you have a yearning to be a lady's maid, my lord?" she inquired caustically when he held up a clean gunna.

"Where you are concerned—perhaps."

Brenna scowled. The man was unnerving. It was even more unnerving to have him touch her, to feel the brush of his fingers against her bare skin as he slid the gunna over her head. The hem slipped to her feet in a whisper of cool linen and the fragrance of flowers, and his blue eyes darkened.

Rye reached for the soft wool kirtle to pull over the gunna. Then he slung her goldlinked girdle around her slender hips.

"Let me do that!" she snapped at him when his big hands could not manage the last clasp of the girdle that cinched in her garments.

To her surprise, he laughed. "Well, I have to admit that you are not likely to bore me with compliant meekness. Aye, I expect to be fielding your barbs for some time to come."

Brenna shot him a baleful stare. It was on the tip of her tongue to tell him to go to the devil, when a timid knock sounded at the door.

"That must be Rachel," she said. "She probably wants to see if I survived the night with a Norman savage."

"Ah, but your night has yet to come, sweet Brenna," he mocked her. "Wait until I bed you to claim survival, milady."

Brenna opened the door for her maid and saw the frightened glance she gave Rye.

"Come in, goose," she said softly in the Saxon tongue. "I am well."

Rachel began to tidy up the chamber, stirring up the

fire and watching Rye from the corner of her eyes as if afraid that he would lift his sword to her.

Rye gave an impatient snort and beckoned for Brenna to help him with his chain mail. "I'll see to my men, then join you in the hall. Here." He handed her the heavy hauberk of mail. "Hold this while I put it on, then lace me up."

"Do I look like a squire?" she asked tartly.

He grinned, raking her with hot eyes. "Nay, milady, you certainly do not. I seem to recall very feminine virtues beneath your gown."

Flushing hotly, Brenna snatched at the hauberk. "Be quiet and put this on." She hoped Rachel had not overheard his crude comment.

Suddenly Rachel gasped.

"What is the matter with you?" Brenna demanded. The girl was staring at the quantity of blood on the sheets.

For an instant Brenna fought the urge to laugh. "The seigneur's arm was cut," she said in a reasonable tone. "That is all. Do not fret overmuch."

It was obvious Rachel did not believe her, but she did not say so. She began to strip the bed. "Aye, milady. But I am to hang the sheets out as proof of consummation."

She'd forgotten that small detail, Brenna realized, and her face flamed. After being spared the bedding ritual—she thanked God for escaping the humiliation of standing naked before gawking onlookers—she had not thought about the importance of the marital sheets as proof of her virginity. Now everyone would assume that he had bedded her.

Brenna looked up to see Rye watching her. Her chagrin must have been reflected in her face because he grinned widely. She was neatly trapped, and by her own hand. If she had not cut him, there would be no blood, and she could have fled to the priests at the monastery and begged asylum, sent entreaties to the pope citing lack of consummation, done anything to escape this Norman earl who was laughing at her.

In the next instant Brenna harbored a flare of hope. If

it was told that the deed had been done, then there was no need to actually go through with it.

Chin lifting, Brenna said haughtily, "Do go see to your men, my lord. They must be afrighted that their precious leader has been murdered in his bed by a Saxon by now, and should be reassured."

"My men fear only God, William, and me," Rye said with the usual arrogance that made Brenna want to slap him. "You would do well to take a lesson from them."

"Anytime I want a lesson in fear, I know well to go to Normans for it," she shot back, and saw his brows lift.

"Perhaps they can school you in obedience as well."

"P'raps. 'Tis doubtful, I think."

Shaking his head, Rye buckled on his sword. "After the morning mass and breaking of our fast, we ride, wife. I hope you ride as well as you argue. If so, we should be at Moorleah by dusk this eve."

Brenna's heart skipped a beat. "Moorleah?"

"Aye. 'Tis where we will make our home."

"But I thought—I mean, Marwald is well fortified and the king wanted you to—"

"Do not try to lesson me on this, Brenna." Rye's voice was hard, all traces of amusement gone. "And be ready when I come for you. What you do not have packed, remains. And if I must carry you over my shoulder and tie you in a litter for the journey, I will do so. You can reflect on what a pretty picture that would make while you decide."

He bent to scoop up the dagger she had used on him, then strode out the door, slamming it shut behind him. Brenna swallowed her dismay. Moorleah, recently rebuilt of stone with great walls and a deep moat. She would be his prisoner if she did not manage to escape soon.

Rye held no illusions that Brenna would submit placidly to his decision in anything, especially to leaving Marwald. He had prepared for this eventuality already and posted an armed guard outside their chamber door.

"Watch her closely," Rye instructed. The man nodded his understanding. It was no secret that his new wife was a rebellious one, Rye ruefully reflected.

Raoul was busily instructing servants to load wagons by the time Rye entered the bailey. All around was the energetic bustle of armed men in the pale, bleak light cast by a hazy sun.

"In that wagon, you dolt!" Beaumont was saying to a man in exasperation. "Do you think your lady will thank you for putting horseshoes atop her clean linens?"

"His lady will not thank him for anything," Rye said with heavy irony. Beaumont turned and smiled in relief.

"Seigneur! I am pleased to see you—well."

"Alive? Is that what you meant to say?" Rye shook his head in disgust. "I understand that you spent the night outside my door like a squire."

He flushed. "Aye, seigneur. In case you needed me."

"And you did not feel the need to investigate at any time?" His breath blew a visible cloud in the early chill.

Shifting uncomfortably, Beaumont blurted out truthfully, "I did think about it once, but as it was a female voice that I heard call out, I did not."

Rye grinned. "I admit, Beaumont, there was a moment when I might have taken your assistance. She's the wildest wench I've ever had the misfortune to meet. And she almost made good on her promise." He rubbed his bandaged arm with an absent gesture.

Beaumont stared at his wound and began to sputter.

" 'Tis only a scratch, Raoul," Rye assured him.

Two carts creaked past, and oxen bellowed loudly. The damp chill of early morning rose off their hides. Rye smiled at his companion. Shaking his head, Beaumont gave a long sigh.

" 'Twas bad of William to force you to this, seigneur."

"He didn't. I chose to do so." Rye looked past Beaumont at the carters mending a broken wagon wheel. "Lady Madelon and my sister now reside at Moorleah, by my command."

For a long moment Beaumont remained quiet, then

he said hesitantly, " 'Twill be good to see your sister again."

"Aye."

Silence fell between them. Both men kept their thoughts to themselves, and finally Rye stirred. Slapping a gauntlet against his palm, he cleared his throat.

"Are the men-at-arms ready?"

Grateful for a neutral topic, Beaumont nodded and began to give Rye the details of their men and arms, and how many horses were fit. Neither of them mentioned Rye's stepmother again.

Engrossed in the outfitting of the men who would be journeying to Moorleah with them, Rye didn't realize how much time had passed. The sun was a hazy orb high in the sky when he paused at last. Flicking a glance at the harried man-at-arms who was trying to explain why so many horses were unfit to ride, Rye grimaced.

" 'Tis of no consequence now, Harald. Take what we need from Marwald. I have other needs to tend."

As he turned, intending to seek out Brenna in the great hall, a youthful voice interrupted angrily, "Aye, Norman, steal our horses!"

Rye halted and turned back slowly to see a red-faced young man glaring at him. He knew without asking that it must be one of Dunstan's sons. The resemblance to Brenna was there in the furious eyes and delicately chiseled features.

"Which of Dunstan's get are you?" he demanded bluntly. The youth's face grew even redder with fury.

Boldly facing the much taller Norman, the youth snapped, "Lord Myles."

"Nay. There are no lords here save me," Rye replied coolly. "You are a brash, braying upstart."

Myles took an impetuous step forward, his hand dropping to the hilt of his sword. He said through his teeth, "I will brook no insults from a Norman!"

" 'Tis fortunate that I am your brother by law, young Myles, or your head might be forfeit for such insolence. There are those men who would not give you margin for your youthful folly."

"I need no margin from a Norman."

Rye kept his voice low. "Do you seek death so avidly? 'Tis certain to come to you soon if you behave with such foolhardy abandon."

Myles swallowed, but kept his hand on the hilt of his sword. "Death is preferable to defeat."

"Is it?" Lyon's lips twitched wryly. "You and your sister must have suckled from the same she-wolf." His narrowed gaze drifted over the youth's length and whip-cord breadth. "Seek death, then, my little gamecock. Or, if you are man enough, seek life."

"In defeat?"

"Nay. If you are so determined to fight, fight with your intellect instead of your insolence. The last rarely wins o'er the other."

Doubt crept into the youth's hazel eyes. "I find it most unusual that you, of all Normans, would counsel wisdom over warfare. You're said to be William's greatest warrior. The Black Lion, they call you, who never leaves a live enemy to fight again."

"In my position, it would be foolish to leave an enemy alive to strike at my back, but I have never killed without need." Rye slapped his thick gauntlet across his palm and regarded Myles thoughtfully. "Are you capable with that sword you carry at your side, or do you wear it just for a brave show?"

Stepping back, Myles drew a thin sword from its sheath. Ignoring the immediate attention that brought from several of Rye's men-at-arms, who came running with drawn swords and fierce expressions, he asked boldly, "Care to test me?"

Rye looked at him a long moment, then signaled for his men to back away. His voice was dry. " 'Twould be murder, and I've no desire to start my day drenched in your blood." Before the youth could react recklessly, Lyon added, "But your courage makes me wonder if you would not do well in my guard. I've need of fighting men who dare much, even if a bit overmuch."

Hesitating, Myles stared at the tall Norman knight with hard eyes. "Are you offering me a position?"

"I'm offering you a chance. Nothing else. If you do not suit as my squire, or if Beltair, my master-at-arms, says you are unfit, you will not be taken on." Lyon flicked his gauntlet against his palm with another loud slap. "Do you care to join us, or do you prefer fighting us with loud words?"

It was a struggle; he recognized it in the boy's eyes—a battle between the desire to belong to a group of men he obviously admired, and loyalty.

"Young Myles, I assure you that though we came to your land as invaders, we stay as countrymen. The Danes seek to plunder England, as does the French king. William has room in his army for fighting men, brave men, but not men who are torn in their loyalties. I have taken your sister to wife, and our sons will not think about who is Saxon and who is Norman. This will be their land, and they will fight to hold it. Will you go against your nephews?"

It was obvious Myles had not thought of that. Rye saw some of the tension ease from his tautly held body as he slid his sword back into its sheath.

"I have seen no evidence of nephews yet," Myles said after a moment, a glint of humor lurking in his eyes. "And my sister will try to murder you in your sleep before you get any sons on her."

"Do you think she will succeed?"

Grinning now, Myles shook his head. "Nay, if I were to bet, my lord, I would bet on you, I think."

Rye smiled slightly. " 'Twould be wise."

"But Brenna will not give you an easy time of it, I vow, so I would not bet much," Myles added. He paused, then said after clearing his throat, "I would like to think on your offer, my lord."

"I offer for any able-bodied man who wishes to join our ranks. You may tell your brothers."

A slight shadow flickered over Myles's face. "I do not think my brothers will come to you, my lord. They are much older than I and have already fought enough battles to hate anything Norman."

"Your brothers would do well to follow your father's

example." Rye's voice was hard. "Dunstan is wise enough to recognize that survival lies in sagacity."

"My father is old and must survive the easiest way he can. My brothers do not feel the same way."

"Then I will deal harshly with them if they raise arms against William."

"They know that, my lord." Hesitating, Myles seemed about to say something, then shook his head. " 'Twill not be an easy decision for me, but I will think on it a while."

"Do not be too long. I leave Marwald within the hour."

"Leave, my lord?"

"Aye. Did you think I would stay here?" Rye gave an impatient shake of his head. "There is no reason to linger now that Lady Brenna and I are wed."

Miles gazed at him with open curiosity. "Do you take her with you?"

"Of course. Where else would she be?"

"We—I had not thought you would want to take her with you so soon."

"Well, I do." Rye half turned to signal an end to the conversation, then glanced back at the youth. A shaft of sunlight glittered in his hair, giving it a rich russet sheen that made him think of Brenna. "Give your brothers my warning," he said. " 'Tis the only one they will get."

The unusual confrontation with Myles preoccupied him until he reached the great hall to find Brenna nowhere in sight. He'd expected her to be seeing to the breaking of the morning fast, and it displeased him that his men would go hungry if she was being too stubborn to see to her duty. Upon questioning a nervous servant, he learned that she had not yet come down from the tower room.

Irritated and suspicious, he took the steps to the new tower two at a time, his prick spur catching in the hem of his mantle as he mounted the winding staircase. Curse her, she had better not waste his time with foolish resistance. Too much time had already been wasted as far as he was concerned. The wedding was over now, and he must turn his energies to more important matters.

There were always the constant rebellions springing up, the Saxons fleeing into the Welsh marches or to the north, past the Roman wall built to keep out the barbaric Celts. It had taken too long to subdue the Saxon barons, and still there were those foolish few who resisted.

Rye thought sometimes that he would never get the smell of burning fields and peasant huts out of his nostrils. It was too deeply entrenched, along with the pathetic wails of the peasants left without food for the winter months. Yet it was those same peasants who hid the barons and rebels in their rude huts, and William knew that in order to vanquish the rebels, all sanctuary must be destroyed.

Grimly Rye had the thought that he must somehow convey that to his wife, that she would realize she had nowhere to go and hide. Tenacious lot, these Saxons, and foolish. When would they admit defeat? Foolish indeed, like that reckless boy, Myles, who couldn't be more than sixteen at best, drawing a light sword on a seasoned Norman knight. Most other men would have obliged him and made short work of the matter, but for some reason Rye had been reluctant.

Perhaps it was because he recalled his own youthful braggadocio, how he'd hated to admit defeat in any form. He still hated it. 'Twas why he'd chosen the winning side by joining with William twelve years before. 'Twas why he had yielded to his king's desire to wed a woman he had not met and did not especially want.

A wry smile twisted his mouth. He desired her, yes, but that was different. A man's desire for a woman could be a thing apart from his life; it wasn't integral to his other needs. He'd always felt a faint contempt for men who allowed women to rule them, had regarded them in the same light he regarded those effeminate men too weak-willed to take up arms in battle.

Years before, he'd seen enough to convince him that if a woman was ever allowed to get beneath a man's guard, that man might as well fall on his own sword. 'Twould be a much kinder death. Hadn't he watched his stepmother slay his own father as surely as if she had struck him down with an axe?

Nay, not for Rye de Lyon the humiliating existence that his father had lived! And the sooner this Brenna of Marwald discovered that she could not disobey him, the better it would be for all concerned.

Rye's boot steps echoed down the stone corridors as he approached the tower chamber where he'd left his wife. He was annoyed at finding the guard gone from the door and made a mental promise to see the man flayed for leaving his post without orders.

When Rye grasped the latch and shoved against the door, it swung open easily. One glance inside the room showed him that it was empty, not only of Brenna and her maid, but of any sign of recent habitation. He swore softly beneath his breath and, turning, slammed the door behind him.

CHAPTER 5

BRENNA HEARD THE harsh rattle of the slamming door and Lyon's furious orders to search the keep until she was found. Hiding in a curtained alcove with Rachel, she closed her eyes at his bellowed orders.

Rachel's hands tightened convulsively in the folds of her cloak, and neither woman dared a glance at the fallen Norman soldier stretched on the floor behind them. It had taken only a little coaxing for the man to drink the wine Rachel gave him, then long moments waiting for him to grow sleepy. They had barely been able to drag the large man into the alcove before Lyon's steps were heard on the stairs, ruining their plans.

"What shall we do, my lady?" Rachel whispered as the shouted commands grew distant.

"Wait until we are certain they are in another part of the keep," Brenna murmured after a moment. She itched to part the heavy curtain and look out, but dared not. It was still too dangerous. If Lyon discovered her before she could reach the monastery—

She couldn't finish the thought.

"And then?" Rachel whispered, her voice quivering, her breath stirring Brenna's hair and making her shiver.

"And then we slip out the side door of the keep. You know the one. Where the lepers come and go."

The side door was almost hidden by full grown bushes on the outside, and tucked behind stacks of supplies in the inner bailey. Brenna hoped that none of the Normans would think to look there.

After several more agonizing minutes passed, Brenna gathered up her flagging courage and gave Rachel a nudge. The guard couldn't sleep forever, and the longer they remained, the more likely they were to be found. She drew the rough gray cloak Rachel had brought her around her frame and adjusted the scarlet leper's cap atop her covered head. Similarly garbed, Rachel met her eyes for a fleeting instant. Then they parted the heavy curtain and stepped into the wide corridor.

Stealing down the spiral staircase that led from the tower wing down three flights, Brenna had plenty of time to consider her actions. It was foolhardy only if she was caught. If she escaped, it would be a brilliant plan.

She held tightly to that thought as they ambled slowly across the muddy yard of the bailey toward the small gate in the low wooden palisade surrounding the stone-and-wood keep. It should be easy enough to exit, then go across the broad courtyard to the gate leading across the outer moat. In the past year or two William had commanded that stone walls be built around the square keep as further protection against raiders. Now she had reason to be glad. Once beyond the walls, only guards atop the flat walkway would see them, and they would give only a cursory glance. Then they would be free.

It was an exhilarating thought.

Even more exhilarating was the first breath of freedom beyond the walls, when the stink of the moat and the chaos of the bailey had been left behind. Brenna glanced down at the long, dirty rags she and Rachel had wound around their hands and arms and feet like true lepers.

"It was the bandages," she said smugly. "No one wanted to come near because of the chance of contagion."

Rachel was quickly stripping away the linen wraps

around her wrists. " 'Tis inviting God's wrath is what it is, my lady," she muttered. "We shall surely be stricken with some dread disease now that we have masqueraded thusly."

"Saint Jerome!" Brenna snapped with exasperation. "It is much more likely that we shall be caught and flogged if we *don't* keep on our leper's rags. Do not remove them, I say."

While they spoke, they scurried over the rough slopes of the ground that fell away from the keep. Of necessity the original site had been built of great earthenworks and wooden walls, borrowing heavily from the surrounding countryside. Here the land was irregular in places, with deep ditches that cut unexpectedly across the terrain. It was easy to fall into one, not seeing it because of the thick underbrush.

Brenna had no intention of keeping close to the road. That would be certain disaster. She prayed she could find their way to St. Giles monastery before Lyon found them. If she could just reach the safety of the church, she would find sanctuary he could not defile. Not even William would go against the Church, though he had no compunction in expelling corrupt bishops from their sees, and abbots from their abbacies.

By midafternoon Brenna had to admit they were lost. Or at least, confused. The gray sky shed fuzzy light but did not give a hint of the sun's position. And the path she had followed had ended in a deep, primeval wood that made her maid shudder and weep loudly.

Hunger pangs assailed her. Brenna sank to a fallen log in the forest.

"Milady," Rachel half sobbed, "what shall we do?"

"Hush, goose! We've been walking only a few hours. I am certain we will find our way soon. Besides, a little travail can do us no harm."

"He'll find us," Rachel said gloomily, sniffing when Brenna glared at her. "Well, he will! And he'll hang us!"

Realizing Rachel was frightened, Brenna tried to keep her voice calm. "Did you remember the sack of food?"

Rachel nodded and drew out a slender cloth sack. She

had brought stale bread and a small round of cheese. It was enough for a light repast but would never last longer than a day. Brenna sighed when she saw it.

"Well, this will have to do. Here. Take a small chunk of the bread and a bite of cheese. We'll drink from a stream. When we find one."

Staring at her mournfully, the slender, dark-haired maid did as she was bid, though her glance was reproachful. Brenna felt a spurt of impatience. It was obvious that her maid had never suffered the privations of hunger or distress. Brenna was used to it. There had been times when she had not dared enter the hall because of the revelry going on and had been too proud to admit her cowardice by asking for a trencher of food.

A little hunger was worth it, if she could reach the monastery before Rye de Lyon caught up with her. Her mouth tightened. Arrogant Norman ass. Did he think all he had to do was command it and it would happen? Did he equate his status with that of God, or king?

Apparently, she answered her own question. It was high time he learned that not every human being danced to the melody of his mandolin. The thought made her smile, and by the time they emerged from the dark, damp wood into the late-afternoon sunlight, Brenna was in a much better mood.

She even recognized some of the landmarks, an old stone bridge over a stream—where they slaked their thirst—and a lightning-struck tree that was twisted and charred. She had ridden this way on her favorite stallion many a time. If she was correct in her estimate, St. Giles was only a mile or two away. They should reach it just after dark.

Turning, Brenna imparted this happy information to her maid and was rewarded with a tremulous smile of relief.

"Thank God, milady! I was truly afeared that we would be eaten by wild animals." She shivered. "There were so many strange noises in the wood. . . ."

"I told you. Wind in the trees." Brenna had no inten-

tion of admitting that she too had worried about wild
boars or other vicious creatures.

The wind had risen, picking at the openings of their
rough cloaks with renewed vigor. With the sun waning,
the air grew chilly. To make matters worse, a light rain
began to mist, dampening their clothes and making the
ground slippery.

Brenna kept doggedly on, her back hunched against
the wind and rain, one hand keeping Rachel moving.
Only a mile or two, she told herself, only a mile or two.

As they topped a rise and stumbled over the rough
ground onto a curve of road, the walls of the monastery
came into view. Brenna heaved a sigh of relief. She'd
begun to think her calculations wrong, and she whispered a quick prayer of gratitude.

As she turned to her maid, a rumble of thunder
sounded. Rachel gasped and crossed herself. Brenna
flung her an exasperated glance.

"It's only thunder."

"Aye, milady. But where there's thunder, there's ofttimes lightning."

The thunder grew louder, shaking the ground.
Brenna glanced up at the ominous sky. When she looked
down again, her heart gave a lurch. Riders. Armed
horsemen; dull light glinted from their weapons, and
from the looks of them, they were in a hurry. Now just
small, dark specks on the road, it was obvious they
would soon be upon them. She could only hope they'd
not yet been seen by the riders.

"Hide!" she gasped out, giving Rachel a shove toward a ditch by the road. "Soldiers!"

She had hoped she was wrong, but her guess was all
too accurate. And not just soldiers, but Rye de Lyon
himself. Her prayer for oblivion went unanswered. He
drew up his sweating, snorting destrier on the road only
a few feet from where they hid on the banks of the ditch.

His voice carried across the sound of wind and whip
of rain.

"Lady Brenna. Come here."

It would be useless to pretend not to hear him,

though Brenna was tempted. She reluctantly got to her feet on the steep slope, meeting his dark, furious gaze with a steady stare.

She saw that he was muddy and wet, his mantle sodden and spattered. His men looked in no better condition. That made her feel a little better, knowing that he was in the same sorry state as was she.

His voice cracked like a whip. "You've cost me an entire day. My men are weary, and so are the horses. Now come here."

"What? Am I a dog, to be whistled to you? A falcon, to be trained to the lure?" Her tone was scornful, her chin lifted high. "I think not, my lord husband. I do not respond to rude commands, but to gentle requests."

Lyon vaulted from his saddle in a move much too quick to be anticipated. In spite of his heavy mail, he was upon her before she could do more than take a quick step backward.

That step put her on undependable ground, and she felt her feet sliding just as he reached out for her. Instead of steadying her, Lyon was caught off guard and went with her, sliding down the muddy slope to the ditch at the bottom.

It did nothing to improve Lyon's already exacerbated temper to end up in a ditch full of water in full view of his men.

Brenna, however, could not help the explosive burst of laughter that erupted from her and didn't stop even when Rye gripped her arms in a crushing hold. He'd stumbled quickly to his feet, his muddy cape tangled around his long legs and his face creased in fury.

"Curse you," he snarled, "if I didn't know better, I would take an oath that you planned this!"

"Oh that I could have!" she said between peals of laughter. "You look like one of my father's pigs!"

This time his grip tightened so painfully, her laughter ended in a gasp. "Lady Brenna," he warned softly, "I do not advise you to say anything else. I might be tempted to do what has been strongly recommended and take my whip to you."

She eyed him. "Would you now? That should prove interesting, my lord husband. Consider how entertained your men would be by the sight of you bleeding like a newly stuck barrow with my dagger in your ribs."

"Have you gone mad, woman? Do you think to provoke me and escape unscathed?"

Leaning close, she said softly, "Do you wish to provide more entertainment for your men, seigneur? Just think how this will be told and retold during the long winter nights. I can almost hear the laughter now."

It was a telling point. With great effort, Rye reined in his temper and abruptly dropped his hands from her arms.

"Get your maid, Lady Brenna. We return to Marwald."

Forcing herself to speak calmly and reassuringly, Brenna helped the weeping Rachel up from the ditch and followed Rye to the road. He'd not bothered to offer a helping hand, but stood in stern, icy silence beside his great destrier. One of his men—Beaumont, she thought—took Rachel up on his own mount with gentle hands, and Brenna was left to see what her husband intended.

"If I were not pressed for time, my lady, you would walk every step of the way back," he said coldly.

"I would prefer that to riding with you," she returned in a sweet tone that made his mouth tighten and the scar on his cheek stand out palely against his dark skin.

Rye made a quick motion with one hand, and his master-at-arms was immediately at his side. "Mount the lady in front of you, Beltair. See that she has no opportunity to escape you."

"Aye, my lord," the huge man replied, and turned to Brenna with an outstretched hand.

She sucked in a deep, furious breath. She was being handed over like unwanted baggage! She might have expected such an insult. Stiffly she put her hand in the older man's and allowed him to put her atop his huge horse. He smelled of sweat and stale beer, and she had the savage thought that she much preferred this crude man to her husband.

Brenna cast a last glance at the monastery walls she had almost reached, and called down a thousand curses on Rye de Lyon's head as the master-at-arms mounted behind her and kicked his horse into a trot. The line of soldiers followed Rye's swift lead, mud flying up from the huge hooves.

On the long ride back to the keep, Brenna had enough time to reflect on her daring. She'd surprised Rye de Lyon with her acid tongue and refusal to cower. It was something to remember for the future. Overused, it would lose its effect. Used sparingly, it could be very effective. She hoped.

CHAPTER 6

CHILLED TO THE bone, Brenna watched Rye warily as he dismounted in the bailey. It was past dark, and the welcoming lights of the keep promised her retribution instead of warmth. She knew she had earned his wrath by her attempt but could not feel sorry for it. She had almost succeeded in her escape.

Rye strode toward her. Without a word he reached up to pull her from Beltair's loose grip. Brenna swallowed the sudden surge of fear at the evidence of his strength as she slid down from the mount, her hands curved over his flexed muscles. His face was shuttered.

"Thank you, Beltair," he said coolly to the master-at-arms. "I admire your fortitude in enduring her company."

"Aye, seigneur," Beltair replied, smiling a little at Brenna's gasp of fury.

Taking her arm in his tight grasp, Lyon ushered her into the keep. Smoke stung her eyes, and she blinked at the assault of light. The smell of food and fresh rushes did nothing to alleviate her anxiety. Across the cavernous hall her father was sitting in his chair on the raised dais. Dunstan rose slowly as Rye strode forward with Brenna in tow.

"I see you found her, my lord," Dunstan said quietly.

Rye slung Brenna in front of him by one arm, keeping a tight hold on her. "Aye, Dunstan, I found her," he said harshly. "I charge you with her care while I see to another matter, Dunstan. Do not let her move so much as an inch, or I will be displeased."

Dunstan stepped down from the dais. "I will keep her by me, my lord, until you come for her."

"I need to wash myself—" Brenna began.

"Nay, lady," Rye said. "Sit in your muddy garments and think about the consequences of your actions. Rebels need neither food nor drink, nor clean garments, but are fueled by hatred and impetuous urges."

"You are truly Norman in your thinking, my lord," she said tartly, "for every croft and field in the land has been destroyed by your hand at one time or the other!"

"And will continue to be, until all resistance is fully quelled." Rye turned on his heel to stalk from the hall.

She allowed Dunstan to seat her in the high-backed chair beside him.

"You needn't watch me as if I intend to bolt," she said calmly as the silence stretched between them. " 'Twould be futile at this late hour."

" 'Twas futile earlier," Dunstan snapped, "but ye're too stubborn a wench to admit it!"

She regarded him with her tawny gaze for a long moment. How she hated him for wedding her to the enemy so that he might regain his lands. "Nothing is futile if it bedevils the enemy. If you'd not lost your manhood, you'd do the same."

Reddening, Dunstan surged to his feet, obviously fighting the desire to strike her. Did he dare? She was wed to the Norman now, and Lyon had made it clear she was his property.

Clenching and unclenching his big hands, Dunstan sank slowly back to his chair. "One day your unruly tongue will make you wish for restraint, daughter," he said shortly. " 'Tis your own stubborn will that ye're wed to a man who frightens ye out of your wits."

Brenna glared back at him. "He does not frighten me."

Dunstan laughed harshly. "Lyon terrifies ye, girl, only ye're too proud and stubborn to admit it."

She sucked in a sharp breath. Was it that obvious? She had not admitted it, even to herself, but her father was right. She *was* frightened of Lyon, of his strength, his anger, the male hunger she'd seen in his eyes earlier. Yea, Rye de Lyon frightened her to the very marrow of her bones. And there was nowhere she could turn for protection. She had only her wits to help her.

Even now, thinking of how he'd held her, touched her, and sparked a fiery response in her body, Brenna trembled. It had never occurred to her that she might experience such a reaction to his touch, and it was confusing and frightening at the same time. She allowed few people to touch her in any way, preferring to keep herself remote, and the forced surrender to his hand had been galling. And enlightening. Since her mother's death, there had been no gentle caresses or soft hands on her, and she'd not known she missed them.

It was something to think about.

Long hours passed. Dunstan sank lower and lower in his carved wooden chair, and the huge fire in the center of the great hall grew dim. Smoke curled to the tiny opening in the roof, blackening the rafters and making the few people left in the hall cough. Most of the keep had retired for the night, save for Ballard, who was not only the minstrel but Brenna's only male friend. He sat close to her feet—not close enough to arouse Dunstan's suspicions, but close enough to smile at her encouragingly as she faltered.

"Milady," he said softly, his knee almost touching the hem of her muddy gown, " 'tis poor sport indeed this eve. Is there ought I may do to help you?"

Brenna managed a smile. "Aye, Ballard. Sing to me. Sing something light and happy." Her father snorted rudely, but did nothing to stop the minstrel as he stroked his lute with a light touch. A pleasing melody rippled from the tips of his talented fingers, and he hummed for a moment before singing a lively ballad about a slave girl who outwitted her Viking captors.

Ballard had begun the tenth verse when there was a noise in the doorway of the hall. Brenna looked up and saw Lyon striding toward them; he'd brought a woman with him, who hung back at the door. A choking constriction kept Brenna silent. Had he brought his doxy to flaunt in her face? If so, he would be rudely surprised to find that she was relieved, not brokenhearted.

When Lyon drew close, giving Ballard such a fierce glare that the minstrel broke off in the middle of the verse and backed away, Brenna held herself with as much dignity as possible. She would not give him the pleasure of reacting.

"Come with me," was all he said, holding out his hand. Rather than risk public humiliation, Brenna stood coolly, ignoring the fact that her gown was stiff and muddy and her hair caked with ditch water and grass. Rye's hand was warm as it enclosed hers in a tight grip, and he pulled her with him to the door.

Brenna was surprised by the sweep of relief that raced through her when she drew close and recognized the hooded woman as the village midwife. Hardly Rye's type to tumble.

"Mistress Maisie," Brenna said in surprise, and slid Rye an uncertain glance. What did he mean by this? He did nothing without purpose, but she was at a loss as to his motive in bringing Mistress Maisie to the keep.

Maisie bobbed in a curtsy. "At your service, milady."

Doubt and curiosity kept Brenna silent as Rye led them to the curved staircase. Torches threw fitful patterns of light over the steps and walls, barely illuminating their path, sputtering and hissing in the gloom.

When Rye pushed open the door to a chamber rarely used, Brenna thought she understood. He intended to imprison her. She halted just inside the door, her stomach knotting with fear. She knew of men who'd kept their wives or daughters imprisoned for their entire lives, existing on the fringe of life until sweet death released them from misery.

Whirling, Brenna yanked her hand from Rye's clasp and glowered at him. "I'll starve myself before I'll live as a prisoner!"

"Will you, milady? I'll keep that in mind." His booted foot shoved the heavy door wider. He looked at Mistress Maisie. "I'll return in a half hour. See that you do as you've been instructed."

Brenna stared as he swung the door shut behind him with a loud thud. She heard the bar drop. Then her startled gaze shifted to Maisie. The woman smiled hesitantly.

"Milady, his lordship wishes me to speak to ye on a grave matter."

"And what grave matter is that, may I ask?"

"The consummation of your vows," Maisie said after a brief pause. " 'Tis concerned, he is, that ye're not well prepared for the night."

It slowly sank in that Rye had brought someone to explain things to her, to ease her fears so that she would not fight him. Her heart thumped with dread, knowing that this night he would not be stayed.

Flinging back her head, she said, "His lordship is only concerned with his pleasure. I know well enough why he brought you, mistress, and though I bear you no ill will, I will not fall meekly into his bed."

Maisie gave her a helpless stare. " 'Tis not just for his own pleasure, milady, but 'tis for your well-being, I'm thinking. He was most specific about what 'tis ye are to know."

Brenna whirled away from her and stalked across the small chamber to the bright fire burning in a brass brazier.

"Tell me this," she said after a moment. "Can you explain how I might keep from breeding?"

Maisie blanched and shook her head. "Nay, milady. He was most hard about that. I am to tell ye only what ye must know to keep yourself from needless pain, and that is all."

"I see." Brenna kept her voice steady, controlled. "I am not to inconvenience him in any way, is that it?" It was appalling, how very young and foolish she felt at the moment. Curse the Norman, for realizing that she knew less than nothing about what was to happen to her.

"Milady—"

Brenna turned. "I don't wish him to be pleased, mistress. I *wish* to inconvenience him. Do you understand that?"

"Aye, milady, but 'tis only your own self that ye spite. He will take ye, willing or no. 'Tis only wise to know how to ease your own comfort." There was a short silence, then she added softly, "Ye must know that the vows have to be consummated for the marriage to be legal and unbreakable."

Oh yes, she knew that only too well!

Brenna turned back to look at the flames licking at the coals. She would be consumed, turned to ashes, just like those coals, just like Lot's wife had been turned to salt at knowing too much.

"Nay," she whispered, "I cannot do it."

She heard Maisie come up behind her, felt the soft comfort of a light touch. Brenna shuddered at it.

"Milady, he must not be as fierce as he seems, else he would not have brought me to ye. Let me tell ye, let me help ye."

After a moment Brenna nodded. "Aye, mistress. Tell me what I need to know. I fear my education is sadly lacking, in spite of all I have seen in my father's hall."

"Did she listen?"

Mistress Maisie looked up fearfully at the huge Norman who had dragged her from her hut in the night. She nodded. "Aye, milord. She listened."

Rye gave a grunt of satisfaction. "Good. Here is your payment, mistress. My man will escort you back to your home."

Maisie stared in astonishment at the silver coin he pressed into her callused palm. "Thankee, milord! Thankee!"

"See that you keep your tongue. My lady will not like having this known about the village."

"Nay, lord, I will tell no one. I have known Lady Brenna since her birth, and I am well acquainted with her pride. I would never shame her."

Rye nodded slowly. He'd half expected a certain amount of loyalty, as both women were Saxon, but there was an air of reproach that he'd even suggested the midwife might betray her lady. "See that you don't," he said, and forgot the woman entirely as he turned to the stairs.

He'd waited overlong already and would have the deed done. Perhaps it had not been kind to allow Brenna to turn him from his purpose on their wedding night, but she'd reminded him of a trapped fox the way she'd fought so hard and violently. Her heart had beat like the wings of a bird beneath his hand, and he'd yielded to pity.

His pity had cost him a day pursuing her. Now he would remove that small barrier that made her skittish as a filly in heat and show her that it was not the worst that could happen to a woman. Indeed, few woman had ever complained of his treatment of them, or of his lovemaking.

Reaching the door to the bedchamber where Brenna waited for him, Rye eyed the guard closely. The man gave him a sheepish look and shifted his feet when Rye stopped.

"Beware gifts from Saxons who seek to escape me from now on, Renaud. 'Twill cost you much more than ten stripes from my sergeant-at-arms the next time."

"Aye, seigneur. I did not think that two such fair women would give me drugged wine."

Rye snorted. "You did not think at all, Renaud. Did you have your weals tended?"

"Aye."

"Good. Allow no one in these chambers tonight, man or woman. I will call you if I need you."

When Rye entered the chamber, he saw Brenna immediately. She stood across the room, her back against a richly woven tapestry. She'd bathed, and her women were still tidying up the room. He stood by the door and waited until they were through, looking so impatient that two of the women began to shake with nervousness.

Brenna stared at him coolly, exhibiting no emotion at all. Rye returned her gaze, leaning back against the wall and crossing his arms over his chest. He'd removed his mail and mantle and wore the long tunic and hose of a nobleman. He'd bathed below, scorning the use of hot water to plunge into the tub of rainwater kept outside the kitchens. A pot of soap and a rough towel had taken care of his body, while his squire heated a towel to soften his beard. Like most Normans, he preferred a clean-shaven face, though at times events rendered it impossible to scrape his beard.

Rye rarely took pains with his appearance, preferring to concentrate on important matters. But he had noticed that several of the serving women below had given him more than one appreciative glance since he'd shed his mail and muddy cloak. A faint smile touched the corners of his lips. There would be little appreciation from his lovely wife, he knew. She looked like a tigress at bay, in spite of her efforts to appear calm and composed.

Perhaps the midwife had well prepared her for what was to come. He certainly hoped so. He'd never forced a woman, never hurt one. He had no desire to begin now, especially with the volatile, beautiful creature he had wed. To him, women were like spirited horses, meant to be appreciated and enjoyed, not mistreated.

Rye levered his long body away from the wall when the last servant had left, and he shut the door and threw the bar. It sounded loud in the quiet gloom of fire and candle glow.

When he turned, he saw that Brenna had moved and was standing close to the brazier. A small table was at hand, and a jug of wine and two goblets flanked a tray of food.

"Do you care to eat, my lord?" she asked quietly.

Rye moved toward her without replying. The firelight behind her silhouetted her slim curves in a way the dark wall tapestry had not, and he felt his stomach tighten with reaction. *Jésu!* she was lovely. 'Twas a good thing for her she had not worn that thin linen gown the night before, or their vows would have been consummated whether she agreed or no. His gaze skimmed over her curves and up to her face; a long silence spun out between them. She looked taut and nervous but did not try to run from him.

"I will sup if you will join me, milady."

Bread, cheese, cold meat, and fruit had been prepared. He watched Brenna warily as she motioned for him to sit and eat. There was no knife to cut meat or bread, for he had given instructions that none be left. Instead the meat had already been sliced, as well as the thick chunks of bread and cheese.

Brenna pushed some toward him, and he saw the slight tremor of her hand. Rye scowled. Damn, that the maid should be so terrified of him! He began to feel churlish and inept as a young boy. He berated himself again for not following his instincts and taking her that first night, when neither of them would have had time for thought. Now he knew that she was expecting the worst, and he wanted it to be much better than that. After all, he did not relish the idea of having to rape his wife every time he wished to bed her.

When he'd eaten—noting that Brenna barely touched her food but drank deeply of the wine—Rye stood up from the small bench by the table. Brenna looked up quickly, her eyes as wide and startled as a young deer's.

"Come here, Lady Brenna," he said softly, and put out his hand to her. She hesitated, then stood and put her hand in his palm. He drew her closer, his gaze focusing on the curves beneath her thin lawn gown. A faint hint of shadows and hollows teased him, and he felt the familiar tightening of desire stir his loins.

Looking at her through the eyes of a lover, he saw her lush beauty, the slumberous quality of her tawny amber eyes, and the promise of her full, wide mouth. Her straight nose was finely molded, her cheekbones high, giving her face a feline appearance that was sensual and appealing.

Perhaps being wed to this silken-skinned creature would ease some of his restlessness. And at least William had not suggested he wed a squint-eyed, skinny girl. He could be satisfied with Brenna, if she would only be tamed a bit. It was disconcerting to have a woman refuse him anything; none had dared for many a year, not since maturity had deepened his voice. Even Lady Madelon was cautious around him, as if she knew the man would not tolerate what the boy had endured. But where that noble dame had been shrewish and spiteful, Brenna was only defiant and rebellious, a wide difference in his eyes.

"Yield, *demoiselle*," he muttered hoarsely, stroking a hand along the curve of her cheek down to her shoulder. His fingers caught in the thin fabric of her gown, a loose gunna that flowed around her body in ephemeral wafts of light and shadow. Toying with the knot that fastened the gown at her shoulder, Lyon feasted his eyes on the slender ivory beauty of her body, the almost translucent hue of her skin. He felt her tremble beneath his touch, knew he unnerved her and was sorry for it.

"I cannot," Brenna whispered, so softly that for a moment he didn't react. He wasn't certain he'd heard her, and looked up from his perusal of her soft breasts. For the space of a heartbeat, he hesitated, looking deep into her golden eyes, cat's eyes, eyes he could drown in if he let himself be so foolish.

"What?"

"I said, I cannot yield to you, milord."

"What the devil do you mean by that?"

A pulse was beating rapidly in the hollow of her throat, creamy and fluttering. Lyon's hands grew tighter around her arms when she dragged in a deep breath and said calmly, "I am sworn to resist, my lord. You are my husband, it is true, but you are not my master."

Fighting the surge of anger that battled with the pure lust heating through his veins, with every beat of his heart and breath he took, Rye replied in a cool tone, "You are wrong, *demoiselle*. I am your husband and your master, not only by decree of the king, but the Church. You belong to me."

"Nay, lord," she said on the wings of a gasp as his grip tightened. There was stubborn mutiny in her eyes as she faced him, and Lyon felt the frustrating thrum of anger begin to overpower restraint.

"Don't say me nay," he growled so ominously that she grew still and quiet for a moment. "I am your husband, wed to you in the eyes of man and God, and you will yield me the bridal rights due me."

"And I am a woman, with rights of my own. You will not have me without my consent."

"On that score, fair lady, you are wrong," Rye said coldly. "I will have you this night and end this farce between us. Do not continue to try my patience."

Dammit, did the wench heed no one? Had she not had the way of it explained to her? Rye was frustrated and angry that she rejected him after he'd taken effort to soothe her offended pride and ease her anxiety. And worse, he was finding it most difficult to school his urges at the sight and feel of her.

Releasing her arms, he took a step back, startling her. She watched him with wide eyes as he shrugged out of his tunic and kicked off his boots. When his hands went to the tapes of his linen chainse and hose, she fled to the far corner.

Rye took his time, stripping off his garments and laying them over a chair, trying to cool his temper before he went after her. Straightening at last, he watched Brenna with a narrowed gaze. She seemed frozen to the wall; the tapestry behind her shifted slightly at a breeze from an unknown origin. It was cold everywhere in the chamber except directly in front of the fire, and he knew the heat could not reach to the corners.

"Come stand by the fire, Lady Brenna."

She shook her head. "Nay. I am warm enough where I am."

A surge of impatient anger shook him, and Rye moved toward her. He refused to play these ridiculous games any longer; he'd done everything he knew to put her at ease.

She sidestepped his approach nimbly, as he had counted on. He was ready when she skittered along the wall, and in a single leap, caught her. She struggled furiously, as he had also anticipated, and he slung her into his embrace and carried her to the bed before she could get enough leverage to do him any harm. He was taking no chances with her nails or feet, remembering the last time.

Flinging her back on the mattress, Rye held her down easily, his face only inches above hers. He recognized the anger in her eyes, and a faint smile curved the harsh line of his mouth.

"I bid you yield the day, *demoiselle*. Your struggle is ended, and 'twill go much easier if you allow me to love you gently."

"Love!" Brenna gave a ragged laugh. " 'Tis nothing to do with love in this bed, my lord, as well you know it. You view me as your property, as no more than a mare to breed. I am a woman, a *woman*, with feelings and desires, not just base urges. Nay, lord, you don't think of love when you think of bedding me."

He stared down at her, at the lovely face that glared at him with open rebellion, and felt that unfamiliar wave of dammed frustration that had dogged him since he'd first touched her. Devil take the wench!

"Call it love or base urges as you like," he said in the cold voice that usually made men take several steps back, "but whichever, your fight is finished."

"Nay—it has just begun." Sudden bright tears hazed her lovely eyes. "I will not yield to force, my lord. You must take me if you want me. Yea, you are much stronger than I, and 'twill be no contest, but know that I will not yield to you willingly."

"So be it," he growled, and sitting up so that his hard thighs straddled her body, he curled his fingers into the neck of her gown and pulled it away from her. She fought him, twisting and turning, managing to evade his grip for several minutes until he caught both her wrists in one hand and pulled her arms above her head. With his weight pressing her into the mattress, Rye methodically stripped away the remnants of her gown.

Half sobbing with fury and shame, Brenna writhed beneath him. His heavy body pinned her, and she felt the insistent nudge of his arousal against her bare thighs. Swallowing convulsively, she closed her eyes. He was huge; he would never fit, but would tear her apart with his swollen organ. Either Mistress Maisie must be wrong when she'd said God had made man and woman to fit together, or Rye de Lyon was uncommonly large. She would not survive the night.

Brenna felt his gaze linger on her bared skin, felt his hands move over her breasts, teasing a taut, beaded nipple between his thumb and forefinger until she bit her bottom lip between her teeth to keep from crying out. Her eyes flew open with shock as she felt a queer, intense tingling in the pit of her stomach.

Rye's darkly handsome face registered her reaction, and his hand shifted to stroke down over the ridge of her rib cage to her belly, lightly caressing her skin in feathery motions.

Shuddering, she squeezed her eyes shut again at the hot evidence of his desire, the fire of him she could feel next to her bare skin. Heated velvet, iron hard and pulsing with life, his stiff body probed against her belly in a slowly sensuous slide that made her breath catch and her heart pound as furiously as if she'd been running. *Madness, utter madness, to seek that touch!*

Even though she'd shut her eyes, Brenna could envision his taut-muscled frame, the powerful set of his shoulders and the flex of smooth brown skin. Shudders ran through her body as he continued to caress her, and she held tightly to her hatred of him as a talisman against his touch. He was the enemy, she reminded herself, the hated Norman foe who'd wrested England from its rightful king, and she would never yield. Nay, never.

His husky voice caught her attention. "Tell me, my lady wife, is your fear because of your maidenhood, or your lack of it?"

She flushed angrily. "I am no Norman whore. I've never given my favors lightly, as your breed seems to expect."

"My breed? 'Tis well-known that all men, Norman, Saxon, or whatever race, seek to lose themselves in a woman's body from time to time. 'Tis a curse more often than not, that a woman rarely refuses."

"You've known whores aplenty, it seems," Brenna said with a contemptuous twist of her mouth. The dark brush of his lashes lifted, and Rye's eyes glittered at her coldly.

"Aye, fair Brenna, I have indeed. Few that I would call lady. Or truthful. Your maidenhood will soon be proved, so if you speak falsely, tell me now."

She stared at him. For a fleeting instant, she thought she saw an avenue of escape. His pride would surely not let him remain wed to an unchaste bride. . . .

He laughed softly, and she saw in his face that he knew her thoughts. "Nay, lady, do not answer. I wish to see for myself if you are virgin. 'Tis a much more pleasant method than listening to a physician's report, and if you are not, then I shall still have tasted your charms."

Stiffening, Brenna swore at him, in French and English and Italian, the words spewing from her in a hot tide of hurt fury and resentment. She detested the feeling of helplessness that gripped her, the awful knowing she had lost control of her fate.

When Rye shifted, spreading her thighs with his knees and leaning over her body, Brenna tensed. For a moment his head was bent, his gaze intent on what his hand was doing, then he looked up at her with a curious expression. His eyes were glazed with hot lights, turning to a blue so deep that it stabbed at her in the dim glow of fire and candles. Oddly, Brenna felt a strange lurch inside, a reaction to the intent expression on his face. For a brief moment he'd looked almost vulnerable, though she knew no Norman could ever feel such a way.

"Yield, sweet Brenna," he murmured, caressing her face with a gentle hand. "I would not be harsh with you, if you will allow me to be otherwise. In truth, I admire your fire and courage as much as I do your beauty."

She turned her head on the pillow and closed her eyes against the temptation to surrender to his coaxing voice and soft words. "Nay, I cannot yield. . . ." She heard his brief sigh, then felt the mattress dip with his weight.

Still between her spread thighs, Rye bent to capture her mouth with his, his tongue thrusting deeply between her parted lips. Instead of repelling her, it sparked a heated quickening inside, a response to the touch of his hands on her breasts, the taste of his lips. Insanity. It had to be insanity to feel anything but hatred for this man, this symbol of ruthless Norman cruelty and dominance.

Snared in the throes of Lyon's passion, Brenna could not understand the flush that swept her body, in spite of Mistress Maisie's information. The midwife had spoken mainly of facts, not the intangibles such as this flaming ache that throbbed moistly where he touched her. His hand dragged back and forth through the nest of red-gold curls at the juncture of her thighs, producing a chain of shivers that made her back arch.

Something was happening to her; she could feel it, feel the starburst of sensation that caused a melting center of fire to spread out from his touch against her. His fingers moved in a clever rhythm that made her shudder, made her thighs open for him instead of close against him.

Rye surrounded her, enveloped her with his hard man's body and his mouth, his searing touch. Gasping for breath, she tried to twist her face away from his kiss; he let her. His mouth grazed her ear, his heated breath whispering over the delicate whorls and making her shiver.

He sat up, his gaze intent on what his hand was doing, that broad hand dark against her pale skin, moving over her to touch and tease and torment in ways she'd never dreamed of. Brenna burned where he touched, her skin quivering with reaction to the scrape of his fingers.

Straining against his grip, her arms over her head and pressed back into the furs on the bed, Brenna knew dimly that she was only making it pleasurable for him with her movements, but she couldn't stop. Something deeply primitive raged in her, out of control and insistent and mind numbing. Had he known she would feel this way? Had the midwife known?

Unprepared, Brenna felt the hot prick of tears sting her eyelids. It didn't help to see his broad chest working in a ragged rhythm, to know that his breath was coming in short pants for air. His eyes, those beautifully wicked blue eyes, were hot and narrowed, glittering beneath the thick brush of his lashes. The sensual line of his mouth was curved in a faint smile that deepened when she glared at him.

"You still deny your own nature, *chérie*," he said in a husky timbre that sent a shudder down her body. "Beneath your cold protests lies a fiery need. Don't fight it. Don't fight me."

Brenna would have raged at him, but his thumb returned to that spot that sparked such fire in her, raking across her in an erotic slide that made her gasp and arch up at him. It was exquisite torment. His body burned hot against her; a flush heated her torso and made her nipples tighten into dark pink buds that tempted him to lean forward again and lavish attention on her breast. He sucked and tugged until she was moaning deep in her throat, a helpless sound that was torn from her very soul.

Flames ripped through her, coiling upward from the center of her being. An odd tightness squeezed inside her, a searing need that made her hips press up, seeking an end to the nameless yearning. She throbbed with it, ached with a fierce pulsation that drowned out everything but the desire to ease it.

Lifting his head at last, his hand still working magic in that shadowed cleft between her thighs, Rye blew softly on her breast and smiled at her gasping shiver. Then he repeated the same act on her other breast, trailing steamy kisses along the divide between them. It was torture, an erotic torture that she'd never imagined the best sorcerer could devise. Nothing in Brenna's life had ever prepared her for this, this mindless response of her body when her brain was drowning in heated oblivion.

It was galling that this Norman had known, that he'd promised her sweet torment and kept his word—Brenna gasped as he moved between her thighs, his rigid organ taking the place of his hand.

Rye was breathing in shallow pants, his corded muscles quivering with the strain of holding her wrists and holding back. She bucked beneath him, heated skin sliding between her spread thighs. A soft whimper escaped her, shaming and childlike. Brenna closed her eyes as he pressed forward.

Now the fiery velvet of him rubbed against her moist entrance as his hand had done, intimately searing and vaguely threatening. This was different. This was what the midwife had mentioned, the moment when he would enter her and penetrate her body.

Yet somehow she couldn't summon the will to continue the fight. Her treacherous body was eagerly waiting, damp and ready and empty, waiting for him to fill her.

Slipping his hard body inside her that first tiny bit, Rye paused, breathing hard, his head thrown back and the strong column of his throat working. Brenna's tight inner muscles closed around him, gripping the end of his shaft in a convulsive movement that made him groan.

"God!" he muttered thickly; his fingers tightened around her wrists; he pressed her more deeply into the furs on the bed. "God!" he said again, the word coming out on a groan.

Slowly, steadily, he pushed against her, squeezing into her with a heavy pressure that made Brenna's entire body arch in an effort to stop the invasion. The delicious slide of him began to alter to pain, sharp and searing.

When he encountered the thin membrane of her virginity, he lifted his head to look at her briefly, a light of triumph in his eyes that made her cry out wordlessly. He kissed her again, softly, almost tenderly, his mouth moving on her lips with a sweet pressure that lulled her into a false sense of security as her body adjusted to invasion.

Then he began to move again. The burning ache between her thighs spread outward, up and sharp and shattering. Brenna fought him, her breath coming in shallow pants for air, her legs drawing up in an attempt to push him away. He held her easily, muttering words meant to comfort her.

"Lie still, and the pain will ease. 'Twill hurt only this once, sweeting. . . . God, you're so tight . . . like a glove around me. . . ."

Brenna tried to hold back her shaming tears, but the pain that was spreading through her intensified, until with another groan, Rye shoved forward in a swift lunge that filled her completely. The invasion tore a scream from her. His mouth found hers again, caught her lips in a surprising tenderness.

Fully sheathed by her body, Rye lay tensely still. His arms were bent on each side of her body, and when he lifted his head at last to stare down into her tear-streaked face, he was frowning.

"I hurt you, I know, but 'twas unavoidable. There will be only pleasure after this time, *chérie*."

Choking on tears and pain and a sense of betrayal, Brenna's head twisted on the pillows. "Touch me again, and I swear I'll poison you!"

To her surprise he laughed softly and shifted his body in a deeper settling. She felt the strong length of him push deeply inside her. He panted with the effort, his hard band of stomach muscles contracting against her belly. His voice was rough with strain.

"Sweet wife, your love talk needs some work."

Staring up at him with hot resentment, Brenna wondered how he could make light of her suffering. She ached inside with the heavy weight of him and was grateful that he did not move for several moments. When she felt his muscles tense again, she stiffened in apprehension.

He pulled her arms down slightly, easing the strain on her, then lowered his head to kiss her. She thought about biting him, but knew he could inflict much more pain on her than she could him, and refrained. Every inch of her felt defeated, surrounded by him. His mouth was warm and soft as he kissed her, and slowly she felt the heat of his lips draw a reluctant response.

Her world was Rye de Lyon, the masculine smell of him, the feel of his hard man's body on her, the swell of him inside her. Her breathing quickened when his hand moved to her breast, teasing the aching nipple into a rigid knot.

Scraping against her sensitive inner walls, Rye began to move inside her with long, sure strokes. At first it was painful, then merely uncomfortable. Then, as his rhythm increased, growing faster and stronger, pushing into her, pulling out, she felt the rising crescendo of anticipation.

It rose on a tide of need, an aching fire that flowed from her belly and through her veins, until she was panting as loudly as he. Someone called out—she?—and Brenna felt his hips recoil against her, felt the shattering loss of her control. Her lips sought his, grazed along the strong line of his jaw, the thick column of his throat, the misted skin of his shoulder, his chest, where the thick pelt of hair tickled her nose. It didn't matter. Nothing mattered but drawing him deep inside her, seeking an end to that nameless ache that threatened to devour her.

Pain and hunger melded together, a culmination that lifted her against him, and she heard his satisfied growl in her ear just before he gave a final deep thrust that felt as if it would tear her apart. The explosion was searing and almost painful, a flood of sweet release that she couldn't escape. His body pulsed inside her, a savage tremor that took her breath away and made him groan again, loud and fierce. His arms went taut around her, pressing against her sides, his breath harsh in her ear.

For several long moments he lay on her, his weight supported by his arms, then he drew back slightly. His dark blue gaze drifted from her face down, lingered on her tight beaded nipples and flushed torso. A faint smile curved that ruthless mouth, and he looked up from her heaving chest to watch her as she worked for enough air to fill her lungs.

"Your passion surprises me, Brenna," he murmured

after a moment. He released her wrists, found her hand, twined his fingers through hers. He was still hard inside her, his body rubbing with every move he made. "Though it should not be such a surprise, I vow, since you fought me with equal fervor."

Her chin tilted slightly. She felt strange, weak and yet restless, as if there was more to come when she didn't know what. Her voice quivered slightly. "In a contest of strength you may have won, but I shall yet bring you low, Norman."

His palm cupped her chin, long fingers gripping firmly. "Rye," he said softly. "Use my name. I would hear it on your lips."

"Nay! Dog! Cur! Those are more likely names for you."

To her surprise and chagrin, he chuckled. "Well, 'tis true I have said in the past that I would be bored by a pious wife. I think now that I spoke hastily. Come, sweet Brenna—show me a little wifely tenderness."

"I'll show you my dagger between your ribs."

"Ah, but then I could not ease the ache inside you near as well, and I know that you have not yet tasted the best." He grazed her lips with his. "Shall I show you what you missed, my sweet? 'Twill give you ease, I vow."

"Show me only your back, Norman. I want nothing from you."

"P'raps 'tis best for now, as you are sore from being broached." He kissed her angry lips quickly. "But soon, my sweet, I shall give you what you don't know you want."

Releasing her chin, Rye rolled from her, withdrawing from her body and leaving her achingly empty. She felt it keenly and scowled at her weakness. She throbbed; ached. Something warm and sticky smeared her thighs, and she wasn't surprised to see the blood. Proof of his taking of her. The loss of her innocence, though in truth she could not remember a time when she had ever felt innocent. Ignorant, maybe, inexperienced, but never innocent. Life had not been kind enough to grant her that.

"Lady wife," Rye murmured after several long moments had passed, "you are now well and truly wed and would do good to think about the future. I may be a stark knight, but I do not mistreat women." He lifted a long strand of her burnished hair and held it up; firelight glinted in the thick waves with a russet sheen. "Admit your yielding, and we will deal well together."

Brenna's throat spasmed with grief. Admit surrender? It would take much more than a simple bleeding to force her to that end.

"Nay, Norman," she breathed softly, her eyes glittering in the light as he turned to her. "I yield to no man. Every time you want me, you must take me with the knowledge that I will fight you every moment, and that I detest you. Do you think because you have used my body you have won me? You have not."

She saw his face tighten, the curved scar flexing with the leap of a muscle in his jaw, and knew he was angry. It was easier to prick him than she'd thought.

He sat up, glaring at her. "You have lost, Brenna. It is useless to keep fighting me. You will only lose every time."

"But I will not surrender."

Swearing, he jerked from the bed. Brenna swallowed the lump in her throat as he towered over her, looking fierce and furious in the play of firelight. Clutching the tangled bed sheets in her fists, she met his gaze steadily. She would not allow him to intimidate her with his size. She'd survived his worst, hadn't she?

But then he said softly, "Your body has already yielded what you won't admit," and she knew he was right. A sweep of despair filled her. How could she combat him if even her body turned traitor?

CHAPTER 7

IT WAS STILL DARK when Brenna woke. Her first thought was that she had survived the night. And Lyon.

The chamber was soft with thick shadows, only a faint glow emanating from the brazier. She felt Rye at her side, heard the rasp of his even breath. He lay between her and the door, and she doubted she could make it without waking him. Most soldiers slept lightly, and he seemed no exception.

Lying still and quiet, she took silent assessment of her hurts. She ached in places she'd never acknowledged until now, and she winced at the memory of how she'd clung to Rye like a besotted fool. It made her want to scream her frustration aloud. Even worse, she must now worry about a babe.

Visions of her mother came back with a rush, the gentle Lady Clarice writhing in childbed, her lovely face blotched with tears and her hands clutching at bedclothes as she bit her lips against a scream. Brenna squeezed her eyes tightly shut against the memory. A stab of panic cut deeply.

Nay, she could not stand it. She could not bear this Norman's child. It would tear her apart, be much worse than his body's invasion had been.

Shifting slightly away from him, Brenna wondered about the man she'd wed. He was fierce, yea, but had shown her an unexpected kindness on their wedding night. None since her mother had shown her gentleness, but Rye had been kinder than her own blood kin. She could not fathom his reasons.

Her father had already told her he thought her mad to resist, that she was a woman and it was her duty to yield. There had been no sympathy for her from Dunstan, but she had not expected any. Nor had she expected Rye's show of concern for her feelings, his muttered reassurances even while he took what he wanted from her.

Brenna worried her bottom lip with her teeth. The man was an enigma. He had no reason to be kind, to have treated her gently, yet he'd not been overly harsh. Most of the men she knew had no compunctions about beating wives or daughters; she had given Rye de Lyon sufficient cause to strike her in the past few days, yet he had not. She had publicly defied him, held him up to ridicule by his men, and he had responded by fetching a midwife to explain what no one else had done, not even her family.

One thing she had learned was that men had their pride. Perhaps fathers could be excused for not giving well-loved daughters a beating, but never a husband. Such a man would be thought weak by his contemporaries. What vengeance could Rye have in mind, Brenna wondered with a trace of unease. He would not show restraint unless he had something in mind to bring her to heel, she was certain.

Blinking against the shadows, Brenna wished she could see Rye's face in the dark. Perhaps there would be a hint of his intentions in those beautiful features. *Beautiful*. Yea, as beautiful as Lucifer, and as proud. Were she anyone else, she might have yielded to his lazy smile, and the hot glances he gave her from beneath the thick brush of his jet lashes. But she was not anyone else. She was Brenna of Marwald and had sworn to fight the Norman invader for as long as there was breath in her body.

Her renewed determination must have transferred to

Rye, for he stirred beside her. Lifting his head, he reached for her and laughed when she resisted.

"Nay, *chérie*," he murmured, his voice hazy with sleep and seductively warm, "do not fight me. There's naught left to save. Your maidenhead is torn, and you are mine. Let me show you what it means to love a man."

"Love?" She managed a laugh that was meant to be scornful but sounded much too shaky. "You speak lightly of it, my lord. I assure you all you will teach me is more hate."

He rolled over, pulling her beneath him in the thick furs. " 'Tis your choice, Brenna. Come, hate me with your sweet body, then."

Though she struggled, refusing to give in to him, Rye won out easily. His strength was too great for her, and he knew how to fend off her blows. Her hands skidded off his taut muscles without harm, though she did manage to tear a few strips of flesh from his chest with her nails before he caught her wrists and held them over her head in one great fist.

"Give over, my fiery vixen," he muttered when she gave a frustrated shriek. His breath drifted over her neck, warm and tickling the wisps of loose hair, and she shivered at what he was doing with his hands.

"Never!" The word ended in a choking gasp as his free hand descended to that shadowy cleft between her thighs and lingered in an erotic caress. His fingers began to stroke with light, teasing motions that sparked a heat, making her quiver with the force of it. "Never," she repeated hoarsely and heard his soft laugh in her ear.

"You already yield, though you deny it. Your body knows my touch, and seeks it eagerly."

"Nay!" Clenching her thighs tightly together, she sought to trap his hand and keep it still. He shoved his knee between her legs and spread them, bending to kiss her mouth as his hand slid smoothly over her sensitive flesh. The dull ache that was inside her subtly altered to a new throb that spread up into her belly. She bit back a moan, and was suddenly, fiercely glad for the dark, shielding shadows. At least he couldn't see her, could not see how he affected her with his touch.

It shouldn't be this way, she thought wildly, jerking her head away from his invading mouth, he shouldn't be able to make her feel this treacherous weakness inside. This was his vengeance, then, this torment that made her body yield to him what her mind would not. She shuddered, thinking it more cruel than a beating would have been.

A silken fire raged in her, hot and humiliating. But this time she fought for and held tightly to her control, not allowing him to guess at the turmoil inside.

Rye's hands and mouth swept her to the very brink of that vaguely threatening release time and again, but Brenna managed to stay the waves of desire that taunted her. She thought of past disasters instead of his touch.

Instead of yielding to that strange fire in her, she recalled Marwald's destruction after Hastings, lonely years in cold Norman keeps; she won the struggle against yielding. 'Twas a hard-won victory, indeed, she thought as she turned her head toward the wall.

Finally, ignoring her stiff resistance, Rye spread her thighs and took her, his body pounding into her until he reached his own release. Then he rested atop her for a long moment, his breath husking over her ear.

"You fight your own nature," he growled softly. He levered to one elbow to stare down at her in the gloom. " 'Tis not ice that runs in your veins, Brenna, but fire. I've felt it in your touch, heard it in your voice. Do not play this game with me. You could win much by gentle yielding."

"Win what, my lord?" Her voice was tart. "Another hour of bed sport? I can well do without that. Go tumble one of the kitchen wenches. I hear they cast admiring glances your way."

"Do they?" She felt the smooth flex of his arm muscles as he tightened his embrace. "Then p'raps I shall. 'Tis certain they will be willing to pleasure a man better than a highborn vixen, I vow."

Brenna fought the urge to rail at him, knowing he

would only take that to mean she cared what he did. She didn't, but he would assume with customary male arrogance that she did.

"Do what you like," she said with casual indifference. "But come to me with the stink of a whore on you, and I will make you sorry."

There was a long moment of silence; she felt the contraction of his stomach muscles against her belly, then, to her amazement, heard him begin to laugh.

"By all the saints, woman, you amuse me as much as you anger me." Rye's laughter rumbled in his chest, and she grew angry enough to try to squirm from under him. He held her easily. "Fiery little vixen," he murmured, still chuckling, and wrapped his hand in her hair to turn her head up for his kiss.

"Nay, my little firebrand," he said when she tried to turn away, "I've no reason to suffer another woman's moods when I have you so easy at hand. And I've come to enjoy our lively romps, though I much prefer your rages to silence."

Brenna would have been happy to tell him that he had just given her another weapon to use against him, but he covered her lips with his mouth and smothered anything she might have said. This time he didn't bother to attempt to arouse her, but slipped his hard body back inside her and took his own pleasure in spite of her fierce struggle.

It occurred to her to resent the way her wishes were ignored, but in the struggle to resist his searing thrusts, she found her control slipping. It was all she could do to hold tight to her hatred.

When the sun spilled over the far edges of land, armed and mounted soldiers bunched in the bailey of Marwald keep; four men flanked Brenna—hard-faced, unsmiling men set by Lyon to guard her. Wagons and carts rumbled in the dawn chill, and somewhere in the entourage, gentle Rachel sat weeping at the uncertainty of her future and her fear of her new lord.

Brenna fought her own fears. She hated Rye with heated fervor at that moment, though she'd known when the first talk of marriage was broached that she was destined to leave Marwald. A huge lump clogged her throat, and she set her mouth in a taut line.

A soldier brought her white palfrey, and she glanced at it. " 'Tis not the horse I wish to ride. Bring my stallion."

"My lady—" The soldier paused, obviously flustered. " 'Tis the horse my lord bade you use."

Stiffening, Brenna glared at him. "I ride much faster on the other. Fetch it for me."

After a moment the man bowed and left, but when he returned, he reported with a wooden face that the seigneur would not allow it.

"Will not allow it?" Brenna saw only a humiliating public defeat at hand if she persisted, so she held her tongue and ungraciously accepted a hand up atop the dainty white palfrey. She arranged her skirts with an irritated flounce and looked up to meet her father's gaze.

He gave her an ironic smile. "Well, daughter. I see that Lyon has managed to do what others have not."

"And what is that, pray?" she snapped.

"Curb thy unruly tongue."

Tapping her riding whip against her velvet skirts, Brenna said as calmly as possible, "The man is a brute and a fiend, but you would care little for that. You have your lands back, and your precious sons roam free to fight for whatever war is declared next. Does it matter that you have wed your daughter to the devil?"

An ugly flush spread over Dunstan's face, and his lips grew taut with suppressed anger. There was something in his eyes that held her gaze for a moment, a flicker of some emotion resembling raw pain, but Brenna could think of no reason for it.

"Ye look unharmed," he said after a moment. "I see no bruises on ye."

"Nay, there are no bruises that I would show the world, that much is certain." Brenna's throat ached, and she felt suddenly like bursting into tears and didn't know why. "Did you wish to be rid of me so badly?" she couldn't keep from asking, then wished she hadn't. Affecting a light shrug, she added, "Not that it matters."

Dunstan struggled silently for a moment, then said, "I have never understood ye, but I do not wish ye ill. Ye were a prize to be won by some man, make no mistake on't. I am old and will die soon. I'm glad that ye have a fierce husband to keep ye safely."

"Who's to keep me safely from him?" Brenna asked around the sudden press of tears stinging her eyes. She blinked them back, refusing to weep like a child.

Wearily her father said, "If ye'll tear down that stone wall ye hide behind, ye won't need protection from him, girl. Think on it."

Whatever she might have responded went unvoiced as Rye approached.

"Fare thee well, my lord," Dunstan said heavily, and put out a hand. Rye took it in his, and the two men exchanged a brief glance of male understanding before parting.

Brenna wondered about that as they rode out of the bailey in the early-morning quiet, the subtle understanding between two very different men. Both had seemed to know what the other was thinking without words, whereas she had trouble knowing how to interpret her *own* thoughts and emotions.

A queer twinge made her flinch. She'd been so angry for so long, 'twas frightening to entertain any other emotion. Nay, she could not bear to think on what might have happened if she had not had her hate to sustain her the past ten years.

Little at Marwald had been as she recalled it; former wood palisades were being replaced by stone; the bedchambers where she'd played as a child were new and covered with rich tapestries and filled with unfamiliar furniture. Only faint echoes of happier times had remained for her—a glimpse of a familiar face or the sweet scent of new-mown hay being stored in the stone warehouses in the bailey.

But now even that small comfort was to be denied

her. Her new home, Moorleah, was as strange to her as Normandy had been, though the keep had belonged to her mother. There had been brief visits there as a child. The wood and dirt donjon was cold and drafty, and the smoke hole in the roof had not drawn properly, filling the hall with thick gray smoke. Moorleah had been in general disrepair, but she had heard that William had begun to restore it for a knight he deemed worthy of such a prize: Rye de Lyon.

It had not then occurred to Brenna that she was to be a part of the prize given to that stark knight who battled so well for his king.

She cast a speculative glance toward Rye. He rode at the head of the column of men, his easy bearing marking him as leader even to strangers. There was an air of authority about him that made her a little uneasy but apparently instilled great confidence in his men.

Shrugging her shoulders under the heavy cloak she wore, Brenna shifted her gaze to the men who guarded her. She wondered sourly if Rye thought she would attempt escape in full view of him and his armed soldiers, or if they were for her protection. She doubted the latter. Who would dare attack William's man?

A fine rain began to mist around her, and she pulled the hood lower to shield her face. In early spring the ground was still frozen in places. Her palfrey stepped in a light, eager prance, as if expecting they would break into a canter at any moment. Brenna smiled wistfully. She had delighted in her early-morning rides, delighted in shocking gentle Rachel by riding a fierce stallion. The animal's temperament matched her own, she thought, and she liked the feeling it gave her to master him.

Which was probably why her new husband forbade her to ride the horse. Men seemed to prefer thinking that only they could successfully tame a spirited beast. Brenna gave an irritated shrug. She would yet show Rye de Lyon that she could master Normans as well as stallions.

The silly females of her acquaintance would almost faint if she shared those views with them, but Brenna had fought popular opinion on most rules as long as she could remember. At times her voiced opinions greatly vexed poor Rachel. A faint smile curved Brenna's mouth at the thought. When they paused at midday to break bread, she expressed her views to Rachel on riding the stallion—more to take her mind off her troubles than anything else.

The slender dark-haired girl looked at her skeptically. "I cannot imagine riding such a bold animal, my lady."

Brenna lifted a delicate eyebrow. "You were brought up in the Norman court, Rachel, where many bold and shocking things happened. Did you not ever dare to do anything . . . unsupervised?"

Rachel colored. "Not until I met you. Since then I have been introduced to an entirely new way of thinking." An irrepressible twinkle gleamed in her eyes as she gazed at Brenna. "And I have found myself in more scrapes than I could ever have concocted on my own."

"Quite true, I vow. I do seem to have a talent for doing what others find obnoxious." Brenna munched on her hard chunk of bread and let her gaze stray to Rye. "I've a hunch that my unsupervised days will be few and far between," she mused softly, unaware she'd spoken aloud until Rachel made an uneasy sound.

"I dare not allow you to draw me in to more mischief, my lady. I fear our new lord and his wrath and would not like to find myself flogged."

"Flogged?" Brenna lifted both brows. "He would not dare. Your father, after all, was a knight of William's. I have noticed that Normans do not go hardly on their own, only on us English."

"Have you also noticed that most men deem it their Christian duty to beat their women?" Rachel asked more tartly than was her norm. "I certainly have. My own father believed it necessary to chastise me twice a week, whether I had displeased him or not. I was glad to be sent to the court."

Brenna was quiet for a moment. A light wind lifted the hood to her cloak and batted it against her face. She flipped the edges away with an impatient hand. The strong scent of damp gorse filled the air, and she let her gaze shift along the horizon. Gentle hills humped in a haze of brown and green in the distance, toward Moorleah, where Rye was taking her. She would be totally at his mercy, with none of her kin to aid her. It was a terrifying thought.

At least, even in Normandy, she'd had her aunt to come to her aid if she asked, though she'd never done so. Just knowing she could was somehow enough. And, admittedly, her Aunt Bertrice was a rather silly woman, affectionate and kind in her way, but forgetting about Brenna's existence until Brenna did something to attract her attention. Many a night had seen a young Brenna lying on her straw pallet in a cold corner of the castle and weeping with fear.

But no more. Now she was grown, and she would not weep when she could fight. Even Rye. He would find no weakness in her. Still—it would be nice to seek solace with someone who cared about her.

Her glance fell on her maid, and she felt a twinge of guilt for ofttimes speaking harshly to her. Rachel was as much a pawn as she was and did not deserve harsh words.

"Rachel . . ." Hesitating, she put out a tentative hand. It was quite uncharacteristic of her to touch someone else, and Rachel had learned some time ago to curb her tendency to offer affection. "Rachel—we are quite alone, just the two of us, in a place very alien to what we've left. Shall we . . . shall we band together, you and I? 'Twould be little enough we could do, but 'twould be a comfort, I think."

Rachel's lovely dark eyes widened, and she smiled with such relief that Brenna knew she'd longed for the same.

"Aye, my lady, I would."

Slowly Brenna put her hand on the girl's shoulder, a gesture of friendship and peace. Her heart was pounding and her mouth was dry, and when Rachel touched her lightly on the arm, she didn't cringe away.

Even though the day was gray and drizzly, it seemed a bit brighter to Brenna. She wasn't certain why, but knew it had something to do with feeling not quite so alone as she had before.

She exhaled slowly and didn't offer so much as a snarl when one of her guards told her curtly that it was time to remount. Perhaps she wasn't overly hospitable, but she wasn't overly hostile, either.

Brenna shot Rye de Lyon a quick glance when she was mounted atop her palfrey again. Perhaps he had not done her such a bad turn by being so fierce. His actions had forced her to reach out to someone else for comfort. Now she would find it easier to resist his efforts to dominate her. . . .

Rye saw the militant gleam in Brenna's eye and knew it for what it was. More stubborn resistance. *Jésu!* did the wench not know how to admit defeat? It galled him. Most men would have bent a knee to him by now, wise enough to take refuge in whatever mercy he offered rather than continue a course of destruction. Yet Brenna of Marwald did not.

A wave of irritation washed through him, and his mouth set in a taut line. Thrice he had taken her, and thrice she had somehow defeated him. He could understand the first time; there was pain involved in the broaching of a maiden. The second time he had tried to ease her fears and give her pleasure. 'Twas her own folly and mulish nature that had prevented it. The third time —bah!

His annoyance increased. St. Jerome! but he should be turning his attention to his business instead of a woman. How could she have pricked him so that he thought about her instead of what was ahead? No mere woman should occupy a man's thoughts beyond physical pleasure, or the remote attention due them. Females were for breeding sons as more knights for the battle, and little else. That had always been his philosophy, and though he desired women, he did not need them beyond casual appetites.

Yet somehow Brenna lingered in his mind. He thought of how soft her skin was, like the satiny furring of a flower beneath his hand, rich and luxurious. Her hair was like silk in his hands, sliding through his fingers and smelling slightly of the perfume she used. He wanted to bury himself inside her lush curves, the tempting body that lay beneath her heavy cloak.

The thought made his body tighten in anticipation, pushing painfully against his chainse and mail. His jaw set angrily. She bedeviled him, even when she was riding her pure white palfrey with an innocent air of silence. 'Twas madness, and for a brief instant of illumination, Rye suddenly understood how other men had allowed themselves to act the fool over a woman.

It was shaming, and he felt as if someone had dashed a bucket of cold water over him. Nay, not for Rye de Lyon the humiliation of being led about like a trained bear! His lady wife had best watch her tongue, or she would find that his forbearance did not extend to suffering her whims for even an instant.

Sliding her another frowning glance, Rye saw that she had pulled the hood of her cloak over her head to protect it from the rain. The loose material hid her face. He was glad. He needed no memories of those fair features to nudge his desire. He would school his urges, as he'd schooled his body for warfare. 'Twas a simple matter of training. He would do his duty by her, but that was all.

Perhaps he *would* go elsewhere for an uncomplicated roll in the straw. Then he would not have to battle the ache she started in him with just a glance. He could ease his body on another and be done with it.

Touching his spurs to his mount, Rye set a hard pace for the rest of the day. He wanted to reach Moorleah as soon as possible, and put as much distance as he could between them. The shrewish wench ignited too many thoughts he should not have.

CHAPTER 8

IT WAS ALMOST DARK of the following day before the weary cavalcade reached Moorleah. The stone structure rose abruptly from the heights of a steep slope, half-finished battlements like great teeth gnashing at the sullen sky. Brenna caught her breath. This was not the place of her memory. This . . . this was a cold, forbidding castle.

Reining his horse close to her palfrey, Rye eyed her coolly. "Our home, my lady." His voice held a hint of mockery that drew her gaze. " 'Tis as welcoming as your bed, I think."

"Do you?" She met his shadowed eyes with an uplifted chin. "More so, I vow."

Gauntleted hands tightened on his reins, and the great destrier tossed its head and snorted dangerously. It was a beautiful animal, but lethal. Trained war-horses were capable of tearing a man to bits with hooves and teeth. It reminded her of Rye.

As her nervous little palfrey sidestepped neatly, Brenna said softly, "I find the Norman castles as cold and empty of comfort as I do Norman knights." She gestured at the towering pile of stone. "Though 'twas once my mother's, I find little in it of comfort. William took it from us and has now given it away. 'Tis not *our* home, but yours."

" 'Twould do you well to remember that," Rye said with a snap, and spurred his horse ahead of her. Brenna looked after him with a faint smile. She could not forget it. She had nothing of her own, nothing. She was a possession, a pawn to be used for barter, and she'd been given to Rye for these towers of stone and wood hulking like a bleak vulture against the horizon. Nay, she was not likely to forget.

A loud creak heralded the lowering of the drawbridge, and as the carts and riders passed beneath the portcullis, a rumble of thunder sounded. Horses trembled and snorted, and men scurried to tasks before the approaching storm. The sky rolled with dark clouds that blotted out the softer hue of early springtime, plunging the bailey into deep shadows.

Torches flickered, and the smell of rain was strong in the air. Brenna followed her escort across a second moat and under a portcullis, then allowed a soldier to assist her from her mount. She saw Rachel hurrying toward her, heard Rye's man-at-arms bellowing orders. Whips cracked, and the rattle of wooden cart wheels over the drawbridge grew louder.

"This way, my lady," someone said, and Brenna turned to see a young page beckoning her forward. Lifting her skirts from the dirt of the bailey, she followed him up the wide steps that led to a gaping portal of the inner keep.

Behind the thick inner walls loomed a huge round tower. It was much lighter than the more familiar *tours* that had walls twenty to thirty feet thick, and would obviously provide sanctuary only as a last resort. The huge outer wall and moat enclosed a vast area littered with outbuildings, the stables, storehouses, shops, and mews. This inner court bore six smaller towers, as well as the huge one still being constructed.

Brenna's eyes widened. A formidable fortress indeed. It should withstand any enemy attack. This castle brought to mind all the great stone castles she'd seen in

Normandy. It was apparent that civilization was reaching this corner of England in spite of resistance.

Rain burst overhead just as Brenna and Rachel were escorted through a huge double wooden door and into a damp, dark chamber lit by flickering torches. A guard stood by the door of the guardroom and eyed them as they entered.

The anxious page ushered them from the guardroom through another door. Long tables had been set up in the great hall, as it was near time for the evening meal, and servants scurried back and forth with trenchers of hard bread and platters of meat and vegetables. The smell of fresh rushes and thick smoke filled the air; a fire burned brightly in the center of the chamber. Smoke rose in a thin curl to reach the hole in the roof, drawing well, Brenna noticed.

Her gaze took in the massive new timbers of the vaulted ceiling, then moved to the hooded gyrfalcons lurking in the rafters. Bells decorated leather jesses attaching the birds to their perches, and jangled each time one of the deadly birds moved.

Deep galleries had been built on three sides of the hall, and a group of musicians gathered in an alcove and played their instruments softly. Drawing in a deep breath at how unfamiliar to her Moorleah was, Brenna's gaze shifted to the end of the hall.

Seated on a raised dais, two women waited in high-backed, carved wooden chairs, regarding the newcomers with grave civility.

Brenna frowned. No one had told her to expect guests, and she wondered irritably if she was to entertain two such apparently noble women no sooner than she entered the keep. She knew what to do; it had been part of her rigid training in Normandy. That she had more frequently than not chosen not to abide by the simple rules of a hostess had been a form of rebellion against her father and king.

Pausing, Brenna flicked a glance toward Rachel, who shrugged lightly.

"Please," one of the women called loudly, "enter and be welcome. Moorleah greets you."

Brenna's frown deepened. Rye had not mentioned any other women who would be living here, but this woman spoke with the air of ownership. Straightening her shoulders and sparing a moment's regret that she had to enter looking like a windblown doxy, Brenna approached the dais.

As she drew closer, she saw that the woman who had spoken was fairly young, probably only a few years older than herself. The other woman had the lines of age in her face, and her patrician features showed no sign of the same welcome.

Executing a polite gesture of courtesy, Brenna looked up expectantly. The younger woman was smiling.

"I understand that Sir Rye—excuse me—Lord Lyon, has just been wed. Would you be his lady?"

Brenna nodded. "I am Lady Brenna. And you?"

Rising from the chair to step forward, the slender young woman put her arms around Brenna before she could avoid her embrace. "Welcome, dear sister," she said softly, "I am Raissa, widow of Count Yves Le Bec and sister to your husband."

Sister? Brenna stood stiffly in the embrace, not knowing what to do or say. She felt a surge of anger at Rye that he had not told her of his family, but honesty demanded that she admit she had not asked. She'd not cared. Now she had a sister by law, and from the resemblance, a mother by law, also.

Brenna felt a stir of uneasiness. The older woman was obviously not pleased; her face was set in cold, austere lines. It was apparent that she had been a great beauty in her day, but Brenna could find none of her son's masculine features in her.

Seeing Brenna's glance, Lady Raissa released her and turned. "This is my mother, Lady Madelon, Countess of Lyon. Or—I suppose now, dowager."

Lady Madelon gave a terse nod. Long fingers drummed on the arm of the carved chair. Her wide, dark eyes raked Brenna intently, from her feet to her face, lingering on her rain-spattered garments.

"I see you bring no great fortune with you," she said at last, her husky voice rich with irony and disdain.

Brenna stiffened at the contempt in her tone. "Should I wear it strung about my neck?" she shot back tartly, then flushed at her rudeness. Unforgivable, under these circumstances. This woman could make her life intolerable if she chose. But then, Brenna could do the same. She'd had long experience with misery.

There was a moment of tense silence, then Lady Raissa gave a burst of choked laughter. "Aye, Mother, 'tis ill of us to judge Rye's lady after days of travel," she said at last, still chuckling. "And from the looks of her, I would say he chose her for beauty, not her wealth."

"Certainly not her sweet nature," Lady Madelon said in a cold tone, rising to her feet in elegant motion.

"Nay, Lady Madelon," Brenna said boldly, "I'm not known for my charity or gentle ways. Some say 'tis a curse, but I prefer frankness to subtleties."

"Do you?" The dark eyes regarded her steadily. " 'Tis well that you remember I am acquainted with all forms of such rudeness thinly cloaked in polite terms. I deal hardly with those who practice it."

"Do not be too hard on yourself, madam," Brenna said in the same scathing tone that Lady Madelon used. "One is never too old to learn manners."

Drawing herself up with a hiss of fury, Lady Madelon looked as if she would like to launch an attack on Brenna, a fact that bothered the younger woman not one whit. She had met women such as Lady Madelon aplenty in the Norman castles and detested each of them fervently.

Things were not off to a good start.

Rye noticed that immediately when he stepped into the hall. His stepmother and his wife were faced off like two weasels, tense and looking as if they would be clawing at one another within seconds. He felt a burst of irritation, then wry amusement. Why not? Had he expected it would be easy, having Madelon and Brenna under the same roof? Nay, he had not been that big a fool.

Striding toward them, Rye reached the four women just as his stepmother took an angry step forward, lifting her hand as if to strike Brenna. That would have been disastrous, and Rye grabbed her wrist before her palm could connect.

"Lady Madelon," he said with heavy irony, "how pleasant it is to see you again."

His stepmother's nostrils were pinched, and her lips were drawn back from her teeth in the suggestion of a snarl. Of course, it would have been ill-bred of her to actually snarl, and Lady Madelon, he reflected sourly, was rarely caught out. It was a tribute to Brenna's sharp tongue that she had managed to provoke that formidable dame to violence within scant minutes of their meeting.

It took a moment for Lady Madelon to control her temper, and when she did, she gave Rye a long, steady stare.

"A fit mate for you," she said at last. "But I always knew you would manage to find a viper to bring into our nest."

A faint smile curled Rye's mouth. He released her hand. "As usual, my lady, you are overly kind. You must have missed me."

"Oh, assuredly." No one could miss the sarcasm in her husky voice. "There has been a scarcity of bastards in Normandy since you left."

"I find that difficult to believe," Rye said coolly, but his eyes were narrowed and hot with anger. "P'raps just a scarcity of noble bastards."

"Noble? Aye, your father certainly thought so. You could do no wrong in his eyes, no matter which side of the blanket you were whelped on."

The bitter words hung heavily in the air, and Rye gave a nonchalant shrug. " 'Tis no secret that my father loved me. P'raps 'twas to make up for the absence of a mother's tender care."

Lady Madelon stiffened. " 'Tis not my fault that the

bitch who whelped you ran off and left you with us. Before God, I would rather she had kept you with her."

"You've made that plain enough for twenty-nine years," Rye said evenly. "But if she had, my lady, who would have cared for you these ten years past?"

A long silence stretched, and Rye could see the appalled expressions on the faces of his wife and sister. Raissa. Thank God, she loved him. She was the only female he'd ever cared about, the only one who loved him unreservedly. The only one who loved him at all . . .

The hellcat he'd wed had made it plain she despised him, and in truth, he had expected no different. But Raissa, she had adored him from infancy. It warmed him, and God knew, there was little enough warmth in his life. His gaze swung back to his stepmother.

He made an impatient motion with his hand. "It grows late, and we have been traveling for two days. Did you get my message, my lady?"

Recovering her composure, Lady Madelon nodded coolly. "Aye. Your chambers have been readied. Your soldiers and squires will sleep on straw pallets in the guardroom, and on the stairs of the north tower. Food has been prepared, and we will be served when you are ready."

Rye nodded. "See that my lady wife has water to bathe before we eat. She will want to change her garments for dry ones."

Surprised by his consideration, Brenna shot him a quick glance. He didn't look at her, but was gazing at his sister with a soft smile that made him look suddenly younger, and very handsome. She'd thought him coldly attractive before, but the glow in his eyes lightened them to a blue as soft as a summer sky, and his sensual mouth curved into a smile that made her heart lurch.

For an instant she felt a surge of pity for him, that he, too, had felt the sharp pangs of loss and abandonment. And he had felt the sense of displacement that she had felt as well, the uncertainty of what the future would bring.

But her pity faded quickly when she recalled how he had forced her to yield to him, and when he turned to look at her, her gaze was cold.

"Shall someone direct me to my chambers, my lord?" she asked stiffly. "Or do I aimlessly wander the halls?"

" 'Tis your choice, sweet wife." He seemed amused at her acerbity. "Do not think to sharpen your claws on me, as you have my stepmother. I will not tolerate it, and you would not like the consequences."

It didn't seem the time to defy him, not with Lady Madelon watching and gloating, and Lady Raissa gazing at her with such a troubled expression that Brenna felt a pang of guilt for her sharp words. She nodded.

"Aye, my lord. I am overtired." It was as close as she would come to an apology; Rye seemed to understand that and looked at her gravely.

"You need not come to the hall to eat if you prefer," he said after a moment. "I will send someone with food to our chamber."

His offer surprised her, and Brenna smiled at him before she thought. " 'Tis not necessary, my lord. I am not that weary." She studied him for a moment, feeling an abstract admiration for his masculine beauty, the perfect arrangement of his features only slightly marred by the thin scar that curved from his left eyebrow to the sharp angle of his cheekbone.

Blue eyes beneath the black brush of his lashes were fixed on her politely, regarding her with a kind of wary patience. It occurred to her that he merely wanted to keep her and his stepmother separated, and she didn't blame him. She had no special desire to trade barbs until she was more rested. Then she would join into the fray with all gusto.

"Do you wish that I should take my meal alone, my lord?"

"Nay, milady. Do as you will. Makes little difference to me."

His careless reply banished the softening she'd begun to feel, and she snapped, "I always do!"

Some of the humor returned to his remote gaze, and

his teeth flashed white in his beard-shadowed face. "I think I already knew that. Your place will be set in the hall, my sweet. Suit yourself."

Though she swung back and forth between "yea" and "nay" with alarming rapidity, Brenna ended by taking her meal in the great hall. There was no point in setting a precedent, not when Lady Madelon would be certain to ascribe her absence to fear or nervousness. Nay, she would be there, and she would act the part of great lady as well as any other woman ever had.

There didn't seem to be much difference to Brenna, between the great ladies that she had known and the lowest serving wenches. Most of them were as petty and selfish as any peasant woman could be, but with more style. Only her mother had filled the description of *lady*, and Brenna had often wondered with a trace of bitterness if that was just a child's fond memory.

Observing Lady Madelon from a distance, Brenna had the cynical thought that the lady was as close to common as any she had ever seen in Normandy. She wondered how the woman had produced such a lovely, sweet daughter as Raissa.

Raissa, a young widow with two lively children, went out of her way to welcome Brenna. It was as if she had taken it upon herself to make up for her mother's lack of welcome, though she did try to explain Lady Madelon's chill reception in a low, confidential tone.

"She's always been the countess, you see," Raissa said during the third course, when hot meat pies, frumenty, and a platter of dumplings were served at the high table. "In Normandy we were always at court. Whenever the duke—your king—holds court there, my mother delights in the gaiety. It helps to make up for the loss of my other brother."

"Other brother?" Brenna lifted an inquisitive brow.

"Yea, Jean-Luc." Raissa stared down at her hands for a moment, then looked up. "He would inherit, you see, as the legitimate heir. When he was killed, my father made Rye the heir. Papa was killed not long after, and my mother has never forgiven either of them for Rye inheriting."

"How was your father killed?" Brenna flushed slightly at the rudeness of her question, but Raissa smiled.

"It was a long time ago. I can speak about it now. 'Twas at Hastings, here in England. He rode into the English shield ring to try to save Taillefer, who was William's favorite minstrel." Her voice shook slightly. "He was slain in the attempt, as was Taillefer."

Brenna was silent for a moment, then said, "I'm sorry. 'Twas a grievous loss, I know."

"Aye. More so for Rye than for me. I loved my father, but Rye spent most of his time with him. And he had to watch him die, you see. Worse, it was not easy at home for Rye." She cleared her throat and cast a quick glance up the table toward her mother. "My mother was very hurt by Papa's liasion with Rye's mother."

Brenna hid her surprise. "They were wed when he had a child with another?"

Raissa looked down at her plate, then back up at Brenna and nodded unhappily. " 'Tis no secret in Normandy, and the public nature of my father's affair with Rye's mother was well-known. The lady was wellborn, you see, and my father appealed to the pope for dissolvement of his vows to my mother so he could wed her." A sad smile curled Raissa's mouth. "It was a great embarrassment for my mother, and even when the pope refused an annulment, Papa continued to see his lady for a time."

"This doesn't bother you?" Brenna stared at the girl in amazement.

"Aye, but it happened before I was born, and I grew up with the gossip. 'Tis common knowledge everywhere, so I am certain you will hear of it before much time has passed."

"Aye, people do like to talk—unless it's *their* secrets being told." Brenna slid a speculative glance at Rye. He'd seated her at his right, his sister on her other side. Lady Madelon sat at his left, and she was engaged in animated conversation with Beaumont. Rye stared moodily into his cup.

Brenna was aware of him the entire meal, gazing into his mulled wine and ignoring everything around him as if he were the only person in the hall. Musicians played gay tunes on a gallery that looked out over the tables, and jugglers, acrobats, and trained animals performed for their lord's entertainment. Rye appeared to see none of them. He ate sparingly, drank sparingly. Most of his attention seemed focused on the dull glitter of jewels circling his goblet.

It was part of Brenna's dowry, the treasure Dunstan had sent with her. Someone had been busy unpacking, she saw; it amused her to wonder who. Lady Madelon, perhaps? Not that it really mattered. She didn't care about the gold plate, or jeweled goblets, or exquisite linens.

She cared desperately only about her freedom.

Tilting her head, Brenna swallowed the last of her mulled wine. A squire moved to refill it.

"Nay," Rye murmured, putting a hand over her cup and gaining her surprised attention and the squire's instant obedience. "My lady says too much wine makes her ill." His lazy smile slanted at her before he returned his regard to the jeweled cup.

Brenna felt the stirring of anger. She was not in the habit of overindulging in wine, but she was damned if she would allow this braying Norman jackal to say her nay!

"Squire," she said, halting the young man with her commanding tone, "my lord is too kind, but I am feeling well. I will have more."

Now she had Rye's full attention. The lazy smile vanished and was replaced by a slight frown. The squire stood in an agony of indecision, his conflicting emotions obvious on his face. Apparently Rye took pity on the young boy.

"As the countess wishes, Gowain. It has been a long day for us all."

Somewhat gratified that he had not argued her command, Brenna's anger ebbed. She had been surly, when she should have held her tongue. It wouldn't do to look too bold, not now, not since her behavior was being observed and noted by many of Lady Madelon's acquaintances. Why give them fuel for their gossip? Her resistance could be done in private.

"Thank you, my lord, for your consideration," she said so sweetly that Rye's eyes narrowed in suspicion. He gave her a long, considering stare, but she only sipped prettily from her goblet and played the part of model wife. It would give him something to think about, she thought irritably. He would wonder what she was planning.

Indeed, for the rest of the evening Rye cast glances in her direction as if wondering when the sword would fall. It gave Brenna a slightly superior feeling, as if she had somehow managed to turn the tables on him.

That feeling evaporated quickly when Rye finally stood, cupping her elbow in his broad palm and lifting her with him. " 'Tis time to bed, wife," he said in answer to her protest.

Music swirled loudly from the gallery above, so that he had to lean close to hear her soft words. "I would like to remain awhile, my lord. The jugglers amuse me."

"Another time." His fingers tightened on her arm when her eyes flashed defiance. " 'Twould be ill advised to offer another protest, milady. See how avidly Lady Madelon awaits your humiliation?"

It was a telling point. Brenna nodded stiffly. "Aye, my lord. I believe I *am* feeling weary again."

Chuckling, Rye pulled her with him, and they crossed the great hall toward the staircase slowly, impeded by the antics of the acrobats and trained dogs. Soldiers and knights were laughing, some of them drunk and grabbing at the servant girls. Loud squeals rent the air, and an occasional yelp of pain cut through the din.

It was nothing Brenna hadn't seen and heard before, but when a particularly overzealous suitor gave a roar and swung his screaming choice into brawny arms, she couldn't help a small gasp of rage.

"Stop him!" she demanded, jerking to a halt and tugging at Rye's arm. "That brute will hurt her."

Rye swung a disinterested glance toward the couple. "I don't think so. Bourchard has been tumbling Daisy for over a year now. She seems to like it."

"Like it! Do you hear her screaming?"

"Does she sound hurt?" His brow snapped down. " 'Tis a game they play, Brenna, that's all. I do not allow my men to harm an unwilling maid."

" 'Tis a shame you do not ascribe to that end yourself."

Jerking her to him, he stared down at her for a moment, his expression cold. "You are no maid. You are my wife. I will hear no more of your shrewish tongue or discuss this matter with you."

Whatever Brenna had been about to retort remained unsaid as she recognized his struggle for control. There was much more to his anger than her barbs, and she remained silent. After a moment he gave a satisfied nod of his head and took her with him up the curved staircase.

Their chamber was large, with a huge brazier in the center to give off heat. A carved wooden bed bore heavy draperies around it, and rich carpets were scattered across the floor. Tapestries warmed the walls, and several small tables bore various items. There was even a chess set on one table, where it looked as if a game had been interrupted and waited on the opponents to return.

Rachel had moved in Brenna's clothing, and the coffers stood against a far wall. Tallow candles gave off plenty of light, and shimmered as Rye shut the chamber door and threw the bar.

Brenna couldn't help a sudden shudder. He saw it and smiled crookedly.

"Still afraid, brave Brenna?"

"Nay. 'Twas just a chill."

"A chill?" He crossed to stand in front of her. "Then let me warm you. What kind of husband would allow his wife to be cold?"

"Norman," she muttered resentfully, but did not

struggle when he pulled her into his embrace. As always, she stiffened.

"Do you hate me so much that you cannot stand my touch, *chérie?*"

She thought for a moment. "Nay. 'Tis not just your touch, but anyone's. I do not like to be fondled."

"As your husband, I appreciate that, but wish you would confine your dislike to others, not me." His voice was wry, and she detected the weariness beneath it. "I am not a man to look without touching. . . ."

"Then don't look," she returned with asperity, and his teeth flashed in the gloom of shadow and light.

"Ah, another challenge, my sweet?" His hand rubbed down her arm in a leisurely caress, and his expression was thoughtful as he watched her shiver with reaction. "P'raps 'tis not your wont to be touched, but you must accustom yourself to my hand on you, Brenna. I will not hurt you."

Her disbelieving stare made him grin again. "If you will allow it, I will prove to you that you can enjoy the union between man and woman."

Brenna strained away from him, feeling his growing arousal against her. "I am sworn to the fight," she muttered, staring at the gilt embroidery on his tunic. She dared not look up at his eyes; her surrender lay in them, for even now, with his hands smoothing over her arms and toying with tendrils of hair at her nape, she could feel the hot magic he worked stirring in her.

Clenching her fists so hard, her nails cut into her palms, Brenna forced her attention away from his caresses. Almost desperately she said, "I thought Normans always had much restraint, my lord. Do your words mean that you could not curb your desire at the mere sight of a woman?"

"I could if I chose." He tilted her chin up on the curl of his fingers to look into her face. "I do not choose to. You are my wife. I have a right to look at you. And touch you."

"Ah, it's so nice to know that just the sight of my

beauty spurs you into boyish rhapsodies of passion, so that you cannot look without touching. . . ."

"Enough." His voice was rough. "Do you think I don't know what you're trying to do?"

"I think you are more boy than man, who cannot hold even his basest desires in check. 'Tis the way of animals, is it not, to act upon urges instead of intellect?"

Dropping his hands away from her, Rye looked at her with furious eyes. "You know how to prick a man, wench."

His low growl made her stomach lurch, but she steadied her hands in the folds of her gown and took a deep breath.

"I mean not to prick, my lord, but to understand. I have seen only men's mindless passion, you see, not this joyful union you speak of."

That seemed to rankle. Rye inhaled sharply, and the skin over his cheekbones turned a dull red that made his dark complexion look ruddy. It was an important revelation to Brenna, who suddenly understood that a man's ability to pleasure a woman upon his whim was important. To fail at it seemed humiliating.

After a moment Rye said roughly, " 'Tis no great feat to curb desire, but 'tis better to be fulfilled."

"If 'tis no great feat, milord," Brenna shot back, "why do you not allow me to see for myself how it is meant?"

"How do you expect me to do that?" Rye's hands loosened on her arms. "If you mean that I should not ever touch you—"

"Nay, not that," Brenna said quickly, "but p'raps show me that you can."

"Can what?" He raked a hand through his hair and stared at her suspiciously. "You're speaking in riddles, and I am too weary to puzzle them."

"Can just look and not touch." She shrugged at his narrowed glance. "You've said you find it easy enough— I would see for myself that you speak the truth."

"What game is this you seek to play?"

" 'Tis . . . 'tis no game, milord, but a test. Can you pass it?"

"A test—I see nothing but a play of straws, *demoiselle*. There can be no conclusions here, as I do not care if you think me too weak-willed to resist touching you. I have gone without a woman for months before, and if you think your beauty so great I cannot resist you, you are misled."

In spite of his angry words, Brenna saw the uncertainty in his eyes. She shrugged lightly.

"Very well, milord. You say you are not overset by my female attributes, and I believe you. 'Tis your choice to touch me at your will."

"Aye," he growled, and as if to prove it, jerked her close, his hands splaying over her back, moving to her breasts to cup them in his palms. Brenna stared up at him steadily. With a soft curse Rye thrust her away from him. "Curse you, woman—do you think you're superior because I choose my own desires over yours?"

"Nay, lord." She cast her eyes down demurely. " 'Tis not my place to think. I am only a woman, in a woman's poor, frail frame. I have no desires save to serve, and I—"

Rye swore horribly. "I've never seen such a harpy. Do not worry about my 'base urges' tonight, *demoiselle*, for I have no desire to touch you. When I do, do not be fooled into thinking I will forgo my pleasure, for I will not."

"Aye, milord," Brenna said, her words meek, but her tone plainly triumphant. Rye shot her a furious glance.

"St. Jerome! but I think that the women in paradise must be all mute, or 'twould not be paradise at all."

"Blasphemy, milord?" Brenna murmured, avoiding Rye as she moved to the opposite side of the big canopied bed in the center of the room.

Giving an incoherent snarl, Rye tore off his tunic and hose and flung them at the clothes pole. Brenna tried not to look when he stalked, completely naked, to the brazier and stirred up the glowering coals into a tidy blaze again. Hurriedly she slipped beneath the furs and coverlets spread over their bed, unwilling to test his angry vow to leave her be for the time being.

She lay stiffly when he came to bed, jerking up the furs over his shoulders and turning his back to her. For a long moment she did not dare move, afraid any movement on her part would precipitate action on his. The fire in the brazier burned low again, the coals like sullen red and gray eyes in the night. Rye's breathing was soft and even.

Scarcely able to believe her good fortune in escaping his devastating attention this eve, Brenna finally closed her eyes in relief. She had won the first match. She must plan for the second, for she had no doubt that he would test her wits greatly.

And, oddly enough, she felt a moment's pique that he'd given in so easily. If he had truly wanted her, truly could not resist her, it seemed that he would have offered more arguments. Puzzled by this contradiction in her nature, it took Brenna a long time to fall asleep.

CHAPTER 9

Rye's abstinence did not last long, Brenna learned to her dismay. With the first gray fingers of dawn lightening the room, he rolled over and took her into his arms.

"Nay, *chérie*," he said softly when she resisted, " 'tis my wont to touch you now."

"Then touch and be damned!"

He chuckled. "You do not lose well, *ma chérie*. P'raps you should lose more often so you will know how 'tis done."

"I seem to have lost only contests of strength against you, but do not intend that it shall always be thus."

His hands moved over her bare body, lightly skimming the curves and hollows with a touch that made her shiver in reaction. "Shall I mark that down for future study? We can have a squire keep a tally stick if you like, of which one of us wins, and which one of us loses."

"Insufferable ass." Brenna squirmed, then sucked in a sharp breath when Rye's hand rubbed down over her belly to the nest of curls between her thighs. "Stop that."

"Why? You seem to like it. . . ."

"Nay, I do not." Brenna caught his hand, but he did not slow in his long, smooth caresses that sparked a raging fire in the pit of her stomach. Her heart beat so hard and fast that it hammered painfully against her ribs, and her breath seemed as heated and labored as a blacksmith's bellows. Her fingers dug into his wrist, but the iron-hard sinews and tendons were not the least fettered by her wild tugs.

Rye's mouth sought and found the rigid peak of her breast, his morning beard scratching her tender skin while his hand continued with the erotic movements until she was almost panting. He lifted his head, then grazed his lips over the arched curve of her throat, nipping lightly.

"Chérie," he murmured against her ear, his breath almost as labored as hers, "do not struggle so hard against me. You cannot win by force of arms and must yield. Give me that sweet yielding, and I will show you pleasure, I give you my promise."

For a moment Brenna couldn't speak. She was afraid any word would reveal her internal struggle, the battle she fought to stay the rising press of fire that made her want to yield. In that instant she hated him, then she admitted to herself that it was her own weakness she hated. That any man could do this to her was shaming, but that it was a man she had sworn to fight and hate was doubly shaming.

"I . . . don't want . . . anything . . . from you," she finally managed to say between clenched teeth. "Leave me be."

"Nay. Never. When I want you, I shall have you, whether you say *yea* or not." His knees nudged her resisting thighs apart as if to prove his words, and he lifted to rest on one elbow and gaze down at her, his body pressing between her legs. Deliberate and slow, he scraped his body over the aching moistness at the apex of her thighs.

Brenna opened her eyes, turning her head to stare at him. The early gray light left one side of his face in shadow; his eyes looked dark and smoky beneath the tangled brush of his lashes, his sensual mouth curved downward in a sulky tilt. For an instant she was reminded of a spoiled, petulant boy instead of a man, and she felt less threatened.

"Get . . . *off* . . . me!" she said with a sudden ferocity that apparently took Rye by surprise. When she shoved hard at him with the heels of her hands, she heard a soft *whoof*! as he tilted backward.

"What the devil do you think you're doing?" He caught her hands in his and pinned her back against the soft weave of linen sheets. The petulant expression had disappeared, and in its place was the angry scowl of a thwarted male.

Brenna glared up at him. "Rejecting you."

He stared at her in amazement. "What?"

"Rejecting you. 'Tis true that you have wed me, but I do not have to obey your every whim. I have my own thoughts and desires and do not intend to submit myself to yours."

" 'Tis the wife's place to submit to her husband, or have you forgotten your wedding vows?" Rye's gaze was narrowed and hot. He pressed her deeper into the mattress. "You gave your oath, sweet wife."

"My oath was not made freely, as you well know." She looked away from his darkening scowl. "You may overpower my body, but you will never overpower my mind and heart. 'Tis not possible."

If she hadn't been so nervous, Brenna might have laughed at the expression on Rye's face. He looked absolutely stunned—bewildered by her words. Apparently no one had ever suggested to him that a female might have such revolutionary thoughts.

When he continued to stare at her without speaking, Brenna took a deep breath and wriggled from under his weight, expecting at any moment for him to jerk her back. He didn't. Instead he remained leaning on one elbow in the wide bed and watching as she reached for her gunna and kirtle hanging on the clothes pole, his eyes narrowed in thought and his heavy brow shading the blue glitter. Even his mouth was set in a thoughtful line, taut as a strung bow and just as tense.

He said nothing until Brenna had slipped her small

kid shoes onto her feet and confined her heavy mane of hair in a net. The sound of his voice startled her. She turned with a nervous gasp.

"I will think on what you have said, but that is all. I do not intend that you shall leave my bed."

"I did not ask that. I asked only for your respect." Brenna curled her hands into the folds of her green velvet gown and met his gaze without flinching.

Rye sat up and flung his long legs over the side of the bed.

"Respect must be earned, my lady. It is not a gift. It is a hard-won reward." He stood up, a magnificent masculine creature exuding power and confidence and raw sensuality, a combination of smooth muscle and bronzed skin and steely determination. He moved to her and took her chin in his hard palm, his long fingers cradling her face. "I do not give respect easily. Nor do I ask it from others. If 'tis your desire to have respect"—his fingers stroked her skin lightly—"then seek it with earnest effort instead of strident demands."

There was something very intimidating about a naked man towering over her. He was too close, much too close, and Brenna found it impossible to reply. She did the next best thing, which was to tilt her chin in the air and give him a level stare that should have been imperious and intimidating but only made him chuckle.

"Ah, *chérie*," he murmured, letting his hand drop along the curve of her throat, "I knew you would not bore me. I did not know you were a rebel baron with so much hellfire in the swing of your skirts, but I should have." He looked amused when she made an inarticulate sound of anger, and bent to let his lips brush across hers. Then he released her and turned away as if she no longer mattered.

Brenna glared at his broad back. Why did even a victory feel like a defeat?

During the week that followed their arrival, Brenna had little time to dwell on what had transpired between them. There was much for her to do as new chatelaine, and she discovered the first day that Lady Madelon had no intention of offering aid in any way. Indeed, that formidable dame did her best to throw out obstacles.

If not for the fact that she knew she had to establish her dominance or spend the rest of her days in misery, Brenna might have allowed the dowager full rein. But to do so would be disastrous, much as she detested the idea of playing the role of Lyon's lady.

Their first unpleasant confrontation came the morning after Brenna's arrival at Moorleah. Following morning mass in the small castle chapel, they broke their fast with a light meal. While squires and servants still cleared the long trestle tables of wooden bowls emptied of porridge, Rye took his leave of the high table. Dogs quarreled noisily for the scraps of hard bread flung to them as the men-at-arms and soldiers rose from tables to follow Rye from the keep.

Lady Raissa excused herself with a brief glance at Brenna, murmuring that she must see to one of her sons, who had taken a chill in the night.

"Should you need me, my lady," she offered before she left, "I will be at your service."

Lady Madelon laughed shortly. "I doubt she will need you to help her choose new garments, or listen to the lutes and minstrels. Go, see to Gilles. He needs his mother."

With a wry smile Raissa left the hall, and Brenna was left alone with Lady Madelon. For a moment neither woman spoke; then Brenna rose from her high-backed chair and stepped close to her mother by law.

She gazed down at Madelon with a lifted brow. "It is my duty to see to the comfort of those here at Moorleah, Lady Madelon, and though I appreciate your kind assistance, I will relieve you of that burden now." She held out her hand with the palm up. "I understand you have the keys to the stores."

Lady Madelon eyed her stonily, fingering the *chauffemains* filled with hot coals that she carried at her side for warmth. "I see no need for you to concern yourself with such. It has long been my wont to abide as head of a household, where you are just an untried girl scarcely out of leading strings. I've no desire to bear Rye's anger should he return to maggoty bread and cold meat this eve."

"Neither do I." Brenna's tone was sharp, and she tamped down her rising irritation with an effort. "I am not so untried as you might think. I was trained in the household of Lady Bertrice Fouchard and know what I am about when I choose to act. The ring of keys, please."

For a moment Brenna thought Lady Madelon would refuse. Then the older woman lifted her shoulders in a careless gesture and unfastened the keys from the girdle around her slender waist.

"Take care you do not earn your husband's wrath, my fine lady," she said with a faint sneer, "for I assure you that Rye can be formidable in his rages."

"Indeed?" Brenna held the key ring in the curl of her fingers and let it dangle with a noisy jingle. "I have seen his angers, madam, and find them worthy of little note."

"Do you now?" Lady Madelon's fingers drummed against the table with a faint click of her long nails. "I wonder if he would be surprised to hear that."

"I doubt it." Brenna's voice was dry. "P'raps you have not noticed it, madam, but I am not one to keep my feelings secret."

Tilting back her aristocratic head, Lady Madelon looked at Brenna for a long moment, her cool gaze assessing as if considering her worth as an adversary. "Be certain that you know which lion's nose you tweak," she finally said in a soft tone that conveyed a malicious tinge of warning, "for you would not be the first maid Rye swallowed without a thought."

"I did not expect kindness, nor am I fool enough to think he will not try," Brenna answered sharply. "But I am not of the mettle of some women. Indeed, I would say that I am more suited to warrior than maid, and your son should watch to his own safety. Do not try to frighten me with oblique warnings, my lady, for I do not frighten easily."

"I never meant to frighten you, child." Her lips turned up in a slight smile. "I merely meant to save you undue pain. 'Tis your choice what you do."

"Aye, my lady. Well I know that." Brenna slid the ring of keys onto her girdle. "I would not have us begin our lives in this keep as enemies, but if you choose it thus, I will oblige you."

"Now I must ask—is that an oblique warning?"

"If you choose to hear it thusly." Brenna forced herself to meet Lady Madelon's icy gaze without flinching. She knew well how it would be if this woman seized the upper hand; she'd seen it happen too often in the Norman keeps where she had spent her childhood, and she had no intention of being a pawn here as well. To her relief Lady Madelon gave a slight nod.

"We shall see who carries the day, child, but I yield now to your position. Do not think I will hesitate to take what I deem my due, however, simply because I prefer more subtle methods."

"I never thought that for a moment."

Brenna did Lady Madelon the courtesy of a brief, polite obeisance, then rose and turned on her heel to stalk from the hall with every appearance of complete confidence. No one could know that her heart was hammering so hard and fast she felt almost faint, or that her mouth was dry. She had not missed the enmity in the older woman's eyes, nor overlooked the thinly veiled warning in her words. War had been declared.

Somewhat to Brenna's relief, she discovered that Lady Madelon was a capable chatelaine, and the warehouses well stocked with stores of food. Most of it was dried and musty by now, as the winter had been hard and bleak, but would suffice until crops could be harvested. In the meantime ships could bring food from sunnier climes to fill the larder, and there were always the forests full of game for the huntsmen to seek should the supply of livestock dwindle.

With Rachel by her side and a young squire scurrying

at her beck and call and making notes on all that was needed, Brenna found that time passed quickly. By the time dusk nibbled at the edges of the sky on the first day, she had made accurate estimates of all the stores and ordered what was needed.

It was not a difficult task, though time-consuming. As most of the keep servants were Saxon, and she spoke English as a first language, she was able to ask pointed questions and listen carefully to replies. Moorleah was largely self-sufficient, as a strategic keep needed to be. Very little was not grown or bred there for food, and even the fuel that lit the fires came from nearby forests. Moorleah's proximity to the sea provided ample fish and access to what goods needed to be purchased, and its location near the intersection of a road leading to London and one to the sea was also convenient.

The week passed quickly with so much to do, and Brenna began to see the wisdom of fortifying Moorleah so well. It was a frequent stop for travelers from the north going south, and from east to west as well. Yea, King William had chosen the right man to guard this position, she thought as she contemplated the full contingent of soldiers and well-trained knights sparring in the field. Rye and his men rode out early every morning, usually not returning until dusk shadowed the sky.

This day, as she saw the fresh rushes strewn upon the floors and the old ones thrown out, she wondered at his late arrival. Deep shadows made it almost dark outside, and he had not yet returned from the sparring field beyond the gates.

Seeing to the proper spreading of the rushes, she did not hear their arrival until a page shouted his lord's safe return, and she paused in her labors. She spared a moment's wonder as to where he'd been, then dismissed it as she beckoned for the page and gave orders to have the evening meal served as soon as her lord and his men entered the hall.

"Aye, milady," the page murmured, then hesitated.

"What is it?" she asked, seeing his hesitation. "Is there aught amiss?"

"Nay, but—" The young boy stumbled to a halt, then flushed and added quickly, "I was told that there is naught ready to eat, milady."

Brenna stared at him. "Impossible," she said in a sharp tone that made the boy blink rapidly. "I gave the cook the menu myself."

" 'Tis what I was told, milady." He backed away, bowing toward her with an air of desperation. "I will see that the cook hears your command."

"Never mind." Brenna slanted a glance at Rachel, who looked just as surprised as Brenna imagined she herself did. "I will question the cook myself."

By the time she reached the cookhouse, she realized that no delicious smells wafted from the huge ovens. Seized with fury, Brenna stalked into the stone building and found the cook cowering behind a heavy table piled high with empty platters and cooking utensils. Firelight from the hearth flickered over his frightened face.

"Where is the meal I bade you prepare?" she asked in a much more even tone than she'd thought herself capable of at this moment. She gestured to the ovens and hearths, where only a single huge cauldron hung. "I see none of the roast lamb, oxen, and pasties I ordered."

The cook, a plump little man with a high forehead and protruding eyes, made a sharp exclamation in some obscure dialect, then swallowed and began again. "My lady, please forgive—I was told that you had changed your mind, and I was to prepare only for the kitchen servants."

Brenna stared at him. "Who gave such a ridiculous order? Did you think everyone else in the keep was fasting?"

He swallowed again and rolled his eyes heavenward. "It is not my wont to question . . . I only obey."

"Again I ask—whom did you obey?"

The cook looked down at the stone tiles beneath his feet and shook his head. "I am not at liberty to say, my lady."

"Are you not?" Brenna controlled an angry outburst with a supreme effort of will. "I see. 'Tis no matter. I think I know who would countermand my orders. Hear you this, cook—from this day forward I am the mistress of this keep, and if you do not obey me, you will suffer the consequences. I will not allow harm to come to you through another's fault, but neither will I bear your insolence and disobedience. If 'twere any other mistress who had to tell her husband and lord he must go without his evening meal, she would see your head roll on the stones of the courtyard."

Shaking, the cook fell to his knees blubbering, and Brenna made an impatient gesture. "Get up, fool! What do you have that can be served quickly?"

"P-p-pottage, my lady. And bread. Greens, mayhap."

"There is dried fish in the stores. Make pasties. They should not take too long. And you'd best bring up plenty of casks from the cellars. P'raps an abundance of ale will ease the hunger for the men, though I doubt that Lord Lyon will be so easy to please."

"Aye, milady." Rising swiftly from his knees for such a pudgy man, the cook raced to follow her orders, and the kitchen came alive with a flurry of activity.

Rachel followed Brenna back to the hall. "Who do you think would give such an order, my lady? His lordship will be most displeased at not having a hot meal ready."

"He'll recover." Brenna was furious and rightly assumed that it must be Lady Madelon's doing. Well, she would not allow her to have the satisfaction of seeing Rye's anger, and her own humiliation at failing.

With that thought in mind, she gave Rachel a swift order and went to head off her husband before he could enter the hall. She found him in the guardroom and waited with wifely patience for him to give her his attention.

Dirt and mud flecked his mail and tunic, and she noted the grime and sweat on his face with a surge of hope. He'd be much more amenable to her stalling tactics if he thought it was for his own comfort. When Rye turned in her direction and saw her waiting, he paused, one hand on the hilt of his sword as she swept him a curtsy.

"My lord," she said sweetly, "I have you a bath poured in our chamber. As it is so late, I thought you would wish to bathe before you took your evening meal."

Rye stared at her for a moment. He still wore his helm, and his eyes behind the noseguard of the metal helmet narrowed slightly with suspicion.

"Did you?" he said casually, removing his helmet with a sweep of his arm and handing it to a squire. "Mayhap you are right." He drew off his thick gauntlets and held them in one fist, gazing at her with eyes the lustrous color of sapphires. His hair was wet with perspiration in spite of the cloudy day and clung to his head in damp black strands beneath the mail coif. Pushing back the coif, he raked a hand through his matted wet hair and nodded. "Do you the honor of leading the way, my lady, as I yield gladly to your arrangements."

With an inaudible sigh of relief, Brenna motioned for his squire to follow and led the way to the sweep of stairs rising to their chamber. Fortunately Rachel had done her work well and already had the huge wooden tub half-filled with heated water. Towels lay on a stool, and a pot of soap lay atop them.

While Rye's squire helped him doff the mail and tools of his profession, Brenna performed housewifely duties that normally would have made her fret with exasperation. She'd never helped the male guests to her father's household bathe as was the norm, nor had she yielded to dictates in her aunt's household to do the same. She'd scorned the practice that bade the women of the household scrub backs and proffer bowls of scented soap.

Now, to her private dismay, she found herself hurrying to do those very things just to escape humiliation. Not from Rye, she told herself. Nay, he could not humiliate her without her consent. It was the desire to evade his anger in front of Lady Madelon that spurred her decision to coax him to a private chamber before it could erupt. There, with none but a few trusted servants to hear, she would let him vent his anger over a meager supper.

It did not occur to Brenna to place the blame where she believed it lay; that would serve nothing but dissension. Nay, she would exact her vengeance in her own way and her own time and let the good dowager stew in her own juices while she wondered what Rye had said to his wife.

The thought put her in such a better mood, that Brenna did not mind when Rye told her to scrub his back. She moved toward the tub without comment as he grumbled, "Gowain will drown me with his clumsy efforts to please. Would that he were so eager about fetching my mount of a morn."

Gowain flushed and took his lord's mail and clothes to be cleaned without offering an explanation.

"P'raps he's less than eager about fetching your mount because the animal is a vicious killer," Brenna suggested, rubbing scented soap across a thick cloth until it was rich with lather. "I've seen wild boars more tame."

Rye leaned back against the high side of the tub. "Do you set yourself up as an authority on horses, *chérie*? I've been told you possess your own less than gentle mount, one that tried to take off the arm of my ostler less than three days past."

"Did he?" Brenna smiled and knelt on a stool beside the tub to lather Rye's back with the cloth. "Saladin has more discrimination than I thought. I had become convinced he was resigned to his new handler."

Snorting, Rye stretched out his legs as best he could in the tub. "Obviously, he is not. I shall school him well, though, and he will not—" He jerked to a halt when Brenna slapped the soapy cloth against his shoulder.

"He is not yours to school, my lord, but mine."

Rye twisted his head to look up at her, and his heavy brow drew down over his eyes. "I do not want you near the animal until he is gentled."

"Would you geld him?" she snapped. "That is the only way I know to gentle a beast with spirit!"

Staring at her with amazement and amusement mixing on his face, Rye shook his head. "Nay, I would not geld a fine horse such as that one, my lady, but I do not intend for my wife to be hurt, either."

"Then perhaps you should geld yourself!"

It didn't help her temper any that he laughed. "Nay, I will not do that, either. There would be too many ladies sighing with disappointment if I did."

"Insufferable, arrogant, conceited—!" She halted, aware of the gleam of laughter in his eyes. And then she remembered why she had invited him upstairs to be bathed and inhaled deeply to calm her unruly temper. It would be foolish to anger him now, when she knew he would be gravely irritated by the lack of sufficient food for him and his men after a hard day's ride.

Swallowing her temper, Brenna amended, "You are probably right, my lord. I would hate for your legion of ladies to be angry with me for encouraging such a course." She scrubbed at his shoulder blades with great vigor, glaring at him when he bent his head to allow her freer access. He truly was a conceited rogue, and she wished she dared dunk him in the soapy water.

Rye captured her hand when it slid over the smooth skin of his back to his chest, and held it imprisoned in his large palm. "Would it not displease you if I were to truly have a legion of ladies, *chérie*?" he murmured, and she stared down at him for a moment without speaking.

"Probably," she answered honestly, too surprised by the question to take time to fabricate the most evasive reply. "Though whether from pride or pain, I do not know."

He tugged on her hand, pulling her around where he could see her face. "Do I have the ability to cause you any pain, sweet Brenna? Somehow, I had thought you incapable of soft feelings toward me."

She jerked her hand from his grasp, her cheeks flaming. "I have no soft feelings for you. But I am not so insensible to my position that I wish to be publicly humiliated by a string of frowsy mistresses and lazy whores in my household."

"If they were wellborn and hardworking, would you like it better?" Rye grinned at her incoherent exclamation. "Do not worry, wife. I have not yet explored all your charms sufficiently to be bored. When I am, then I will seek others to amuse me. For now—you suit me well."

Seeing the sudden hot gleam darken his eyes to a smoky blue, Brenna tried to evade his sudden grasp. After a week of his passion in the wide bed of their chamber, she knew that look well. It was usually the same; he tried to coax her with sweet words and caresses, and when she still resisted him, he ended by taking her. Rarely did she allow herself to feel anything, even when her body betrayed her with involuntary response.

Snaring her arm, he pulled her inexorably toward him.

"Nay, sweet love, do not flee yet. I have more in mind than a bath, I vow, and the hour is yet early."

"My lord!" she gasped out when he drew her slowly down on her knees beside the tub, "my maids. The hour —your meal waits below—"

Flicking a careless glance toward Rachel, who stood frozen in place with Rye's clean garments in hand, he said roughly, "Leave us."

Rachel hesitated and glanced at Brenna. "My lady?"

Stiffening with outrage that his command might be weighed less important than his wife's, Rye leveled a fierce glance at the quivering girl and snarled, "Get out!"

With a squeak of dismay, Rachel flung his clean clothes toward another stool and fled, lifting her skirts in both hands as she skimmed over the floor with the other two maids close behind. The door slammed shut behind them.

Though she should have been furious with him, Brenna felt an irrational spurt of amusement well in her. For some reason the memory of the horror and terror on poor Rachel's face as she cast Rye's clothes in the air struck a chord of laughter, and she bit her lips against it. Perhaps it was just a nervous reaction to the strain of her situation, but Brenna found she could not contain the waves of laughter that bubbled inside.

A small snort escaped her, then a snicker, and when she looked away from Rye and tried to regain her composure, she was horrified to hear a strangled giggle burst from her throat. Rye's hand curled around her wrist more firmly, and he reached out wet fingers to hook beneath her chin and tilt her head back toward him.

To her relief, laughter danced in his eyes as well. "I hope the maid does not hurt herself in her fright. I only desired privacy."

In between gasps of laughter, Brenna said, "P'raps she thought you would drown her if she stayed."

"I may have. She was right to flee so quickly." Rye released her hand and leaned back in the tub again. He laid his arms atop the edges and smiled at her as she yielded to laughter.

Aye, she was a beauteous wench when she smiled as she was now, merriment lighting her cat-gold eyes and flushing her face; she was fair, indeed, and he wondered if she had guessed how her beauty affected him. Besides the obvious, he reflected, feeling his body tighten in response to the direction of his thoughts.

It had not left him in a good mood to have Brenna haunt his thoughts all day, and he had worked himself and his men doubly hard to try to drive out any thoughts of her. It had not helped, save in leaving his men so weary they would not think of mischief for the eve. 'Twas likely they would be so weary as to seek only their straw pallets for the night instead of livelier amusement.

Rye allowed Brenna to finish bathing him without comment, though it was difficult for him to keep his hands from her in the process. He was certain it was the sight of his body's rebellious response to her presence that had finally ended her laughter, and thought wryly that she had not seemed to change her mind about their couplings.

He'd not expected wild enthusiasm from an untried maid—especially not this one—but neither had he expected such continued resistance. After all, once she realized she could not fight him, it would be much more clever for her to bind him to her than to annoy him with her refusals, and he had decided that for all her rebellion, Brenna was intelligent. Few women would have been able to stay him from his purpose, and she had managed it with her clever, wicked tongue. He'd known even while she was doing it what she was about, but had allowed her to succeed by his own folly. She'd deserved her reward, but tonight—he deserved his.

Rye rose from the tub and stood still while Brenna dried him with a towel, then took it from her to dry his hair. He accepted without comment her offer of mulled wine, and when he had crossed to the brazier, where she had placed his garments on a stool, he caught her hand.

He pulled her to him and saw her quick, wary glance. A faint smile curved one side of his mouth upward. "I find myself needing more than wine and food right now," he said softly, and held her fast when she tried to pull away. "Do not flee, *chérie*. I will not hurt you."

"I'm not afraid of you."

Her answer was quick, too quick, and he wondered for a moment why she would still fear his touch. He stroked a hand up and down her arm and noted her shiver.

" 'Tis as I said before—you fear yourself. Come. I will show you a sweet vengeance against me."

Brenna looked up at him from beneath the sweep of her long lashes. Her eyes glittered like gold. "Vengeance?"

"Aye. 'Tis one every woman wields against a man, some more so than others." He grinned. "I see that notion gives you great interest. Learn this lesson well, Brenna, and you will have a formidable weapon, indeed."

She did not struggle as he led her toward the wide bed in the adjacent chamber, but shot him several wary glances that made him smile. She scowled.

"I do not trust you."

"So I see." He took her hand in his, his palm covering

her entire hand, and moved it over his bare chest, down the ridges of muscle to his flat, taut belly. He couldn't help sucking in a sharp breath at her touch and briefly closed his eyes. When he opened them again, she was staring up at him with an interested expression.

"See?" he asked ruefully. " 'Tis not so very difficult to torment me."

Brenna's quick downward glance brought a deep flush to her cheeks, and she jerked her eyes back to his face. "Does it torment you? To have me touch you, I mean?"

"Aye, milady, most assuredly." He moved her hand down, until her fingers found the shape of him. This time he bit back a groan of satisfaction as she curled her hand around him and stroked lightly. He felt his body leap in response, and heard her small gasp of—dismay? Pleasure? He couldn't tell. It was certainly a pleasure to feel her willing hand on him this way, though he knew to go slowly or he would frighten her away like some fey forest creature.

Keeping his voice soft and soothing, in spite of the increasingly ragged tempo of his breathing, Rye whispered, "I see that you learn quickly, *chérie*. Already I am in deep torment."

"Good." Her voice was oddly thick, soft, sounding like warm honey to his ears. "Does it get worse when I do this?"

Rye's fingers curled and uncurled at his sides, and he thrust himself into her clasp when she tightened her grip and slid her hand up and down in the motion he had shown her.

"Aye," he said on a groan, "aye. *Jésu!* but you go too fast . . . stop, before I forget myself." His hand moved to hold hers, and Brenna drew in a ragged breath and removed her hand.

"That was easy," she said softly, adding, "is that all there is to it?"

"Nay, my lady. There are many ways to torment a man, and that is but one of them. Do you seek to learn more?"

He hardly dared hope she would say yes, but to his

intense surprise she hesitated, then nodded. "It has been said that the key to power is knowledge, and I have never been one to pass up an opportunity to learn what will serve me well."

Refraining from reminding her that he had tried on more than one occasion to tutor her in the skills of love, Rye shifted so that she stood next to the bed.

"This involves much more than just me, you know. For a man, seeing is almost as much torture as touching."

"Ah. I recall your telling me that."

His hands moved to her girdle, and he began unfastening it without speaking. He half expected her to protest, but to his surprise she said nothing as he removed her girdle, gunna, and kirtle, leaving her in her stockings and shoes. He stared appreciatively at her lithe young body, the high firm breasts and narrow waist, the slender curve of her hips, and the downy luxury of her woman's mound. It made him react in the expected and time-honored way of males, and he saw that she absorbed his reaction silently for a moment.

"I had thought," she said at last, "that you could not possibly increase, but I see that I was wrong."

Rye hid a grin. "There's a lot to learn at first. Come. Lie down, and I will show you things about yourself that you do not know."

She shook her head. "Nay, I wish only to know about you this eve."

Shrugging, Rye did not argue. The time would come when she would not say that, and he knew it much better than she. He dared not shatter this easy acquiescence with hasty words or impetuous acts.

When he lay her on the bed and removed her shoes and stockings, letting his hands caress her shapely calves and thighs, it occurred to Rye that he was probably doing himself more harm than good with this sensual tutoring. She was obviously intent upon using it against him, and like a fool, he was giving her the sharpest of weapons. Still, he was not exactly a novice in sexual matters and had never had a woman succeed in mastering

him. He was confident that he could counteract any na-
ive attempt by Brenna to control him in this manner.

It wasn't until she gasped softly as his hands moved to
touch her lightly that he began to have the first pangs of
serious doubt. Then it struck him with almost painful
clarity that never before had he gone to such extreme
measures to seduce a woman he could have at any time.
After all, did her pleasure really matter but as a sop to his
vanity? Nay, yet he yearned for her to feel the same rush-
ing sweep of ecstatic oblivion that he pursued.

And he had no intention of stopping until she did.

CHAPTER 10

FIRELIGHT PLAYED OVER the figures on the huge canopied bed in a twist of rose hues and purple shadows. Brenna lay quietly beneath him as Rye stroked her quivering body with an experienced hand, seeking and finding those subtle spots that would coax the most response from her.

"I thought," she murmured at last, her breath soft and heated, "that you would show me how to torment *you,* milord."

His laugh was low and husky. "Aye, *chérie,* but to do that, you must first know how it is to *be* tormented."

A throaty gasp drifted in the air between them as his hand found and caressed her, lingered between her thighs. Rye lavished kisses on her breasts, his mouth tracing paths from one to the other in a silken trail of fire until she was moaning and reaching for him.

Bed sheets were wadded hopelessly beneath them when he finally drew back and levered his body up to gaze down at her with blue eyes smoky with passion. Desire seemed to blur his features into a more gentle expression, but Brenna recognized the appraising look in his eyes and bit her lower lip. This was not going at all as she had planned.

"Leave me alone," she said sullenly, and he laughed.

"Nay, sweet wife, I will not. Nor do you want me to. Your body yearns for my touch, despite your sharp tongue's denial."

Rising to his knees on the bed, Rye straddled her body and caressed her quivering curves for a long moment, watching from beneath half-closed lids as she tried to avoid his touch.

"Why," he murmured with a quizzical glance, "did you provoke this moment if you did not want it, *chérie*?"

She grabbed and held his hands still, struggling for a steady breath as his palms cupped her breasts. "I didn't provoke this. I merely—"

"You merely lured me to our chamber for a private bath and seductive promises you did not mean," he finished for her with a moody smile. "I see. You've made no secret of your dislike for this, Brenna. 'Tis why I was surprised at your suggestion."

Dragging his thumbs across the beaded tips of her breasts in a lingering stroke that made Brenna writhe, Rye lowered his lashes to watch the caress, then lifted them in a slow sweep to gaze at her flushed face.

"Do you fear that I will tell others of your desire for me, *ma chérie*? I would not. 'Twould be our secret, and one that I would cherish."

"I . . . do not . . . desire you," she forced out, and saw the corners of his mouth turn up in a knowing smile.

"P'raps not in some ways, but in this way you do."

Brenna squirmed, her eyes half-lidded with passion and her lips parted. She put out her tongue in a purely female gesture to wet them and snapped, "What do you want of me?"

Spreading his dark hands on her pale, creamy flesh, Rye lifted his lashes to give her a brooding stare. "I would hear you say that you want me, *chérie*. As I want you."

Her eyes widened. "Would you?" She pushed at his hands and tried to twist away. "Nay, lord, you will not hear it."

"Yea, I will hear it. P'raps not willingly, but you will say it to me, sweet wife."

Some of Brenna's passion cooled as she glared up at him with angry eyes. "Vain Norman! Do you think that I yield so easily to your touch? I do not. Nay, though I admit that there is much about this that surprises me with the depth of sensation you are able to arouse, I have no doubt that any other man as skilled as you in the arts of sexual matters could do the same. P'raps I should see if—"

Her words ended in a gasp as Rye snarled savagely and leaned over her, gripping her wrists and pinning her to the feather mattress with a quick motion.

"Do not say it, Brenna," he warned so menacingly that she couldn't speak. "Do not ever say that you would take another man into your bed. You are mine, and there will be no other. Ever. Do you understand?"

"Do you love me so much?" Brenna taunted despite the surge of apprehension he provoked with his fierce glare.

He released her wrists. "Nay. But I hold what is mine, and you belong to me." His touch was possessive as he ran his hand over her body, his expression daring her to argue the point.

Brenna smiled slightly. "Nay, lord," she said softly, "I do not belong to you. My body, p'raps, but not my heart. That you have not won, and that is what must be won to have succeeded in keeping me."

Lowering his body over hers in a slow, deliberate scrape of bone and muscle over her soft curves, Rye said, "I will win all, *chérie*, make no mistake about it." His mouth captured her lips in a lingering kiss that Brenna could not avoid.

She wanted to rage at him, to rail that he would never have her as he seemed to think, but already she knew that part of her had succumbed to Rye's determined assault. Why else would she go to such lengths to avoid his anger? To want his respect, and have her foolish heart lurch when he slid her a speculative glance? 'Twas madness indeed that made her think softly of him at times, and she vowed to renew her barriers against him.

It was a vow that she found most difficult to keep as Rye plundered her mouth with his tongue, forcing a heated response from her. With a sense of chagrin, Brenna found her arms around his neck, her body arching to receive him, and heard her own soft cries in the shadows. It was vaguely shaming that she could not hold to her resistance, that he could so easily make her respond with caresses and kisses.

Then, as that silently acknowledged admission of her softness toward him sparked an even deeper sweep of emotion in her, Brenna felt a tremor begin to shake her body. Rye must have felt it, too, for he muttered love words in her ear that she'd never heard before, his voice thick with passion as he urged her to yield to what she felt.

Gasping, Brenna tried to hold to her resistance but found that it had dissolved, leaving only Rye in its wake, Rye and the searing thrust of his body that took her higher and higher. Just when she thought that she could bear the tension no longer, that she would snap with the strain of it, he lifted her hips in his hands and forced her over the edge of control and into shattering release.

Brenna cried out, clutching at him with her hands, panting in short, gasping breaths as the waves swept over her. She shook from head to toe with the force of her climax, half sobbing as she clung to his broad shoulders.

"I didn't know," she couldn't help saying in tear-choked whispers, "I didn't know. . . ."

Rye kissed her gently, holding her against him, murmuring in her ear that it was all right.

" 'Tis the reward I wanted you to have, *chérie*," he said softly. He smoothed back damp tendrils of her hair from her face, brushed his hand over her closed eyes. "Don't weep, my love. *La petite morte*—the little death —is what we all seek."

With her eyes still closed, Brenna could not answer. When Rye began to move inside her again, seeking his own reward, she knew she'd lost an important battle as she rose to meet his body with willing passion.

When Brenna awoke, the fire had burned low, and she was jerked wide awake by the realization that Rye's men-at-arms had not yet eaten. She sat up with a sudden movement that woke him.

"Where are you going?" he murmured, reaching out for her.

Brenna pulled away, suddenly shy at facing him. "Your men have not eaten, milord. I would see to them."

Rye's voice was thick with sleep and satisfaction. "I am certain Raoul has given the order. Stay here with me."

"But, lord, 'tis my duty to see to them." Brenna avoided his reach deftly as she slid from the bed. "Would you have it said that your wife was so poor a mistress she preferred lying abed with her husband rather than feed hungry men?"

Laughing, Rye said, "Aye. I would, indeed, prefer it to be said that my wife preferred my appetites to those of my surly men-at-arms. But," he said, cutting across her angry protest, "I do not want it put about that you are lazy. So go, give Raoul the order to have the men's food put out, then come back to me."

Highly resentful of his arrogance and the way he expected her to leap at his command, Brenna murmured a noncommittal reply as she slid her gunna and kirtle over her head and reached for the linked girdle that held her ring of keys. As she left the chamber, she glanced back at him and saw him watching her. She shut the heavy door on his lazy gaze and half-mocking smile. A hot flush stained her cheeks, and she wondered if he was thinking of her surrender.

She should have thought of another way to stall him, but that had seemed the swiftest. It would have been even more shaming for him to discover Lady Madelon's trick, and the empty tables for hungry men.

When she stepped into the hall, she found men-at-arms still drinking pitchers of ale and goblets of wine. Beckoning to Raoul Beaumont, she managed a smile when the Norman came to her side.

"Sir de Beaumont, the seigneur wishes that the men eat now. I have given orders that your meal shall be served, and I hope that it is palatable for having been kept so long."

"I was about to give the order," Beaumont said with a relieved smile, "but did not wish to gainsay Lord Lyon. He is not unwell?"

"Nay, just weary, I think." Brenna's cheeks flushed as a knowing expression slowly settled on Raoul's face.

Saying nothing, the Norman knight bowed slightly, and when he smiled at her, Brenna felt some of her chagrin fade at his pleased expression. Impulsively she smiled back, and Beaumont stepped closer.

"He is not as fierce a lord," Beaumont said softly, "as you had feared, I hope. Methinks he dwells upon your fair face at length when we ride away from you, milady. I've not seen him so smitten before."

Brenna stared at him. Smitten? Rye de Lyon? Nay, not that savage knight. Irritated, perhaps; lusty, even. Never smitten. The very notion would have shocked her if it was not so amusing.

"You do not know your lord as well as you think, Sir de Beaumont," Brenna said. "He does not pine for me."

"Nay, not pine, p'raps, but he definitely thinks of you while we ride, milady. I know this, as we have discussed it a time or two."

"When—while hunting for me the day I escaped?" Brenna asked sharply. "If he spoke of me at all, 'twas not with a soft tongue, I vow."

Laughing, Beaumont agreed, "Not that day, for certain, my lady. But when we train, and when we visit the villages to hear what we can of the outlaws who roam and ravage the land, he has spoken of you several times."

"Has he?" Brenna felt her interest quicken. "In what manner, might I ask?"

Shrugging, Beaumont seemed to search for words. "It would be disloyal to reveal what he might not want told, Lady Brenna, so if you do not mind, I will only say that he spoke well of you."

"I suppose I should be satisfied with that, but I am not as content with mere words as another maid might be." Brenna pleated the folds of her gown and frowned down at her feet, feeling Beaumont's curious gaze on her. She looked up at him after a moment and managed a careless shrug of her shoulders. "He's merely interested because I do not play his game, Sir de Beaumont. He only seeks a way to pass the time."

"I do not think so, but I do not presume to know his mind." Beaumont stepped closer to Brenna. "My lady, I would be so bold as to beg a boon of you concerning your maid."

"My maid?" Brenna's brows lifted. "Do you mean Rachel?"

"Aye, milady." Beaumont flushed deeply, and his honest face bore such an expression of acute suffering that Brenna took pity on him.

"Rachel is an exceptional girl, and well-bred. Did you know one another in Normandy, perhaps, Sir de Beaumont?"

"Aye, milady. Not well, but we know many of the same people in Normandy. And I was acquainted with her father." He took a deep breath. "I wish to pay court to her, with your permission."

"I see. Rachel has been my mainstay since we left Normandy," Brenna said, regarding him thoughtfully. "I would not want to see her ill-used."

Looking askance, Beaumont hastened to assure her, "Nor would I, milady. She is a fair maid, and gentle."

Brenna nodded. Raoul de Beaumont was a nobleman, she decided, in every sense of the word. He was not coarse or brutal like so many men she knew, nor did he have Rye's ferocity, for all that he served him so well. He would be a good match for Rachel, and she hoped suddenly that her maid found the happiness that she could not.

"You have my leave to pay her court, if that is what you wish, Sir de Beaumont," Brenna said at last. "Of course, the rest is up to God and the maid."

Beaumont grinned and swept her a courtly bow. "So I am made to understand, milady. Thank you for your generosity."

Smiling, Brenna said, "It is not misplaced, I am sure."

Some of Brenna's pleasure dimmed as Beaumont left and she turned to survey the hall. Though she lingered a while to be certain the cook had, indeed, obeyed her instructions and served a decent meal to Rye's men, Brenna was well aware of Lady Madelon's fine hand behind the furtive glance she received. The servants waited to see who would win out, dowager or new wife.

Irritated, and knowing that it was the people who would suffer in any case, Brenna guarded her tongue when Lady Madelon pointed out that it was not exactly a meal fit for men who had ridden hard all day in search of Saxon rebels.

"Outlaws," Brenna corrected with an insincere smile. "I understand that there are few rebels protesting William's crown these days."

"Yea, outlaws or rebels," Lady Madelon said with a shrug, " 'tis little matter. Soldiers need more than pottage and a few pasties to fuel their rides."

"I agree." Brenna met her gaze with a lifted brow. "And I intend to see to it that the men-at-arms are well fed."

Gesturing toward the long tables, Lady Madelon murmured, "Hardly a hearty fare at this meal. Where is your husband, that he does not partake?"

"Resting." Brenna saw the annoyance in Lady Madelon's eyes and did not say the words that trembled on the tip of her tongue. She would not yield to the impulse to lay the blame for meager fare where it belonged. Nay, she would allow Lady Madelon to snare herself in her own foolish traps.

Drumming beringed fingers against the wooden table, Lady Madelon's mouth settled into a thin line. "He rests much for a man who is overlord. Should William discover that his man lies abed like a slug, he will be most displeased."

"I think not, for William would be the first to enjoy hearing the reason for his vassal's weariness." Brenna let the double-edged rejoinder sink in, then added when Lady Madelon's eyes flashed angrily, "Lord Lyon will not be glad to hear that anyone would attempt to cause him trouble, I think. 'Twould be wise if we were to warn those who are foolish enough to try it."

"Would it? I'll keep that in mind," Lady Madelon said sharply. "Not that he would listen to sly suggestions one might whisper into his ear of a night. You forget, milady, that I have known Rye since he was an infant. I am well aware of how his mind works."

"Is that so? Odd, then, that you should so foolishly risk his anger."

Laughing, the dowager lifted her aristocratic chin in a haughty gesture. "He would not offer me insult. In his youth, he was trained well to respect me."

" 'Tis not a respect he feels for all women," Brenna pointed out, "and I think you depend on his childhood needs too greatly."

"Do you forget that I was the only mother he ever knew? He has not forgotten, I am certain, and will allow me much more freedom than he would any other woman. Save, perhaps, my daughter, whom he adores." She stepped close, each word heavy with sarcasm. "You, however, do not seem to be high in his favor, except as a bed partner."

Curling her fingers into her palms so deeply that she left half-moon cuts in the tender skin, Brenna said, "I was under the impression you were not a very good mother, Lady Madelon. He's spoken of a lack of affection, I believe."

"Affection? For the bastard son of my husband, who was begotten of a highborn whore? Nay, there was none, nor will there ever be. But respect—aye, he was taught that lesson early."

"You will find, I think, that respect instills much less leniency than love," Brenna said slowly, realizing as she said the words that it was true. Her gaze lifted, and a faint frown creased her brow as she said, "Beware, my lady, that you do not mistake his generosity. It could be quite unpleasant for you."

Not waiting for the dowager's reply, Brenna moved from the high table to the lower, passing between the rows of men wolfing down platters of fish pasties and rounds of hot bread covered with stew. There did not seem to be any complaint in the lack of quality, as there was plenty of quantity, and she felt a wave of relief that she had avoided Rye's displeasure in front of his stepmother and men.

Feeling the sharp bite of weariness at last, Brenna turned toward the stone steps that led to the bedchamber she shared with Rye. She'd been awake since before first light, thanks to Rye, and had accomplished much in the long hours between dawn and dusk.

It was not, Brenna reflected as she mounted the stairs, as easy as she'd always assumed it would be to take over the many tasks of running a large household. From the first small meal to break their fast, to the meal served at ten in the morning, were only a few hours. That meal was the large meal of the day, and the evening meal was usually much lighter. In between, her hours were filled with the supervision of stores, weaving of cloth, making of garments for servants as well as members of the higher class, then seeing to the proper care of those who might have taken ill or injured themselves. It was a dizzying task, and she wondered why she'd not recognized that in her days spent in Normandy.

This week had been a lesson in humility as well as an education in housewifely arts. Even more of an education had been her reaction to Rye, that almost painful shattering of her senses into something she'd never dreamed existed. How had he done it? Made her feel that mindless ecstasy that wiped away all her resistance?

It should have left her feeling used and helpless, yet instead, she felt an odd anticipation at the thought of sharing his bed again. That morning at mass she'd prayed for the strength to resist, yet even as she had, she'd known that God might frown upon a wife's resistance to her husband. It left her feeling even more confused than ever.

A frown still creased her brow as she reached the door to the chamber she shared with Rye. Before she could touch the latch, suddenly Rachel sped down the corridor, almost knocking her down, her pansy-soft eyes wide with fright.

"Oh! There you are, milady—quickly, there is need of you in the nursery."

"In the nursery?"

Nodding, Rachel clutched at her hand, drawing her along up the stairs. "Aye. Young Gilles, Lady Raissa's son, has cut himself and is like to bleed to death if you do not help him."

"What has been done?" Brenna asked as she scurried at her side, their steps echoing in the wide halls.

"Nothing. He will allow no one to touch him, but hides in an alcove and howls."

"*Jésu,*" Brenna muttered, "is there none who can soothe the child?"

"I fear he is too afrighted to heed us, milady."

"What makes you think he will listen to me?" Brenna asked in surprise.

" 'Twas Lady Raissa's idea, to fetch you. She said you would have a calming affect on the child."

Brenna doubted it. She'd never been good with children, not quite knowing how to talk to them. But if Raissa wanted her there, she would go.

Lady Raissa knelt near a wall, where an overhang formed a small alcove. Crouched back in the recess was the six-year-old boy, Gilles.

An expression of relief crossed Raissa's face as she looked up and saw Brenna standing in the open doorway. "Lady Brenna. Gilles has cut himself and won't allow us to tend his hurt. See what you can do, I beg of you."

Her glance shifted to young Gilles, who obstinately avoided his mother's frantic efforts to soothe him. Moving toward them, she asked, "What kind of hurt?"

"A dagger." Raissa's voice trembled as she gestured to her son. "He was told not to play with it, but he did, and now he has a cut that threatens to bleed him dry."

Seeing the bright smears of blood on floor and walls and Raissa's gown, Brenna approached slowly. There was a chance the boy had severed a main artery, which would require more than her few skills to tend. Her thoughts were obviously echoed by a nursemaid, who sobbed and said the cut would have to be cauterized, else the child would die from loss of blood.

"Fetch a hot knife, milady, and lay it against the cut to seal it," she whined.

"Fool," Brenna snapped softly at the woman, who gave a shriek in French and English. "Stop your silly prattle, ere you frighten the child out of his wits. Stop it, I say!"

Backing away, the nursemaid cowered from the flare of anger in Brenna's eyes.

Brenna turned back to Raissa. "Fetch some boiled water and clean strips of cloth, please. And send Rachel for my bag of herbs. She knows where it is."

Without waiting for a reply, Brenna crossed to where the boy hid in the stone recess. He was scooted back into the shadows, so that only a pale glimmer of his face showed in the cleft. Brenna knelt close and folded her hands in her lap.

When she felt the boy's attention rivet on her, she said without preamble, "I cut myself on my brother's dagger once. Would you like to see the scar?"

When Gilles finally mumbled assent, she held up her arm and drew back the sleeve to her kirtle. "See? It is pale now, but it was once very evident. My father tended the cut for me."

After a moment the small voice quavered, "Did it hurt very badly? To have it tended?"

"Not as badly as it hurt to cut it," Brenna said in a frank, calm tone. "And my father told me a story while the physic tended me, so that I hardly felt it at all."

"What story was that?" Gilles scooted a small bit closer so that she could see the tear streaks on his round, boyish face. Blue eyes that reminded her of Rye were hazy with tears and pain, and she felt an unexpected surge of tender pity for this frightened child.

" 'Twas the legend of King Arthur. You've heard of him, of course."

When Gilles shook his head, Brenna feigned astonishment. "You've not? By the Holy Rood, young Master Gilles, I'm amazed. King Arthur was one of the greatest knights to ever live."

"Greater than Rye de Lyon?" came the indignant query, and Brenna swallowed a snort of derision.

" 'Tis said that he was great indeed, but of course, your uncle has not lived all his life yet. Fame oft grows after death, you know."

Gilles nodded, sniffing and clutching at his torn and bleeding arm. "Then I am certain Rye de Lyon will one day be greater than this King Arthur."

"Most assuredly," Brenna said, wondering why small boys always had to be so literal. She could recall similar discussions with her brothers in their youth. "But would you like to hear of this great king? He was only fifteen when he pulled the sword from the stone to become Britain's king, you know, and ruled well and wisely for over twenty years."

As Brenna spun tales of Arthur and Mordred and the Ladies of Avilion, Rachel arrived with the bundle of herbs and her satchel of healing supplies. It didn't take much to coax Gilles from his lair, and soon Brenna was cleaning and binding his cut with strips of cloth soaked in herbs. Tannin from the gall of an oak helped to stop the bleeding, and she saw that though deep, the cut had not severed an artery.

"Will you tell me more, Lady Brenna?" Gilles asked when she had tied the last strip of cloth around his arm. "I want to hear about the Lady of the Lake. And the Ladies of Avilion."

"Later." Brenna smiled at his expression of dismay. "I will soon run out of tales if I spin them all now, Master Gilles. Let us leave something for another day."

"Then you will come here again?" Gilles's smile was

hopeful, but his eyes were already beginning to drowse from the effects of the herb she had given him to drink.

"Aye, I will come again. Next time I will tell you about the great battle fought between Arthur and Mordred, and how Merlin the magician helped the young king."

From the open doorway Rye's voice drawled, "Did you tell my nephew that Arthur was king of the Britons, and as such, helped drive out the pagan, barbaric Saxons, *chérie?*"

Annoyed, Brenna turned and snapped, "Saxons and Britons melded to become one people, as you must know."

"Aye. Just as Normans and Saxons will now mingle to become one nation," Rye returned with an amused smile. A mocking light glittered in his eyes at Brenna's incoherent exclamation. Ignoring it, he pushed away from the doorway and crossed the room to kneel beside them. "How did you manage this, Gilles?"

The boy looked slightly abashed. "I played with the dagger Grandmère told me not to play with," he mumbled without looking up at his uncle.

"Did you? 'Tis certain that your punishment for not obeying was swift then, as the cut must pain you."

"Aye, milord." Gilles lifted his head after a moment, and the trace of a grin flickered briefly on his lips. "A cut is much better than some punishments, I vow, as your lady told me such a fine tale of knights and battle."

Throwing Brenna an amused glance, Rye stood up and raked a gentle hand through the boy's dark hair. "Aye, but your good fortune may not hold once your grandmère hears of your disobedience. You'd best devise a method of recovering her good graces rather than think of old tales of British kings and forgotten glory."

" 'Tis not forgotten," Brenna pointed out, irritated that he dismissed the tales of Arthur so lightly. "The legends of King Arthur and his knights will be told and retold as long as there are men who desire to be reminded of love, honor, and courage."

"Indeed, *chérie?*" Rye lifted her to her feet and pulled

her next to him. "P'raps you are right, though I oft wonder if honor will be an advantage or a fault a hundred years hence."

"What do you mean by that?"

"Steady, my fiery little Saxon, I only meant that there are men for whom honor means very little, I fear. Witness the outlaws who devastate their own kind, plundering and killing innocent serfs to strike back at William."

"And you are certain 'tis Saxons who ride across the fields and burn huts?" Brenna asked sharply.

He regarded her coolly. "Aye. I am certain."

Brenna bit her tongue to keep from saying something too rash and saw Raissa's guarded glance at her. Poor Raissa. She detested conflict and avoided even the hall to keep from confronting her mother.

Raissa made a gesture of peace now, putting her hand on her brother's arm to draw his attention from Brenna.

"Milord, I have a plate of comfits. Honeyed dates, all the way from the Mediterranean. I remembered that you like them."

Rye's expression softened. "Yea, Raissa, I do like them. Why have you kept them from me so long?" he teased, and was rewarded with a relieved smile from his sister.

"So you would have them now." Raissa bundled a sleepily protesting Gilles off to bed with his nursemaid in charge and produced a brass plate of sticky dates for Rye. "Would you have one also, Lady Brenna? I wish I had more than mere dates to offer for your kindness and expertise in caring for Gilles."

Waving a hand, Brenna said, "I am glad I could help. You owe me nothing, Lady Raissa."

"Please—" Raissa put out a hand. "Let us not be so formal. Call me Raissa, and I will call you Brenna. After all, you are my sister now."

Slightly startled, Brenna managed a nod, not sure if she wanted to be so familiar with Raissa. Despite her reluctance to like anything Norman, she'd found that the gentle young woman was nothing like her mother or her half brother. That by itself was in her favor, Brenna reflected with a cynical smile.

Feeling awkward and uneasy, Brenna sat stiffly on a stool near Rye, as he would not allow her to leave but made it plain with a gesture and firm tug on her wrist that she was to stay. The easy patter of their conversation flowed around her, and despite the fact that she knew none of the people they spoke of, and recognized only a few names from her past, she began to grow more relaxed. Somehow just being in Raissa's company had a softening effect on anyone she came in contact with. It was a trait that perplexed Brenna, and she was still puzzling over it when she heard that soft voice rise in protest.

"Rye, nay! Do not promise me to d'Esteray, I beg of you. . . ."

"Steady, Raissa," he soothed her. "I merely mentioned his suit to you. Your mother is pressing me to agree, but I can find no good in it."

Strained, Raissa looked down at her twined fingers. "I do not like him, for more reason than your quarrel with the man." She shuddered. "He is . . . there is something evil about that man."

Rye's voice was hard, his eyes cold. "Yea, I agree. He and I have never been able to stomach one another's company at even the best of times, so I wanted to be sure you were not fond of him."

"How can you say that!"

Grinning, Rye said, "There are times it's hard to read a woman, sweet sister. And some women find the most unlikely suitor desirable."

"Men and women," Brenna put in sharply, "look for quite different things in a mate, I believe."

Rye's blue gaze shifted to her, his brow lifting. "Do they, my sweet? What do you look for?"

"That is a moot point now, my lord, as you are well aware. Like most women, my wishes were not taken into consideration."

"Probably best, or you would have wed a Saxon rebel

and found yourself swinging alongside him from a gibbet, I'll warrant."

Brenna glared at him. Raissa quickly intervened by asking Rye if he'd had more news of d'Esteray's activities.

Rye shook his head. "Nay, not since I disabused him of the notion that he would take my lands from me. He's not a forgiving man, I fear."

Laughing, Raissa said, "It could have something to do with the fact that his father attacked your back and was dishonored by all."

Rye shrugged. "And it could have something to do with the fact that I was forced to kill him for it."

Staring at Rye, Brenna saw the faint flicker on his face and wondered at it. Did he regret killing the man? He gave no indication of it, yet spoke calmly. War was a way of life, and hotheaded knights frequently quarreled among themselves. Hadn't she seen her brothers quarrel often?

Lost in thought, Brenna slowly became aware that Rye was speaking to her.

"Pardon, milord," she said with a faint flush, "I was not listening."

" 'Tis evident, sweeting. I merely made mention of the May Day festival the village has planned. What do you know of it?"

Shrugging, Brenna smoothed her hands over her velvet garments in a stalling gesture. "Not much, but that the townsfolk enjoy morris dancing and a sapling festooned with ribbons. My mother was used to crowning a Queen of the May for them, and they made much of it."

"Oh, Rye," Raissa said with a delighted clap of her hands that made Brenna think of a child, "how wonderful! We shall do the same. I think if we only try to make the people feel that we are one of them, instead of against them, then perhaps they will be more accepting of us."

"Aye, then p'raps they will reveal the hiding place of

the men who outlaw," Rye drawled, his gaze coming to rest on Brenna.

She felt a flash of anger. "You would trick them into it, milord? How noble. Were we not speaking of the lack of honor earlier?"

"I only seek to save them from their own," Rye said in a flat, cold tone that made her pause. "Those outlaws kill and starve their own kind without regard, and I would see them destroyed before they can ruin the crops that are yet to bud in the fields. Would you have the people starve next winter? Without a good harvest they will. Their kine will go hungry as well, and there will be no milk for the babes, or salted meat for pottage. Is that what you wish?"

Turning away, Brenna did not answer. It was apparent that she and Rye would never agree on a subject, especially the difference between Saxon and Norman.

Night lay softly on the land. Lights from the village glowed in erratic patterns. The huge stone castle that sprawled atop a rise overlooking the town glittered with torches marking its presence. A light rain fell, making the stone walls shine in the fireglow.

"It puts me in mind of a huge vulture," a shaggy-bearded man said in a growling mutter to his companion, who shrugged. They huddled in a copse of trees for warmth, and rain dripped in a ceaseless patter from leaves overhead.

" 'Twould be even worse if we were foolish enough to defy the Black Lion," the youthful companion said after a few moments, and earned a wrathful glare.

"Aye, and have ye gone over to the Normans then? 'Tis said ye talked with him that day at Marwald, even drew your sword, yet now ye prate of caution?" Snorting angrily, he shook rain from his beard and grabbed the youth by his drenched cloak. "If ye're thinking of allying with the enemy, lad, 'tis best ye had your throat slit now instead of later."

Fixing him with a steely glance, the boy reached up to

uncurl the fingers tangled in his cloak. "I never said I was an ally of Normans, but I see no sense in earning the Lion's anger without cause. Show me a cause for it, a cause that will help us, and I will draw my sword on him again."

Sitting back, the older man stared at young Myles in the misty gloom. "Ye're not afraid, I'll grant ye that," he said grudgingly, "yet I cannot be certain of your true goal. Tell me."

"Peace," Myles said simply. "I long for it, want it like a drowning man wants fresh air. I've not known it for most of my life, Whitley, and it beckons to me as if a ghost whispers in my ear."

"Peace." Shaking his head, Whitley looked past his younger brother toward the castle rising like a specter in the night. "Peace. Yea, I can remember peace of a sorts, but not as you mean. We had freedom to do what we pleased, to choose our own men. That was peace."

"Nay, brother, that was petty wars. One thing you must acknowledge about William, is that he has brought law to the land. P'raps not the kind of law we sought once, but a kind that allows our women to travel freely without fear, and our merchants to go from one end of England to the other without losing their gold."

"Not lately," was the dry response.

"The outlaws will be caught." Myles's gaze held Whitley's. "They will be caught and hanged, and 'twill be their own fault for not heeding warnings."

"Ye're with him, just like that bitch of a sister of ours, ye're with the Normans." Whitley's mouth tightened, and he growled, "If ye were not my brother—and mayhaps even then—I would see ye dead by my hand before I let ye cast your lot with that bastard earl!"

"Do you offer a challenge?"

Grimacing, Whitley held up the stump of his right arm. "Aye, a sorry match I'd be even for a weedling youth. Nay, Myles, I do not offer you a challenge. But I cannot say the same for the others. Watch your back, if ye align with the Normans, 'tis all I can say."

" 'Tis enough." After a moment Myles lay a hand on

his brother's shoulder. "Try not to hate so hard, Whitley. 'Tis bound to end badly for you if you travel that course."

"But I am bound to it, as ye are bound to your quest for a peace that will never be."

Both men fell silent, and the rain pattered down as they huddled in their cloaks and waited for dawn.

CHAPTER 11

In the days that followed, Brenna found a routine that kept her hours busy. From morning mass at dawn to the first breaking of fast to the noonday meal, she scurried between duties with an agility that would have astounded her Aunt Bertrice. Brenna had never been known for her domesticity, and she often thought of her aunt's reaction should she ever hear how involved her niece had become with the proper weave of cloth or the contents of a stew. It was enough to make her laugh at herself at times, that small knowledge of how she had changed since her marriage to Rye.

Rye. The most difficult and alien of all males she had ever encountered. He rode hard all day in pursuit of the outlaws, and his temper was never predictable when he came in at dusk of an evening. Brenna had learned to be cautious around him, and when she thought of how she once would have tweaked his temper without regard, she felt a twinge of chagrin.

It wasn't that she was really afraid of him; nay, not that. Instead she avoided any confrontation with him, not wanting to listen to Lady Madelon's amused comments about her inability to manage her household or her husband.

There were times Brenna wished she could tell that formidable dame exactly what was on her mind, but she knew 'twould only cause more trouble. Trouble, she had found, came oft enough on its own, without her calling it.

"Does it never cease raining in this cursed land?" Rye demanded of no one in particular as he dismounted late of an eve. The bailey was loud with the clamor of returning men-at-arms and weary mounts.

Turning toward his lord, Raoul de Beaumont laughed. "I vow, seigneur, that the very skies weep with chagrin o'er England. 'Tis not the sunny climes I long for, yet 'tis what makes the land so green."

"I'd trade green land for blue skies any day," Rye said in a growling mutter as he began to pull off his gauntlets and lift his muddy metal helm from his head. He looked around with an impatient glance. "Where is my squire?"

"Here, lord."

Turning, Rye swept the unfamiliar youth with a sharp glance. "You are not Gowain."

Bowing, the young man said, "Nay, milord. He is down ill. Beltair sent me in his place to tend you." He reached out and took the muddy helmet, tucked it under one arm, and waited with outstretched hand for the heavy gauntlets.

"I know your face. You are Myles, the youth who pulled his sword on me at Marwald."

"Aye, milord. I hope you have forgiven me that foolish play."

Rye studied him for a moment, blue eyes narrowing with thought as he took in the neat garments, tidily cropped mane of red-blond hair, and respectful mien.

"Time will tell that, Myles. So you are squire now, at my advice. Tell me—what does your sister say?"

Myles shrugged. "I have not seen her, save from a distance. Our paths have not crossed, and Beltair keeps me too busy to seek her out of an eve." The boy smiled.

"In truth, sire, I am not eager to hear her words when she discovers I am now in your camp."

Rye's grin lightened his muddy face, and his eyes were pale with amusement. "Nor I. 'Tis not often she curbs her tongue when moved to speak, and I am ever grateful for her silence."

Myles bowed slightly, then looked up at the earl with a lifted brow. "Do you hear it, then? Her silence? If so, I must admit that you have accomplished what none in our family were ever able to do."

"Do not be fooled, little Saxon. Lady Brenna keeps her own counsel only by choice, not by intimidation." Rye's tone was dry. "I do not flatter myself that I have had any to do with her softer nature."

A wide grin spread across Myles's face, and he took the gauntlets from Rye. "P'raps love has softened her."

"Love?" Rye shook his head. "Nay, I do not think love has aught to do with it."

Myles made no reply but followed Rye into the keep to help him remove his heavy mail hauberk for cleaning. Dim torchlight lit the dark guardroom, and just beyond in the hall could be heard the sounds of music.

"Minstrels?" Rye asked Myles, who nodded.

"Aye, milord. Ballard from Marwald, who was always Brenna's favorite, came this morn to sing her songs."

Rye's mouth tightened into a grim line. "At whose request does the fair Ballard come to Moorleah?"

After glancing at him quickly, Myles shrugged. "I cannot say, milord."

"I remember Ballard. He sang songs of a Viking slave's rebellion to your sister, very unwisely, I must say."

"Brenna needs little coaxing to be rebellious." Myles met Rye's narrowed gaze. "She's always been unruly, ever since our mother died giving birth. Brenna was there when she died and saw the whole of it. She took it very hard, I know, lord, and has not been tractable since."

For a moment Rye looked at Myles with a thoughtful

frown. "I would hear more," he said slowly. "P'raps 'twill help me understand why she fights me so."

Myles shifted uneasily and cast a quick glance toward the curtained doorway leading into the crowded hall. " 'Tis not my place to bear tales," he said finally. "You should ask Brenna."

"And do you think she would tell me what I need to hear?" A faint, hard smile curled Rye's mouth. "Nay, lad, she would not, and you know it. Tell me this—was she always so filled with hate toward your mother's people?"

"Nay, lord. There was a time when Brenna bore no ill will toward any man. But that was before the Normans came hard on the heels of our mother's death. It was a bad time for us all. I can still recall how she looked, hiding behind old Gytha, our mother's maidservant. Soldiers rode into the stockade and captured Moorleah without much of a struggle, as my father and brothers were still in hiding after Hastings." Myles paused, and a bleak shadow darkened his eyes. " 'Twas a bad time, my lord. The men were rowdy, as soldiers often are, and hungry for more than food."

"They did not touch her," Rye said sharply, and felt a wave of relief when Myles shook his head.

"Nay, lord. But there was a young girl from the village. Hlynn. She was Brenna's only friend after our mother died, and though she was a bit of a tart, she was not a harlot. P'raps you can imagine what happened to a young, pretty girl when the Normans rode into Moorleah."

"And Brenna saw it."

Myles nodded. "Aye, lord. The girl survived the day, but she did not survive the babe nine months hence."

Rye remained silent. He thought of the girl he had wed, and her stark terror and insistence that she would not bear his children. 'Twas easy to see why she felt as she did, and he suffered a pang of guilt for his failure to understand.

"Shall I bring your gear to your chamber, my lord?" Myles asked, and Rye nodded.

"Aye." He wiped his face clean with the strip of cloth Myles gave him, then bent so that the youth could slip a fresh tunic over his head. Pivoting on his booted heel, Rye stepped to the heavy curtains, then paused and turned. "Myles. My thanks."

Myles didn't reply, but a faint smile slanted his mouth as he stood in the guardroom and watched Rye disappear through the doorway.

Jugglers, acrobats, and musicians entertained what looked like all of Moorleah. Trained dogs leapt through hoops and climbed small ladders, and dancing girls bent and swayed to the tune of a lute.

As he wended his way through the press of guests and retainers, Rye was approached by his master-at-arms. Beltair spoke freely, as he usually did to the man he'd fought side by side with since he was a youth. Much older than Rye, the grizzled Norman lessoned him on occasion, as he would have an untried lad.

"My lord, do you think it wise to trust a Saxon whose brothers ravage the land?" he asked bluntly. Rye paused to look at him closely.

"Do you find Myles dishonest?"

"Nay, but I do not trust his kin."

Rye's smile was slow. "Nay, no more do I, and that includes my wife when it comes to loyalties."

"Your wife?" Beltair's eyes narrowed slightly. "I find it difficult to imagine that any woman would gainsay you, my lord."

"She does not. She prefers deviling me, but that is not in question here." When Beltair just gazed at him with a troubled frown, Rye added, "Do not fear. I know how to tame the wench, and how to guard her loyalties. No woman will be able to deny my rule."

"Aye, lord," Beltair said with a lift of his brow that made Rye scowl.

"Do you doubt it?"

"Not if you say it, seigneur."

"See that young Myles is well trained, but do not trust him overmuch. We will see if he can be trusted with the passing of time."

Bowing, Beltair murmured, "As you say, my lord. I am certain he is as well disciplined as his sister."

Rye stared after him for a moment, wondering why there had been such a mocking disbelief in Beltair's expression. Did he think Brenna able to avoid yielding? If he did, he misjudged his lord more than he ever had before.

Scowling, Rye pushed his way through the crowd, pausing to greet important guests, chafing at the delay in reaching his wife. She was seated with Lady Madelon at the high table. Brenna wore a gown of yellow velvet and had ribbons twined in her hair and dangling in intricate loops. For an instant Rye had the angry thought that she dressed so for a minstrel, but would not for her husband, then dismissed it from his mind. She was his, and he would remind her of it if she was foolish enough to forget even for a moment.

When he approached the high table on the raised dais, Brenna stood, indicating that he take the chair she sat upon.

"My lord," she murmured without looking at him, her eyes averted. "I did not expect you so soon. Someone should have told me you were here."

"Blame the new squire." Rye took the chair, watching as Brenna seated herself gracefully on a low stool nearby and folded her hands in her lap. She played the part of docile wife well in front of Lady Madelon, and he recognized her game for what it was. Not that he blamed her. He would do the same if faced with Madelon's meddling ways and vicious tricks. Yea, he'd played games of his own as a youth, just to escape his stepmother's sharp tongue.

A servant quickly brought an aquamanile, a bronze water holder formed in the shape of a grotesque animal, for him to wash his hands, then he dried them on a clean strip of linen. With a goblet of wine at his right hand and a steaming plate of boiled beef and vegetables in front of him, Rye finally turned his attention back to Brenna.

She sat tall and straight, her glorious mane of hair tumbling in neat curls over her shoulders and back. It was obvious to him that she was doing her best to ignore him. He reached out to stroke his hand along her arm.

"My sweet, tell me how we are so fortunate to have all these guests in the hall this eve."

"I am not one to question Normans' motives, Lord Lyon," she said sharply, "so I have not asked why they came."

"Ah, but not all the guests are Normans, I am made to understand. Do I detect some from Marwald, p'raps?"

"Aye." Her voice was sullen, and she shifted slightly so that his hand fell away from her arm. "Ballard, from Marwald, my old minstrel, came with the Lord of Halstone Hall to honor us with music, my lord. 'Tis his habit to travel about singing ballads of the land, and he thought you would be pleased."

"Did he? And if I am not?"

Brenna gave him a quick glance. Rye saw the confusion darken her eyes and felt suddenly spiteful at his attempt to spoil her pleasure.

" 'Tis no matter," he said softly, "as long as you enjoy his songs."

Brenna half turned, and a startled smile curved her lips and made him think of how soft and sweet they were, and how he'd thought of her during the long day spent riding after raiders who disappeared as if wisps of fog.

"My thanks, my lord."

Rye sat back in his chair and regarded her for a moment without speaking, savoring her lovely face and the slight smile lingering on her lips. Aye, she was a beautiful wench indeed, and though her moods were hard to fathom, he could not recall ever having been so drawn to a woman before. It was somewhat unnerving to consider that this one Saxon woman with years of hatred behind her should be the one to play upon his affections most hardly.

Rye managed a careless shrug and turned his attention to his goblet of wine. When several guests were presented to him, he made the necessary comments without conscious effort. Brenna, with the faint fragrance of lavendar soap lingering around her, kept his mind only half on his duties as lord of Moorleah.

It was enough to make Rye long for the days before he'd met this fiery Saxon, those days of untrammeled peace of mind. Now he frequently found himself mired in unfamiliar emotions he couldn't understand. 'Twas enough to make a man surly, indeed.

His gaze came to rest on Ballard, the fair-haired minstrel from Marwald who stood boldly before the high table with a lute in his hands. Ballard's clever fingers coaxed a melody from the strings, and his fine voice lifted in a song about invincible Norman raiders.

It was obviously a song meant to flatter the Normans, yet it rankled that they were still considered to be foes after near ten years in the land. Rye's brow drew down in a scowl as he sipped at his wine. After a few more verses Ballard ended the long ballad with a quick paean to the king.

Ballard bowed deeply from the waist before Rye. "I hope my songs please you, Lord Lyon."

"They please my wife better, I think." Rye saw Ballard give a start of surprise at his rudeness and felt Brenna's angry gaze on him. Knowing he was behaving churlishly did nothing to improve his mood.

"Then I apologize for not pleasing you, seigneur. Do you have a song you wish for me to sing?"

Rye shifted. "Aye. Sing of King Arthur, if you will."

"King Arthur?" Ballard seemed taken aback. "I will be delighted to do so, my lord, though I did not know there were others who would enjoy such tales."

"Do you think only the Saxons have heard of him? His ballads are sung in Normandy also, though I admit they were brought to us by Saxons. Sing, Ballard, and entertain the hall with tales of love, honor, and courage."

The echo of Brenna's words to him in the nursery was not lost on her, and Rye felt her smile more than saw it. He kept his attention on the minstrel, and on his goblet of wine while Ballard spun melodies of Arthur, Mordred, Merlin, and the Ladies of Avilion.

The guests were highly entertained. When the central fire had burned low and the candles grew short, Rye finally gave the signal to retire for the night. He stood up and held out his hand to Brenna.

"Come, wife," he said, his standard invitation to bed. She put her hand in his palm after only the briefest of hesitations, and he heard Lady Madelon laugh.

"Aye, my lusty son, 'tis easy to see that you have tamed the Saxon rebel with kisses instead of killing. How noble. But is it wise? I should watch to see that she does not put a dagger in my back, were I you."

Rye's gaze was hostile. "You are not I, Lady Madelon, but I heed your warning only as I have always done. Which is to say—not at all."

His rebuke was plain enough to make Lady Madelon's face pale with rage, and her mouth tightened into a thin line. "I see. You have chosen this Saxon over your own kind then, my fine lord?"

Turning to face her, his hand holding tight to Brenna's when she would have pulled away, Rye said in a low, fierce tone meant only for Lady Madelon, "I have been at great pains to stress that there should be no more 'your kind' or 'our kind' talk, my lady. We should be one. William is king by right and might, and all of England should bind as one to a mutual cause. Your words are careless and seek to rend asunder what William would make whole. I suggest that you mind your tongue more carefully, ere you find your welcome at Moorleah grown thin."

Recoiling, Lady Madelon said in a pitiable tone, "Aiee, that an old woman should find herself abandoned in this day is most grievous, Lord Lyon! Do you think, how would it look to others for you to cast out your father's wife in her latter days?"

"Anyone knowing of your backbiting ways would commend me, madam, so do not think to play upon my sense of duty. I have little where you are concerned, as you well know the reason."

Lady Madelon met his hard gaze for an instant, then looked away. Her fingers curled into her palms, and she sat stiffly silent as Rye took Brenna's arm and led her from the high table. When he glanced back, he saw the dark enmity in her gaze, and knew his stepmother would take vengeance for his insults at first opportunity.

"My stepmother will seek to harm you, Brenna," Rye said once they were alone in their bedchamber. "Through you, she will strike at me, I think."

"Lady Madelon and I have our own private battle, my lord. Do not worry that I cannot deal with her, for I have found it best to ignore what I can of her tricks, while yet undoing what can be undone behind her back."

Looking up at her, Rye's hard mouth curved slightly. "I forgot for a moment that my wife is well capable of dealing with other shrews."

"Meaning that I am one, my lord?"

His mouth squared into a grin. "At times, yea. But a fairer shrew I have yet to see."

Brenna's voice was tart. " 'Tis a backhanded compliment, indeed, my lord. I am strained not to throw myself at your feet with joy at your high regard."

Laughing, Rye straightened from untying his cross garters and walked over to where she stood. Clad only in his loincloth, he reached out to pull Brenna to him, holding her against his bare chest. "Yield, *chérie*," he murmured in her ear, "yield all to me."

"I already have, my lord." Brenna felt a wild urge to relax against him instead of resist his embrace, but fought against it. "I defer to you in every matter large or small, and I yield to your word as final."

" 'Tis not what I mean and you know it," he muttered. His arms tightened, holding her so close against him, she could feel the rise of his passion between them. Her eyes closed briefly, and she held to her restraint.

There were times he made it most difficult to resist him. Even in his foul humor this eve, his obvious dislike at finding Ballard present in his hall, he'd tried to please her with a choice of song. She wasn't certain why, but that he had done so surprised her. Even more surprising were his brooding gazes on her, the way he watched her when he thought she did not notice.

She'd noticed. Aye, she'd noticed well. And wondered at it. Could he feel a softening toward her despite his rough manner? 'Twas something to think on.

Putting her palms against his chest, Brenna summoned the willpower to say softly, "Please, lord, I have not yet washed, or tended my nightly duties."

Rye's arms did not lessen their grip around her, and he lifted his head to stare down into her face. "Am I not a *nightly duty* as well, my sweet?" he mocked. "Would you deny your husband his rights?"

"Nay, lord, I would not." She shook her head, knowing that a refusal would only make him more determined. "I only ask that you allow me to complete my other, less important, duties first."

Rye released her. "You should be a courtier in William's court, sweeting. You have a facile tongue when you wish."

"If you say so, my lord."

Rye stared at her with a frustrated gaze, and Brenna knew she had succeeded with honeyed words where open rebellion would have earned her a pitched battle. Another lesson learned in dealing with this Norman knight, she thought as she turned toward the chamber door. If she fought him openly, he sought to break down her barriers with a determined assault. If she resisted his efforts with tact, he yielded more easily to her wishes. Yea, an important lesson indeed.

Before she reached the door, a sharp rap sounded upon the oak surface. Brenna was aware of Rye's immediate reach for his sword even as he called out, "Enter."

Her gaze shifted from Rye, who stood with sword in one hand, to the opening door, then her eyes widened.

"Myles," she breathed, feeling as if she'd been struck in the chest by a mallet.

Her brother threw her a quick glance, then turned his

attention to Rye, still standing with drawn sword only a few feet away.

"I brought your cleaned armor, my lord," he murmured. "Is there anything else you wish?"

"Aye. Come in and close the door." Rye relaxed, sheathing his sword with a metallic rasp of steel. His gaze shifted from Myles to Brenna. After a moment of tense silence, he explained, "Myles is my new squire, Brenna. As you must have guessed by now."

"So I see." Brenna stood stiffly, not knowing what to say or do. Only two of her brothers garnered any real affection in her, and Myles was one of them. They were close in age and, though separated for many years, had managed to keep contact when possible. Now here he was, in the service of the Normans, and she wondered why. Myles had been fierce in his Saxon loyalty in spite of being held hostage by William.

Shifting from one foot to the other, Myles gave his sister a wary glance as he seemed to deliberate on whether to speak or hold his tongue. Rye watched them with an irritated frown.

"Well," he said, "do you not have words of greeting for one another?"

"Of course," Brenna said quickly, and nodded at her brother. " 'Tis good to see you well, Myles."

"And you, Lady Brenna."

Myles still stood awkwardly holding the cleaned hauberk and gauntlets in his arms, and when Rye made an impatient gesture and told him to put them down, he did so without delay.

"If there is nothing else, milord?" he began, and took a step toward the door.

Rye's voice stopped him. "There is something else. I've no objection if you wish to speak with your sister. Since you are at Moorleah by your own choice, you might tell her thus so she does not think you have been coerced."

Brenna looked at him. "This is true, Myles? You came of your own accord?"

He nodded. "Aye. Your husband offered me a position as squire should I be suited for it, and I thought 'twould serve me better than roaming the forests or listening to our father's tales of past Saxon glory."

"You would think," Brenna murmured, "that Dunstan would be too busy to dwell on his own history."

Myles grinned. "When I left, he was most busy indeed. I think the king has set him to building new roads as well as walls, and he was most put about trying to find expert stonemasons."

"Was he?" Brenna was intrigued by the mental image of her blustering father caught up in such a task, and smiled. "That should keep him too busy for tale spinning, I vow."

"Or anything else," Rye put in dryly. "William has a unique method of engaging his vassals in tasks that will consume their time to the extent they can do little else."

"Meaning that this is only a way of keeping my father from plotting rebellion?" Brenna turned to ask mockingly. "I do not think William need concern himself with one wornout old man like Dunstan. Rather, he should concern himself with his own barons who seek to drag him from his throne."

"Ah, 'tis good to see you leap to the defense of your father at last," Rye said with a grin. "I have oft wondered at your lack of loyalty to the man who gave you life."

Stiffening, Brenna said quietly, " 'Tis none of your affair, my lord, whether I cherish my father or not."

"Is it not?" Rye murmured, stepping close to her. He put a hand under her chin and lifted her face to his when she would have turned away. "I think it is, *chérie*. If you have no loyalty to kin, you will have none to me. Or to the children we will have."

Brenna jerked away from his touch. Her cheeks flamed with hot color. Aware of Myles's close regard, she did not yield to the scathing words on the tip of her tongue, not quite certain of her brother's reaction should Rye choose to retaliate.

"I place my loyalty carefully, my lord," she said after a moment. "And I do not place it easily."

"So I am made to understand." Rye looked from Brenna to Myles. "And you, young squire? Are you of the same mind?"

Myles gave the earl a cautious glance before he nodded slowly. "Aye, seigneur. It took much thought to seek an employment in your keep, but I chose well, I think."

Rye gave a satisfied nod. "You did. 'Twill mean the difference between life and death in the end. Should you have chosen the life certain outlaws have chosen, you would find yourself hanging from the castle gate where they will soon dangle."

Myles ducked his head to stare at his feet, his reply almost inaudible. "Aye, lord. As you say."

"Give over," Brenna cut in sharply. "He is here, is he not? Do not try to make overt threats when there is no need for it."

Rye's gaze shifted to her. He took up a goblet of wine from a table and sipped it before he said, "Why do you think I make threats, *chérie*? 'Tis common knowledge that I seek the outlaws who prey on their own kind, and I simply saluted your brother's wisdom in joining our forces."

Brenna saw Myles's discomfort and guessed at the reason.

"As squire, he will be cleaning swords, not wielding them." Her brow lifted. He tested Myles, 'twas plain, and she hoped her brother was wise enough to see it also. If Myles sought to spy for the outlaws, he would be killed with them. Brenna's stomach churned with anxiety, and she tried to hide it as she turned back to her brother.

"I am glad to see you so well, Myles, and pray that you will seek me out when your duties permit. I cannot show you many kindnesses, you understand, or it will only go hard with you should your peers object."

Myles grinned. "Already Gowain makes loud noises since I was chosen by Beltair to take his place, and the leech is hard put to keep him in his sickbed. I will be once more serving mutton as soon as Gowain is able to rise, never fear."

Rye listened as they talked, and when the conversation turned to questions of those left at Marwald, he ambled in the direction of the garderobe. Brenna immediately took advantage of his absence.

"Myles," she said quickly, "you must do nothing to earn his suspicion, do you understand? Our brothers— what news of them?"

For a moment Myles hesitated. Then he said slowly, "I left Whitley in the forest beyond Moorleah. He and Ridgely plan another raid, I think, but would not tell me too much. I know nothing of Rannulf or Corbet, save they ride with them at times."

"Fools, all of them."

"Aye." Myles nodded wearily. "So I told them, but they do not listen. We should be glad Guy and Wulf are still in Normandy as William's hostages, 'ere they yield to the same madness that infects our other brothers."

"Guy and Wulf are young yet, still serving as simple pages," Brenna murmured, and Myles gave a short, bitter laugh.

"There's not much time for childhood in this world, my sweet sister. Have you forgotten?"

Brenna thought then of how young Myles had been when he was forced from his home after the Saxon king's defeat. Six was a young age to be taken hostage at sword point and bade go to a foreign land with invaders. Guy and Wulf had been too young to realize danger, but not Myles. Nay, it had not been easy for him in those long years after being forced to live with the enemy, but he had somehow survived. She hoped that he would not yield to the rebellion of their other brothers.

As if reading her thoughts, Myles said softly, "There will be naught we can do if our kin are taken, Brenna."

"Do you seek to warn me not to try, Myles? Do not. I am not so big a fool I would risk my own neck just to keep just retribution from men who refuse to listen to common sense. Although I would hope that Lyon will not allow his anger to spill over on those undeserving of it."

"He does not seem that kind of man. 'Tis why I sought service here."

Brenna gazed at him for a long moment, noting how he'd filled out in breadth and height since last they'd been together. He was fast becoming a man, despite his tender years.

"There were other reasons you came here," she said after a moment, glancing at the arched doorway where Rye had disappeared. The garderobe was not far away, and she expected him back at any moment. "What are they?"

"You are too suspicious," Myles said softly. "But you are also right. I came for more than that. Now is not the time to speak of it."

"When?" she asked urgently. "Do not be a fool, Myles. Lyon is not a gentle man. He will deal most harshly with you if you are—" She broke off when she heard Rye's steps in the hall and said loudly, "Tell Ballard that I most enjoyed his playing this eve. I look forward to hearing more, if he is to linger for a time."

Myles shrugged. "I do not know his plans, but I will relay your message." He glanced at Rye, who sauntered through the door with a leisurely tread, hitching up his chausses as if he had but answered nature's call. "My lord, it is late, and I am to tend you early on the morrow. If you have no more need of me—?"

Waving a hand, Rye said, "No more tonight, squire. Leave us now."

When Myles left with only a smile and brief glance at his sister, Brenna could feel Rye's curious gaze on her. She shifted slightly so that her back was to the door as it closed behind her brother.

"I am weary also, lord. If you do not mind, I shall seek my bed."

"Our bed." Rye's eyes narrowed slightly when she drew in a sharp breath. "Must it always be the same? First you avoid my touch, then you seek it eagerly before the night has passed. When will you admit to your softer yearnings, Brenna?"

"You confuse wifely attention with an emotion I do not feel," Brenna said stiffly, wondering why he persisted in trying to coax emotion from her. Couldn't he be satisfied with the passion she could not deny? Must he have it all?

"Nay, *chérie*," he was saying with a trace of a smile on his hard mouth, "I do not confuse it. I am well aware of what you feel and am quite content with it. What bemuses me is your unwillingness to admit to that flame that sears your flesh when I touch you."

Brenna fought a wave of irritation. Curse him, for forcing her surrender then mocking her for it. Her struggle always ended the same; surrender came in a heated rush of passion and blazing desire, and she was left lying awake many a night thinking bitterly of her self-defeat at his hands.

"Brenna," Rye said softly, "I do not mock you. I only seek to understand."

She looked away from his penetrating gaze. "I cannot explain what I do not understand myself," she said after a moment. Her slender shoulders lifted in a slight shrug. "If you seek understanding, I am afraid you ask the wrong one."

"That much is obvious." Rye reached out for her, ignoring her efforts to resist, and she found herself pulled against his hard-muscled frame in an inexorable grip. He did not loosen his grasp, not even when she turned away from his searching kiss.

Patiently he gripped her chin with his fingers and turned her face back to him, lowering his head to capture her cold lips with his. His kiss was searing, consuming. It melted her reserve within the space of a few minutes, and she was barely aware of the incoherent protests she made when he lifted her in his arms and bore her toward the huge bed.

CHAPTER 12

EARLY-SPRING SUNSHINE filtered slowly across the rolling hills of land. Fingers of light sifted through new green leaves and, diffused by mist, gave an almost ethereal quality to the village.

Wooden benches had been set up beneath the leafy arms of a huge oak, and Brenna was seated with Lady Madelon, Raissa, Gilles, and Rachel. A silken canopy was swagged over them, and those of the village gathered in the open square to celebrate. Music swirled from lutes and mandolins, and a troupe of acrobats performed.

A tall sapling stood in the village green, and rosy-cheeked girls garlanded it with flowers in the soft press of sun and wind. Ribbons had been tied to branches, and children stood eagerly waiting the dances that would celebrate the coming of spring.

"A pagan custom, Father Gutierrez says," Lady Madelon observed with a disdainful sniff. " 'Tis a day dedicated to heathen gods."

Brenna gave her a sharp look. "Aye, the goddess Flora, I am told, of Roman times. She smiled upon the fruits and flowers of spring and summer. Do you wish to leave this pagan celebration, milady? No one will mind, I assure you."

Lady Madelon's mouth settled into a taut line. "That would suit you well, wouldn't it?"

"Very well, milady." Brenna met her quick glance with a slight smile. "This is a time of merriment, not dour faces and sour dispositions. As for Father Gutierrez, he frowns upon everything human. He believes only in the purging of the soul."

"He is a man of God," Lady Madelon said stiffly. Her hands curved into the folds of her elegant velvet gown. "Do you blaspheme the Church?"

"Far from it. This is just a family custom, milady, begun by my mother to amuse the peasants. She saw it in Italy and enjoyed it so much she brought the custom to England when she came to marry my father."

"Ah. I had forgotten that your mother was Norman," Lady Madelon said. " 'Tis what saves you, I suppose."

"*Saves* me?" Brenna's brows drew into a knot over her eyes, and she glanced from Rachel's strained face to her mother by law, then back. Her little maid looked worried at the confrontation, as well she should. Lady Madelon had a habit of taking out her temper on servants. Brenna swallowed a harsh reply and merely said, "Aye. My Norman blood saves me much, I vow."

Deliberately turning her back to avoid any further conversation, Brenna rose and went into the crowd. On impulse she caught the hand of a small child and pulled her toward the group beneath the tree. Bright ribbons fluttered in the wind, strips of colored cloth dancing enticingly just above the girl's head.

"Would you like to touch one?" Brenna asked, and when the child nodded shyly, Brenna lifted her to touch the end of the snapping ribbon. Laughing, the child put a chubby arm around Brenna's neck to hold on as she reached up and out, watching the ribbon lick the ends of her fingers in the press of wind.

After a moment Brenna returned the child to her mother with a smile. The woman swept her a deep curtsy.

"God bless ye, milady," the peasant mother said

softly, "and I hope ye soon have your own happy babe
to hold in your arms. . . ."

Brenna's smile vanished, and she turned blindly away,
motioning for Rachel to hand out the little cakes that
had been baked for the villagers. A babe of her own.
Nay, not that end, she prayed. Never that. She could
not.

Somehow she managed to force smiles and respond
with a gracious comment when needed, but the gaiety of
the day had been tarnished by a simple well-meant comment. Only Rachel and Lady Raissa noticed, and the
latter came to her with an anxious expression.

"You are unwell?"

"Unwell?" Brenna echoed, then shook her head.
"Nay, no more than usual. More weary than I am accustomed to feel, p'raps, but not unwell."

"Ah." Raissa swept a hand toward the villagers and
children dancing about and laughing. "This was much
needed to restore their spirits, I believe. Since the outlaws have been so predatory, the people have been afraid
and unhappy. Now they look positively carefree."

Brenna nodded and watched as a boisterous group of
young people grabbed the ends of the trailing ribbons
and began to dance in couples. The May Day celebration
had the air of a festival, with music and games and per-
formers. The only sober note was the armed soldiers
who patrolled the area, and those she'd not been able to
avoid. Rye had not yielded an inch in his determination
that there would be soldiers, or there would be no celebrations.

"Nay, sweeting," he'd said. "I will not risk my family
or my people to the outlaws should they seek to disturb
your plans. My men will be there, or you will not."

Brenna had stopped her arguments before he'd re-
scinded his permission for the May Day. She'd begun to
recognize that obstinate light in his eyes and knew he
would not be turned from his decision. So she had re-
verted to her newly discovered tact to persuade him not
to have mounted soldiers line the village and thus de-

stroy the holiday mood. And she had also persuaded him to show himself to the villagers in a more lenient mode.

" 'Twill not hurt your reputation as a man who seeks to rule, my lord," Brenna had coaxed, "but only add to it as a lord who cares about his people's welfare in more than terms of what they can produce for the storehouses or the coffers."

Smiling, Rye had allowed her to coax him into appearing at the May Day celebration, but he had not yet shown.

"Where could he be?" young Gilles asked his mother. Raissa assured him he would be there soon.

"Your uncle is a very busy man," Raissa said, stroking back the boy's hair, "but he always keeps his promises."

Brenna shivered. Raissa was right. Rye kept the promises he made, or he did not make them. And hadn't he promised to make her yield all to him? There were times she feared he'd already reached that goal, for even now she watched for him as eagerly as his nephew.

Fool, she berated herself without a hope that she would stop listening for the sound of his voice or watching for his tall frame among the milling soldiers. She was growing besotted, and though she fought to remain aloof, she found her resolve growing weaker every day.

Rye was not the man she'd once thought him to be; or rather, he was much more than the man she'd thought him. He governed justly, allowing the people to punish those among them who broke the laws, and not imposing a harsh Norman justice. Instead, Saxon chastised Saxon, an act that did much to instill confidence in their new lord's laws of justice. Aye, Brenna mused, he knew how to govern men, but there were times he knew little of women.

Instead of coaxing cooperation from Brenna, he demanded it, and that she could not tolerate. When he made a request of her, she was quick to comply, hoping to show him that he received much more with softness than he did by demands, but he seemed to miss the point of that lesson more times than not.

Yet here she stood, waiting for him as if she were a simple maid in love.

Love. Could she be? The thought stunned Brenna, and she must have made some sound, because Raissa turned to look at her.

"Did you speak, milady?"

"Nay," Brenna replied, trying to ignore the faint flush that crept up her neck. Her fingers caught in the material of her gown, and she managed a smile. "Here comes your brother."

Rye approached with an easy stride, head and shoulders above most of his men and the villagers. He wore a scarlet mantle over his mail, and though Brenna had hoped he would wear more elegant garments, she was satisfied that he had at least come to the village. Behind Rye, Raoul led his lord's huge destrier. Brenna caught Rachel's quick glance at him and hid a smile behind her hand. It was obvious to anyone who cared to look that the slender maid was quite taken with Raoul de Beaumont.

"Rachel," she leaned forward to say softly, "do see if Sir de Beaumont would care to have some refreshment. There is wine for the men in the baskets beneath the trees."

"You've seen to every detail," Raissa remarked with a smile. "I commend you, Brenna."

Only Lady Madelon voiced a complaint, and she waited until Rye had come to put a possessive hand on his wife's arm before she spoke.

"So, my lord, I see that you have been reduced to consorting with serfs since wedding a Saxon. But 'tis all that should be expected, I vow, from a lowborn knight."

A moment of shocked silence enveloped those close enough to hear, and Rye turned slowly to bend a steady stare upon his stepmother.

"Only you would be rude enough to make such a comment, Lady Madelon. You show your lack of manners with every word lately, it seems. If you are so unhappy here, you are free to return to Normandy."

There was nothing in his face to indicate that he was

less than serious, and Lady Madelon must have realized that she had overstepped the boundaries of common sense with her rudeness.

"I beg your pardon, my lord," she forced out, her eyes lowering from the harsh look he gave her. " 'Tis my frailty that bids me be so ill-tempered lately."

"You are ill, madam?"

Lady Madelon looked up at Rye, and only those who knew her well could see the hatred in her gaze. "I would not bother you with such things, when there are many important matters to take up your time."

"If you are ill," Rye said less harshly, "then you must seek care, my lady."

"Aye, lord. Thank you for your kindness."

Brenna regarded Rye's stepmother for a long moment. She knew very well that Lady Madelon was as fit as usual but had only sought a way out of the mire her hasty words had created. And she knew from the faintly sardonic set of Rye's mouth that he was aware of the ploy also. But there was little to be gained from a public confrontation, especially with all the villagers gathered to greet their new lord in an entirely new manner.

"The man you have set as mayor to the village is here to present you with a gift, my lord," Brenna said softly, and felt Rye's gaze shift to her. Her heart lurched. He looked every inch the lord today, every inch the Earl of Lyonfield and now Moorleah. William had chosen well, though a few months ago she had not thought so. These past weeks had been quite enlightening, Brenna thought.

"A gift?" Rye repeated in surprise.

"Aye, to honor you as their lord. 'Tis a ceremonial gift, you will see."

The mayor, a portly man with a full head of blazing red hair that matched equally bushy eyebrows, knelt nervously to present Rye with a huge basket. He cleared his throat and indicated the contents with a gesture.

"Here, my lord, is a sheaf of wheat, to signify that we till the fields for the good of all. There is barley, corn, and"—he dug into the basket, and after a brief skirmish, brought up a squawking chicken—"fowl, to share your table. What is ours, lord, is yours, and we share gladly with the man who has brought justice to our land."

Rising, the mayor gestured to a small girl, who tugged at a bright ribbon bound to a lamb.

"This is my daughter, and she wishes to give you her pet lamb from our flock as a token of our good faith."

The girl seemed less enthusiastic than her father, but the lamb was obviously reluctant. It bawled loudly, and balked when the child tried to tug it forward. Near tears, she glanced up at the man seated in a high-backed chair and lisped, "Daithy won't come, my lord. Thees thcared."

"Is she?" Rye glanced from the mayor's crimson face to the child, then to the lamb. "Then let Daisy stay with you until she's not so scared," he said after a moment. "I give her to your care."

The child's face brightened, and she nodded. "Aye, milord, I will thee that Daithy ith cared for."

"I trust you to do so." Rye looked back at the mayor. "And I will justify your faith in me as your overlord when I bring you the outlaws who ravage your fields."

Bowing, the mayor looked up at Rye and said, "I know you will, my lord. 'Tis said that you are a man who does not fail."

Brenna stiffened, and Rye turned his eyes to her. She saw the grim purpose in his eyes, and knew that this time he would bring back the outlaws who dared to burn crops and villages, though her own brothers might be among them. There was nothing she could do, and she knew that she had made her choice.

The shock of it reverberated in her mind as she realized how far she had come in the six weeks she had been wed to Rye de Lyon. She was deliberately choosing Norman justice over Saxon kinship. It was as heartrending as it was confusing.

It was early. The sun had not yet burned off the morning mists that shrouded wood and fields. Rye's destrier snorted softly and stamped its great hooves against the still-damp earth. Huge oaks shadowed the mounted, mailed knights as they waited, and faint sounds of bird calls drifted on the breeze.

Leaning close to Rye, Beaumont murmured, "Do you think 'tis birds who make that sound?"

"Nay, 'tis a signal. That must mean our quarry does not know we are here. But that's a matter of little consequence, since we are hardly trying to hide."

Shifting in his saddle, Rye let his gaze move from the wooded copse to the clear land beyond. Furrows ran across the fields, and tender shoots greened the brown earth with new life. Thatched cottages were clustered on the far side of the fields, and thin curls of smoke drifted from open holes in the roofs.

It was the first week in June, and Rye's efforts were finally about to be rewarded. Two days before, a man of the village had come to warn his lord that he had overheard the plans of the outlaws to ravage this distant village. Though frightened, he considered it his duty to stop them. Rye had assured him he made the right choice, as the next village might very well be his own.

Now he waited impatiently for success.

Rye and his men had ridden out from Moorleah well before first light the day before to snare these outlaws who planned to ravish village and fields, and now the trap was nearly sprung.

On the opposite side of the copse that ran between the fields and village, more knights waited. And at the end of the funnel through which Rye intended to herd his quarry, a band of soldiers lay hidden to cut them off should any reach that far. Rye intended they should not, but he'd planned for all possibilities.

"I was told," Beaumont remarked, "that there are forty or more outlaws. They are armed with swords, but for the most part carry scythes and axes." He gave a scornful laugh. "Truly fearsome, I vow."

"Do not underestimate them," Rye replied. "They have managed to outwit us at every turn so far, and have wrought devastation upon the land so successfully that I began to fear we would never be able to catch them. I will not feel safe until we have them beneath our swords at last."

Tightening his knees, Rye urged his mount a few steps deeper into the wood, his every sense attuned for the signal he sought. He didn't know what he waited for, only that he would recognize it when it came. He always did; it was a trait instilled in him by his early masters, that telltale sign of movement from one's enemy, and he had learned his lessons well.

When it came, a faint, muffled sound, he jerked into action. Bringing his left arm up in a quick signal, he spurred his destrier forward just as armed men emerged from the wood to race across the fields toward the thatched huts just beyond.

"*Jésu,*" he breathed softly. These were no simple peasant warriors. These were trained knights who had descended into outlawry, as he had guessed. He saw from their concerted moves with swords, axes, even scythes, that the men knew what they were about when it came to warfare. Already the first wave of his men had joined them in battle, and the noise was as fierce as the fighting.

Swords clanged harshly; hoarse bellows rent the air as men met with savage force. With the mounted Normans waging a fierce assault rife with the frustrations of the past months, the outlaws had little chance of success. Yet they fought well and savagely, giving no quarter.

Rye spurred his mount into the thick of the fray, taking a cut on one arm from a scythe before he mowed the man down with a downstroke of his sword. He swung it with swift efficiency, hefting the heavy blade with the easy, practiced motions he'd learned as a youth. This was work he knew well, and he recognized in the enemy that they, too, had learned it well.

Behind Rye, Beaumont guarded his back while battling a heavyset outlaw armed with a sword. The man was obviously a trained knight and brought Beaumont down in a quick motion that made Rye turn his destrier toward them.

The war-horse had been schooled in warfare as well

and kept the enemy at bay with lethal hooves and teeth while Rye swung his sword. In a few quick strokes Rye killed the man and was off his horse to see to Beaumont.

Ignoring the battle still raging around them, he knelt and lifted him, his hands searching for the wound he'd been dealt. Smiling weakly, Beaumont pushed aside his helm and grimaced as Rye found the deep slash in his side. His eyes were bright with pain when he looked up at Rye.

" 'Tis not a deathblow, seigneur. I shall live to fight again."

Rye made his own assessment, noting that though the wound was deep, it had missed vital organs. He felt a wave of relief that was almost crippling in intensity and knew then that this loyal Norman knight meant much more to him than he had allowed himself to think about.

"Aye, Raoul, I think you are right. You just wish to lie abed and have the tender ministrations of your lady, I think. 'Tis a sorry state for a knight, to go to that end to gain his lady's kind attention."

Beaumont looked up at Rye's teasing words and must have seen some of what he felt. He kept his tone light.

"Sorry, indeed, lord. But worth it, I think." Grimacing at the pain his movements brought, Beaumont managed to sit up while Rye beckoned a soldier to his aid.

The sounds of the battle were diminishing, and though the outcome had been a foregone conclusion with so many armed and mounted Normans catching their quarry in the open, Rye could not help a feeling of relief that it was over. He would have lost much in the loss of this one knight, he reflected, as he gave orders to herd the surviving outlaws into a group and tie them together.

"Pile the dead outlaws beneath a tree," he commanded, pushing his helm to the back of his head, "and see to those most wounded. Call a priest for those who wish one."

One of the prisoners lifted a bloodied head at Rye's last command, and a fierce light sprang into bloodshot blue eyes. His voice rang out, loud and mocking.

"A priest, Lord Lyon? Do you consider that Saxons have souls, then?"

Rye flicked him a cold glance. "Some of them. Others seem to have lost theirs, but 'tis not my place to judge. That I leave to those better qualified."

"Aye," came the bitter retort, "so you should. For a man said to confer with the Dark One, 'tis not fit that you should judge other men, even Saxons."

Rye felt a spurt of anger and stepped close to the man, raking him with a narrow gaze. "What is your name, bold Saxon?"

Straightening as best as possible considering he was bound hand and foot, the Saxon met Rye's stare without flinching and said, "Ridgely, son of Dunstan from Marwald."

"And you lead these men?"

Ridgely glanced around. "I did. There do not seem to be many left to lead, I fear."

" 'Twas by your choice, Ridgely of Marwald. Did you not heed my warnings to the end should the assaults on innocent villages continue? If you had," he continued without waiting for an answer or denial, "you would have saved many lives. Including your own."

"You would put the brother of your wife to the sword?" Ridgely mocked, his eyes burning with hatred. "I vow, even the shrewish Brenna will mislike that act."

"Nay, I would not put you to the sword." Rye hefted his sword into the air in an agile swing, then plunged it into the ground between his spread feet. He fixed a fierce stare on the startled Saxon. "I will give your fate into the hands of those you have wronged, Ridgely of Marwald. 'Tis up to the peasants who have suffered your cruelties if you live or die. A jury of men shall be selected to decide your fate."

Ridgely swallowed, and his chest rose and fell rapidly. "I am the son of a Saxon baron. I have no peers to—"

"Wrong." Rye cut across his words angrily. "Your peers are those whom you have plundered these last months. By not swearing an oath of fealty to William, you have lost claim to noble title as well as any lands in

England. Therefore, 'twill be your peers who decide your fate."

Pivoting on his heel, Rye stalked away, leaving the Saxon outlaws to consider their futures and fates. He went to Beaumont, who had been laid gently upon a litter to be taken back to Moorleah. He knelt beside him, peeling off his gauntlets and pulling off his helm.

"I shall see to you as soon as I return, Raoul."

"You go to run down those who fled, my lord?" Beaumont gave him a worried look from eyes hazy with pain and clutched at his mail-clad arm. "Set a good man to watch your back. When word gets out that you are set on such grim justice, there will be those who seek your death at any cost."

" 'Tis no different than it has always been. Don't be an old woman." Rye smiled to ease the sting of his words and saw Beaumont's faint grin. "All the outlaws must be brought to justice."

"Aye, lord. Though I think 'twould be best just to hang those men or put them to the sword. An example of Norman justice should prevail."

"But William wishes for this land to be one, Beaumont, not Norman or Saxon. In this case, since the hurts were done to Saxons, Saxons should deliver the justice."

Standing, Rye gave the signal for Beaumont's litter to be carried away. Pulling his metal helm and coif back over his head, he shoved his hands into his heavy gauntlets and took the reins to his destrier. As he swung into the highbacked saddle, he caught Ridgely's gaze bent on him.

"Any words for your fair sister?" he asked, tightening his hold on the reins as the destrier pranced eagerly.

"Aye—" Ridgely paused, his eyes alive with hatred. "Tell her that I'd sooner see her dead than wed to a Norman bastard. . . ."

The last words were whispered hoarsely. A wave of savage fury surged through Rye, and he fought the urge to use his sword against the insolent Saxon outlaw who used such strong words. Only iron restraint kept his sword sheathed and his fury contained.

Whirling his mount around, he snarled to his sergeant-at-arms, "See that the leader has ample time to regret his war against peasants, Beltair. Put him alone in a cell, so he has no distractions."

Rye spurred his destrier toward the soldiers, who gave chase to the outlaws fleeing toward the armed men, waiting there beyond the fields.

Pressing a hand to her aching back, Brenna straightened slowly from where she'd been bent over a large vat.

"My back aches," she murmured, and heard Rachel's soft sound of sympathy. She flashed her maid a smile. " 'Tis all this bending and mixing, I vow."

Moving the vat closer to the edge of the long table set up in the kitchen, Rachel cast her a glance.

"Do you think so, milady?"

"Of course. What else could it be?" Brenna peered into the metal cauldron at the noxious mixture. In the past week she had begun to notice a difference in her body that was as confusing as it was frightening. She tired easily. Her back ached. Her appetite waned, especially in the early mornings.

She'd not spoken of it to anyone, but Rachel had noticed, as she did now.

"Milady—come, sit down for a time. I will see to the mixture for you."

Brenna frowned slightly. She glanced at the others around her to see if they had noticed her infirmity, but no one looked her way. Turning back to Rachel, she gave a nod of her head.

"Aye, I know you will take charge for me, Rachel. 'Tis just that this concoction needs to be right, or it will not remove candle wax or wine stains from our garments."

Rachel cast a doubtful glance at the vat of fuller's earth and lye. "P'raps a soaking in warm wine for a day or two would help those most stained."

"P'raps," Brenna agreed with a sigh. "Most of Rye's heavy garments have already been laden with bay leaves and packed away in cypress chests, but these—!" She shook her head. "He's most careless with his velvet tunics."

Rachel watched silently as Brenna shook out an elegant tunic embroidered with gold gilt thread on sleeves and hem. Her brow was furrowed in thought, and after a few moments passed, she blurted, "Does your lord know about the babe, milady?"

Pausing, Brenna turned slowly to face her. "The babe? What do you mean?"

Rachel gestured hesitantly. "Your babe, milady."

"My babe?" Brenna lowered the velvet tunic to the worktable set up at the end of the kitchen. "You are mistaken. I have no babe."

"Aye, milady," Rachel mumbled, looking down at her folded hands.

Brenna's mouth felt suddenly dry, and a wave of nausea welled in her throat. She'd suspected, but until now had not put into voice her fears. The wooden spoon she'd been using to mix the powder slipped from her hand and clattered against the edge of the vat. She looked up at Rachel with a stricken expression.

"That's it, isn't it."

It wasn't a question, but a statement, and Rachel bit her lower lip and nodded.

"Aye, milady, it would seem so. Your symptoms rival those of my stepmother when she was breeding."

A shudder of fear trickled down Brenna's spine. A babe. She'd tried to ignore the symptoms, but now it was impossible. "Speak of this to no one, Rachel. I wish to hold the knowledge to myself for a time."

"Aye, milady, but should you need help—"

"I will ask you, I promise." She paused, sucking in a deep breath. "Do you mind—? I will leave this to you. I wish to be alone to think."

Without waiting for Rachel's worried reply, Brenna left the vaulted kitchen and made her way outside into the bailey. Men-at-arms were riding across the inner bridge. Behind, in a scraggly line, half walking, half stumbling, were the outlaws. Litters bore the wounded.

Brenna stopped a man-at-arms and inquired anxiously, "My husband—where is he?"

"Gone after the rest of the outlaws, milady." The grim-faced soldier smiled slightly. "I vow he will not return on a litter, so set your fears to rest. The earl is the fiercest fighter in all of England and Normandy."

It was little comfort. Brenna turned, one hand lifted to her throat as she looked at the prisoners. She gasped. She could not mistake her brother as he stalked at the head of the line, his tall frame unbowed and his face alive with hatred. He was glaring at her.

"So, she-wolf, it seems that you have mated with the lion and brought shame to our house," Ridgely snarled, his voice rising above the crowd in the bailey. A soldier cuffed him, but he only reeled and did not fall, his intent gaze unwavering as he stared at his sister.

Putting a hand over her mouth, Brenna felt a wash of emotion drown her contempt for her brother. He was bloody and furious, but seeing him somehow reminded her of happier times. There had been days when they had all gathered to celebrate the first of May, and their mother had led them in laughter and songs and dancing. Ridgely had been clumsy but most enthusiastic at those times, and somehow that memory made up for the later, harsher memories of him as a crude, brutal soldier in her father's keep.

She walked to where he stood. "Ridgely—"

"Nay! Do not offer sympathy now, sweet sister. You've had none before."

"That's not fair," she said calmly. "I've hardly seen you since I returned from Normandy; you were not oft at our father's table of an eve. I am sorry to see you like this, but you brought it upon yourself with your burning and killing and looting of innocent people."

"Innocent?" Ridgely laughed harshly. "They've thrown in with the devil, Brenna, as have you. Rye de Lyon has put more villages to the sword of late than I have ever burned fields, and if you do not believe me, ask him. He is an *honorable* man, is he not? Or so he claims. Ask him. Ask him if he has put those villages to the sword or torch, and then mayhap you will know what brand of Norman justice you have helped bring upon our land."

Backing away, Brenna agonized with indecision. She only half believed her brother. Ridgely had never been a kind man, and her momentary pity was obviously misplaced. Rye could never have put a village to the sword, not as Ridgely claimed. Nay, hadn't she seen him deal kindly with those of the village? Even a child's pet lamb stirred his sympathy.

Aye, she would ask him.

CHAPTER 13

STILL SHAKEN BY the encounter with her brother, Brenna walked blindly toward the door of the keep. As she passed a litter that had just been lowered to the ground, a hand reached out to snag her skirts.

"Milady," came a hoarse voice, and she halted to look down with surprise at the litter's occupant.

"Sweet Mary in heaven, it's Beaumont!" Brenna knelt by his side immediately. "You've been wounded. Let me see your hurts."

"Nay," he protested weakly, " 'tis not for the eyes of a lady. . . ."

"Don't be foolish, Beaumont." Brenna brushed aside his hand and peeled back the edge of his mantle to look at the sword cut. Forcing a smile, she assured him, "I have tended many such wounds, I promise you. I will not make it worse."

"I was not worried about that, milady, but . . . do not heed the words of an angry man."

Brenna looked up at him in surprise. "An angry man?"

"Aye. The outlaw. I heard . . . what he . . . said." Grimacing with pain, Beaumont clasped Brenna's fingers with a bloody hand and held tightly. "War makes men do things they would not do otherwise. Remember that, milady."

Slipping her hand from his clasp, Brenna gauged the depth and seriousness of his wound and motioned for him to be lifted and taken inside.

"I will tend him myself," she told the man-at-arms, who nodded and bent to lift Beaumont's litter. Brenna followed close behind as two hefty soldiers carried Beaumont up the stone steps and into the keep.

As they entered the dimly lit guardroom of the keep, Brenna's attention was focused on the wounded knight. She paid scant attention to those around her, nor did she dwell on what had occupied her mind so completely a short time before. Beaumont's injuries precluded all but the necessary work to save him.

Snapping orders at startled servants, Brenna soon had hot water, clean strips of cloth, and her bag of herbs. She also had a frantic Rachel at her side, and she gently drew the girl away from Beaumont's pallet.

"If you are too stricken to be of use, Rachel," she said softly, "I will find another. Do you wish to remain?"

"Oh, milady," Rachel said in a breathy gasp, "do not send me away. I will not cry out or get in the way, I swear it."

"I didn't intend to send you away to be hurtful, but to spare you pain," Brenna assured her, touching the girl on her arm with a light gesture. "And if you cannot bear it, I cannot take the time to tend you."

Rachel swallowed. "I will bear it."

Lifting her hand, Brenna said, "Very well. You may stay. But quickly, fetch more cloths for me while I examine Beaumont more closely. The wound is long, but doesn't seem to be that deep. I need to see it more clearly."

Kneeling beside him again, Brenna concentrated on the fallen knight. Sweat beaded on his forehead, and she wiped it away with a cloth.

"This will hurt, so I shall give you a draught to ease your discomfort," Brenna murmured, and added when he gave a protest, "I can work better if you are not in pain, sir. Please do not refuse it."

Links of chain mail had been embedded in the deep sword slash, and as soon as the draught began to make Beaumont drowsy, Brenna began picking out the tiny pieces of metal. It was tedious business, and she was careful not to miss one as she worked. Rachel sponged away the flowing blood as she cleaned the wound, and when all the metal was gone and Brenna was certain no vital organs had been damaged, she took up a needle and thread to close the wound.

It was a grim task, and several times Brenna had to pause and take a deep breath, fighting the nausea that clogged her throat. Rachel put a steadying hand on her shoulder and offered to take over.

"I can sew a fine seam, milady, and should be able to make short work of one knight, I think."

Brenna looked at Rachel's pale face and shook her head. "Nay, though I am certain you would do well. I will finish it."

When she was through and Rachel was binding Beaumont's wound with long strips of cloth, Brenna stumbled to a low bench and sank gratefully to its hard surface. It had taken more out of her than she'd realized it would, but she was glad she had done it. Beaumont was a favorite, and she would not have trusted his wound to the clumsy but well-meaning efforts of the men-at-arms.

Putting her face in her hands, she drew in a deep breath. She was shaking, and when she felt a hand upon her shoulder, she looked up with a startled gasp.

Raissa smiled at her. "You are overweary. Come with me and I will see to your welfare. 'Tis not good to tire so much in your—at this time."

"At this time." Brenna met Raissa's sympathetic gaze and saw that she knew. "It seems that all at Moorleah are aware of my condition," she said bitterly. "Why am I so slow to guess what others have known?"

"Because you did not want to see it." Raissa offered

no other comment, and after a moment Brenna sighed and stood up.

"You are right, Raissa. I did not want to know it. I do not want to know it now. If you don't mind, I need to seek my peace in private."

"Of course. I understand. If you need me . . ." Her words trailed into silence, and Brenna gave her a fleeting smile as she turned away.

Though aware of the troubled expression on Raissa's lovely, usually serene face, Brenna could not manage a soothing word but went alone up the wide stone stairs across the hall. Beaumont would be in the best of care with Rachel at his side, and in truth, none would have hovered over him near as close as her young maid was doing now.

She sought peace and quiet in her chamber, closing the massive door behind her and leaning against its solid oak surface. She stood that way for a while, thinking back to her early days, thinking of her mother.

Instead of recalling the anguish of her loss, her thoughts centered on the happier times, when her mother had laughed with her children and played with them of an eve. A babe had usually dangled on Lady Clarice's knee, fat and smiling, and Brenna closed her eyes as she tried to recapture the content she'd felt then.

Some of her inner turmoil eased as she thought of those days, and she recalled her brother Myles as a babe, then Guy and Wulf, both still William's hostages in Normandy. She bore Guy affection, but the child Wulf had been the one to end her mother's life, and she'd not been able to bear the sight of him for some time after. Now she regretted that selfishness. It had not been his fault; she'd been too young and immature to recognize that.

Pushing away from the door, Brenna crossed to the small writing desk where implements lay. Sitting down on the stool, she sharpened a quill and took up a clean sheet of parchment. She would write them, especially Wulf, and let him know that he still had kin who thought of him.

Brenna stared into the flickering flame of a candle for some time before she lay her quill down without having penned a single word. Wulf was unknown to her; he had spent his entire life without the affection of a sister and, more than likely, had no need of it now.

Forcing her thoughts back to her own situation, Brenna faced the knowledge that she could not make up for those lost years, and she could not make the child that grew in her fade away by doing her duty for another. She buried her face in her hands and shivered.

What would Rye say when she told him? Would he welcome the news of a coming child? Or would he resent the need for abstinence it would surely cause? She wasn't certain. Though he had oft teased her about bearing children, he was not a man who seemed to enjoy them. Nay, he more frequently enjoyed his sensual pleasures of an eve and might take it amiss that his passion would be curbed.

Fretting, Brenna rose from the stool and began to pace the cold floors of the chamber. Light still filtered into the room from the slits, and she could see that the day had lengthened into late afternoon. Soon it would be dusk, and Rye would return from hunting the outlaws.

Should she tell him at once? Or worse—risk the chance someone else might do so? Lady Madelon would surely take vicious pleasure in relating the information in the worst manner possible if she delayed.

Walking to the window, Brenna laid her flushed cheek against the cold stone ledge and stared at the green hills beyond Moorleah. A child. Her child. It lay within her now, proof of Rye's passion.

"Sweet Mary," she whispered, shivering with fright at the thought of giving birth. "How can I stand it?"

It was almost a week before Rye returned, and it was near dusk when the inner bailey echoed with the sounds of the creaking portcullis gate and the muted rattle of chains and jangling of harness. Chained prisoners were yanked to a halt in the bailey, and servants ran to light torches as saddle-sore Norman soldiers dismounted.

Rye swung wearily from his destrier and gave the reins into the keeping of Gowain, who waited for him.

"Good eve, seigneur," the young squire said, and smiled when Rye gave him a questioning look. "I am well, sire."

"So I see." Rye pulled off his helmet and handed it to him. "And your temporary replacement? Is he back in the kitchens?"

"I hope so, seigneur," Gowain muttered, then looked down at the ground when Rye's brows lifted and his mouth curled into an amused smile.

"You do not like him, I take it, Gowain?"

" 'Tis not that, sire, but—" He halted, gave a sheepish grin, then finished, "But 'tis only that I don't want you to get too accustomed to another squire yet."

Clapping a hand on the youth's shoulder, Rye assured him, "You suit me well, Gowain. And I can find another knight for young Myles to serve." Peeling off his heavy gauntlets, he handed them to Gowain. "How is Sir Beaumont?"

"Doing much better, sire. Your lady tended him well."

"My lady?" Rye paused in unbuckling his armor. "Do you mean the Lady Brenna?"

Shifting from one foot to the other, Gowain nodded. "Aye, lord. She is an able surgeon, it seems."

"Is she." Rye shook his head. "And I thought she would be furious that her brother is among those captured—tell me, Gowain—what other miracles have occurred while I was away?"

"None that I know of, my lord."

The boy looked more puzzled than anything else as Rye strode toward the keep with his armor unbuckled and loose. Gowain followed swiftly after giving the great destrier into the keeping of a groom, intent upon his duties. By the time he caught up with Rye in the guardroom, Beltair was confirming the squire's answers.

"Aye, seigneur, the Lady Brenna tended Sir Beaumont most well. Though still sore, there is no fever, and the cut shows no sign of poison."

Rye looked bemused as he allowed Gowain to strip him of his armor and weapons. "Take the sword to my chamber, lad," he said absently when he was attired in a fresh tunic and had washed his face and hands. "I will be up later."

He went first to see Beaumont, who lay upon a fat pallet stuffed with straw and covered with rich furs and soft wool blankets. Rachel sat beside the stricken knight, spooning a light broth into his mouth. When Beaumont noticed Rye, he flushed and caught Rachel's hand.

"No more, sweeting," he murmured.

"You must." Rachel flashed Rye a quick glance but did not move from her position beside Beaumont. "It will give you strength, even your lord will say that."

Amused by Beaumont's embarrassment as much as Rachel's unusual temerity, Rye nodded agreement. "Aye, Raoul, the maid is right. A hearty meat broth will make your blood strong. I will wait until you have eaten all before we talk of outlaws and battles."

Still flushed, Beaumont silently allowed Rachel to finish spooning the dark beef broth into him while Rye leaned against the stone wall and watched. Finally, when the girl had given him the last bit and insisted that he drink all his herbal draught, she gathered up the empty dishes and left, promising to return.

"I have a feeling, Beaumont, that your nurse will run me away with a straw broom if I linger too long and tire you out," Rye jested, then laughed aloud at Beaumont's chagrined expression. "I do not mind. Indeed, I am glad that you have received such excellent care."

"I have that, my lord. What news?"

"The outlaws are either dead, captured, or fled. For the most part, I think we have ended their days." Rye sat down on the stool Rachel had vacated. "I'm afraid that my wife's brothers are among those captured. Two got away, but I have two of them below and know not how to tell her."

"She knows." Beaumont smiled at Rye's surprise.

"She knows of one, anyway. Ridgely, late of Dunstan. He met her in the bailey and berated her for having a Norman husband. I fear that she will question you on certain matters of war when you see her again, so be prepared."

"Matters of war?" Rye's surprise must have shown, for Beaumont grimaced as he nodded.

"Aye, seigneur. The man spoke of the Saxon villages that we burned in the past, and I think Lady Brenna takes it amiss that you have done such . . ."

His words trailed into silence, and Rye nodded. "Who knows what the lady will find at fault? She ever surprises me. I cannot imagine that she thinks I have never slain her countrymen, however, or done my duty. No one is that blind to the fortunes of war."

"P'raps not, my lord. She did look rather distressed, I think, so I just wanted to warn you." Beaumont hesitated as if about to add something, then pressed his lips shut.

Rye sighed with resignation. "There is more, Raoul?"

"Nay, sire, not from me." Beaumont looked down at his blanket-covered feet and refused to meet Rye's steady gaze.

"Not from you," Rye repeated slowly when his knight did not look up at him again. "I see. Well, I suppose I must expect the worst from my fair wife, so I might as well get it over with quickly." He grinned when Raoul looked up at him. "The worst is best over with the soonest, I think. I have been gone for six days and would have this behind me if she is overset because of her brothers. Even Lady Brenna is not foolish enough to think I could let them go free."

"And the other?" Beaumont pressed. "You will tell her how we were forced to burn Saxon villages that harbored the enemy? 'Twas years ago. Surely she will not hold that against you now."

"With Lady Brenna all conjecture is useless. She ever surprises me."

Rye rose, promising to visit Beaumont again soon, then left him behind as he strode toward the curved steps leading to the second floor of the keep. He passed Rachel as she returned to her knight and smiled to himself at the budding romance between them.

In her chamber Brenna waited for Rye. She knew he was back, as Gowain had brought his sword. That had been a good hour before, and she fretted anew. If he had met with Lady Madelon in the hall, that cruel dame would certainly have found a way to tell him of the coming child. Brenna prayed that he would seek her out first.

She lifted a length of soft material that Raissa had given her to sew tiny shirts for her babe, and felt a wave of resentment. She did not want this child. Nay, more than that—she was *afraid* to have this child. The knowledge that she was pregnant did not ease her fears, but increased them until she wanted to scream her terror aloud.

Nay, she'd not forgotten how her mother died, nor had the horror of Hlynn's death faded with time. Both women had soaked a bed with their blood, and one of them little more than a child herself. Shuddering, Brenna began to pace the floor of her room as she tried to forget her mother's pale face, tried to block out the still vivid echoes of her screams as the child tore her in two. . . .

"*Jésu!*" she whispered, putting her icy palms to her hot, flushed cheeks. Was this the reward she received for allowing that fierce Norman in her bed? She should have fought him to the end, until he killed her for her defiance. Surely that would be a kinder, swifter death than the ones she'd seen.

Yet she'd not continued her fight. Nay, she had craved his touch, the sweet, hot magic he could make her feel with his mouth, his hands, his body. It was the devil's doing, just as the priests had said. And now she would suffer the penance for lying in Rye's arms and loving him.

Shivering, Brenna stared into the growing shadows of the chamber, lost in fear and dread anticipation. She did not hear the chamber door open until Rye shut it, startling her.

"Did I frighten you, *chérie?*" he asked, crossing the room toward her. "I thought nothing could frighten you, especially not a Norman."

"Not usually," Brenna managed to answer steadily, though her heart was racing madly and her pulses had leapt at the sight of him. Damn the cur for being so handsome and smiling so winsomely when she was trying to remain calm. It was as if he knew her intentions and sought to stay the words before she could say them.

She rose and faced him with a tilted chin and amber eyes gleaming with determination.

"I have something to say to you, my lord," she began, but he put up a hand to stop her.

"Wait, Brenna, until I have said what I must. Then I will hear you." He stepped close, looking down at her with a fading smile. For a moment it looked as if he meant to take her into his arms, but instead he put his hands behind his back and held her gaze with an intent stare. "I know that you have words for me, *chérie,* but I wish to say what is on my mind. Then, if you are still reluctant, I will hear you."

"Very well," she said, wondering if he already knew. Perhaps Lady Madelon had managed to tell him after all.

For a moment Rye hesitated, then said, "I know what upsets you, but 'tis something you must bear. You were aware when this all began what could come of it, so I will hear no complaints now."

Brenna's eyes widened, and she felt a sudden lurch in the pit of her stomach. He did know. And he sounded so cold, so harsh. Did he not care for her feelings at all?

"Nay," he admonished when she opened her mouth to speak, "do not protest yet. Hear me out. I know you hate this situation, and I am sorry for it, yet I will hear no rebuke nor suffer the sharp side of your tongue for it. 'Tis the way of life, and you must accept it. When one errs, the retribution is ofttimes swift and irreversible. This is what has happened now, and I expect you to keep your own counsel. I will witness no tears nor hear your pleas for mercy. The outcome has already been decided."

Swallowing the thick lump in her throat, Brenna asked when he paused, "May I ask what the outcome will be?"

Rye seemed to consider a moment. "Yea, I suppose 'tis only fair that you know first. Banishment is not too great a price to pay for the brief rewards gained from the play, and 'twas a just end that I suggested to all."

"To *all*." Brenna stared at him blankly. "Do I take this to mean—there are others you have . . . placed . . . in this same position?"

His eyes narrowed for an instant, then he said with a trace of impatience, "I was warned you might bring this up. I will not be chastised for what has gone before, Brenna. 'Twas before I knew you, and there are things that a man does that a woman has no right to demand explanation for. You cannot understand what—"

"Cannot understand!" Brenna's tightly held control vanished like smoke in the wind. Fury raged in her, fury and pain and outrage that he would treat her pregnancy in such a light, as well as the fact that he so casually dismissed other women he'd gotten in the same condition. He took a cautious step backward when she advanced, and Brenna did not realize her hands had clenched into fists until she shook one in his face.

"You abominable, insufferable boor! How dare you come in here and prate about your . . . your *conquests*! And to abuse innocents so easily—aye, I was right when I first named you a common murderer! You are just that! And worse! Why—"

"Brenna," Rye broke in grimly, " 'tis best you watch your unruly tongue before you find yourself locked in this room until you've come to your senses. I've no mind to listen to your foolish prattle about things long past, or things that cannot be changed now."

"Oh, you've no mind to listen, have you? 'Tis a sorry state then, my fine lord, because you'll have a long time before you find peace here. Nay, p'raps never!"

Whirling away from him, Brenna snatched up a cloak from the clothes pole and started for the door. Rye caught her as she swung it wide open, one broad hand slamming it shut with a resounding thud that echoed through the keep. His arm braced the door, and he shoved his other palm against it when she twisted away, pinning her between his hands.

"Wife, you try me sorely," he snarled, and grabbed her arm when she turned with it uplifted as if to strike. "I would not suggest you do anything so foolish, either." He yanked her close, and the scar on his cheek stood out in a livid streak against the taut skin stretched over the bone. "This is none of your affair, and I—"

"None of my affair!" She jerked free. "You prating baboon, whose affair would it be if not mine? Do you deny the blood kinship that will tie the bond? You cannot. Nay, though I once raged against it, and denied it even to my own self, I find that now the deed is done, I can no longer deny that blood bond. That you can so easily dismiss such an important tie is only indicative of your shallow nature, and the fact that I misjudged you completely. I thought—" She paused and took a deep breath. "I thought p'raps there was honor in you after all. I am deeply disappointed to find there is none."

"Are you?" His eyes flashed dangerously. " 'Tis a regret I share, madam, though not for the same cause. I thought you capable of understanding the nature of war, and would know that I would never willingly cause you or yours hurt. Yet neither will I ignore my duty."

"War?"

"Aye, you are not such a fool that you think I would allow my enemies free to harm me again? Nay, I would not do such a foolish thing. Unfortunately, it seems that your Saxon serfs are not of the same mind. Therefore, banishment seems more than a merciful end for outlaws who—"

"Rye—what are you talking about?" Brenna's hands twisted into the folds of his tunic, and she stood up on her toes to repeat softly, "What are you *talking* about?"

Almost shouting now, Rye bellowed, "Your outlaw brothers! What the devil did you think, madam? And I do not intend to—why do you look at me like that?" His furious question only added to Brenna's irritation. He scowled when she snapped an oath at him, and his mouth tightened. "Pray, enlighten me as to the cause for your anger, then, if not for your brothers?"

"I thought you knew. I mean, 'twas certain from what you said that you had heard—" She stumbled to a halt and pressed her hands tightly together. "Do not glare at me thusly, or I shall never be able to say it. St. Jerome, Rye, give a care! You are hurting my arm."

He released her arm. "Say it and be quick, or I may yet shake it out of you," Rye warned between clenched teeth.

Brenna sucked in a deep breath and steeled herself for his reaction. "I was talking about our babe, not my outlaw brothers."

For a long moment Rye didn't say anything. Brenna stood in frozen silence, watching him warily. Nothing showed on his face, no reaction at all. He looked down at her with an opaque gaze that revealed nothing. Even his voice was flat and calm.

"Our babe?" he repeated slowly. "You are with child?"

Brenna faced him unflinchingly; her tone was as bitter as she felt. "Aye, lord, so it seems. I'm certain you have proved your manhood now and will be pleased."

For a long moment he stared at her. "Aye," he said finally, "I *am* pleased at the news. A child is welcome to me."

"Is it?" she mocked. "How wonderful. Now everyone but the one who must suffer and bear the brat is delighted. The entire castle can rejoice at the news."

Rye stiffened. "It is a time of rejoicing, Brenna. Most women give thanks when they find that they are not barren."

"P'raps you haven't noticed, but I am not like most women." Tilting back her head to meet his narrowed gaze, she held back the wild hurt that she wanted to fling at him, the terror she felt at the very thought of bearing a child. He would not understand. Worse, he would not care. If she died in childbirth, he would marry again. A man must have heirs. 'Twas the way of life, and she had been a fool ever to think he might care if she was frightened. He did not. He thought only of a child.

"Aye," he said bitterly, "I have noticed that you are not like most women. To my sorrow." He caught her when she spun around to leave. "Nay, sweeting. I would hear your intentions."

"I don't know what you mean."

"Don't you? What of the child? Do you mean to bear it safely?" His voice grew harsh. "I would hear what you intend."

"Would you? How novel that you wish to hear how I feel for a change." Brenna gave a careless shrug that infuriated him; she could see the anger flare in his eyes and recklessly pushed him further. "Nay, lord, I owe you no answers. If I decide to bear this Norman brat, 'tis my business. After all, *you* have no say over my body now, not in this way."

His grip tightened on her arms. "Brenna, I will not allow you to do harm to yourself because of this. Do not think it for a moment."

"Do you intend to stay with me every hour then, my lord?" she shot back, jerking free of his grasp. "I cannot think how else you would stop me from doing anything I wanted to do!"

Two fine white lines bracketed his mouth, and his face was paler than usual. Brenna felt a spurt of fear at the fierce look he gave her and took a backward step.

"Damn you, Brenna. I will not allow you to harm yourself or my child."

"And how do you think you can stop me?" she flashed. Fear made her reckless, fear and the driving desire to hurt him as he had her. "Do you think to threaten me with a beating, as my father often did? What manner of punishment will you contrive, my lord? Come —let me hear your threats!"

" 'Tis no threats I make, but promises," Rye said coldly. "Since you make no secret of your reluctance to bear my child, I will make no secret of my intent that you shall do so."

"You cannot stop me from doing whatever I wish to do, my arrogant Norman husband. Do not think it."

His hands flashed out again to grip her by the shoulders, and he promised softly, "Yea, wife. I not only can —I will."

"And that is all you think about?" Her throat ached. Did he not think of her and how she felt? Her pain? Her fear? Did he not care if she died giving birth to his heir, or did he care only for a child he'd never seen?

He made an impatient motion with his hand. "I don't know what you mean."

"Aye, 'tis plain enough." Brenna stiffened, summoning rage to replace the pain his indifference caused.

Rye's eyes narrowed slightly, and he stood looking at her with a trace of wariness. "You speak in riddles, madam. I shall be plainer. You will not leave Moorleah without a companion of my choosing. I will not chance the safety of my unborn child with a woman who has stated her distaste for motherhood."

Brenna shrugged. "As you will, my lord." She turned away before he could see the naked, raw pain in her eyes and wished that God had been kinder in the manner children were brought into the world.

CHAPTER 14

"WHO IS MY JAILER today, Raissa?" Brenna mocked. "You?"

Raissa stirred uneasily. "Do not be too hard on my brother, my lady. He worries about you."

"So I see. He worries so much I cannot visit the garderobe without someone tagging along. It's become embarrassing, and I assure you that poor Gowain was near apoplexy at the mere notion of being so near my lady's privacy."

Brenna's voice was harsh, and her eyes flashed angrily as she faced Raissa. Rye's sister shrugged helplessly.

"If you would but tell Rye you mean the child no harm, p'raps he would—"

"And how do you know I mean the child no harm?" Brenna gave an angry laugh. "Mayhap I do. Am I not the evil witch he thinks me? Could it be that Rye de Lyon is wrong? Nay, do not suggest it to him. Your head will roll for it."

"You wrong him. He is not as harsh as he seems. If he appears to be cold at times, 'tis because he has never known tenderness."

"And he is the only one who has suffered? I suppose he thinks his suffering is all that matters."

"That's not true."

Raissa's quiet voice penetrated some of Brenna's anger. Brenna turned to look at the young woman.

"My lady, do but think about what little I have told you. Rye never knew a mother's tender love. At least you had ten years to hold dear. He had nothing but a father's careless hand, and a foster mother's hatred. My father had his good qualities, but he never really understood what he'd done to his son by loving him more than his legal heir. My mother made Rye suffer in any way possible for it, yet he has never turned her out when he could do so."

Brenna turned to look out the slit window for a moment. "I know you think me hard, Raissa, and I'm sorry for it. But I cannot undo what was done to him. I cannot undo what was done to me."

"I know that. So does Rye. Has he asked for your tenderness? I don't think so. He asks only that you care for his heir as he wishes he'd been cared for. His mother cast him away. He does not want you to do that to his child."

Near tears, Brenna couldn't reply. She wished she could find it in her to hate Rye, but she couldn't. Nor could she hate the child growing in her, the innocent life that terrified her as much as it intrigued her.

When Raissa sighed and moved to the door, Brenna turned. "I will not hurt the child," she said softly. "But neither will I make promises I may not keep. He will have to content himself with that."

She turned back around to gaze out the window and heard the door close softly. Lost in thought, she did not hear it reopen until Rachel's worried voice came from just behind her.

"Milady?"

Startled, Brenna turned. "I'm sorry. I did not hear you enter, Rachel."

"So I guessed." Rachel spoke softly. "It's been a week since you and the seigneur argued, milady. Don't you think it's time to end this play? He will not give the word to release you from being guarded unless you seek him out to make amends."

"Make amends?" Brenna's brow lifted. "There can be no amends in this, Rachel. He has set a guard upon me at every hour, and I find that hard to forgive. There is nothing to be said between us."

"But, milady, he has been so worried—"

"Faith! Must I listen to even you plead his cause?" Brenna glared at her. "Have you taken his side in this, too?"

"Nay, don't think it, milady! 'Tis just that I hate seeing you so miserable, when you could be free if you would only say the word he wishes to hear."

"Give my oath not to disobey him, you mean," Brenna mocked. "Aye, he would enjoy that, I vow. Well, I will not do it."

"You would stay inside until the babe is born?"

"If he decrees it. 'Twas his decision, not mine."

Rachel threw up her hands in despair. "I will not mention it again."

"Thank you."

"But it's only fair to tell you that your husband paces the floor and snarls at any who dare approach him. I think he would like to release you but does not know how without being made to look weak."

"Do you? Interesting. Unlikely, but interesting." Brenna's hands clenched in her lap. Rye's order that she be confined had hurt more than her pride, but she was loathe to admit it to anyone, even gentle Rachel.

"I don't think it unlikely. I think it's true, milady."

Brenna looked up at Rachel's troubled expression. "I know you do," she said gently. "You're a good friend, and I am glad you're here with me, though I think it unfair. You should take the freedom I offered you."

"I could not enjoy it, knowing you were watched like a bird in a cage, milady." Rachel smiled when Brenna reached out to touch her lightly on the cheek. "Besides, who would serve you as well as I?"

"No one, that is true. Can you see old Gwyneth climbing these stairs three times a day?" Brenna managed a laugh at the jest, for Gwyneth weighed more than most men and was as cranky as an old boar. In the past months she had come to depend on Rachel much more than she'd ever considered she would, and now that Rye had locked her away, that dependence had grown deeper. The bond of affection forged between the two women had grown strong as well.

"Lady Raissa and Lord Lyon quarreled most bitterly about your being watched," Rachel commented after a few moments had passed.

"I'm certain Lady Madelon enjoyed that," Brenna remarked dryly.

"Aye, she did. Lady Raissa chastised her for being so glad about your situation. Then they quarreled, too, and even young Gilles was heard to complain that his uncle had grown cruel of late."

Brenna shook her head. "It sounds as if my husband has his hands full even without my being there. I wonder if he wishes I were free?"

"If I hear one more remark about my wife," Rye warned Beaumont, "I will set the guilty man to cleaning out the garderobes and make certain his next joust is waged with a gomph stick." He stared across the bailey, watching as rain pounded the dirt into mud. It was the inactivity the rains had forced upon him that made his temper so taut, he told himself, and he leaned against the stable wall.

Raoul simply looked at Rye without commenting. His steady gaze finally penetrated to his lord, and Rye turned to stare back at him with narrowed eyes.

"I take it that you disapprove as well, Beaumont."

"Have I not indicated so, my lord?"

"Nay, not in words, but your every action screams of your disapproval." Rye kicked viciously at a pile of hay and watched as it lifted on the wind. "So what is your suggestion? I'm certain you have one. Every man in the keep seems to have one, though none dare say it to my face."

"Leave her be."

"Leave her be." Rye glared at him. "Aye, and allow her to harm herself or my child? Nay, Raoul, that is not a good suggestion at all."

"She would not harm the child. I do not believe it. No woman would harm her own child."

Rye fixed him with a brooding stare. "You think not? Do you recall those barbarian women who threw their children off high walls rather than risk invaders' mercies? I do. I can still hear those screams . . . nay, Raoul, though I do not think Lady Brenna as afraid as that, I do not trust her not to attempt some foolish act that will do them both harm. She has told me she fears what lies ahead, and I do not know how to ease those fears. I've done all I know to do."

"She feared the wedding night as well," Raoul pointed out, "yet nothing came of it."

A faint smile curved Rye's mouth, easing the sulky line into grim amusement. "Nothing but a fierce battle. She lost it, aye, but I dare not risk her waging war against me like that again."

"I think you underestimate your lady." Raoul finished cleaning the leather harness he held and laid it aside, wincing slightly as he rose from the bench where he sat. It was obvious the wound still pained him, but he was able to complete light tasks with no problem.

Rye watched him for a moment. "I will think on it," he said finally. "P'raps you are right."

Surprised, Beaumont only nodded speechlessly, and when Rye strode out into the rain and crossed to the keep, he smiled.

Rye cursed the rain, his wife, and himself. He took the steps to the keep two at a time and was thoroughly soaked by the time he reached the heavy door. When he stepped into the smoky, dim-lighted guardroom, he found Myles waiting.

"I would have a word with you, my lord," the youth said as Rye shrugged out of his mantle.

"Speak. I have a notion you will whether I give you permission or not."

"Aye, 'tis true." Myles drew in a deep breath and

took the drenched mantle Rye handed him. "I do not think Brenna should remain confined."

"No? You are not alone in that theory. I've yet to be shown a good reason for her release, however." Annoyed by the opinions and interference of most of the keep, Rye's voice was cold and harsh. Dammit, must he be set upon by each and every inhabitant? The next thing he knew, even his destrier would voice disapproval. Worst of all was the nagging voice inside him that whispered they were right.

"Brenna may be a bit fiery-tempered," Myles was saying, "but she is not vicious. She would never harm herself or an innocent life."

"You did not hear her threats, Master Myles. I did."

The cold finality of Rye's tone penetrated to the youth at last, and his temper flared. "Devil take you, seigneur, have you never said things in anger? Have you never been angry enough to say things you don't mean?"

"Yea, I've been that angry," Rye growled softly, "but I am rarely foolish enough to promise things I've no intent of doing."

"You might take into consideration that my sister is more volatile of temper and frequently makes threats she does not mean."

Fixing the youth with a cold stare, Rye said, "Do you want me to take the chance that she means it? If I do, and she meant her hasty words, think on the consequences."

"I do not think she would do herself or the child any harm, my lord. No matter her words."

Looking past him, Rye said bitterly, "I wonder if I dare risk it. When it would be too late, would I regret my leniency, do you think?"

For a moment Myles gave no answer; then he said softly, "I see your dilemma, seigneur. And I cannot say what is best."

"Aye, and neither can I."

Rye strode from the guardroom and crossed the hall, bound for the stairs that led to the small east tower. When Lady Madelon barred his way, he was tempted to push her aside and continue, but years of habit bade him pause to hear her out with the courtesy drilled into him as a child.

"Yea, my lady? What do you wish of me?"

"Lord Lyon," she said briskly, "a word with you, if you please."

"Aye, and why not?" Rye muttered, allowing her to draw him to a covered alcove where none could overhear. He was impatient at the delay and shifted from one foot to the other as Lady Madelon turned to face him.

" 'Tis about your wife. . . ."

"Nay, madam, I've heard enough from others about my wife, if you please," he interrupted. "I'm weary of more discussion about her release."

"Release!" Lady Madelon laughed shortly. "Nay, Rye, 'tis not her release I seek. You are wise to keep her under guard. I simply wish to commend you. She has been a fomenter of trouble since you brought her here, setting the servants against one another, yea—even against us. Have you not noticed how they are different since she came?"

Rye frowned. "I was not here much before she came, so I cannot say, madam."

"Nay, p'raps not here at Moorleah, but in Normandy you were accustomed to the obedience of servants. Here the lowliest squire is wont to argue a command." Madelon gave a light shrug. "Would your former servants have dared to voice disagreement with you? Nay, but these do."

" 'Tis not completely unexpected that they would not be happy with their lady's situation," Rye pointed out. "This was her mother's keep at one time, and they are all Saxons."

"Her mother wasn't."

Rye couldn't argue that. Brenna had made no secret of the fact that she resented her mother's keep being given as a bride-gift by William. Would she go so far as to sow seeds of rebellion in the servants?

Lady Madelon was quick to press the advantage she must have seen in Rye's scowling expression.

"I've heard whispers, my lord. 'Tis said that there are those who would follow your lady rather than you should she raise her hand against you."

"And you do not think my men-at-arms capable of defending themselves against simple serfs armed with a few pitchforks?" Rye asked coldly. "Not even my Saxon wife would be so foolish."

"Nay, not foolish enough to set servant against soldier perhaps, but would she be clever enough to call in some of the rebel barons and have the servants open the gates to them? Think of that."

"Have you heard of such?" Rye stared at her in the dim light of a wall torch. He knew well his stepmother's habit of malicious manipulation, but what she suggested now was treason. Would she be wicked enough to invent such a tale without reason? "If you have, my lady," he said slowly, "I would know your sources."

"Father Gutierrez."

Rye gave a start. "Moorleah's priest?"

"Aye. He hears much in the confessional but is not at liberty to reveal his sources, of course. However, he has grown concerned enough to confide that trouble may brew if you do not exercise caution."

Rye clenched his fist, feeling suddenly as if he had been struck in the pit of his stomach. It was possible that Brenna may try such a thing, but he had not really thought she would go that far. Not even as vengeance against the Normans. Not even as vengeance against him. . . .

"I will take precautions," he said at last, and lifted a brow when Lady Madelon made a sharp exclamation.

"If you do not take action at once, all may be lost!" she added when she perceived Rye's attention. "Has she got you so fooled already? She has had much time to set her plan in action, and you should not delay a moment. . . ."

"Do you think even the Lady Brenna a magician, that she could foment rebellion under the eye of my guards, Lady Madelon?"

Bowing her head, Lady Madelon murmured, "As you

will, my lord. But be careful she does not lead you by the nose."

Wheeling, Rye stalked from the alcove and to the tower stairs, his steps brisk and angry. He did not see the faint smile hovering maliciously on his stepmother's lips, but it would have made little difference if he had. His own doubts raged anew.

When he slammed open the door to Brenna's chamber, Rye saw her head jerk up in a startled reflex, then her gold eyes widen. For an instant a smile hovered on her lips, but as she gazed at him, that smile faded and was replaced by a watchful expression.

"Greetings, Lord Rye." She set aside her needlework and stood in a slow, graceful motion. "You seem overset."

His frown deepened. This calm was unexpected. Where was the raging virago he'd come to expect?

"Aye," he said shortly, "I find that your supporters lurk around every corner and behind every door. 'Tis enough to make the most peaceful man short-tempered."

"Oh? Then, as you are far from a peaceful man, you must be fit to burst by now." Brenna's smile flirted with the corners of her mouth, and his gaze lingered on her lips for a long moment. When he heard a polite cough, he looked up to see Rachel standing nervously by the far wall; he jerked his head to dismiss her.

"What game do you play, wench?" he growled when Rachel slipped silently from the chamber. With an effort he kept his thoughts from returning to memories of Brenna's mouth on his, of her soft, satiny skin beneath his hands. "Do you seek to sow dissension in my household?"

"How would I succeed in such when I am watched so closely, my lord? Do you ascribe magical qualities to me, mayhap?"

Her words so closely echoed his own, that Rye felt suddenly foolish. He'd allowed Lady Madelon to raise doubts where there should be none, though he reserved any final judgment until Brenna's loyalty could be proved. And it was certain that Brenna did not look guilty of more than boredom.

Smiling, he said, "Nay, no magic, little one." His eyes fastened on her hungrily when she moved toward the window, away from him, yet he felt her presence as powerfully as if she were nestled under his arm. Rye put his hands behind his back to keep from going to her and taking her in his arms, when to do so might brand him weak. So he contented himself with merely gazing at her from across the small chamber.

"Why are you here?" Brenna murmured after several silent moments had passed. She waved a hand to indicate the four solid walls and mounds of needlework. "As you can see, I have little to occupy my time—plotting of rebellion aside, of course."

"I came to release you from your guard, if you would but offer a simple oath," Rye said when she had turned to face him. He saw her eyes widen, the long, thick lashes shading the golden depths beneath.

"Release me, my lord? Against all advice, I am certain. Why do you offer my release? Do you think I have mended my murderous ways?"

"I never thought you contemplated murder. I only wanted to keep you from doing something foolish that might result in your own harm, or that of our child."

"Our child. *Our* child. 'Tis comforting to know that you include me. For a time now I have considered that I was only a mistaken vessel for *your* child. 'Tis all I heard of, it seems."

Flushing slightly, Rye met her clear gaze. "You must admit that you threatened—"

"I threatened to do whatever I wished," she cut in. "You supplied the rest of the threat yourself."

"You've frequently said you have no wish to bear my child."

"Aye," she agreed thoughtfully, and moved to stand behind a chair. Her fingers curled into the grained wood of the back, toying absently with the intricate scrollwork. "I did say that many times. And I meant it when I said it. I'm finding it difficult to recall exactly when I said I would murder your babe, however."

Rye made an impatient gesture. "I never said you would go so far as to murder the child. But as you do not want the babe, I meant to safeguard your life and that of my heir. 'Tis a normal reaction, I think."

Brenna looked up at him, and he kept his expression set into stern lines. "Not *want* it?" she repeated slowly, her eyes widening to huge amber pools that soaked up the light from window and lamp. Long lashes lowered to shutter her eyes for a moment, then she blinked. " 'Tis difficult to tell you how I feel, my lord, when I have not sorted out the tangle myself."

"Not so difficult, I would think, when faced with the alternative I offer you," he said shortly. He tried to see beneath the mysterious shadows in her eyes to her thoughts.

"Alternative?"

"Aye," he said roughly, wondering at the pain he felt like a raw wound in his chest. Was it so hard for her to bear his child? Did she hate him that much? He'd not been able to conceive of such dislike, even in this fiery Saxon wench who defied him at every turn.

"I do not want my child ignored like an unwanted mongrel," Rye said after a long, tense silence, "and if you think to cast him aside, I would know it now."

Brenna didn't answer. Her face paled, and her eyes looked like burning amber pools. Rye waited, and when she didn't reply, he gave her a slight shake.

"Well?" he demanded. "Do you think to mother the babe or shun it?"

Jerking away, Brenna's mouth curled with rage. "I will care for any child I birth, my lord, never fear. What must you think of me, that you would ask?"

Rye raked a hand through his hair. " 'Tis a custom among noblewomen to hand the child to another to give suck, and ofttimes that child is left to its own devices. I merely mean to learn your intentions."

"Norman noblewomen must be rare mothers, indeed, that you think I would be so cold!"

Rye's mouth twisted in a sardonic smile. "I've had some experience with Norman mothers, *chérie*, but have yet to see how Saxon women treat their young. You must forgive me for relying on what I have seen rather than guessed."

"And you think me like Lady Madelon?" Brenna demanded angrily.

"Nay, but p'raps you might be as careless with your child as my birth mother was with hers," Rye snarled in a bitter tone, unable to stop himself. He saw Brenna's surprise and held tightly to his self-control. Curse it, he had not meant to give so much of himself away, the pain and rage he'd felt at being abandoned by a careless mother.

"I assumed your mother died," Brenna said after a moment.

"She did—when I was fourteen. Old enough, I assure you, to feel the pangs of abandonment. If not for my father . . . but none of this is what is important now. I ask you—what are your intentions?"

"My lord," she said softly, "I will not see my babe go to another. I will nurture any issue of my body, whether I want the babe or not."

"Are you certain?" Rye released her arms, and looked down at her for the space of several heartbeats. "And if you find that you do not care for motherhood?"

"Regardless, I will keep my child with me. Do you still dwell on words spoken in haste, anger, or fear? Do not." She smiled slightly. "I am ever speaking too hastily, I think."

Rye's expression softened. "I did not come up here to dispute what has been said or not said. I came to release you, if you would but promise that you will not try to do anything foolish enough to cause harm."

Winding a silken curl around her finger, Brenna gave it her full attention until Rye made an impatient sound. She looked up at him coolly.

"And if I don't promise?"

"Then I suppose I would leave you to your own company—and that of your guard."

"I see." Brenna shrugged. "Very well, my lord. I agree."

He eyed her suspiciously. "You agree to what?"

"To promise that I will not attempt harm to myself or the child. Does that not satisfy you?"

"Aye, it would if I believed it."

An amused smile curved her generous mouth. "You insist upon hearing it, then do not believe it. You are a puzzle, Rye de Lyon."

"Swear that you mean your words, madam, and I will accept your oath."

She met his gaze steadily. "I swear on my mother's grave that I will not attempt to harm myself or my child."

Rye felt slightly ashamed but nodded grimly. " 'Tis done. You are free to go where you wish without escort." He cleared his throat, then said, "William comes tomorrow. I would have you in the hall to greet him."

Brenna stiffened, and the look she flashed him was furious. "William? Here, at Moorleah? What an honor for you, my lord."

"Not as much an honor," Rye said ruefully, "as expense. He brings a great many people with him. Fortunately, most will be quartered in the village. We are expected to entertain only his immediate household."

"Which is why you are so anxious to release me from my self-imposed exile, I presume."

"Not at all. Beaumont is an able steward, I've discovered, and has made most of the arrangements."

"I will attend you, my lord, but do not expect miracles. I'm not overly fond of your king."

"So I understand." A faint smile pressed at the corners of his mouth. "Tomorrow should prove a most interesting day."

" 'Tis good to see you looking so well, Lady Brenna," Raissa said with a fond smile.

Brenna nodded and managed a smile in return. She was nervous. Meeting the king after all these years—the man who had ruled her life for so long—had her poised between outright defiance and stark terror. She wished she had the courage to throw his meddling into his teeth, but on the other hand, knew that it would only complicate her life even more. There was nothing she could do about his interference. He was, after all, the king.

"Is the king here yet?" she asked softly. Raissa shook her head.

"Nay, but Rye has gone out to meet him. He will be here anon, and we must be ready." She took Brenna's hand and flashed her a look of surprise. "You are so cold. Are you afraid?"

Brenna surprised herself with her truthfulness. "Aye. William frightens me with his power to do me more ill."

"More ill?"

With an impatient shake of her head, Brenna said, "It does not matter now. My own chamber has been prepared for the king's comfort this eve, with fresh linens on the bed. He will sleep in my own bed. 'Tis a strange feeling—" She halted abruptly as Raissa watched her and asked calmly, "Has all else been done?"

"Yea, and well. Young Beaumont has outdone himself in his efforts to please William. He probably wishes to press his suit with the king and thus seeks his favor."

"Press his suit with Rachel, I presume," Brenna began, but before she could continue, there was the clamor of raised voices and the unmistakable sound of armed men in the guardroom.

"They arrive," Raissa said with a gasp, and moved to the dais where Lady Madelon already waited in regal splendor.

Brenna's gaze shifted to that noble dame, and something inside her rebelled. She would not sit and wait for William like some fawning lackey. Nay, not Brenna of Marwald, whose life had been manipulated by that stern Norman with no thought of her feelings whatsoever.

Brenna turned and fled to an alcove nearby and slipped behind the heavy curtains. Her heart was pounding fiercely, and she felt a spurt of foolishness that she would hide like a child to watch as William arrived. The group of men were richly garbed, and the light from fire and torches glinted from gold-encrusted cloaks and tunics as they began to fill the hall. Brenna saw Rye at once, laughing as he listened to the banter around him.

Her breath caught. He looked so resplendent in his scarlet tunic and long cloak. Knee-high boots of fine leather covered his calves, and he wore a sword at his left side that had a jeweled hilt. For some reason, seeing him garbed so richly made her uncertain of him. It was as if he belonged in this elegant crowd, and she did not. He laughed and moved easily, and jested with the king.

It was easy to tell which one of the men was William. The tallest of all of them, his broad shoulders and stately aura was easily recognizable. Brenna pressed against the cold stone around her and stared at him, filled with resentment and awe. He *looked* like a king. Sharp-featured, with an aquiline nose and short-cropped hair, William moved with easy grace to the raised dais.

Lady Madelon and Raissa dipped in a deep curtsy, not rising until the king bade them do so, their obeisance graceful and lovely. Brenna knew she could not have managed it and was glad she had hidden at the last moment. To curtsy to the king would be hard enough, but to pretend a respect she did not feel would have been impossible. She would have revealed her anger and hate for him, and Rye would have been furious. Yea, 'twas much better that she remained hidden.

Brenna waited for the right moment to leave her hiding place and flee, but it never seemed to come. Too many people milled about in the hall, making a stealthy exit impossible.

"My lady?" a deep voice said softly. Brenna swallowed a gasp of dismay as she turned.

"Oh, 'tis you, Ballard." She felt a wave of relief. "I am so glad. I thought 'twas someone else."

"And who would be looking for you behind heavy curtains when the king is present?" Ballard teased, but there was a puzzled light in his eyes as he observed her.

Brenna flushed. "I do not want to see him."

"The king?" Ballard guessed. "Aye, I can understand your not wanting to meet him. 'Twould be hard for you."

She pleated the folds of velvet gunna between her fingers as her glance shifted to where William sat in the high-backed chair Rye usually used. She didn't see her husband and wondered if he had left the hall. If he had, she didn't know where to go.

"Ballard, where is Lord Lyon?"

The minstrel shrugged. "I do not know, my lady. P'raps he has gone on some errand for the king."

"And left him alone?"

Ballard laughed. "He is hardly alone, fair lady. There are enough eager nobles surrounding him to fill the royal palace. I daresay our William does not miss his host."

"Nay, but I do. I do not want to chance an encounter with Rye until . . . until later."

Ballard's shrewd eyes regarded her for a moment, and he seemed to consider. "Would you like to leave the hall unnoticed?"

She nodded. "Yea, I would like that above all things right now. I don't feel ready to meet William. I'm afraid I could not guard my hasty tongue, and my husband would not be pleased."

"And that disturbs you." Ballard reached up to graze her cheek with his finger, startling Brenna. "My lovely lady, I do not know of any man who could be cruel to you."

"P'raps you do not recall my father that well," Brenna said tartly, and moved away. Ballard's hand fell to his side, and his mouth twisted in a wry smile.

"Aye, 'tis an unpleasant memory. There were many times I had to leave the hall to keep from offering a challenge on your behalf."

Brenna frowned. "What do you mean?"

"It pained me greatly to see your father use you so roughly, my lady. The only reason I remained so long at Marwald was to do what little I could to distract him from his abuse."

"You did that for me?" Brenna's eyes widened. "I never knew."

"Nay, 'tis not something a common minstrel would confess to the lady he loves from afar."

Brenna shifted uneasily. "Such conversation between us is unseemly."

"I understand." Ballard took a step away from her, and his smile was sad. " 'Tis enough for me to do what little I can to give you aid, my lady. May I escort you to the chapel, p'raps? It would be quiet and peaceful there, and you could remain as long as you wished."

"Of course. The chapel—why did I not think of it?" Brenna murmured. She darted Ballard a curious glance. He'd never revealed by word or glance that he cared for her in any but the most platonic way, and to discover that he carried a secret affection for her was disturbing. She knew that some great ladies enjoyed a light dalliance with minstrels and knights, but she'd always viewed them with scorn. Now, to have a handsome minstrel declare his love for her was faintly flattering. Not that she would act upon it.

"Here," Ballard was saying as he slipped out of his long cloak and held it out. "Wear this to disguise yourself. It has a hood. No one should notice you in the confusion."

Brenna allowed him to drape it around her, glad he stood between her and the hall. Ballard's large frame blocked her view of the crowd and kept them from recognizing her. The heavy wool covered her from head to foot, and she clutched it tightly as she allowed Ballard to escort her from the curtained alcove. No one even glanced at them as they made their way through the crowd.

"This way, my lady," Ballard said softly, and put an arm around her waist to steer her toward another alcove. He reached around her to open the door, and it creaked loudly as he swung it back.

Brenna felt a blast of damp air sweep over her, smelling of rain. Ballard was close behind her, so close she heard his quick exclamation brush past her ear. She turned, startled.

Then her breath left her in a rush as she saw Lyon spin Ballard around, his face contorted with rage.

"What is this?" he snarled at the minstrel. "Do I find you sneaking out with my wife, by God?"

"Nay, my lord," Ballard said quickly, making no move to the sword at his side. It was obvious to even the most unobservant that Rye held tightly to his temper, and any sudden move might be wrong. "Not sneaking. I was merely escorting your lady wife to the chapel."

"To the chapel?" Rye's incredulous gaze snapped to Brenna, where she stood immobilized in the open doorway, the wool cloak flapping loudly around her ankles. "Do you feel you must go to pray in disguise, madam? Do you think God would not know you?"

"Don't be a fool, Rye," Brenna said sharply, seeing that unless she did something to distract him, Rye was likely to set upon poor Ballard. Characteristically she chose inflammatory words to distract him from his real purpose. "I simply decided that I did not desire to meet your king, 'tis all. An hour spent in the chapel praying for his soul should suffice."

"God's eyes, Brenna, but you're treading where you should not," Rye grated softly. His gaze flicked to Ballard, who still stood with a wooden expression, his stance poised as if for flight. "Go, minstrel. And do not come near my wife again, or I shall see you hanged for it."

As Ballard bowed and backed away, Brenna glared at Rye. "Do you wish to frighten away every friend I have, my lord? Is that your intention? I wonder if you realize how very foolish you sound when you make those threats."

Rye reached out to draw her to him, his hand hard on her wrist. He pulled the outer door shut, then tugged back the hood to Ballard's cloak until Brenna's hair shone in the torchlight. The coronet of flowers she wore slipped slightly, and she adjusted it, faintly regretful that the lovely blossoms had been crushed by the weight of the hood.

"I do not make threats," he said finally, and she heard the barely repressed rage in his voice as he struggled to remain calm. "I make promises, betimes, but I do not make threats. That is for beardless boys and foolish women to do."

"Counting me among the latter, I suppose?" Brenna swallowed her next comment at the quick, hard look he gave her.

"Come, wife," Rye said evenly. "The king wishes to meet you."

"I do not wish to meet him."

"That is not a choice you were given. You will meet William, and you will behave as you should, or before God I will see that you are sorry you did not."

Brenna's chin lifted, and she made no answer as Rye pulled her with him back into the hall. To the most casual observer it would seem, perhaps, that he was merely escorting his wife to meet the king. Only those who knew them well would realize that Rye was furious with Brenna.

Brenna intercepted a worried glance from Rachel and was aware of Beaumont's concerned approach.

"My lord," he said softly when he reached Rye, "the king has asked for you."

"And so he will have me." Rye smiled grimly. "I merely went to fetch my wife, who has grown suddenly shy. 'Tis a puzzle, is it not, Beaumont?"

"Loose my arm," Brenna said in a low voice to Rye. "I am able to walk."

"You are able to do anything, sweeting." Rye's brow lifted in a sardonic gesture as he released her. " 'Tis what worries me."

They had arrived at the front of the dais where William sat. Caught up in their private battle, they did not realize how quiet the hall had grown, or that William was looking at them with a thoughtful smile, gesturing for the man behind him to quiet.

"Well?" Brenna prompted her scowling husband.

"Do you intend to present me, or must I present myself to your precious overlord?"

"Brenna—"

His voice was a low warning that she ignored. The hours of uncertainty, fear, and resentment made her incautious, and Rye's apparent belief that she would be so foolish or licentious as to sneak off with a minstrel had fanned the flames of her wrath. Her voice was a low whisper.

"Go ahead, Lord Lyon, preen before the man you revere as if he were God. Present me to him and behave as if you were a fearless knight. Only I will know the truth."

Moving with jerky motions that did not disguise his rage, Rye presented Brenna to the king and stood stiffly to the side as she managed a deep curtsy. His face reflected his fury when she said nothing to William's greeting, but kept her eyes downcast. Custom decreed that she remain in her curtsy until the king bade her rise.

"By God, madam," Rye ground out in a savage mutter, "you'd best be civil."

Brenna's head snapped up. "Civil? Or do you mean servile? Speak plainly, my lord."

Laughter gleamed in William's eyes, and only an iron control kept it from erupting as he viewed the domestic squabble between his favored knight and his new wife. He gave the signal for Brenna to rise. She did so and moved to the side with the other guests.

"Before God," he murmured to a dismayed Raissa, "I would not have thought any woman reckless enough to taunt the Black Lion."

"Lady Brenna has more courage than most," Raissa answered helplessly. Her knuckles whitened as she gripped her wine goblet, and Lady Madelon was almost choking with embarrassed rage.

"Aye," William replied with a low laugh, "I'd say she does. Or lack of fear, at any rate."

"Lack of common sense 'tis more the truth of it!" Lady Madelon snapped furiously. "The Saxon bitch may find her back striped for her if she continues with this folly."

William regarded Madelon with a lifted brow. "Somehow, my lady, I doubt that."

Lady Madelon ignored the warning pressure of her daughter's hand on her arm. Her venom was obvious to all those within earshot as she said, "I tell you that haughty slut will be fortunate if she is able to walk when he is through with her."

"Do you think so?" William's voice was cold. "I do not think he will harm one hair on her head. And I usually know my man."

Lady Madelon, sensing the king's displeasure, forbore further comment. Raissa tried to breach the void with desperate conversation, but she fell silent as the king rose to his feet.

"Lady Lyon," William called, beckoning Brenna forward. "Please do me the honor of sitting at my side." His amused gaze shifted to Rye, who stepped forward with a bow. "I was beginning to think you had hidden such loveliness away from me, Lyon. I am certain you do not mind if I become acquainted with your wife."

"Nay, sire," Rye replied.

William indicated to Lady Madelon, seated on his right, that she was to give up her seat. She did so immediately, flushing an ugly crimson.

Brenna's heart thumping erratically, she allowed William to seat her next to him. She could feel Rye's furious gaze on her, willing her to behave herself. It would serve him right if she made the king so mad he deseisened Rye of every possession he had, she told herself, even as she knew she would never do such a thing. Still, it was a pleasing fantasy to envision his torment at such an event.

"My husband is, as usual, most considerate," Brenna said sweetly. "I'm afraid that I became suddenly shy at meeting you, sire, so do not blame him for my tardy arrival."

The glib lie fell readily from her tongue, and she saw that William was not fooled by it; his dark eyes gleamed with laughter at the discomfort of his earl, and there was a hint of appreciation at Brenna's daring.

"Lovely lady, I will acquit him of wrongdoing at your request. He should be grateful for such a loyal wife."

"I'm certain he is, sire." Brenna dared not glance at Rye, who was now seated on the other side of the king, to gauge his reaction to her impudence. He would make her suffer for it later, she was certain. His eyes had darkened to a blue that was almost black, and the tight look he gave her held a promise of retribution in it. Brenna almost looked forward to it. She had a few things to say to her noble husband that should singe his ears.

William of Normandy, Brenna discovered, was adept at drawing out reluctant conversation. He spoke easily of his family, of his wife Matilda and his growing brood of children. All in England knew William's reputation as a faithful husband; indeed, no man dared force a free woman to have sex against her will, under threat of castration. Though William was known to be a stern and violent king, Brenna found that he could converse lightly when he chose.

She thawed slightly toward him, at least enough so that she could make decent replies to his questions. It wasn't until he asked casually, "How fares your family?" that her old resentments surfaced again.

"Not as well as in the past," she said tartly, and saw his brows lift. She immediately regretted her quick tongue and hoped he would not pursue the matter. Unfortunately, he did.

"Lord Dunstan is ill?"

"Nay, sire. I spoke too quickly. 'Tis just that I know nothing of my brothers, so did not know how to answer."

"Do you still hate all things Norman, my lady?" William was asking in an idle tone that did not disguise his interest.

It took Brenna a moment to form a reply. "At times, sire," she said honestly. "I cannot help but recall how I was taken from my home to a land of strangers, nor can

I forget the things that happened when the Normans came to Marwald."

"War begets brutality. One cannot condemn an entire nation for the actions of a few."

"A child knows only what she sees. I have never forgotten the events of that day."

"Does not your husband prove that all Normans are not to be blamed for the cruelty of a few?"

Brenna smiled ruefully. It was true that Rye had never been deliberately cruel; nay, he had never laid a truly harsh hand on her, and she could not say the same for her own father.

"You are wiser than I ever credited you being, sire," she answered.

"From you, Lady Brenna, I accept that as high praise. Would that I heard such sweet words from my Maud. She ever bedevils me with her temper."

"A wife, I have heard it said," Brenna ventured with a sense of mischief, "is only a reflection of her husband. If this is true, mayhap it is your own nature you see in the queen."

William laughed aloud. The sound drew Rye's attention, and he looked up to see Brenna laughing with the king. Damn her, he reflected moodily. She ever surprised him. Any other woman could be cowed with sharp words or threats, but not that flame-haired witch who bedeviled him at every turn. And here she was bewitching the king himself.

By the time the meal had ended and the entertainment grown stale, Rye's temper had cooled, and he'd realized that he had indeed behaved foolishly about the minstrel. Married to a lovely termagant he might be, but he had no reason to believe that he had been cuckolded.

Rye returned from accompanying William to the master chamber to find Brenna in the dimly lit corridor.

"Well, madam? Why do you wait here?"

"I don't know where to go," she said simply. "Beaumont planned so well that he forgot to tell me where we are to sleep. Perhaps I am to go to the ladies' quarters with the others."

"Nay." Rye's hand cupped her elbow and turned her. "Come with me."

She offered no protest but tried to keep up with Rye's long strides as he left the corridor and moved to the far stairwell.

He pulled her with him up the wide stairs and shoved open the door to a tiny chamber. It was empty save for a straw pallet like those the servants used.

"This is where we are to sleep?" Brenna asked, dismayed.

" 'Tis better than the stable." Rye's short reply sounded overloud in the small room; his voice echoed from the stone walls.

"Not by much," Brenna muttered, and began dragging off the coronet of wilted flowers she wore.

Rye watched her impassively. The single torch in the room shed feeble light yet was enough for him to recognize the familiar curves that haunted him. He set his teeth.

"Did you enjoy William's company, sweeting?"

"Aye, better than I thought. I still do not like him, but I can tolerate him better than most Normans."

"Including your husband?"

"If you will recall, my lord, I warned you not to take me to wife. 'Tis only your just deserts that you are now receiving. Are you enjoying them?"

A faint, secret smile quivered on her mouth, and Rye was suddenly provoked into action. Damn her for making him feel like an untried youth!

" 'Tis just what I intend to do, sweet wife," he said, and saw a flare of dismay light her eyes. "I will enjoy my just deserts this eve, I vow."

He strode to her and took her into his arms, ignoring her startled protest as he ground his mouth down on her half-open lips. She was as sweet as he remembered, and after a moment of brief struggle, she did not resist when he took her to the straw pallet and laid her down.

For the first time Rye did not attempt to soothe her

with gentle caresses. He was not brutal, but neither was he tender. He took his pleasure, then rolled away from her on the straw pallet and put an arm over his eyes. Now that it was done, he felt a pang of remorse. She was, after all, pregnant with his child. He should have left her alone.

Brenna stirred, sitting up to look at him in the dim light. "I apologize, Rye."

He returned her gaze with narrowed eyes, suspecting a trick. "What do you mean?"

"Merely that I taunted you when I should have held my tongue. I owe you an apology, and I have now given it."

"Before God," Rye muttered as she drew a blanket up and over them, "I will never understand women."

Brenna laughed softly. "You may thank your Maker for that, my lord. 'Twould probably curdle your brain if you were to manage it."

Because he suspected she was right, Rye remained silent. He lay for a long time, relishing the warmth of Brenna's soft body next to him, inhaling the faint scent of lavender that emanated from her hair. Lady Madelon was likely right. He was obsessed with her, and if he did not watch his step, he would end up looking a fool. He tried to remember if he had ever expected love from a woman and knew that he had not. Yet somehow, for a short time, he'd hoped he might find that gentle emotion with this one woman. He was a fool indeed, Rye thought bitterly.

Raissa was waiting anxiously the next evening when Brenna came to the hall. Her sweet face scanned Brenna as if searching for sign of injury, and when she saw her hale and hearty, she relaxed.

" 'Tis welcome to see you looking content, Lady Brenna," she said, leaning close to smile at her.

Brenna took her seat next to Rye and smiled at his sister. King William had the place of honor, and on his other side sat Lady Madelon and a baron who had traveled with the king.

"I am glad to be here," she said honestly. She couldn't look directly at Rye. She was afraid others would remark on it, and she wasn't certain how she should feel about him. She'd expected anger from him the night before, but not the almost desperate passion he'd given her instead. It was a riddle without a solution. Even the day had been spent differently, as Rye had insisted she accompany them to visit a nearby village. Though she wasn't certain for the reason, she felt the king's visit had something to do with the bandits that still preyed on the land.

Servants approached from the unoccupied side of the high table, then genuflected with their heavy platters of broken meats. Wine was poured from jeweled flagons into goblets at the high table, and into wooden cups at the lower.

Distinguished guests were seated on the banquette at the wall side of the high table, looking down on the tables that had been placed perpendicular to the high table. Huge salt cellars of silver divided the lower tables between upper and lower classes, with the lower class being seated below the salt. A nef, or silver ship containing spices, was placed on each table, near a maple mazer. Each pair of guests shared a wooden bowl, or at the lower tables, a hard trencher of bread. All brought their own knives but were supplied with spoons.

Brenna recognized some of the guests, but not others. These were the barons who had been away, fighting campaigns for William, and had returned to find a new overlord at Moorleah. Now they came, ready to do homage to Rye de Lyon and offer their military service should he need it.

Managing a smile for Raissa, Brenna was well aware of Rye on her other side. She gave her full attention to Raissa.

"How is Gilles? And little Perin?"

"They are both well," Raissa replied, "though Perin grows so quickly, he will soon rival Gilles in size." She smiled at Brenna. "Gilles asks about you frequently. He is enamored of the tales of King Arthur now and insists upon being entertained with recounts of knights of old."

"I believe I shall one day be sorry I ever mentioned it to him," Brenna said with a laugh. "But he grows as well and will soon be interested in other things."

"Soon Gilles will be sent for training to the keep of a nobleman. Rye tells me he has made arrangements with St. Aubin, who is here this eve, to accept Gilles in his household."

"St. Aubin? Already?" Brenna looked toward the men. "I had not thought 'twould begin so soon—how old is Gilles?"

"He's soon seven years, but arrangements must be made early before there are too many young boys and no place for him." Raissa looked away, biting her lower lip. "I know it to be silly, but I worry about the time when it comes."

"Of course you do." Brenna glanced at Rye, but he did not appear to follow their discussion, and she looked back at Raissa. " 'Tis customary, I know, for boys to be sent away for training, but p'raps if you mentioned to your brother that Gilles is still so young, and with the boy's father dead and his paternal family so far away—"

"I did," Raissa cut in softly, "but Rye is correct when he says it is even more imperative for a boy brought up among women to be taught the ways of a young man. Since my husband died when Gilles was so young, it would be distracting to have his mother fretting over him."

"Then Gilles is to leave soon?"

"Not soon, but within the next year. He must gain his knighthood, as his father's lands were left to the eldest son by his first wife. Gilles has only my few dower lands, and must win his own one day, so Rye would have him begin his training early."

"Is that why you are here, instead of with your son's kin?"

"That, and because . . ." Raissa halted and flung

Brenna an embarrassed look. "My mother had no one to turn to after her holdings were razed in Anjou, you see, so we came to Rye for succor. He has our father's lands —who held to them as well against King Henri as Rye does against King Philip, another greedy ruler." Sighing, Raissa murmured, "I grow weary of constant war over land and power, and the hardships it puts upon those of us who seek only to raise our children to adulthood. I fear for my sons, but I would fear more for daughters, who might be wed to harsh men just to ally lands and titles."

"That seems to be a woman's lot," Brenna agreed, and her gaze slid to Rye. She could have been wed, as Raissa had been, to a man much older, who already had heirs for his lands. Young Gilles would not find it easy to make his way in this world, and his uncle's power would be a great advantage to him.

Thinking of her father, and how Dunstan had been William's hostage in a time when death seemed imminent, Brenna spared a moment's gratitude for the security she now had. Though she was subject to the whims of a husband, that husband was not as harsh as he could have been. Nor did he mistreat her family, though she was sorry for her brothers' plight. They had brought it upon their own heads, she knew, by not taking the mercy offered them. William dealt harshly with rebellion and expected his earls to do the same. Rye would not have kept the king's favor long if he had been less than just to the outlaws. Open rebellion against the king would have earned them death; outlawry had earned them two score of stripes on their backs and banishment from England.

Brenna had not witnessed their punishment and was glad she had not. She'd not have been able to bear the sight of her brothers being used so harshly, though she thought it well deserved.

She slanted a surreptitious glance at her husband and found his gaze resting on her. She refused, flushing, when he lifted his wine and offered her a sip.

"You seem solemn, *chérie*. Why so? Are you not glad to be free of your guard this past day?"

"Aye, I am well pleased to be free, my lord. I merely wonder why you keep staring at me."

"I missed your sweet temper." Rye laughed at her quick frown. "P'raps I missed your sweet body more," he added in a low tone that made her flush deepen to a scarlet shade. He stroked a hand down her arm, ignoring her stiffness as he lifted her wrist and turned her palm up to kiss it. Murmuring against her palm, "I did miss you, sweeting, though I cannot say I missed your prickly temper," he seemed to wait for her anger.

Brenna withdrew her hand and met his blue gaze with a careless shrug that hid the tumult he caused with his touch and words. "Do I dare admit that I have not missed your pricking words, my lord?"

"As I have ofttimes said, you would dare anything." Rye sat back in his chair and let his gaze drift past Brenna to where William sat deep in discussion with one of his vassals. After a moment he said softly, "I wonder if you would have wed me were it not for William's command."

"Of course not," Brenna replied. "Why?"

"Just a thought."

Rye turned to answer a question from another, leaving Brenna to muse on his enigmatic remarks. He was in a strange mood, she decided, probably brought on by her behavior the night before. Odd, that she'd felt no anger toward him when he'd taken her so roughly and without gentle words. Odder still, that he seemed to regard her more gently, as if ashamed of his actions. That was nonsense, of course. Rye de Lyon would never feel remorse for his actions, particularly toward a woman.

There were times she wondered why she cared if he felt any tenderness for her. Hadn't he made it plain he wanted only an heir from her? Why should she care?

And more confusing, she had begun to wonder about the new life she carried within her. While she dreaded the coming ordeal, there was an odd expectancy mingled with her apprehension. When she sat dreaming at the window, she found herself wondering if the child was a boy or girl, and if it would look like its sire. Would the babe have that same ebony hair and stimulating blue eyes? Or would it have softer features, with a crown of red-gold curls and eyes as yellow as a cat's?

Brenna stifled a sigh and dragged her attention back to her surroundings. She drifted often now, caught up in what was going on inside her body, as much a prisoner of it as she was an interested observer.

"Milady," Lady Madelon was saying in a honeyed tone that immediately made Brenna wary, "tell me of your health. There has been no illness of a morning?"

"Some," Brenna admitted. "It passes quickly."

"Ah, how fortunate you are. I remember when I had my son. I was so ill for so long—but of course, the women of Normandy are more delicate, and not as used to birthing babes as are Saxon women."

Brenna stiffened. "How unfortunate for you."

"Some would say we are more gently made, and not as sturdy. I knew at once that you would breed well. You are near tall as a man."

"Mother," Raissa put in, "do you think this conversation suitable for the table?"

Lady Madelon looked surprised. "Oh? Is it not? I am certain I was just trying to impart my concern for my daughter by law. After all, she will bear the next heir to Lyonfield. Let us hope she survives it."

The last was a careless sally, but the effect on Brenna was startling. She stood up with a wrenching gasp, and her face grew so pale even Lady Madelon was surprised.

Madelon's brows lifted, and her eyes narrowed maliciously. "Of course you will survive, child. Most women do. 'Tis only the pain that makes some succumb to death rather than—oh—have I distressed you?"

Brenna pushed back her chair before a squire could do it for her and moved blindly away from the long table. Though she hated giving Madelon more ammunition against her, the cruel comments brought to mind too many of her own fears to bear them.

Before she reached the doors from the hall, Rye caught up with her.

"What is it?" he asked, and there was such concern in his voice that Brenna forgot her resistance and turned into the comfort of his embrace. Her words were muffled by his rich tunic.

" 'Tis nothing, my lord. Nothing you would understand."

"I might. The babe? Are you ill? Let me take you to our chamber and fetch Rachel to assist you. Brenna—" He pushed her away and tilted her face up to look at her. "You would tell me if you felt ill?"

"Of course." She flushed slightly. "I gave you my oath on it, and I would not disregard it."

"Well, I did not expect you to yield easily, I suppose. Ah, sweeting, do not startle me like that again. I thought you had become ill."

"Nay, I only need to have some privacy for a moment," she said lamely, offering the only excuse she could contrive on such short notice. "To—to visit the garderobe."

"Ah." Rye nodded understanding. "Then you will return."

"Of course." Over his shoulder Brenna saw Lady Madelon gaze at her with speculative eyes and knew that she had fallen into her trap. It didn't help to know that her cruel words fell on fertile ground. She *was* frightened, and to hear how she would suffer only made it worse.

She managed a reassuring smile before she continued down the torchlit corridor to the alcove concealing the garderobe from view.

When she returned, Rye smiled at her, and she was aware of William's regard as well. Several of Rye's vassals were present, and one of them, Sire de Searcy, earnestly sought the king's ear for a project he was considering.

She found it difficult to eat, though the cook had done well with the dishes. They included peacocks that had been roasted, then refeathered so that they looked almost alive on huge platters; desserts that had been fashioned into clever shapes; and puddings steaming in gigantic bowls. Wine flowed freely, but Brenna had no stomach for it and was glad when the meal was over and the tables were being cleared.

Raissa's soft hand on her arm gained her attention. The young woman whispered, "My mother seeks to drive a wedge between you and Rye. Do not allow it. She is jealous of his affection for you."

Though she doubted that was the cause, Brenna whispered her thanks for Raissa's peace-making efforts.

Rye leaned against the high back of his chair as squires and servants moved aside the lower tables. Scraps were given to the poor and bones to the dogs, as was the norm. Guests washed their hands at the lavabo, while the aquamanile was offered to those from the high table.

Several tense minutes passed for Brenna. She wanted desperately to forget Lady Madelon's terrible words, but her hands continued to tremble. When she saw Raoul de Beaumont approach, she drew in a breath of relief at the diversion. Beaumont stepped onto the low dais and murmured into Rye's ear for a moment. After bowing to the king, he joined the vassals seated at the high table. The king watched silently.

It grew quiet in the hall, with even the musicians quitting their instruments. A fight erupted between two of the hunting dogs and was quickly hushed with a well-placed boot and a last startled yelp.

Rising from their benches, the vassals approached the dais from below, bowing first to the king, then to Rye. Finally Rye stood, beckoning them forward.

" 'Tis a law, that there be no lord without land," he said in ringing tones, "and no land without a lord. A fief is more than land; 'tis a representation of a vassal's rights, and his obligations. Besides the armed knights each vassal swears to render, I charge that each of you shall be expected to attend court when summoned to be a judge in a case against your peers. Your taxes shall be assessed according to the size of your holdings. St. Aubin," he said then, gesturing, "you hold the largest demesne, and as such, shall pay me homage first."

Stepping forward, St. Aubin, a man almost as large as the earl, knelt before him and placed his clasped hands between his lord's. Saying, "Lord, I become your man," he then took the oath of fealty.

Lifting St. Aubin to his feet, Rye gave him a ceremonial kiss of acceptance, then repeated the procedure with each vassal. One by one the men swore fealty to him, accepting him as their new overlord, while King William witnessed the ritual.

Brenna remained silent as the powerful barons came and bent the knee to her husband, though she wondered with a trace of grim amusement if she should feel such satisfaction at seeing these men bare their heads and offer fealty to her husband. It was a double-edged sword, she mused, this humbling of Normans in her presence. She, a Saxon, was wed to a Norman earl, yet by that very token, accepting of the same homage due him. If Rye were slain, these men would be forced to pay their child the same homage, in fact, gave oaths that they would do so.

Oaths, she had learned, were oft broken in times of war and conflict, but the vassal who broke his sworn oath to an overlord was rarely trusted to give another. Men lived by those sworn words, and the breaking of a bond was a serious affair.

When the formalities of fealty were over and the vassals accepted William's kiss of peace, Rye gave the signal for lively entertainment to begin. Music piped, and with a swirl of diaphanous silk, dancers skipped between the wooden benches, slender bodies gleaming in the light of torch and central fire. The tempo of mandolins, lutes, and horns escalated, and so did the writhings of the dancing girls.

Brenna had viewed dancing girls before and admired their lithe movements; now, however, she tensed when Rye exchanged a laughing comment with Sire de Searcy about the charms of a supple young dancer.

Grinning, de Searcy observed, "She is very agile, don't you think, my lord?" and Rye agreed with a bawdy remark that made Brenna burn with silent anger.

As if sensing the attention of the earl and his vassal, the dancing girl bent and swayed with increasing sensuality as she approached the dais. Her movements were even more enhanced by the floating silk veils and skimpy costume she wore, and her eyes were heavily outlined in kohl.

Stepping lightly, she skipped across the stone floor in time with the music, and as it played faster and faster, her feet moved more quickly, giving the observers ample chance to glimpse the flash of her slender bare legs as the silk lifted and swirled. Sweat misted her body, and the gleaming flesh of her bared midriff and round breasts promised ample delights to the man who wished to taste them.

A faint feline smile curved the dancer's lips, as if she knew she aroused the men who watched, and with a toss of her long dark hair, she pranced directly to the dais. Tiny silver bells gleamed and jangled around her ankles, and her bare feet slapped the stones. Silk swished in a mist of scarlet color, and tawny flesh beckoned.

Then, as Rye and de Searcy still smiled their pleasure, the girl boldly stepped up onto the dais, stepping lightly between Rye's outspread legs in a flash of near-naked legs. Sire de Searcy roared with appreciation, but Rye sat with a lifted brow and his mouth still curved in a slight smile.

To Brenna's chagrin he made no move to halt the girl, but watched as she undulated in the erotic movements of the dance, lifting her arms over her head and twining them in a sensual glide, then bending to expose the full charms of her young body. At this close range, the silk costume bared more than it hid, and Rye seemed to enjoy the view.

Growing even bolder, the girl spun about to let her arms drop over the earl's head, drawing him into a light embrace and laughing sultrily as she pressed his face to her bosom.

Sire de Searcy gave another roar of approval, and even William smiled. When Rye made no effort to extricate himself, but allowed the girl to writhe upon his lap and caress him with silk veils, Brenna could not contain her fury.

She stood abruptly, capturing her husband's attention as well as that of a startled de Searcy. "I think I shall retire for the evening, my lord," Brenna said stiffly, not looking at either Rye or the smirking girl. She made a quick curtsy to the King. When she moved past Rye, he caught her hand, still not dislodging the panting girl from his lap.

"The evening is not yet ended," Rye said. "Linger."

"I do not wish to linger." Brenna still refused to look at him, though she felt his intent gaze upon her. "I wish to retire."

Leaning forward, Rye set the girl on her feet. "And do dishonor to our king and the men who have come to swear me homage? Nay, milady, I must insist that you reconsider and stay a while longer."

She removed her hand from his grasp, and he did not try to keep it. Pleating the folds of her gown with her fingers, Brenna said haltingly, "I feel ill, milord, truly I do. I do not think even your most sensitive vassal would wish to see me faint at your feet."

"Take your maid with you," Rye said after a moment, and gestured to Beaumont. "Find the Lady Rachel and bid her see to her mistress," he told the knight. "I will be occupied for some time here." Rye intercepted Brenna's quick glare and added, "With the king and my vassals."

Brenna fled the hall in relief as soon as Rachel came to her, though Beaumont went with them as far as the door to the chamber she shared with Rye.

"I've put your things back in here, milady," Rachel said when the door had shut behind them. "Lord Lyon bade me do so."

Sinking to the stark comfort of a hard chair, Brenna buried her face in her palms. "You did well, Rachel. I am overweary, 'tis all."

It wasn't at all the truth, but she had no desire to explain her reasons for fleeing the hall when she wasn't certain of them herself. That they had something to do with Rye's reaction to the nubile dancing girl was a part of it, but not all. Lady Madelon's vicious remarks had left her feeling confused as well.

Did Rye de Lyon harbor soft feelings for her? If so, why did he not reveal them himself? Why did he switch back and forth between harshness and tenderness as erratically as a willow limb in the wind?

"Damn the cur," she muttered, and did not realize she'd spoken aloud until Rachel came to her side.

"I saw the girl dancing, milady, but 'tis of no moment, I am sure. She only teased him, and he would not—"

"I am not at all sure what he will and won't do, I'm afraid," Brenna snapped. "He certainly seemed not to mind her efforts. P'raps as my form thickens, he will choose another. 'Tis done frequently, I know."

"But not always." Rachel hesitated, as if seeking more comforting words. "And I think him a more honorable man than that."

Brenna looked at her consideringly. "Do you, Rachel? I thought you feared him."

"I do. But not so much that I think him wicked and a dishonorable man."

"Dishonor does not always mean the same thing to a man as it does to a woman," Brenna muttered. She looked down at her hands, twisting in her lap. "I ofttimes wonder what it does mean to him. He spoke of justice, of Norman and Saxon living in peace, yet tonight he asked his vassals to swear to him they would bring men to war when he called."

"Milady," Rachel reproved, "you know that there are always wars, whether great or small. Greedy men will always want what is not theirs."

"Aye," Brenna admitted with a sigh, "I suppose that is true." She lapsed into silent contemplation, wondering if her brothers had been banished only to seek more vengeance against the Normans. Would they be so foolish? Is that what Rye expected?

"Shall I fetch you a soothing herbal drink, milady?"

Rachel was asking anxiously, and Brenna shook her head.

"Nay. I just need to seek my bed, I think. There has been too much excitement this day."

Rachel smiled. "For me as well, since the king approved Raoul's suit. I shall be able to see him much more now. With all the outlaws captured and punished or banished, your lord will be more often at home too. 'Tis well that you rest, so—milady! Are you unwell?"

Standing abruptly, Brenna made a helpless gesture. "Do not speak to me of the outlaws, please. I know you mean well, but I must—tell me, Rachel—can you find the squire known as Myles and bring him here?"

"Myles?" Rachel shifted nervously. "Are you sure it would be wise, milady? I know he is your brother, and that Lord Lyon does not mislike him, but—"

"Please, Rachel. Rye will be some time below with the king and his barons, so it would be a perfect time to speak with Myles in privacy."

Reluctantly Rachel went to seek out the squire in the kitchens, but it took her the best part of an hour to bring him back. Brenna was pacing impatiently when the door to her chamber swung open and Myles entered. He looked wary and glanced about the lamp-lit room.

"You sent for me, Lady Brenna?"

"Aye, come in, quickly, and shut the door behind you." She put up a hand to stop Rachel. "I wish to speak with him in complete privacy, please."

Rachel's dismay was obvious, but she nodded and left, closing the door with a soft thud. Brenna turned back to her brother.

"Tell me, quickly, of our brothers. Any news?"

"Why this sudden concern?" Myles asked carefully. "Did you have a change of heart?"

Waving an impatient hand, Brenna shook her head. "Nay, I just wish to know of them. All I now know is that they were whipped, then banished. Do you have word of their whereabouts?"

"Brenna . . ." Myles paused, and shook his head. "I do not wish to discuss them with you."

"What?" She stared at him in disbelief. "Do you think I would betray them? Or my husband?"

Spreading his arms, Myles said with a helpless shrug, "I know only that you are not in favor with Lord Lyon right now, and that you might do or say anything."

Glaring at him, Brenna snapped, "Do not think me fool enough to play the traitor with either kin or husband! 'Tis only that I fret about their actions, that is all. Do they intend to start another rebellion? Must I ever watch for my brothers to be hanged on some gibbet, or from a town wall?"

Myles looked down at his feet and sighed. "I do not know their intentions, only that they feel betrayed by you and me. Whitley threatened once to see me dead before I put in with the Normans, but I do not think he really meant it. He had ample opportunity, yet let me go."

"Whitley—does he fare badly in exile with his stump?"

Shrugging, Myles raked a hand through his hair. "He does as well as can be expected. He cannot bear weapons as well, of course, though he has learned to use his left arm instead. 'Tis Ridgely we should fear, and Rannulf and Corbet as well. They are dangerous, to us and to your noble husband."

At his last mocking words, Brenna shuddered. She'd known it. There would be repercussions; her brothers were violent men. They had lived so long with violence, and with a need for vengeance, that she feared they were no longer cautious.

"What can we do?" she whispered, and Myles strode to her and took her by the arms.

"Nothing. Do not even think of it. They will not listen to anyone, so do not try. Let them reap what they sow. It is all we can do."

She shook free of his grip. "Do you not care what happens, that they can destroy us with their rebellion?"

"They cannot destroy us, Brenna. Only themselves. Did your husband berate you for their actions?"

Shaking her head, she said, "Nay, he did not."

"He will not. You should trust the man you married more than you do." Myles gave a short, bitter laugh. "If *I* do, I cannot see why you refuse."

"You trust Rye de Lyon? *You*, Myles, who once swore to fight the Normans to your dying breath?"

"I was too young and foolish to realize the truth of it. Now that I have served in his keep, and heard his men speak of him, and seen his justice firsthand, I know that I have chosen well." Myles smiled at his sister's skeptical gaze. "Our own father bade me follow him. He said that Lord Lyon was a man worthy of respect."

"Is that why you came here?"

"Partially. Another reason is that I drew my sword on him in our bailey the day after you were wed and dared him to fight me."

Brenna's eyes widened. "And *that* is why you chose to follow him? Because you fought him and lived?"

"Nay, because he was kind enough not to fight me," Myles replied with a rueful grin. "I was angry, and very foolish. He could have split me in two with that great sword of his, and I would not have been able to put a scratch on him. Instead of shaming me, he offered me a post as squire. I thought about it a long time before I came here."

"Well," Brenna said, "you are a bit old to be squire, I vow. You should be training for knighthood, if you can coax our father into sponsoring you."

Still grinning, Myles lifted a foot to show her the silver spurs attached to his boots. "I will be, soon. I've earned the right to carry a shield and to wear a knight's helmet. Though I can wield a sword, I am to tilt at the quintain and learn the lance from Sir de Beaumont."

"Sir de Beaumont?" Brenna's brows rose. "He is a fair and noble knight."

"I agree."

"Then you will not ride with our brothers if they bid you come to them?"

Surprised, Myles demanded angrily, "Is that why you sent for me? To find out if I intend to betray your husband with treachery?"

"Nay, do not scowl at me so. I merely fear that you may find yourself caught up in something you cannot escape."

"As you are?"

Startled, Brenna met her brother's gaze, saw his eyes drop deliberately to her middle, and flushed.

"Yea, I am caught up, 'tis true. I may soon find that my husband does not desire my company. If he has not already reached that decision."

"I do not think he has," Myles said in amusement. "Not if the past week has been any indication. He has fretted like a boar in rut. I am amazed that he took so long to find an excuse to free you."

" 'Twas no excuse he needed, only my oath not to attempt escape," Brenna said bitterly. When Myles looked surprised, she managed a faint smile. "He harbors a suspicion that I may find a way to do myself and the babe harm. He cannot believe that my mood has changed, and that my threats were only angry words."

"A common mistake, I think." Myles laughed at her quick frown. "You rage often, fair sister, and mere men might not realize your threats meaningless, especially as you are not known to make empty promises."

"Well—" She paused, then said lamely, "I have changed a great deal of late. More than the obvious. P'raps things are not as I once thought them."

"P'raps." Myles gave her a mocking smile. "And p'raps you have grown up a little. Whichever, I must leave here and tend my duties, or Beltair will be looking for me with a stout cane. I do not need any stripes laid upon my back for avoiding my tasks, nor do I feel I need any more of that worthy man's discipline."

Laughing, Brenna kissed him quickly and said, "You've changed, too, little brother. I do believe you are learning responsibility."

"St. Benedict! I hope so," Myles said fervently. "I grow weary of toting water buckets and doing the work of a page."

When Myles had gone, Brenna lit another oil lamp, making a face at the foul smell as the reed wick finally caught and flared with feeble light. Vegetable oil was better than fish oil but gave just as little light. Torches burned better, but smoked horribly and dripped hot pitch onto the floor and unwary persons. Beeswax candles were too precious for any but royalty, and the tallow candles they used at Moorleah were in short supply at the moment. More were to be made as soon as she set the servants to it.

"Lady Madelon," Brenna told Rachel when she returned to the chamber, "must have forgotten to order tallow poured into the candle molds."

"It seems odd that she would, as she is trying to prove to Lord Lyon that she is a better mistress than you," the girl said, smoothing back the furs and wool covers on the bed. "If the smell of the lamps makes you ill, I can look for candle stubs."

"Nay, 'tis not necessary." Brenna looked at the bed and wondered when Rye would come to their chamber. Was he still with the dancing girl? Had he gone with her to some shadowed corner of the keep to taste her sultry charms? The thought of him holding the dark-haired dancer made Brenna's teeth clench with fury and pain.

Rye had thrust the girl from him as Brenna left and did not allow her in his lap again. Instead he shoved her toward a willing, delighted de Searcy, who took immediate advantage of the girl's alluring charms and spirited her away to a distant, more private corner of the keep.

Though he gave his attention to King William, Rye found it wandering at times to his red-haired wife. She'd looked angry and disturbed at the girl's play with him, and though irritated, he was impatient to go to her. He chafed at the delay forced upon him by hospitality's conventions, and watched as the tallow candles grew shorter and shorter and the barons grew more boisterous with free drink and lively entertainment.

A jongleur chanted interminable tales, *chansons de geste* and poetic romances, while striking melodies on his vielle and inviting the audience to sing the refrain.

Merry it is in halle to hear the harpe, / the minstrelles synge, the jongleurs carpe.

Rye drank wine mixed with honey, ginger, and cinnamon as he smiled politely and made conversation, and when he finally perceived that his vassals had passed the point of coherence, save for those who had already retired along with the king, he rose from his chair. Few noticed as he crossed the hall, paused to ensure that all the doors were barred and his defenses manned with sentinels, then moved to the staircase. Sounds of music followed him as he mounted the spiral steps.

By the time he reached their chamber on the third floor of the keep, nothing could be heard but a muted melody, and that not clearly. Rachel lay on her straw pallet in the outer room, and Rye ignored her as he stalked toward his chamber and pushed open the door.

It was almost completely dark in the room. Only a faint flicker of light showed him any direction, and that from an oil lamp on a low table. No embers burned in the brazier to give off heat and light, and it was cool in the chamber in spite of the warm weather without the keep. Rye could barely make out Brenna's covered form in the wide canopied bed across the room.

Shrugging out of his garments, he aimed them at the clothes pole without pausing to see if they landed well and walked naked to the bed. Brenna had her back to him, the covers pulled up well over her shoulders. Her hair fanned out over the pillows like silken fire, and he gave a sigh of pleasure.

He had missed her more than he'd wanted to admit; it was only right that she be back in his bed. As his eyes adjusted to the lack of sufficient light, he saw that her back was rigid and knew she was awake. He smiled. She was angry, but he could deal with that. Most of their evenings began this way, with Brenna angry, resisting his touch until he gentled her with hot kisses and caresses.

Lifting the covers, he slid beneath and reached for her. She shrugged off his hand, and he leaned forward to brush the hair from her neck and kiss her nape. His lips moved leisurely along the span of sweetly scented flesh, tasting, teasing as his arms circled her unyielding body in a light embrace. Her hair was fragrant, smelling of the soap she used.

Spreading his hand over her belly, Rye rested his palm against the gentle swell for a moment. He could feel her heart race beneath his forearm and knew she waited for him to offer some word of comfort. He tried, but he could think of nothing that she might want to hear, that might ease her fears or give her solace.

He'd never felt his lack of easy conversation with a woman more keenly. Sighing, Rye turned Brenna to her back. Her eyes were wide in the shadows, muted gold and shiny with emotion. He wondered what she was thinking and stroked back the hair from her cheek before he bent to kiss her.

Desire rose hot and heavy in him, and his abstinence pricked him harshly as he tried to take his time with her, to arouse her to the point of surrender. She made no effort to avoid him, but neither did she yield to passion.

"Nay, sweet Brenna," he murmured when she closed her eyes, "you won't escape me that easily." One hand moved to tease a budded peak of her breast, while his mouth gave ardent attention to the other. He threw a leg over her thighs when she gasped and tried to roll away, scraping his free hand down over her body to the damp cleft between her legs. "See?" he said softly when he touched her, "your own body betrays you with a longing you would deny."

Shuddering, Brenna moaned when he began to caress her sensitive woman's mound. Rye's tongue flicked over her taut nipple in lightning strokes that made her writhe, and his hand manipulated the fiery center of her with such expert care that she was soon reaching for him.

"Damn you," she whispered huskily as she clutched at his broad shoulders, "damn you. . . ."

"If this is damnation, *chérie*, I do not mind it at all," Rye said between kisses. "Aye, I will seek it eagerly."

When she cried out, her body arching under him as

she surrendered to the sweep of ecstasy he provoked, Rye gave in to his own passion and slid inside her with a smooth thrust that buried him to the hilt. Sheathed in her warmth, he held tightly to control as her body pulsed around him in velvet contractions. He waited until she relaxed, sobbing into his bare shoulder, before he began to move.

Slowly at first, then more rapidly, Rye moved in the erotic rhythm of pleasure; he felt Brenna's response before she did, felt the tightening of her body begin again. She was panting for breath, no longer resisting him, but yielding to him without thought. It was exhilarating. It was sweet ecstasy that soon brought him to his own release, and as he surged powerfully against her, feeling her body melt around him, Rye knew that he had never felt such intense pleasure before wedding this rebellious woman.

Perhaps, he thought hazily when he allowed himself to relax in satisfaction, Lady Madelon was right. Was that so bad, to be attracted to one's wife? In this way, at any rate. And he would never be foolish enough to yield to the pleasure of the body over the warnings of the mind. Yea, if this was the rewards of being besotted, he might find it a pleasant pastime.

"Sleep, *chérie*," he murmured gently when Brenna shoved against his chest with her hands. "The night is long, and we may yet seek more pleasure."

Trembling, she allowed him to hold her in his embrace, and it occurred to him just before he drifted into sleep that she had not argued with him.

CHAPTER 15

"A TORCH DANCE !" Raissa exclaimed, clapping her hands together with delight. She gazed happily at the line of dancers with lit tapers in their hands. The hall was filled with guests and Moorleah's inhabitants, and the warm July weather lent a festive air to the evening that had not been present since the king's departure the month before. Raissa laughed. "I've not danced thus since I was a young maid."

"And you are so old now," Brenna teased, smiling fondly at the young woman. Her gaze took in Raissa's high color, sleek, dark hair, and shining eyes; Rye's half sister was a lovely woman. Offers had been made for her hand, and as the widowed sister to a powerful earl, she would bring much to the man who married her. Several suitors had traveled to Moorleah or sent their offers by courier.

Leaning close, Brenna whispered to Raissa, "Now that the evening meal is done and we are to play, who will you choose to dance with you? Lord Pierre Réchin, perhaps? He is very handsome, and still young. Of course, Geoffroi le Bressan is a bit older, though not as handsome, don't you agree? However—he is very rich."

Laughter danced in Raissa's eyes as she listened to

Brenna's teasing words. "What say you, Brenna? Do I choose beauty over wealth in a husband, as well?"

"Do you get to choose?" Brenna's brow lifted. "I heard your brother say he was still considering your match, but I never heard him say you were being consulted."

"True enough." Raissa smiled. "He will choose wisely, I am sure. Rye knows the advantages of having a contented wife."

"I hope you aren't suggesting that *I* am content," Brenna said more sharply than she intended, and Raissa gave her a hurt look.

"Aren't you? I have seen my brother soften in the past month, and he ever lingers near your side."

Shifting uncomfortably, Brenna murmured, " 'Tis concern for the babe, I perceive."

"You know that's not true." Raissa met her lifted gaze with a smile. "You've pierced my brother's armor, Brenna. I believe he loves you."

"He loves what is his, as a rich man loves his gold." Brenna looked down at her hands, feeling Raissa's troubled eyes on her. She glanced up and shrugged helplessly. "I do admit that I have soft feelings for him, if that is what you are trying to discover with this roundabout play of words."

"It was." Raissa smiled impishly. "I'm glad. He needs your tenderness more than he will show."

"I've seen nothing in his manner to indicate that he would welcome softness from me. Surrender yes, but not soft words of love." Shrugging to ease the pain those words cost her, Brenna added lightly, "Of course, your brother would not show you that side of his nature, I am certain."

"I am well aware of Rye's manner toward women, as I have had some years to observe. You are the first woman he has sought to please in any way but the most casual." Raissa leaned forward and lowered her voice. "He's never been kind to women before, as it was not his nature. I do believe my mother had much to do with that side of him, but he has never said. I've told you how she treated him most cruelly as a young lad, and it hardened his heart toward our sex."

A faint smile curved Brenna's mouth. "If your mother gave him cause to distrust women, you are the only reason he has any softness at all, Raissa. I've seen how he loves you and am glad that you love him as well. No one should be alone in this world, left to face their fears without a hope of help." Impulsively she put her hand atop Raissa's. "If he has been kind to me in ways, I owe it to you."

"Nay, sister, you owe it to the courage he admires in you, the fire that tempers his steel. That is what attracts my brother to you—your strength."

"My strength?" Brenna stared at her in surprise, hardly hearing the music or people around her. "I am not strong, but weak."

"Not where it matters—in the heart. You have a strong heart, Brenna. You love fiercely and loyally, and the man who wins that love will win much. Rye can see this in you; any man can see it."

"You observe much," Brenna said slowly. "I'm not certain you are right, but I will think on what you have said."

"And you will dance at my wedding?" Raissa asked in a light tone, steering the conversation back to safer topics. "I should know the decision soon."

Shaking her head, Brenna said, "You will be fortunate to know his name before the wedding."

"Rye will tell me. He does consult me, though when it is time to make the final decision, his opinion will weigh more than mine."

"He will force you into marriage with a man you do not want?" Brenna asked, angry sparks beginning to flash in her tawny eyes. Raissa's situation too closely paralleled hers for her to be comfortable at the thought of the sweet girl being forced to wed a harsh man just for lands and profit. Her hands clenched into fists in her lap, and she slid a quick glare toward her husband.

"Nay," Raissa said swiftly, putting a hand on Brenna's arm. "He will not. He has said that I will be at liberty to refuse any husband he chooses, but he asks that I consider my choice carefully." She smiled at Brenna's anger. "Don't worry so about me. Rye will not allow harm to come to me or force me into a marriage I do not want."

"He did me," Brenna muttered, then flushed when Raissa arched a brow.

" 'Twas different," Raissa reproved. "You had to wed the king's man; think about the consequences had you wed a man who might have dealt harshly with you."

Staring at her, Brenna realized that Raissa was right. Rye, though harsh enough in a way, had not been cruel to her, or locked her in a cell as he might have done.

And if she was to be honest with herself, she would admit that she had gradually begun to care more deeply for him. It was galling that she had begun to love the man she'd sworn to hate, but she had. Not just his touch —though her body craved that despite her efforts to resist—but his crooked smile, and the way he'd begun to linger near her side more and more often to listen to her, made her soften toward him. Her heart lurched when he spoke to her, and her breath caught at his attentions.

"Uh-oh," Raissa said with a laugh, "I see your husband looking this way, and he has a gentleman with him. I do believe that we are about to be asked to join the dancers." She glanced at Brenna with an anxious expression. "Do you feel well enough to dance?"

"Of course. My sickness of mornings has largely passed, and though 'tis hard to credit my condition with my still slender appearance, I feel well."

Lady Madelon approached as Brenna said this last and gave a malicious laugh upon hearing her words. "Wait until you are overlarge, my lady. Then see if your husband waits you so eagerly, or if he seeks his pleasure in another's arms. I warrant he'll not linger long at your side when his arms will no longer go around you."

Brenna gave Madelon an even stare. "Do you? I assume you speak from your experience with your own husband, my lady."

Stiffening, Lady Madelon glared at her. "Remember this, you impudent Saxon slut, that the acorn never falls far from the tree. Rye's father was a man who could not be loyal to one woman, and neither will he be. Do you think your charms so endurable that he will never look elsewhere? You fool only yourself if you do."

"Mother," Raissa interrupted, rising to her feet to take the older woman by the arm, "do not spread your hatred and pain to others. What happened with my father was many years ago and should be forgotten."

Shaking free of her daughter's clasp, Madelon said in a low, harsh tone, " 'Twill never be forgotten, not as long as I draw breath. Nor will I allow his misbegotten son to forget how he came into this world!"

Brenna lapsed into silence. In a way she understood Lady Madelon's pain and shame, though she could not accept her abuse without speaking out. It would be difficult for any wife to accept her husband's child with another woman, especially a woman who had stolen his affections. Yet even so, it was not the child's fault, and the part of Brenna that demanded justice could not condone Lady Madelon's abuse of a helpless lad who'd had no fault in his birth.

"Lady Madelon," she said softly when Raissa gave a cry of dismay, "I am sorry for your pain, but I will not allow you to spread your venom in my hall. And I do not wish to suffer my lord's chagrin at your hurtful words, so I advise you to keep your silence in his presence. He may treat you with courtesy as his mother, but I feel no such compunction to do so."

Lady Madelon met Brenna's coldly determined gaze, and her eyes narrowed slightly as she apparently saw no weakness there. "So, my fine Saxon upstart, you declare war between us."

"Since the first day I arrived, madam. I am aware of your fine hand in some of the problems that have arisen in my household, but I have allowed you free rein. No more. I shall take you to task the next time I find droppings in my grain, or sour wine in my casks, or my servants sent on silly errands to delay some necessary task. Do not think to earn sympathy from your son because of it, either, for he is not as blind to your nature as you may think."

"I never thought he was," Lady Madelon said stiffly. "I have only sought to remind him of the generosity of his father in leaving his lands to a bastard, and to remind Rye of his duty toward his father's widow."

"He is not a man who needs to be reminded of his duty," Brenna said shortly. "He knows it well. Too well at times, I vow. Do you think a weak man could have held his father's lands against the odds that Rye faced? Nay, yet he has held them well and earned more lands besides. Do not belittle his achievements, my lady."

"Ah, how you've changed your tune in the past three months, my eager Saxon slut," Madelon sneered. "Now you defend your lusty husband. Does he play the bed-game that well, to make you rise to his defense against a woman who seeks only to keep him in favor with his king?"

"He plays the bed-game well enough," Brenna stepped close to say, her temper flaring that this woman would bring up such a subject in public. "But 'tis not what gives me cause to defend him behind his back. Normans prate long and hard of justice, but rarely have I seen it, save in the man you call your son when it pleases you, yet speak of him as enemy when it does not. He seems to have a sense of true justice I find lacking in most, especially those who use the term *bastard* the loudest. Perhaps you should look to your own life before you are so free with labels, madam."

"Do you dare attempt to lesson me?" Madelon shook with fury. "I do not countenance haughty words from a common—"

"Common?" Brenna broke in, her eyes glittering with anger like orbs of gold. "An accident of birth made you noble, madam, not your nature, I vow. I've seen more regal behavior in the lowest serf than I have in you."

Hissing with rage, Lady Madelon drew back a hand as if to strike, but Raissa quickly grabbed her wrist.

"Mother, curb your temper! Rye approaches, and I do not think he would like to hear us squabble like she-cats, nor less would he appreciate hearing the reason for it."

Raissa's desperate words penetrated Lady Madelon's rage enough that she lowered her hand, but her fingers were still curved into talons as if to claw at Brenna. It would have been obvious to a blind man that there was dissension between the women, and Rye was clear-sighted.

"So," he said pleasantly, "do I interrupt a discussion about something important?" He caught Brenna's arm when she shifted away, pulling her gently to him. Garbed in a rich velvet tunic of bright red embroidered with glittering gold threads and tiny figures of prancing lions, he looked every inch the fine lord he was. His gaze moved to his wife, and his brow lifted questioningly.

"Woman talk, my lord," Brenna said, and flicked Madelon a glance that dared her to contradict her.

"Woman talk?" Rye's mouth curled with amusement as well as disbelief. Something shadowed his eyes as he met Brenna's gaze, but his words revealed nothing of his private thoughts. "Would you not prefer dancing to talking, my sweet? And Raissa, I have been bold enough to promise a dance to Lord le Bressan."

Raissa smiled prettily and put her hand in the palm the baron stretched out to her. "I accept, Lord le Bressan, with great pleasure." She stepped daintily to the middle of the cleared floor of the hall with the tall, lean Norman, who looked down at her with a pleased smile.

Left alone with Rye and Lady Madelon, Brenna wondered uneasily if the older woman would take the opportunity for further insult, but she did not. She merely moved to take a seat in the chair Brenna had abandoned.

"Come," Rye said, amusement edging his voice as he looked at Brenna, "dance with me, my sweet."

"How do you know I won't blow out your taper, my lord?" Brenna retorted, accepting the lighted taper he took from a squire and gave to her.

"Do you think you can, *chérie*?"

Smiling impishly, she said, "Aye, when I choose to do so."

Rye laughed and took her hand as he led her in the steps of the dance. The torch dance was a favorite of most in the hall, as it allowed not only lively dancing, but a game. The one who held the last lit taper was the victor, and there was much merriment as tapers were blown out by dancers. People dodged and ducked, holding candles high over their heads, shielding the tiny flickering flames with upheld palms when possible, swirling away when not. Hot wax spilled to the rushes and on clothes, but no one seemed to mind in the excitement of the play.

"Here," Raissa said, coming quickly to Brenna, "relight my taper for me!"

Giggling as she touched the flaming wick to the still smoldering taper Raissa held, Brenna said, "Do you dare cheat, my lady?"

"If I can," was the merry reply, and amid much squealing and laughter, the game continued.

Finally winded, only Rye, Raoul de Beaumont, Brenna, and the Baroness of Stutely held lit tapers. Brenna saw Rye bearing down at her with a determined expression, and she allowed Beaumont to wheel her away in the steps of the dance.

"Quickly," she cried, laughing. "Don't let him catch us!" Barely managing to elude Rye, Brenna skipped down the length of the hall with Beaumont.

Other dancers, still moving in the steps of the dance, laughed at the play between the earl and his wife. Flashes of red tunic dogged Brenna's heels as Rye pursued her, and as she dipped and whirled, watching the flickering flame of her candle, she saw him from the corner of her eye. It was hard to concentrate on the dance steps while keeping the flame alive, harder still to keep another from blowing out her taper.

She whirled, saw Rye advancing toward her, and pivoted on her toes to skip away, Beaumont laughing behind her. She was panting, and her gown clung to her in damp drapes of fabric as she exerted herself. Rushes clung to her feet as she moved and shifted, aware all the time of Rye's determined pursuit and Beaumont's grinning countenance. It had somehow become more than just a game to her.

He pursued her in play as he did in reality, and she was equally determined that he must put forth all his effort to capture her attentions. In the dance she could step under her partner's outstretched arms, pivot, take three steps, then turn again. Instead she ducked under Beaumont's arms and turned in the opposite direction, barely avoiding Rye, who took advantage of poor Beaumont by blowing out his taper as he turned. The Baroness of Stutely, a tall, willowy brunette with a sweet face, managed to elude Beaumont's effort to extinguish her taper, only to come up against Brenna.

Laughing, Brenna quickly blew out the taper, saw the expression of laughing dismay on the baroness's face, then turned again. This time she came up against Rye's broad, inflexible chest.

"I have you now, *chérie*," he said, bending a bit to blow out her candle. But Brenna took in a quick breath and extinguished the taper he held at arm's length. The expression of shock on Rye's face sent her—and Beaumont as well as the rest of the hall—into gales of merriment.

"Well done," Rye said ruefully, grinning at her. He held up his taper for all to see, the thin curl of smoke still rising from the blackened wick. "And to the victors go the spoils."

Still panting and out of breath, Brenna asked with an impish smile, "And what do I win, my lord?"

She looked up at him and saw a quick flare in his eyes that made her breath catch, and wondered if he could tell that she loved him. Aye, she admitted to herself with painful reservation, she did love him, though she wondered if it was not too late. This was her secret, an admission she would make to no one else. Aye, she loved this fierce Norman warlord despite her vows not to, and it frightened her at times.

"You have won," Rye was saying, his smile crooked as he grasped her still-lit taper and held it high, "and you and Beaumont are King and Queen of the Festivities."

"Truly?" Brenna could not hold back a delighted laugh. "Do you hear that, Beaumont? We are to rule the evening's play! What say you, gentle knight, to a game of blindman's buff?"

When the lively game began, with Beaumont and Brenna presiding and naming le Bressan as the first to wear the hood over his eyes, Brenna had time to catch her breath. She was more winded than she wanted to admit, having used quite a bit of energy in the torch dance. Sitting beside Rye's favorite knight on the dais, Brenna happened to catch Rachel's eye as she glanced their way.

On impulse she leaned close to the Norman knight and whispered in his ear, "I feel a bit weary after such play, Sir Beaumont. Do you think Rachel Vernay would mind taking my place on this seat?"

Startled, Raoul flashed her a quick glance and a smile, then nodded. "She could be persuaded, perchance. But you do the honor of asking her, milady, as I would not want to be thought presumptuous."

Within the space of a few minutes, Rachel—blushing —had taken Brenna's place in the high-backed chair on the dais. Brenna moved back against a wall, watching with a fond smile as her maid cast shy glances at the handsome knight sitting beside her.

"Matchmaking, *chérie*?" a deep voice inquired at her side, and Brenna looked up to smile at Rye.

"P'raps. Though I would not have thought of it if they had not thought it first, I think."

Rye cupped her chin in his warm palm and lifted her face to his. "Would you not? Only a blind man could ignore what shines in that maid's eyes when she looks at Raoul."

"Does it displease you?"

He shook his dark head. "Nay, not at all. I am fond of Sir Beaumont and would see him content."

"And you think Rachel would be content?" Brenna asked.

" 'Tis not important what I think." Rye shrugged

when she stared at him in surprise. " 'Tis most important what Rachel thinks."

Smiling, Brenna allowed Rye to pull her into a light embrace. Her heart quickened at his proximity, the strength of his sturdy body beneath her hands, the spark of interest she recognized in his eyes. There were times when she felt a sense of chagrin that she held such tender emotions for a Norman, and times when she felt a pang of dismay for her rejections of him in the past. She had behaved badly, had been the shrew she was named so loudly, yet Rye had persisted. P'raps he had not vowed love, but neither had he been cruel. Shame made her look away from him and say the first thing that came to mind.

"And you, my lord?" she murmured before she could stop the words. "Is it important to you what your wife thinks?"

He seemed surprised. "Aye, sweeting. If you are not of a like mind concerning the two, why have you gone to such lengths?"

"I did not mean Rachel and Raoul," Brenna said quickly, and felt her face flame at his scrutiny. "I spoke of you. I wonder at times if you truly care what thoughts fill my head."

Rye didn't answer for a moment; he gazed at her in the shadow of the wall. They stood some few feet behind the dais where the others sat and were alone in the midst of a crowd. Few paid them any mind as they sought their frolic in the games, free-flowing wine, and platters of sweetmeats being served by harried squires and laboring maids. As the music swirled and laughter pervaded the hall, Rye seemed finally to perceive Brenna's mood.

"Chérie," he said softly, his fingers caressing the tilt of her chin in a lingering touch, "I always care what thoughts fill your mind. Have you not guessed that there is more in my attentions than just your welfare?"

She looked up at him, hardly daring to hope he held her in affection. "Duty, I know, weighs heavily upon you, but I would know, Rye, if you think softly of me because of the babe."

"That, for certain," he replied, then smiled at her quick, downcast look. "But before the babe I felt a tender warmth for you that I cannot deny."

Brenna gave him a searching look, trying to see if he was only teasing her again. At his steady regard she knew he was not.

"I, too, feel warmth toward you," she admitted, "though at times you do not deserve it."

Grinning at her tart amendment, Rye held her hard against his body. "I vow that your words are the closest I shall come to hearing sweet romance from you."

"You haven't exactly impressed me as a lovesick swain, yourself," Brenna pointed out. Snuggling close to him, not caring who saw or remarked upon it, she curled her fingers into the rich velvet of his tunic. She felt the quickened pace of his heart beneath her hand, felt his arms tighten around her.

"P'raps I can impress you more completely in the privacy of our chamber," Rye said in a rough voice that betrayed the passion he felt, and Brenna rubbed her cheek against his chest.

"Do you think so? What would our guests think, my lord, if we took our leave so prematurely?"

"That I wanted to lie abed with the most beautiful woman in all of England," Rye replied with a grin, ignoring Brenna's faint flush. "And they would be correct in that guess. Come, sweeting, we will never be missed."

Laughing, they stole away from the hall like two guilty children, holding hands and running lightly up the wide stone stairs that led to their chamber. Brenna felt a surge of love so strong as to be almost overpowering, and when Rye closed their chamber door and took her into his arms, she wondered why she had delayed so long in loving him.

"There are times," she murmured as he laid her gently on the canopied bed and began to peel away her garments, "that I can act the absolute fool."

Engrossed in the satiny skin revealed with the removal of each layer of clothes, Rye was breathing more heavily than he had while dancing the strenuous torch dance. A faint smile curved the hard line of his mouth when he pulled away the last garment and sat back on his heels, and he looked up at her flushed face at last.

"Aye," he agreed, "you can act almost as big a fool as your husband, *chérie*. Pray that we have learned our lesson well."

His big hands cupped her breasts, grown much larger in the past weeks, with the creamy globes blue-veined and ripe in his palms. He caressed them softly, watching his hands as he did, his breathing growing apace with his movements. Then, stroking downward, he slid his palms over her belly in gentle caresses before touching the red-gold nest of curls below. Brenna squirmed beneath his touch, and her eyes lifted to his face.

"My lord—are you not overdressed for this play?"

Laughing softly, Rye lifted a dark brow. "Do you seek to tempt me, wench?"

"Nay, lord." She smiled at his disappointment. "I seek to do much more than just tempt you. . . ."

With a deft motion she turned and rose to her knees, her hands moving to the gold clasp at his shoulder. She unfastened it, holding his gaze with her eyes, seeing his eyes darken with passion as she pulled away his mantle, then sought to unbuckle the wide leather belt that circled his lean waist.

Grabbing her in a fierce embrace, Rye muttered against the rich, fragrant wealth of her russet hair, "Sweet lady, I think we may yet find that elusive contentment that I've heard can exist between lovers."

"I'm depending on it, Rye de Lyon," Brenna answered, tossing aside his belt and tugging at his tunic. "I assure you, I'm depending on it."

CHAPTER 16

SUMMER LENGTHENED INTO fall, and the harvest came in
with great abundance, promising plenty for the long
winter to come. The depredations of the outlaws had
been long and hard but had done no lasting damage to
the lands of Moorleah. As was the norm, the serfs labored three days for their lord, three for themselves, and
rested on the Sabbath.

The stores at Moorleah were filled nearly to bursting,
and Brenna saw to the placement of the supplies. On
one day of the week peasants were required to bring to
the keep a small portion of their yield, sheaves of corn,
chickens, cakes of beeswax, or in lieu of such, a few
coins. This kept the castle well supplied and provided for
the lean times to come when it would be doled back to
the very folk who brought it.

Grain was ground at Moorleah's gristmill, wine made
in the castle winepress, and bread baked in the castle
ovens, all for a small fee that went into the castle coffers.
Men labored to build stone walls, roads, and new buildings for the abundance of foodstuffs being collected.
The castle even collected from the village fish pond a
certain share of the fish, though a much larger share was

garnered from the sea and fishermen, salted, and kept in huge barrels in the stores.

Rye, as designated by William, kept detailed ledgers of every sheaf of wheat, sow, or lamb, and was responsible for the census of his people. It was a full-time task, and one he was glad to share with his stewards and the priest.

The only custom Rye scorned was the heriot and mortuary by which he was to claim the best beast at a serf's death and allow the rector to claim the second-best.

"Nay," Rye refused. " 'Twill be hard enough to make it through a bitter winter if the family must give up its best to one who has plenty."

Brenna grew even more impressed with Rye's sense of justice as time passed and began to fully realize the nature of the man she'd married. Aye, he was harsh with those who had earned it, and his temper ofttimes was much strained by Brenna's occasional sharpness, but on the whole of it, he was a more tractable knight than he'd been in the past. No longer did Rachel tremble in his presence but saw in her lord a kindness beneath the gruff exterior.

Though Rye retained a certain wariness, and had never said aloud that he loved Brenna, she began to feel that he did. That certainty lent her a serenity she'd never felt before, and for the first time since she was a small child, Brenna radiated contentment.

The only thorn in her newfound happiness was Rye's stepmother, and that dame still sought to prick at Brenna with the few weapons at her disposal.

"You've grown as large as a she-boar," Lady Madelon commented one crisp afternoon when the ladies of the keep sought fresh air atop the castle walls. "How much longer do you think Rye will seek your bed?"

Giving Lady Madelon a startled glance, Brenna glimpsed Raissa's indignant face and the matching anger on Rachel's. The responses of her two friends made her more accepting of Madelon's attempts to prick her, and she shrugged lightly.

"I cannot imagine why you would be interested in where your son sleeps, my lady. Unless, of course, you feel the need to share, however remotely, someone else's happiness?"

"Happiness?" Lady Madelon's face had mottled into an ugly shade of purple, but she did not back down. Waving a painted fan bought in London, she gave a derisive snort. "He only sports for now. I know him, and I know his nature. You are a fool if you think he will not leave your bed as soon as you can no longer serve his needs."

Pushing at a heavy strand of hair escaped from its neat knot on her nape, Brenna searched for a neutral reply to silence Madelon. It was growing more difficult to field the woman's barbs; with her growing belly and more lumbering gait, she felt clumsy and unattractive. Only Rye's ardent attentions at night when he sought her company in bed made her feel better, and she couldn't help a small prick of disquiet at the thought he would soon find her bulky shape repugnant.

"Really, Mother," Raissa put in when Brenna lapsed into silence, "I do not know why you must torment her with your ridiculous notions."

"Ridiculous?" Lady Madelon waved her painted fan of thin shell more vigorously. "I seem to recall another man swearing fidelity even as he sought his pleasure in the bed of a highborn Norman whore."

"At least," Brenna observed with rueful humor, " 'twas not a Saxon who stole his attentions."

Furious, Lady Madelon rounded on Brenna. "Do not think to play the fool with me, Brenna of Marwald! I know your game and recognize your ends."

"Do you?" Brenna's temper, held tightly in check, began to rise sharply. "Then, pray, tell me what I seek to gain by being loyal to my husband. Wealth? Nay, not that, for he willingly sees to my needs. Power? I think not, for as his lady I have more power than I ever wanted. Yea, my lady, I think I have much more than I ever dreamed of having and am well satisfied." She waved an arm to encompass the lands beyond the castle walls, the rolling hills and forests rich with fall hues of red, yellow, and brown. "Moorleah once belonged to my mother, 'tis true, but 'twas never a home to me. Now I find to my amazement and delight that I view this cold stone domicile as more home than I've ever had."

Lady Madelon's voice vibrated with spite. "Yet 'tis not your home, but his, and once you are gone, he will share it with who pleases him."

"You speak easily of 'once I am gone,' but I see no evidence that he wishes me away. Do you know something that I do not?"

Madelon leaned close. "Who says you will survive the birth, little Saxon whore?"

Brenna paled but faced her defiantly. "If you survived giving birth, madam—and we've all heard how delicate you are—then I assure you that a common Saxon wench has a much better chance of mothering her babe."

Laughing cruelly, Madelon shook her head. Malice sparked in her eyes, and she mocked, "Do not equate inner strength with common blood. The two do not mix. You are a common wench, for all that you pretend to nobility. And if you do survive the birth—" She paused, then shrugged. "It will be a miracle, I say."

"You speak as if you wish me gone yourself, milady. Do you intend to suggest it to Rye?"

"Once you birth that brat, my fine Saxon, he will find a way to rid himself of you. William bade him build and hold these lands and sire a son to follow. 'Tis the way of Normans, to ensure the lands stay in their family. Why do you think my husband left his lands to a bastard?" She gave a harsh laugh. " 'Twas not out of fondness, but the need to keep the lands away from those who would take them. Rye but seeks the same end, to keep these lands for his heirs."

"You speak of me," Brenna said with an angry toss of her head, "as if I am but a brood mare. Yet when he wed me, he did not know if I would ever give him a child. Nay, in my anger I swore I would not."

"Yet here you are, just as Rye said you would be, heavy with his child, his heir."

Brenna tried to ignore the tingling of alarm that beat

in her brain and felt Raissa's anxious gaze on her as she shook her head.

"You lie, Lady Madelon, and other than satisfaction at having sown seeds of discontent, I cannot imagine what you hope to gain with your malicious words."

Shrugging, Lady Madelon smoothed the velvet of her gown over her knees and looked out over the walls to where Rye and his men-at-arms trained in the field. Clods of earth churned beneath the great hooves of the destriers as the men made mock battle in the late autumn sun.

"I think," she said into the tense silence that crackled with her hatred, "that you know my reasons but do not wish to see them."

"I only know that you wish to make us both unhappy. I will not allow it," Brenna said in a flat, calm tone that did not, thankfully, betray her inner turmoil.

"Mother," Raissa begged, her voice breaking with her distress, "please do not speak so cruelly! I cannot bear it if you continue, and—"

"Silence," Lady Madelon snapped at her daughter, her dark gaze turning to the slender girl. "You have a new life ahead of you, and when you marry le Bressan, you will leave here for his house. What do you know of what I will have to bear once you are gone?"

Shrinking back, Raissa said in a low tone, "That is not for some time yet, and I did ask that you go with me."

"And what did my noble bastard stepson say?" Madelon demanded harshly. "Shall I tell you? He said that he would not wish to inflict a disruptive scold into the household of the king's vassal, and that he would shut me into a nunnery if I would only agree."

Paling, Raissa whispered, "Nay, he did not say it like that. He only suggested that you would be more content in a quiet, peaceful place where you could spend your days in comfort."

At that Brenna understood the motives behind Lady Madelon's fury and relaxed slightly. It was a dreadful misunderstanding, and when she explained it to Rye, he would ease the dowager's mind, and perhaps her venom.

But Rye, Brenna discovered, had no intention of easing Lady Madelon's mind.

"Nay, she is quite right," he said bluntly, "though I cannot like her habit of eavesdropping."

Brenna looked up from the small garment she was sewing for the coming child, watching Rye in the early-evening light that streamed through the window of their chamber. "But Rye—you would put her aside?"

He met her gaze with a lifted brow. "Defending her, my sweet? I thought there was little love between the two of you."

"There is no affection, that is true, but just to put her away like an unwanted, frayed garment . . ."

"She's made her own choices." The stubborn set of Rye's mouth should have warned Brenna, but when she offered the argument that it would be unkind to shut away the woman who was his father's widow, he growled at her to leave the topic alone.

"Lady Madelon has caused more trouble here than I care to discuss with you, Brenna, and though I appreciate your belated, misguided compassion, I caution you to keep your tongue from matters that do not concern you. This is men's business, not to be meddled in by a woman."

Angry now, Brenna carefully set aside the linen shirt and rose from her chair near the brass brazier. "Men's business, you say? To put aside a woman into a nunnery? Is that what you consider men's business?"

"Leave off, Brenna," Rye muttered, not meeting her eyes as he raked a hand through his thick black hair. It had grown down over his ears again and curled on the nape of his neck in tiny wisps that normally would have beckoned her attention. Now, however, she gazed at him with growing consternation.

Lady Madelon's situation too closely paralleled her own should Rye decide to put her aside. It was common for a wife to flee a brutal husband and take refuge in a convent, even more common for that woman to take the veil to keep from finding herself ordered back to the husband and risk being killed, or allow herself to be put aside. Many a wife had chosen the veil over being murdered, and now Brenna began to wonder if Lady Madelon was paving the way for her own removal.

Doubts assailed her, though she admitted to herself that it was unlikely. Rye treated her with genuine concern and tender care, and she could not be mistaken in that. He was not always sweet-tempered, but neither was she.

"Don't worry," Rye said, seeing her troubled face, "I won't force her to it, only suggest most strongly that she seek her peace in the nunnery of her choice. I've even offered to settle lands and vineyards on the chosen nunnery, or arrange a marriage for her, but she has refused my offers."

"She does seek discord, it is true," Brenna agreed, "but I think banishment a harsh reward."

"Banishment?" Rye gave her an astonished look. "I do not seek to banish her, but to put her where she will not cause more trouble. I know my duty to my father's wife and will not shirk it."

Brenna recognized the growing irritation in his voice and decided to hold her tongue. Nothing would be gained by pricking his temper further, and in truth, she did not know why she defended a woman who only sought to hurt her.

When she quieted, Rye looked at her with a soft smile. "Brenna, I think you have changed more than just in your round form," he teased. "I detect a tenderness in you that was not there when we first met."

"Do you?" she murmured, flashing him a fiery glance that made him grin. "Be certain you do not feel the sting of my tongue when you least expect it."

"Ah, I look forward to the flick of your tongue," he jested, laughing when she flushed. "Still shy, *chérie*? I vow, you are the only woman I've ever known who can be so filled with child, yet so easily embarrassed."

"It's the company of Normans that sets my face afire," Brenna retorted, but her eyes began to gleam with amused lights as Rye chuckled at her display of temper.

"Let me set more than your face afire, my sweet," he said with a meaningful glance at her rounded breasts, and when he pulled her to him, she forgot all about Lady Madelon and her own doubts.

Brenna's newfound contentment was not marred until her brother sought her out one chilly autumn eve, coming to the chamber she shared with Rye.

"Myles," Brenna said with genuine pleasure, trying to heave her bulky form from the chair to stand.

"Nay, please do not rise," Myles begged, eying her with trepidation. "I fear you will harm yourself in the attempt. I came only to bid you farewell for a time, as I must leave Moorleah."

"Leave? But why, Myles? I thought you were in training to Sir de Beaumont as a squire."

"I am." Myles's mobile mouth tightened into a taut line that made his young face look suddenly older and harsh. "I cannot explain but knew that you would worry if you heard of my absence."

Grabbing at his arm, Brenna said with a cautious glance toward the open door, "Is it our kin who draw you away?"

Myles gave her a sharp look. "Why do you ask that?"

"Because I can think of little else that would make you risk your position as knight," Brenna retorted. "You've heard something, haven't you?"

"Aye," he admitted after a moment, and knelt close by her side to speak softly. "They're planning something rash, Brenna, and I must stop them before it's too late."

"Too late? What can our brothers do that will not end in their untimely deaths?"

Raking a spread hand through his silky russet hair, he muttered, "Raise an army and seek to join forces with King Philip of France. You know he would leap at the chance to prick William."

Brenna felt a stab of fear. Still clutching his arm, she said earnestly, "Do not risk yourself by warning them, Myles."

"Warning them?" He stared at her. "I go to stop them, not warn them, Brenna. I do not want their disloyalty to reflect on Lord Lyon; therefore, I want to be far from his demesne when I seek an end to their treachery."

"How did you hear of this?"

Myles gave a start at a noise in the corridor, but when no one came within sight, he whispered, "I saw Rannulf in the village last week. He sought to enlist my aid."

"How?"

His mouth twisted bitterly. "By threatening to expose my part in the raids this past spring if I do not open the castle gates one night to allow them inside."

Brenna felt faint, and the child within her moved in a strong motion that made her clutch her belly. Myles gave an alarmed exclamation, but she shook her head.

"Nay, 'tis just an active babe. Listen to me, Myles, you must tell Rye. . . ."

"Nay!" His face whitened. "I cannot. He trusted me, you see, and I do not wish to admit that I participated in the raids that I find shameful now. It was only a few, and long before I came here, but I am afraid that—Brenna," he said swiftly, grabbing her arm and holding it tightly, "do not betray me to him, swear to me you won't!"

"Nay," she gasped out, "I won't. But please—trust him. He will not deal harshly with you if you tell him the truth of it, Myles."

"I dare not risk it." Myles gave her the look she knew as his most obstinate, and she felt a sinking misgiving that he was risking much more than Rye's displeasure.

"When do you go?" she asked miserably.

"This eve, after the midnight hour."

"But what is your plan? How do you hope to stop them from accomplishing their ends?"

Myles hesitated, then shook his head. "The less you know about it, the less you will fret. Do not believe all that you hear, and do not trust anyone but your most loyal servants. Do you understand what I am telling you?"

A frown creased her brow. "Are there those in this keep who would harm Rye?"

"A man of his prowess and power will always have grim enemies that seek his destruction. Rye de Lyon is capable of dealing with them, but you are a liability he cannot risk." He caught her hand. "Brenna, do not do anything foolish, or you might risk your husband."

"I don't understand. . . ."

"Pray God I'm wrong, but if I'm not—" He paused, then said, "Trust *no* one, do you hear?"

"Yea, I hear, but I do not know whom you mean."

"That's the crux of it—neither do I. I only know that there is someone here who stirs trouble with both hands."

Rising to his feet, Myles looked behind him, then bent and kissed his sister on the forehead. At that moment, with his sword at his side and his young face set in lines of grim determination, he looked much older than the seventeen he'd just turned. Brenna's throat closed with fear for him, and she clung to his hand until he pulled free.

"Fare thee well," she whispered as he stepped to the door and peered out, then turned and blew her an impudent kiss on his fingertips before leaving. She stared at the spot where his mantle had whirled in a splash of bright blue velvet and felt the nameless dread that had once dogged her days steal into the marrow of her bones.

Danger and death stalked her family again, as it had in those days she'd thought gone forever.

CHAPTER 17

"MORE OUTLAWS?" BRENNA repeated, feeling an icy chill grab at her heart. "But Rye—are you certain?"

"How certain does one have to be in the face of burned huts and dead or raped serfs?" he asked bitterly. Donning his mail chausses, he pulled them over his legs and tied them at his waist. He already wore the leather *aketon*, or tunic over a woolen shirt, as well as a padded cap over his head.

Brenna watched with a leaden heart as he accepted the help of his squire into the mail hauberk. Gowain laced it in the back as Rye reached for the coif of chain mail that he wore over his head. Such armor denoted his intention to engage in fierce battle, and she tried not to protest. It was his duty as overlord to keep his people safe, and the depredations of the outlaws were a deliberate flaunting of his authority as well as injurious to those he'd sworn to protect.

"Where do you seek them?" she asked when she knew she could speak without pleading.

"Beyond Haverleigh, to the north." Rye tugged on the conical helmet and lifted up his sword as Gowain buckled on the thick belt that would hold the leather scabbard.

" 'Tis a far distance," Brenna commented, and earned a glance from Rye.

"Aye, it is. But not far enough. It's as if the bandits want me to follow them." He flicked her a glance, then said in a heavy voice, "You know that your brother Myles is gone from Moorleah."

Brenna couldn't meet the steady blue gaze he bent on her but looked away and murmured, "Aye. So I was told."

"Do you know where he went?" he asked sharply, and when she shook her head, he muttered a soft oath.

"Curse it, Brenna, I thought the boy loyal. Beltair has told me—but that is of no matter now."

Stepping close, Brenna put a hand on his mailed arm as he stuck one hand into a heavy leather gauntlet. "Please, Rye, beware of a trap."

"Do you think I haven't thought of that?" he returned shortly. "I have. And you might as well know—I suspect your brothers of being behind these latest assaults."

Brenna nodded. "I suspect the same."

Startled, Rye peered at her closely. The nasal, or strip of metal that guarded the nose from sword cuts, hid his face, but she could see the surprise in his expression.

"Do you? You do not object?"

"Yea, I object." Her chin lifted angrily. "I object to men slaying the innocent and preying on those weaker, just to draw out an enemy. Oh yes, I object most heartily, my lord, and I hope you find them and stop them."

Rye smiled faintly. "You ever astound me, my sweet."

"Why should it surprise you that I do not approve of slaughter?"

"If you will recall, I once chastised you for not having any loyalty, then endured your ire because you did not care for my treatment of your kin. I can never be sure of your temper."

"Be certain of this—" Brenna stepped close, looking up into his brilliant blue eyes. "I will pray every moment for your safe return, my lord, and will light so many candles in the chapel that Father Gutierrez will think the altar on fire."

Chuckling, Rye pulled her to him, jerking off his helmet to kiss her hard. When he lifted his head, his eyes were smoky with passion, and his smile rueful.

" 'Twas not well advised to kiss you so long, my sweet, as I am almost swayed from riding out to do my duty."

"Come back to me safely, and I promise you another kind of ride that has nothing to do with duty," she whispered against his lips.

"In your condition, *chérie*, I fear we must wait a long time for your keeping of that promise." Rye gave a lengthy sigh tinged with regret and set her back from him. Bellowing for Beaumont, he stalked swiftly from the guardroom with Gowain hastening to follow.

Brenna watched from a parapet as the armed soldiers and knights rode out of the keep. Shivering, she paid no attention to the harsh bite of the cold or whip of the wind and continued gazing in the direction the men had gone till only the faint mists could be seen lying on the land.

Few men remained, except for the guard Rye had left to protect the keep in case of attack. Those men were soldiers trained to defense, led by Beltair, the crusty sergeant-at-arms who'd been with Rye for many years. Inside the keep itself, however, the only males to be seen were those young enough to serve as pages. Even the squires were gone with their lord.

The hall felt strangely empty, though there were plenty of servants scurrying about, stirring up the central fire so that smoke rose in thick clouds toward the hole in the high ceiling, carrying platters of food to the lower tables. Dogs quarreled noisily over scraps in the rushes, and Brenna made a mental note to have them set loose in the keep after dusk instead of chained as usual. If Rye was not there, and the keep guarded with a contingent of soldiers, she wanted as much warning as possible should an enemy try to sneak in. She'd not forgotten

Myles's bitter words about their brothers' efforts to sneak into the gates at night.

It was enough of a worry, that she sought out Beltair to tell him of her disquiet.

"I have fought many battles, my lady," the old soldier assured her, "and I know how to defend a keep. Do not worry about your safety. Your lord would not have left you to a man who could not protect you."

There was an implied rebuke in his calm words, and Brenna managed a smile. "I apologize if I have offended you or cast aspersions on your ability, Beltair, but it was made known to me that at one time outlaws planned to sneak through the leper gates by stealthy means."

"I understand, my lady." Beltair's manner was short, but respectful. "I have already set guards in every tower and seen to those possibilities."

"Thank you," Brenna said, "and forgive a nervous woman her fears."

Bowing, Beltair's crusty face eased into a slight smile that softened his harsh countenance. "Your lord would never take a chance with so precious a jewel, Lady Lyon, so do not worry overmuch."

It was much easier to hear his reassurances than it was to heed them, Brenna thought as she went about her daily duties. She was so much slower these days, that it took twice as long as normal to complete the simplest task.

"I rival Rye's destrier in size," Brenna muttered when Rachel had to help her up from a low bench. " 'Tis no wonder he seeks danger instead of our chamber."

Laughing, Rachel held to her arm as she escorted her to the room where the looms were set up. Cloth was being woven on a horizontal loom, and several servants sat on stools, weaving industriously. Their hands flew nimbly at the task, and the soft, muted sweep of the shuttle across the warp filled the chamber. Distaffs and carding devices were set up on the far wall, and the room was in neat order.

"You're doing a splendid job," Brenna approved as a girl glanced up at her shyly. The wool was soft and fine and was producing a superb quality of cloth. Brenna paused to discuss the pattern with her, then moved on.

By the time she'd finished inspecting the material, the smell of shorn wool and the fluff in the air had made her seek a chamber without chaff. She paused to breathe deeply and cast Rachel a rueful glance.

"No one ever told me I would be so uncomfortable with my burden," she commented. "I wonder do I bear a babe with more than the normal legs and arms."

" 'Tis good that the child is lusty, Mistress Martel said. A weak babe could not survive the winter months."

Brenna could not suppress a sudden shiver and glanced up to see Rachel's frown. "A chill," she explained, "from remaining too long on the walls."

Rachel nodded. She, too, had stood on the parapets and watched the men ride away. Her heart had gone with Raoul de Beaumont, though no banns had been posted, nor offer made.

"Shall we sit by the fire in the hall, milady?" Rachel asked, and they made their way down the curved staircase.

Brenna bit back a frustrated groan when she saw Lady Madelon in the hall, seated on a cushioned chair. No one sat close to her, and to withdraw now would seem rude, so she sighed with resignation and moved across the hall.

"Good day, my lady," Brenna murmured as Rachel helped her sit down in a high-backed chair made comfortable with stuffed cushions. "I hope you're faring well."

"Well enough," Lady Madelon answered in a civil tone, but her eyes were sharp as she observed Brenna. "Is it near your time?"

The question, on the surface, was innocent. But as the wedding had been in late March, and it was now October, any babe born now would have been conceived before marriage. Brenna's chin lifted slightly.

"Nay, milady, I still have some time left before the child is due. By the midwife's calculations, it should be born near Christmas."

"Christmas?" Madelon gave her a shrewd glance. "That is over two months away. You're much too large to have that long a time left to you."

"Nonetheless, that is the time the child is due."

Brenna leaned close when Rachel murmured softly to her and nodded her acceptance at her suggestion. When the maid brought a goblet of warm herbal drink for her, Brenna took it gratefully. She shifted uncomfortably in the chair and tried to appear interested in the chess game two soldiers were engaged in at one of the lower tables. With the raw, chilled weather, all sought warmth in the keep.

Even Father Gutierrez, Moorleah's priest, sought warmth and comfort in the hall, his *chauffe-mains* dangling from his side to keep him warm. He had been, these past days of rain and wind, conducting morning mass in the hall so that the ladies would not have to brave the elements. An altar had been set up in a small chamber and draped with cloths.

Brenna found the priest a pleasant companion, witty and filled with amusing anecdotes, and enjoyed his company. She smiled when the priest badgered a soldier with genial humor into playing him at chess, and the two men bent over the board with avid attention. Gutierrez pushed back his heavy cowl and propped his chin on the bridge of his hands as the soldier promptly took his bishop.

Lady Madelon did not seem to find the priest's presence as entertaining and grumbled that he should be tending to his business instead of drinking wine and playing chess.

"You would have a man of God live like a monk who has taken the vow of silence?" Brenna inquired with a shrug. "I do not think him blasphemous."

"Do you not?" A faint smile curved Lady Madelon's mouth as she regarded Brenna. "That is very interesting, milady."

Frowning, Brenna turned away from Lady Madelon's cold eyes and vicious tongue. There were times the woman made her feel threatened, and lately she detected more hatred than usual in her manner. She shivered.

"Cold, milady?" Rachel asked, and offered to take her chair closer to the central fire.

"Nay, I am not that chilled. Do not bother yourself."

Garbed in layers of heavy wool, Brenna wasn't as cold as she might have been otherwise; her only complaint was that her shape made it necessary to sit propped on cushions instead of sitting up properly. She alternately cursed Rye for causing her condition, and missed him.

"If you weren't so slender," Lady Madelon observed in a voice that set Brenna's teeth on edge, "you would be better able to carry children. Your hips are too narrow. If I'd seen you before the wedding, I would have warned Rye about your improbability of carrying a babe to full term."

"Would you?" Brenna asked sweetly. "How kind of you to think of my welfare. I vow, if anyone had been bold enough to speak out and save me from a marriage I detested at the time, I might have kissed her feet."

Smirking, Lady Madelon observed, "Some Saxons have tried to rise above their stations by marriage but must always pay a heavy price in the end."

"Aye," Brenna agreed, wishing she felt well enough to slap that dame's aristocratic face, "but I was fortunate in being chosen by a man who brooks little resistance. To that end I am now well content with my lot. It seems that he was the more farseeing of the two of us, for he once said that I would feel this way."

Sitting back with a jerk of irritation, Lady Madelon snapped, "You rattle like an empty gourd, spewing phrases to his glory that none has ever said. You cannot be foolish enough to think I believe in your devotion."

"Madam, *you* cannot be foolish enough to think I care what you believe," Brenna retorted, goaded beyond endurance into being rude. She'd tried to ease the tension between them in the past weeks, noting Raissa's dismay and Rye's growing annoyance, but devil take the woman, if she would not try the patience of a saint! And

Brenna, for all that she had tried hard to curb her natural temper, was far from saintly.

Leaning forward, Lady Madelon fixed Brenna with a hot glare and said slowly, "One day, my fine lady, you shall regret your haughty words."

"No doubt. I certainly regret a few other things that have been thrust upon me of late." Brenna turned her back to Lady Madelon and beckoned to Rachel. "I would go to my chamber now, Rachel. Please see that the evening meal is as I ordered it."

Never having forgotten Madelon's interference with the cook, Brenna always ensured that the meal was being prepared on time and as she ordered. There had been no more skimpy fare.

By the time Rachel had helped Brenna to her chamber and eased her onto the bed, dusk shrouded the land. Weariness and cold seeped into her very bones as she lay back on the thick feather mattress. The bed cords creaked with her movement, and Brenna couldn't help a laugh.

"I never thought I would be in danger of ruining a bed with my bulk," she observed.

Rachel smiled as she stripped away Brenna's stockings and shoes, then reached to help her out of her overtunic.

"Nay, with Rye gone I need the extra warmth," Brenna murmured. "Besides—I do not feel like going to the trouble of undressing and dressing. I'm certain I shall be roundly chastised for this laziness, but the day has been long."

"No one would chastise you, my lady." Rachel tucked a thick fur pelt around Brenna's feet and legs. "Shall I bring more coals for the brazier, and perhaps move it close to the bed?"

"Aye, that would be nice. If it's this chilly in the autumn, what shall I do this winter?"

"Cuddle up to your husband, and after Christmas, to the babe," Rachel answered promptly.

A faint smile curved Brenna's mouth, and after Rachel left, she closed her eyes and tried to envision the child she carried beneath her heart. Dark hair, and bright blue eyes like brilliant jewels, kept appearing before her, and she hoped their child would bear Rye's coloring. She'd once asked Rachel, did she not think their lord was the most well-favored man in all of England, and then laughed at the maid's expression.

"Except Sir de Beaumont, of course," she'd amended, and Rachel had laughed and nodded.

"Aye, milady, the most well-favored. 'Tis his eyes, I think, that brand him as remarkable."

"Yea," Brenna had murmured. "Even his scar only makes him more attractive. It lends a rakish air that is quite appealing, I think."

This night, as she lay dreaming of him, drifting in and out of light slumber, she eased her fears with memories of his increasingly loving attitude. Would he ever admit to that kind of emotion? she wondered. Or ever feel it? 'Twas one thing to have a softness for her, but quite another to love her as a man should love a woman.

Patience, she scolded herself, *patience.*

One day Rye would love her, and he would tell her so without her ever having to ask. She knew it, and knew that she could then tell him of her own love for him.

CHAPTER 18

THE QUIET OF the night was broken by a shrill yell, and dogs began barking in a chorus of snarls and yaps. Brenna, jerked wide awake, sat up so quickly the babe kicked out in protest.

"Rachel?" she called out, frightened by the sound of more shouts, then the clash of arms. "Rachel!"

"Aye, milady." Rachel scurried toward her from her straw pallet on the floor near the door. With Rye gone the maid had spread her pallet inside the chamber in case her lady needed her in the night. Now she hurried to her side.

"What are those noises?"

"I do not know, but I can see if you—"

"No. Don't leave me. Here, help me up. . . ." Brenna struggled to the side of the bed and swung her legs over the side, taking Rachel's arm to help rise.

By the time she stood on her feet, there was a pounding on her door that made it rattle on its frame. Frightened, she exchanged a quick glance with Rachel, seeing in the light of a hastily lit candle her own fear mirrored in her eyes.

"Open!" bellowed a deep male voice, and Brenna shivered when she failed to recognize it.

"What shall we do?" Rachel wailed, twisting her hands together and glancing about the chamber.

"If there are men this far into the keep," Brenna said calmly, though her legs were shaking and she was trembling from head to foot, "then there is nothing we can do but open the door. See to it, while I ready myself."

Armed with a dagger in her hand and one concealed under the loose material of her sleeve, Brenna waited as Rachel swung open the chamber door. To her relief it was Father Gutierrez, and he strode swiftly into the chamber, glancing about him.

"Lady Brenna, you must hurry," he demanded, "so that I can get you to safety."

"What has happened?" Brenna asked anxiously as she put her hand on his proffered arm. "Who has dared to attack us here?"

"I know not. Come. Quickly," he said impatiently.

Rachel accompanied them, and as they made their way down the dark corridors of the keep to a small doorway that had been built into the corner tower, Brenna heard the unmistakable sounds of battle. Her breath caught as the din of clanging swords and yelling men grew louder.

"This way," Father Gutierrez said, thrusting aside a heavy curtain to pull her through. Torches dimly lit a narrow stairwell that dipped steeply, and Brenna held to his arm as he helped her down the steps.

When they emerged from the keep into the inner bailey, the sight that met her eyes was chilling. Soldiers fought armored men; some of Moorleah's men-at-arms having been surprised on their pallets, they were only half-dressed.

"Who has attacked us?" Brenna asked again, but in the clamor of swinging swords and shouting, the priest did not answer.

She clung to him as they made their way to the chapel near the far wall, and the wind whipped cruelly at her bare legs as she stumbled along. Rachel held her other arm, and when they finally stepped into the safety of the small stone building, Brenna heaved a sigh of relief. Surely those men who attacked them would not violate

God's house. Even among harsh, cruel men, few dared anger the Church and risk God's vengeance.

"Come with me, Lady Brenna," Father Gutierrez said, and pulled her toward the back of the chapel where his own compartments were located. He shoved open a heavy door and thrust her inside. A fire blazed, and Brenna moved toward it gratefully, holding out her hands.

Shadows danced across the tapestried walls, and as she grew warmer, she took notice of the gold and gilt furnishings. It was a rich chamber, decorated with statues of ivory, gold, and bronze. Luxurious furs and embroidered hangings were everywhere, and Brenna marveled that the priest had fared so well.

Wax candles burned instead of tallow, and there were no smelly oil lamps to foul the air. Yea, the priest had done well, indeed.

"My lady," Rachel whispered timidly, "I do not like the feel of this."

Brenna gave her a sharp glance. In her fright and the effort it cost her to hurry in her condition, Brenna had not paid the same attention to detail as her maid had done. Now she saw the reason for Rachel's concern.

Turning slowly, Brenna faced an armed, mailed soldier, who grinned at her insolently.

"Lady Brenna of Marwald and Moorleah, wife of Rye de Lyon?" the man asked boldly, and when she nodded, he strode forward. "I take you as prisoner, my lady, and will treat you with kind attention as long as you do not resist."

Brenna stared at him. His words made little sense to her in her extremity, and she glanced helplessly at Father Gutierrez. The priest lifted his sloping shoulders in a shrug.

"You are prisoner, Lady Lyon, and best go quietly."

It took Brenna a moment to realize that the priest had not offered a protest but, indeed, seemed to know that she was to be taken. Myles's final warning to her came back in a rush, and she remembered his worried expression when he'd told her to trust no one. Perhaps he'd suspected the priest but had not wanted to believe that a man of the cloth would behave so treacherously.

Father Gutierrez observed her from beneath hooded lids with a quiet regard that finally penetrated her stupor. He did not look away, nor seem in the least surprised by what was happening.

Taking a step forward, Brenna looked at him, her amber eyes sparking angrily as he met her gaze. "I see," she said quietly. "This is all a ruse, a trap to take me and hold me as prisoner against my husband's actions. I do not know who is behind it, but I have my suspicions, Father. I do know this"—she stepped so close her hands brushed against the rough wool of his habit—"that the thirty pieces of silver you have no doubt taken for this deed is not enough. Rye will hunt you down, and he will run you through with his sword, priest or no."

Gutierrez took a step back and swallowed heavily. "Do not make idle threats, milady. Your husband is far away from here, and by the time he returns, you will be safely hidden." He pulled a rolled sheet of parchment from his wide sleeve and spread it on a nearby table, bringing a candle close for her to see. "This is a list of demands to be met, and you will make your mark at the bottom."

"I will not." Brenna stood stiffly, barely glancing at the document. She could read fairly well, but the words seemed to be in Latin instead of French or English, and she had never been taught that script.

A soldier she'd not noticed stepped forward at a signal from the priest and took Rachel by the arm. The girl screamed as he tore at the neck of her gown, curling his fingers into the material and tugging it away. Sobbing and fighting, Rachel could not avoid his hands. The man was grinning, obviously enjoying her struggles, and Brenna made a small sound of horror.

"Enough!" she said as the man began to push Rachel on her back, intent upon raping her there in the priest's own chamber. Fury rode Brenna hard, fury and fright, that these men would stop at nothing. "Enough," she choked out. "If you will release my maid, I will sign."

She signed with a flourish and wondered if Rye would know that she had been forced. Surely he would realize the truth.

As the soldier came close and Father Gutierrez began to roll up the parchment, Brenna said softly, "I will see you all hanging from the castle walls before this is done and do not envy you your deaths."

Pivoting on her heel, Brenna had the satisfaction of seeing the priest's face turn pale. He gave a signal with one hand, and the soldier took her by the elbow. Another man came to take Rachel, and they were escorted from the chapel to a gate in the wall just behind it. Hoods were put over their heads, and they stood shivering.

"Milady," Rachel sobbed, clinging blindly to Brenna's arm, "are you all right?"

"Yea, I am well," Brenna said softly, "but I have not felt such rage in my entire life. If I were not encumbered with child, I swear I would slit the gullet of every man who has dared touch us. . . ."

"Silence!" a soldier growled, and lifted Brenna in his arms.

She couldn't help a gasp and felt the hard comfort of a cart beneath her body as he laid her roughly on the straw bed. Blinded by the hood, choking with fear, she felt a thud next to her. More straw was piled atop her, and she felt its gentle, prickly weight with dread. They were to be taken away from Moorleah, and that suspicion was confirmed when the cart jerked into a creaking roll.

Rachel's muffled voice reached her ears. "Are you well, Lady Brenna?"

"Of course. Do not worry. The straw is a nice enough bed. And warm."

Lying cushioned on straw, unable to see, and the noise of the cart so loud it drowned out almost everything, Brenna lay wondering what had brought her to this end. Who meant to harm Rye? That someone did was obvious. She was a pawn—not the first time a woman had been used thusly, but Brenna had never considered that she herself might suffer such a fate.

There was plenty of time to think in the hours that followed her abduction, and her frantic thoughts skipped to her brothers, among them Myles. He would never have allowed this to happen if he knew, so she was certain he had been taken, or at the worst, killed. Myles would have found a way to warn Rye, she knew. She couldn't be that wrong about her own brother.

Crouching in the dirt of a rude hut, Myles listened to his brothers with an impassive expression. No reaction was revealed, none of his thoughts.

"Here," Rannulf said, "the earl rides to hunt down the men we set upon Haverleigh." He scratched in the smooth dirt with the point of a stick. "And here we wait until they are fresh from battle, wounded and weary. Then we set upon them."

"And after that?" Myles asked, lifting his head to gaze at his older brother. "What do we do if we manage to take the Black Lion of Normandy?"

"Use him as barter, of course," Rannulf replied in a voice rich with satisfaction. "We will use hostages just as William does."

"What do we gain?"

A frown creased Rannulf's brow, and he tilted his head to stare at his younger brother for a long moment. "There are times, Myles, when you sound as if you do not approve. Are you with us as you said you were?"

"I swore it, didn't I?" Myles looked at him coolly.

"Yea, you swore, and you gave us vital information. But there are times I doubt your loyalty."

Myles looked round at Rannulf, Corbet, and Ridgely. All looked at him steadily, and he rose from his crouch and drew his sword.

"Let the first man who doubts me test my skill with a blade," he said boldly, "and my steel shall speak for me."

Laughing, Corbet observed, "You are a strutting little cockerel, that's for certain. Your months of training with the Black Lion have made you cocky."

"Nay, brother, they have made me strong." Myles looked at his brothers. "There is one less of us now, with Whitley dead, and we do not need to be quarreling among ourselves."

"He's right," Ridgely said after a moment, lifting a tawny brow. All the brothers bore a strong resemblance, with fair hair worn long in the Saxon mode, and heavy beards on their jaws. They were big men, brawny and thick with muscle. Myles showed the same promise in his slighter frame.

"Aye," Rannulf said slowly, "p'raps he is. If we are to take back that which is ours, we must be united."

They returned their attention to the plans being made and were still engrossed in the details when a commotion sounded outside the hut. Myles jerked to his feet, as did his brothers.

Sticking his head out the door, Rannulf bellowed, "What goes?"

"A messenger," came the reply from one of their men, and Rannulf looked surprised.

"A messenger?" He exchanged quizzical glances with his brothers, who looked equally puzzled. Turning back, he bade the man, "Bring him to us."

The man was brought to the hut, looking nervous without his weapons. He was ringed by several roughly dressed men, the Saxon outlaws who followed Dunstan's sons.

"Who are you, and what do you want?" Rannulf demanded, and the messenger bent a knee.

"I bring you an offer."

"An offer? Of what? Who would make us an offer?"

Drawing in a deep breath, the soldier replied, "We have your sister hostage and would barter with you for her."

Myles growled an oath and took a step forward before his brother put out an arm to stop him.

"Barter for our sister?" Rannulf repeated, and a slow smile curved his mouth. "How did you come by her? And why?"

"Faith," Corbet muttered, "knowing Brenna, they

are anxious to rid themselves of that vile-tempered shrew."

The messenger looked up. "She does have a sharp tongue, it is true. But my master bade me offer her to you in an exchange."

"Exchange?" Rannulf looked interested. "Let us hear more of this. . . ."

Brenna glared at her captor. She was seated in a low wooden chair, with Rachel at her side.

Smiling faintly, the man facing her said, "You are a pawn, milady. Your wishes are of no moment here. You will do as you are bid or suffer the consequences."

"Do you think to escape my husband's wrath, sir? I vow, you will not be so pleased when he comes for me."

"If he can find you." The man shrugged. "England is not so well occupied that your presence here will be marked. It is possible that you will linger here for years without him knowing your location." Shifting position, he moved to a table and poured a goblet of wine, sipping at it as he regarded her over the rim. "Your best option is to placate us, milady."

"By writing a letter that he will see through at once?"

"Nay, by writing a message that will bring him to his knees."

"Why do you think I would do such a thing?" Frustration filled her as she met the man's implacable gaze, and she tried not to let it show on her face.

"Because you have no choice."

The blunt words filled her with cold dread, and she let her gaze shift around the chamber of the small square keep where she'd been taken. Rachel made no sound but sat as stiffly as she, her face strained.

Brenna cleared her throat. "Who are you? I would know who I am dealing with."

"Not that it matters, but I am the Count d'Esteray, of Anjou, now of Hemphill."

"What do you here?" Brenna asked with a frown.

Laughing, the count said, "I seek to increase my lands

and fortune, Lady Lyon. Hemphill is mine by my labors. And I have an old score to settle with your husband."

Brenna regarded him silently, her mind racing as she frantically tried to think of a way out of her situation. If this man was bent on vengeance, it would not matter to him what condition she was in as hostage. Nor would it give him pause to harm Rachel in the process.

"What could my husband have ever done to you?" she asked in her haughtiest tone. "And why would you think he cares about my welfare? I am just a nuisance to him, as you probably are aware. King William forced us into marriage, and there has been no love lost between us."

"Even if that were true," d'Esteray said, gazing at her swollen belly pointedly, "you bear a token of his attention that will surely bring him to me. No man desires that his heir be taken."

Shrugging carelessly, Brenna laughed. "You have been misinformed, sir. Rye de Lyon has said time and time over that he does not care to have half-Saxon brats tagging at his heels. I do not think he will concern himself for long with an unborn child that he did not desire."

An ugly expression creased d'Esteray's face. His hand clenched into a fist, and he swore softly.

"I know that you lie, milady, and I swear to you that I will make you sorry if you continue! Lyon bears you some affection, and he will come for you. When he does . . . when he does, I will cut him to pieces, just as he did my father. Your husband ruined me, milady, taking lands that should have been mine when my father died. Instead he laid claim to them, and William took them from me."

"What lands are those?" Brenna frowned, twisting her hands together when d'Esteray laughed cruelly.

"What lands, milady? Why, Moorleah, of course. . . ."

"You lie," she whispered. "Rye was given those lands by William in reward for his fighting in Anjou."

"Aye, that and the fact that when William came over

to beat Harold, Rye de Lyon was the knight who marshaled the forces that took Marwald, as well as Moorleah. Yea, I can see that you did not know. 'Twas your husband who savaged your lands and leveled your keep, and he would have stayed to settle his claim if not for William's desire to have him fight for him in Normandy."

It made sense. Rye, ever obedient to William's wishes, would have waited for his reward. After all, by then he had inherited his father's lands and would have to see to them before the less important estates going to ruin in England. Brenna felt a pang of betrayal. He'd never told her. He'd never revealed by word or deed that he had been a part of those mail-clad men who had terrorized her early days.

Grief rendered her incapable of speech for a moment, and she heard d'Esteray's bitter words through a haze of pain.

"I will lure Rye de Lyon here to Hemphill and will slay him," the count was saying, striking one fist into his palm. "I have waited overlong for this and planned it too well to fail now. And you are better bait than I had first thought, I am assured, so do not think to sway me."

"Better bait?" Brenna repeated numbly.

"Aye, at first I had planned on taking his sister as the lure, but was persuaded after his marriage that you would suffice much better."

"Persuaded? By whom? Father Gutierrez?"

"Nay, that prelate is only a pawn," d'Esteray said with a scornful laugh. His eyes narrowed thoughtfully, and he kept his gaze on Brenna for a long moment. "Who, milady, do you think hates you enough to see this through? And who is it who bears your husband little affection?"

Rachel made a small, strangled sound, and d'Esteray smiled. "See? Even your simple maid knows."

"Lady Madelon would not be so foolish," Brenna said, but knew even as she said it that Rye's stepmother would not hesitate to do him harm.

Moving to where she sat, d'Esteray reached out to

trail a finger along the curve of Brenna's cheek, laughing when she jerked away.

"Do not be so haughty, my beauty. Once your brat is born and buried, I intend to take you to wife myself. Part of my just due, don't you think?"

"Your just due," Brenna grated, "will be a sword in the belly. And if Rye fails to do it, William will succeed. You are a fool, sir, a dead fool."

"William?" Another laugh erupted from d'Esteray. "Even now your own brothers seek to bring the French king to rout William from England, thus gaining even more land and wealth. Those fools—your brothers are too stupid to know that Philip will not honor his promises to return England to the Saxons, but will put his own mark upon it if he can wrest it from William's iron grip. Aye, with Saxon rising against him here, and his armies beleaguered in Normandy, it will be only a matter of time before William must choose between the land of his birth, and this wet country he took by trickery."

As much as Brenna would have liked to have England in Saxon hands again, her loyalties were torn. Less would she like to have the French king, Philip, as monarch, and even though she felt angry because of Rye's part in the razing of her home, she loved him. She was wed to him, and she had his child beneath her heart. Nay, she would not willingly betray the man she loved.

After several moments of silent thought, she looked up at d'Esteray. Rachel gasped when she said, "So, my lord, how do you wish me to help you snare the man who burned my home and took my lands away?"

A frown creased Rye's brows into a knot, and he slid Beaumont a thoughtful glance.

"Do you not think it strange that these outlaws tarry, Raoul?"

"Aye, seigneur. They linger overlong instead of fleeing like hares from what they have done."

Rye's knees tightened, and his huge destrier moved in

a restless prance to one side. Holding his shield on his left arm, and his lance in his right fist, Rye regarded the men in the field beyond him. They ran, as he'd expected, when confronted with armed soldiers, but they did not flee as they had before into the glens and woods that hid them so well. The outlaws had lingered in a still-burning village until the Normans had ridden almost upon them, then fled to the north across bare fields.

With the fields fallow, it was easy to see their path. Garbed in bright colors for outlaws, they made excellent targets for arrows, Rye thought, and motioned for his master-at-arms to attend him. Within moments the archers had strung their bows and loosed a volley of arrows.

Surprised by this tactic, the outlaws dispersed into the woods at last, and Rye smiled. "They are too obvious, Raoul. We are to follow. See? They make no provision for our pursuit but seem almost to invite it."

Beaumont agreed, adding, "We have used that ploy before too, and if done just right, it works. These men expect us to follow so they can turn on us with more men and cut us to pieces."

"My thoughts exactly. Shall we do as expected?"

Startled, Beaumont blurted, "My lord? Surely you do not mean . . ."

"Nay, I do not mean we are to be cut to pieces. I mean we are to let them think we do not see through their ploy, then turn the tables on them."

Grinning, Beaumont nodded. "I relish the opportunity to feel my blade cut into men who think us fools."

Spurring his destrier, Rye gave the signal to charge, and bracing his lance against his booted foot, he led his men after the straggling outlaws. They caught some of them at the edge of the woods and quickly disposed of them with lance and sword. Rye fought furiously, feeling a certain satisfaction in slaying men who preyed upon the innocent.

Having left soldiers behind to stall a retreat from the enemy, Rye swept a line of men to left and right while he and Beaumont moved down the middle of the open field toward the outlaws caught out in the open. A man turned, deciding to make a stand, and braced his lance against the ground while gripping his sword with his other hand. Rye's lance took him full in the chest before he could do more than offer a single thrust, bearing the man back to the ground. Jerking his lance free, Rye wheeled his mount to meet the swing of a sword, parrying it with his shield, then jabbing his lance again and again.

Drawing his sword, Rye hacked about him without pause, hearing the chaos of battle rage louder and louder as he fought viciously. Even in the chill air, sweat streamed under his helmet, wetting his face and blurring his vision.

It wasn't until the worst of the fray was over that he wiped a hand across his eyes and turned to survey the field. It was littered with bodies, most dead, some dying.

"Beaumont," he said tersely, "strip the dead, tend the wounded. And bring me any man able to talk."

"Aye, milord." Beaumont wheeled his weary mount to see to the earl's orders. By the time he brought Rye three men still able-bodied enough to be questioned, the prisoners knew what was intended. They cast fearful eyes toward the bright fire blazing, and the irons thrust into the flames.

Rye smiled pleasantly. He was bareheaded and leaned upon the hilt of the sword he'd thrust into the ground as he regarded the wary men.

"Are you chilled?" he asked, and swept a hand toward the fire to be certain they saw their possible fates. "I will be glad for you to warm yourselves once you have given me a few answers to things that puzzle me."

One man fell to his knees, ignoring the curses of his fellows. "Milord, pray forgive me!" he choked out. His hands were tied behind him, and his head was bowed. Blood streaked his face and arms, and his garments were tattered and torn.

Looming over him, Rye asked almost gently, "Who leads you?"

The man looked up with glazed eyes. "Leads me?"

Nudging him with a booted foot, Rye's gaze shifted to the fire, then back. "Aye, who leads the men in their raids against the villages?"

There was an instant's hesitation as the prisoner gave a quick glance at the fire, then back at Rye.

Beaumont stepped close, snarling, "Do not be so patient with a brigand like this, my lord. Let me apply the hot iron to his face until he feels more talkative."

The effect of Beaumont's words on the prisoner were immediate. Babbling almost incoherently, the man spouted names and places in an endless stream. Rye had to stop him twice, for speaking too swiftly to follow.

Then, nodding with satisfaction, he exchanged glances with Beaumont. "It seems that the Saxons were too lenient with the outlaws before. Now these men will see William's justice at first hand."

Stepping back, Rye gave the order for the prisoners to be tried by the surviving villagers they had raided, then hanged from the trees as a warning to others.

"If they are not found guilty," Rye said grimly, eyeing the townsfolk clustered within hearing, "I would know why. Mayhap some of the raiders who prey upon this land come from this very town."

It was an oblique warning that none of the villagers missed. As Rye mounted and rode away with most of his force beside him, he saw the soldiers left behind begin to swing hemp ropes from sturdy branches. Before the day passed, the trees were heavy with convicted outlaws left as an example of swift justice.

"They grow ever bolder, milord," Beaumont muttered. "I still think we should just slay them instead of bothering with a trial. It's only a mock trial at any rate, for every man can see that the raiders caught in the act are guilty."

"Therein lies the lesson, Beaumont. Even a guilty man gets a trial, thus proving to one and all his guilt, and he must reflect upon his eventual fate while he hears the evidence against him." Shrugging, Rye nudged his destrier into a faster pace. "Now we will give that same kind of justice to Dunstan's sons. . . ."

The band of knights rode at a fast pace toward the deep woods where they'd been told the outlaws made their camp, pausing only to rest their mounts before riding again. Rye rode at a furious pace, determined to catch the men who ravaged his lands, and his wife's brothers or not, he would show them no mercy when he caught them.

CHAPTER 19

"MILADY?" RACHEL'S VOICE was a soft sob, and Brenna summoned her strength to answer kindly.

"Yes, Rachel, what is it?"

"Do you think . . ." She paused and gulped. "Do you think that we shall be rescued?"

"Of course." Brenna injected more assurance into her voice than she felt, not wishing to be subjected to fits of hysteria when she felt so bad herself. "Do you doubt Rye de Lyon for an instant? I do not. When he discovers that we have been taken, he will hunt down those foul enough to have committed this deed and take us from them without delay."

Brave words, she reflected as Rachel nodded, biting her lower lip and fretting even with Brenna's assurances. But she had to believe her own words or go mad. Rye would find her, would take her away from the madman who believed he could actually take Lyon's wife.

D'Esteray's casual reference to her "born and buried brat" had frightened Brenna almost into incoherence, and it had taken all her willpower to remain calm and pretend an emotion she did not feel. She had lied glibly to d'Esteray, telling him she wanted vengeance for Rye's razing of her childhood home, when she'd only sought to learn what she could.

Unfortunately d'Esteray was more clever than to reveal any plans, merely saying that he was delighted she saw the sense in his intentions. Brenna had forced herself to stay still when the man had stroked her cheek again and said that she might make a dutiful wife after all, though he had heard tales of her temper.

Looking down, Brenna had murmured, "All exaggerated, my lord. 'Twas only my husband's nature that brought out the worst in me."

That had pleased d'Esteray, and he'd spoken of the power he would have once his enemy was in his hands. With the Lady Brenna as his wife, he would have the lands of Moorleah, and whatever King Philip sought to bestow on him in gratitude for his efforts.

Once he'd gone, barring the door on the outside to lock them in, Brenna had turned to Rachel in despair. "D'Esteray is completely mad," she'd said. "He can never hope to accomplish any of those ends."

Poor Rachel was no help at all, Brenna quickly found, and she sought to soothe her while she tried to think of a way out of her predicament. Weary, and with the child she carried kicking energetically, she found thinking a more laborious process than it should have been.

Still, before the night was spent, Brenna had formed a plan of sorts.

Quiet hung heavily in the dense wood. Muted calls of birds warbled from the empty trees, and beneath the feet of man and beast, dead leaves rustled in thin whispers. Here and there came the muffled jangle of bits or spurs, and the creakings of saddle trappings. A horse snorted, and in the back of the line of mounted troops, a man coughed.

"Can we be certain of our direction?" Beaumont grumbled to no one in particular, though his question was directed at Rye.

"Certainty is rare," Rye responded. His destrier

picked carefully over fallen limbs and thick underbrush that straggled across the narrow path, and there was an air of waiting that dogged him with tension.

It was near dusk, and the outlaws' lair should be nigh. His men were weary from the previous skirmish, and some had wounds that left them sore and stiff. Yet he did not dare turn back, knowing that should any have escaped and gone to warn the outlaws, he would lose whatever opportunity he had to take them unawares.

The still air was chill, and breath blew in frosty clouds in front of horses and men, yet Rye pushed on with no hint of pausing for night. It grew dark more quickly in the forest, but when he considered stopping, he caught a faint whiff of smoke.

Reining in his mount, he said softly to Beaumont, "I think we have found our quarry."

As the troops came to a halt behind him, waiting for instruction, a loud bellow rent the air. Men swarmed from trees and hollows, waving swords, and the battle was joined at once. Rye's reactions were swift, as were those of his men, all trained well.

Sword met sword, and lances jabbed with lethal fury as the men closed with one another. Horses screamed, men gave voice to hoarse shouts, and Rye swung around him with his sword. They had been expected, it was apparent, and he gave little thought to the reason as he fought furiously. Behind him Beaumont guarded his back while fighting men bent on reaching the leader, and Rye began to realize that there was more to this assault than on the surface.

Along with the outlaws there were mailed knights, men who fought as ruthlessly as the earl's troops, and it soon became obvious that Rye's men were in danger of being cut to pieces. Marshaling his troops, Rye bellowed orders that kept them from being divided and slaughtered, and Beaumont rode to see that they were passed to the rearguard.

Falling back, offering puny resistance to the attackers yet not giving too much quarter, Rye's men retreated slowly to the edge of the forest. Triumphant, the outlaws and French knights followed, seizing their advantage and giving enthusiastic pursuit. It seemed to be a complete rout, and the assailants savored the coming victory and spoils that would be theirs.

But as the struggling combatants reached the clear edge of land that fringed the forest, and broke into the clearing with clashing swords and shouts, men swept down from behind low hills to join the fray. More mounted men circled in from behind, catching the outlaws in a vise.

Pandemonium broke loose, and Beaumont found it most difficult to keep up with his earl as he fought. Rye was not wont to press inexorably forward in a battle, mowing down his opponents in a straight line as was usual, but instead rode hither and yon, giving his sword and strength where it was most needed. Ofttimes, he saved one of his men from being butchered, and they looked to their lord with eager determination.

When Rye came up against a mounted blond giant clad in light armor and wielding a massive sword about him as if it were no more than a thin willow switch, he knew immediately that this was one of Dunstan's sons. The blond giant bore too great a resemblance to his kin.

"Dunstan's get," he growled, and saw recognition light the giant's eyes.

"Aye! Rannulf, late of Marwald, soon to be lord of the keep you share with my sister," came the taunting reply.

Swinging around with a grin and blood-lust in his eyes, Rannulf lashed out with the sword, opening a shallow gash in Rye's arm as he instinctively shifted away. Grimacing against the pain, Rye thrust forward with his blade, but it was deflected by Rannulf's shield. His sword slid away in a harmless blow. Disengaging so quickly that his opponent had no opportunity to bring up a defense against his return, Rye thrust his sword forward again, this time managing to inflict a wound on Rannulf's exposed leg.

Blood gushed, and with a grunt of pain the blond giant covered himself against further attack with the flat of his blade, deflecting Rye's swift return. Bringing up his sword in a high arc, Rye brought it down in a wicked slash that would have severed Rannulf's arm if he had not brought up his shield just in time.

The force of the blow, though deflected, was enough to wrest the sword away and leave him weaponless, and Brenna's brother fumbled for the mace he carried at his belt, taking advantage of Rye's time-consuming upswing for a death blow. As Rye brought down his sword to smash it through his helm and skull, the heavy metal ball at the end of the chain came up and caught him on the shoulder, delivering a punishing blow that sent him reeling and destroyed his aim.

Plunging and squealing, Rye's destrier reared up with gnashing teeth, was caught by the weight of its unbalanced rider, and fell heavily, hooves thrashing and flailing dangerously. Though wounded, and more than a little stunned by the fall, Rye tried to roll clear, hoping desperately that he could remount. A mailed knight on foot was in dire peril during a battle and easy to ride down and dispatch with sword, lance, or mace.

Stumbling, the destrier managed to rise, but Rye was not able to grasp the pommel of his saddle to remount as he saw the silver glitter of a sword swing above him. He ducked the swing of the sword Rannulf had reclaimed, and pivoted on his feet to bring up the shield attached to his left arm, thrusting up and hard with his blade.

Rannulf's destrier reared, screaming, hooves slashing at him as Rye managed to slice into the beast with a blow that sent the horse to its knees. When Rannulf rolled clear in a single motion and heaved to his feet, he faced Rye in the midst of battle.

The odds were even now, and Rannulf laughed as he began to circle slowly.

"So, my fine earl, you come to slay the bandits and stay to spill your own blood, I see."

Panting, Rye tried to gauge the strengths and weaknesses of his opponent while stalling for time. The first battle had sapped his own strength, and the long ride had not given him rest. He knew that Rannulf was aware of this, as he must be aware of his fate should he fail.

"A scratch does not send me whimpering from the field as it does puny Saxons," Rye returned coolly. He bent his head toward Rannulf's bleeding thigh. "Do I see your blood staining the field also?"

Growling an oath, Rannulf swung his sword at Rye and missed, the effort sending him slightly past. Rye's quick sword flashed up and slipped under Rannulf's shield, barely grazing his ribs as it was deflected by reflexive action.

Obviously this blond giant was unused to a man who was his equal in battle, and slightly disoriented, Rannulf swung around to face Rye again, fury riding his features.

"Bastard earl," he snarled, "you have purchased your fate this day for certain."

"Then come," Rye taunted, "give it to me if you can."

Breathing heavily, Rannulf swung his sword again, lifting it over his head and bringing it down in a glittering arc to cleave head or arm or shoulder. Moving agilely, Rye pivoted away in a graceful motion, turning and swinging his sword to catch Rannulf across the back of his neck. If he had not been so weary, his blade would have cut through the mail and severed the Saxon's head. The sharp edge was not quite aligned, and the mail held its strength so that Rannulf was only slightly cut.

Uttering a hoarse oath, the Saxon staggered forward as the blow sent him reeling, but Rye had foreseen such an event and caught him with a booted foot behind his leg, bringing him crashing down to sprawl his length upon the damp ground. With a swift motion Rye brought the point of his sword to rest against Rannulf's throat, the tip pressing harshly against the mail links protecting him.

"Yield, Rannulf of Marwald," Rye said evenly, "or die."

Glaring his hatred up at Rye, the Saxon's lips drew back over his teeth. "Nay, I will not yield to any man."

Rye felt a wave of reluctant admiration and recognized in this man the same spirit he'd seen in his sister. Brenna bore that bold courage of heart and will and would not have bowed the knee to any man who had not earned her deep respect. That he knew, as fully as he knew that should he lose her respect, he would lose her affection.

Hesitating, Rye stared down at Brenna's brother with an unfamiliar sense of indecision.

Bloody, bruised, and with shallow cuts over his head, shoulders, and torso, Myles of Marwald looked up to see Rye de Lyon leaning on the sword he had pressed to his brother's throat. Though angry with Rannulf, Myles could not stay quietly back and watch him die.

Scrambling to his feet, ducking the swing of a sword and parrying swiftly, Myles shouted, "My lord! Wait, I pray you, Lord Lyon!"

A sinking feeling gripped Myles when Rye's head turned, his blue eyes chilling to ice as he recognized him.

"So, little traitor," he growled, the scar on his face a livid red against the darker skin, "you broke your oath."

Reaching him, Myles dropped to his knees, his sword still in one hand, blood staining the steel. "Nay, lord. Not as you think." He was panting and out of breath, scarce able to lift his head to look up at the earl.

Rye laughed harshly, his sword point still at Rannulf's throat. "At least your brother who is about to die is more honest than you. And honorable. He's not given an oath."

As the battle around them slowed, Rye's men overpowering the outlaws and taking prisoners, Myles knew he had only a few seconds to convince Rye he was telling the truth. His tawny head bowed, and reversing his sword hilt-first, he held it out to Rye.

"Lord, I yield the day. But in truth, I was not fighting against you. I came to learn what I could, and—"

"Save your breath," Rye said with a contemptuous

sneer, and beckoned a man forward to take Myles's sword.

Desperately Myles blurted, "You must listen! Brenna has been taken, and if you don't—"

Rannulf kicked out with one leg, striking Myles on his shin and shouting, "Shut up!" as best he could with the tip of Rye's sword still pricking his throat. The mail kept him from being pierced, but a strong man had only to lean on the hilt until the blade choked the breath from him.

"It's true, lord!" Myles persisted, choking back a moan as his brother's foot slammed into his injured thigh.

Increasing the pressure of the sword he held, Rye snarled at Rannulf to be still before he spitted him, then looked back at Myles.

"You lie, little Saxon. I left Brenna at Moorleah with Beltair as guard. No man could get into that keep without a fight, and Beltair is too wily an old fox to allow that."

"Mayhap you're right, lord, but—no, don't let them take me away until I tell you!" he begged as two men-at-arms came up and dragged him roughly away. Hanging between them, struggling, Myles managed to break free and throw himself back at Rye's feet, clasping the earl's mail-clad legs with desperation. He could see the startled expression on Rye's face and said quickly, "The priest! Gutierrez was meeting with—" Kicking back, he managed to knock away the man-at-arms who reached for him, turning swiftly back and saying, "Curse you, listen to me! Lady Madelon and your priest plotted with d'Esteray to use my brothers to get to you. . . . He has her, my lord! I swear it on my mother's grave, if you will only listen. . . ."

By this time the two men-at-arms had managed to drag Myles back, cuffing him viciously and slamming him to the ground. Rye watched impassively for a moment, then gave a curt order.

"Let him up. I would hear more."

Beneath the point of Rye's sword, Rannulf panted for

breath, snarling as the tip lifted slightly to allow him to breathe, "He's lying, and if you are fool enough to listen, you are fool enough to die."

Rye flicked him a cold glance. "For the moment you are saved, Rannulf. Don't think I won't slit your throat if you annoy me, however."

"Do you think I fear death?"

"Nay," Rye said with a slight smile, "but I think you fear the kind of life I might give you."

The implications were enough to silence Rannulf, and he cast sullen glances at his younger brother as Myles was half dragged, half led to a nearby tree to converse with the earl.

Fully aware of his brother's malevolent stare and Rye's distrusting gaze, Myles tried to get his breathing under control so that he could speak coherently. He ached all over, and the bruises and wounds he'd suffered began to hurt.

"Speak, before you're hanged with the rest," Rye said in a cold voice, and Myles sucked in a deep breath.

"D'Esteray has Brenna and holds her until you yield."

Rye's facial muscles altered slightly, and the men who were near took instinctive steps backward at the look of ferocity he directed toward Myles.

"How do I know," he asked in a soft tone that fooled no one, "that you do not lie?"

Seized with uncontrollable trembling, it took Myles a moment to reply. "You do not. You must trust me— nay, lord! If you kill me now, you may not learn the truth until it's too late. . . ."

Rye had taken a step forward, a dagger in his mailed fist and his arm lifted, but jerked to a halt. "Very well," he said after a long moment had passed, "I'll listen to the rest. But if you lie, Myles, there is nothing that will save you."

Shivering in relief, Myles nodded. "Yea, lord. If you will but listen, I have a plan that might save my sister."

* * *

Brenna, her poniard clutched tightly in her hand, sat stiffly in the high-backed chair and awaited d'Esteray's return. She'd not been searched and had not had to yield either of the small daggers she'd thought to grab the night of her abduction. Rachel carried the other, hidden in the wide sleeve of her kirtle.

"It has been a week, milady," Rachel said softly. "Do you think they'll come?"

It was the same question—couched in different terms, but the same question. Brenna sighed.

"Yea, Rye will come."

The sound of the bar being lifted from outside the door was not comforting. The two women exchanged glances before composing themselves. Brenna held tight to her self-discipline, hoping d'Esteray would not see through her ruse until she was able to turn it against him.

The door swung open, and she glimpsed two men as they entered, one tall and blond, the other the dark d'Esteray.

The man with d'Esteray was her brother. She was at first overjoyed, then stunned into silence as Myles gave her a cold glance and said, "Lord Lyon will be happy to pay well for her, though I don't know why."

Count d'Esteray smiled at Brenna, who sat with widening eyes. "Look, Lord Myles, I don't think the Lady Brenna knew of your defection to the rebels."

"She should have. I tried to tell her often enough." Myles shrugged. "She was fool enough to be swayed by Lyon, but I was more clever. Now the time for vengeance is here, and Lord Lyon thinks I'm with him." Hazel eyes came to rest on Brenna's shocked face. "Rye de Lyon believes me to be bound by my oath, but he discounts the oath I gave to my kin long before."

Brenna felt the beginning of fury escalate. Her mouth tightened, and her eyes began to glow with rage.

"Traitor!" she couldn't keep from snapping, not caring what d'Esteray thought at the moment. Her throat tightened with pain as Myles merely smiled, a thinning of his lips into a curve of indifference.

Laughing, d'Esteray observed, "Why young lordling, your sister does not seem glad to see you."

"Nay," Myles said, "she does not. P'raps 'tis because she knows the reason I'm here."

Stiffening, Brenna wondered wildly how she could have been so wrong before she snapped, "It should be obvious that I care little for the reason! You are cut from the same cloth as the rest of my kin, so I'm not surprised that you have been as treacherous."

"Which leaves you where, Brenna?" Myles shrugged at her furious oath. "You were traitor to your own land, so do not rail at me for the path I have chosen."

Aware of Rachel beside her, shivering with terror and confusion, Brenna drew in a deep, calming breath. Her plan was futile now that she'd allowed d'Esteray to recognize her anger, so she took another path.

"If I must choose, Myles, I will choose a man who has kept all oaths given, or not given them at all. It seems to me that honor belongs to those who live it, not speak of it so lightly."

"Enough," d'Esteray said roughly. "I weary of these interminable discussions. Now that you know your husband is surrounded by those who seek his downfall, my lady, p'raps you will cease your resistance. I have a document for you to sign. Your brother is to deliver it."

Glaring at them both, Brenna shook her head. "Nay, I will not sign."

" 'Tis useless to refuse. Myles has informed me of Rye de Lyon's every move, how many men he has called to arms, and his route to reach here. It seems that he managed to *persuade* your brother Rannulf to divulge the information he needed, so he will be here within the week. I must be ready, and I must have a lever to use against him. You will sign, or I will send him pieces of you."

Brenna shrugged. "If you send one lock of my hair, you will not be able to find a hole deep enough to hide in when he comes for you." Her steady gaze obviously unnerved him, and when d'Esteray muttered a low oath and stepped back, Myles laughed.

"You allow my sister to frighten you, d'Esteray? I vow, I should have stayed with the Lion. He, at least, never feared her pricking words."

Flushing, d'Esteray snarled, "Do you suggest that I kill her?"

Something flickered in Myles's hazel eyes, and he said quietly, "Nay, never that. But I have a better plan than the one you would use."

"Always men have better plans." D'Esteray glared at him. "You've seen her; you know your sister is well, so we shall go to my chamber and hear this 'better plan' you tell of."

Myles nodded and slid Brenna a cool glance. "Aye, and it will work much more quickly than sending messages back and forth."

"We'll see, Lord Myles, we'll see." D'Esteray shot a fierce glance at Brenna. "I would enjoy bringing Lyon low, but do not think me fool enough to trust either of you."

"Trust no one, my lord," Myles said before Brenna could comment. " 'Tis always much safer."

"Yea," Brenna whispered huskily. "You speak the truth."

Myles flushed slightly but ignored his sister, keeping his eyes on d'Esteray as he moved to cup Brenna's chin in his palm.

"She is lovely, Lord Myles," d'Esteray murmured, "and when I take her to wife, I will use her well."

Stiffening, Myles said curtly, "You must see her husband dead first, my lord."

D'Esteray laughed. "Aye, and to that end you will aid me."

Brenna jerked away, striding to the window slit at the far side of the room. Oiled cloth covered it, allowing in a diffused light but no view of the outside. "I cannot think why you would find an advantage in wedding me. After all, I am not a great heiress or well-dowered, and until I was wed to Rye de Lyon, of little consequence at all except as King William saw fit to use me as a pawn." She turned to look at d'Esteray, ignoring her brother.

"I told you—"

"You told me," Brenna interrupted, "that I was the lure to draw your enemy. After that end there is no further use for me." She shrugged. "William will not release my lands to you, and in truth, I have none once my husband is dead. Moorleah was not dowry, but prize."

D'Esteray's face tightened with anger. "You are not so big a fool that you do not know the man who holds lands and power, holds kings in thrall. William has his hands full across the Channel and soon will have his hands full here in England. One small earldom will not save his kingdom for him, nor lose it. If he does happen to be driven back to his duchy in Normandy, then I will be rewarded. If he does not"—d'Esteray shrugged again—"then he will have more to ponder than the loss of Moorleah."

Brenna snarled, "You stupid toad! Does William strike you as a king who fears his vassals and barons? Nay, he does not. Mistrusts them, perhaps, but never fears them. Are you so certain he will not protest the taking of lands he gave as a prize?"

"Not under the right circumstances." Smiling, d'Esteray added, "Philip has long yearned to have William under his heel, and with enough men and arms, I can aid him. William will have to turn like a terrier to every keep that rises against him. Half your Saxon barons are now in France, and they will be only too glad to war against the bastard duke, I assure you."

Forcing a bright smile, Brenna said, "Aye, and I pray that we both survive what will surely befall, my lord."

Startled, d'Esteray, who had been turning back toward Myles, whirled around. "What do you mean?"

With tawny eyes wide in innocence, Brenna said, "Why, only that should my husband's forces fail to find and take me back, thus avenging the insult you have done him, my father's forces will surely join up with the king to seek out the man who has dared take his daughter."

"Dunstan. I had not considered . . ."

"You forgot my father? Oh dear," Brenna said with a

shake of her head, "that was most unwise. He was a powerful baron in his time and, with William's aid, has grown in power again. I understand that he commands more and more vassals as he proves his loyalty and can summon several thousand men to his banner."

"Several thou—" Staring, d'Esteray seemed not to grasp this for a moment. His face paled, and his hands shook with visible tremors as he regarded Brenna through wide eyes. "I have not heard of his newfound favor, my lady."

"Had you not? Someone must have been remiss."

"Aye," he growled, "and I can imagine why. I would never have undertaken a doomed project just for the sake of vengeance alone. I have men who will war for me, and the mercenaries I pay, but—several thousand!" He turned to glare at Myles. "You did not tell me of Dunstan."

Myles shrugged. "My father vacillates, battling his own oath to William with loyalty to his sons. I daresay he will drag his feet in aiding Lyon."

"And your brothers?"

"My brothers bring their force of French knights and outlawed Saxons to your aid. They will come in the cover of night, and we will let them in the postern doors."

Smiling, d'Esteray nodded, swinging his gaze back to Brenna. "You see, my lady? We shall win, after all."

CHAPTER 20

STILL CLUTCHING HER poniard in her hand as if for reassurance, Brenna heard a faint sound at the door. She tensed, peering through the darkness toward Rachel. It had been a week since Myles had come to her chamber, and time had passed with agonizing slowness.

Now, quivering in the dark, she waited.

The scratching sound grew louder, then there was a soft rasp that made her shudder. She felt Rachel's hand grasp her arm, and her grip on the small dagger tightened as the door to their chamber swung slowly open.

A shadowed figure paused in the opening, and as Brenna readied herself for whatever was to come, she heard Myles's familiar voice whisper, "Brenna? Come quickly if you would be safe."

For a moment she remained still. Anger flooded her, mixed with pain that the boy she had trusted betrayed her love. Myles stepped into the room, and the faint light from a torch in the corridor glittered from the blade he held.

"Brenna," he called softly again, insistently, his tone growing sharper. "Do not tarry, or all will be lost. Rye is here for you, but I must take you to him without being seen by d'Esteray. Brenna!"

Loathe to trust him, yet afraid not to, Brenna took a deep breath and tightened her grip on her poniard. If Myles betrayed her again, she would kill him with her own hand.

"Here," she answered softly, and stood, Rachel clinging to her arm.

Searching in the shadows, not daring to light a taper, Myles reached for her. His voice quivered with relief.

"I began to think you would believe my words to that knave. I am glad to see that you do not. Come quickly, and you can—"

"Wait." Brenna's voice stopped him. "How do I know you do not play me false again?"

Impatient, Myles said roughly, "Because I swore to your husband I would bring you safely to him or surrender my own body to the rack. Do you think I would take such risks if I play you false?"

"I do not know what to think." Brenna put a hand on the rise of her belly, then said, "Lead on, brother. If I am to die, it might as well be while trying to escape."

"Sweet Mary, but you make me feel like a churlish knave myself," Myles grumbled. "I'm guilty of trying to persuade pig-headed men to another course, but little else. Come."

Brenna and Rachel followed Myles down dimly lit halls to a small curved flight of stairs. Gripping her tightly by the elbow, Myles helped his sister navigate the steep steps in safety. He seemed to know where he was going, and when they emerged from the keep into the inner bailey, a blast of icy air hit Brenna.

Shivering, she bit her lip to keep her teeth from chattering too loudly as she followed, Rachel in her wake. A current of tension filled the air, and she heard muffled noises and vague rumblings.

"Where are we?" she leaned close to whisper in Myles's ear, and he put a finger to his lips. Motioning her forward with one hand, he led her to a small gate in the curtain walls. The hinges had obviously been well oiled, as it opened without a sound.

Thrusting Brenna through the opening, Myles held

the door wide as someone grabbed her. Fear flooded her, and she began to struggle, opening her mouth to cry out.

"Quiet, *chérie*," a voice growled in her ear, and Brenna felt a wave of relief.

"Rye," she whispered, looking up at his dark, familiar face. Her throat clogged with love for him, and the relief of being in his arms again made her cling to him with both hands. She kissed him wherever she could reach, the bottom of his jaw, the mail coif around his neck, his broad chest. She felt his laughter, and he kissed her quick and hard.

"Wait." Enveloping her in a smothering clasp, he then put her away from him. "There is little time. Do as you're told for once, and make no sound," he said against her ear.

Nodding, Brenna allowed a man to lead her and Rachel away from the walls, stealing through the dark night. She glimpsed a line of men that stretched along the foot of the high walls, blending in with the dark stone and brush to be almost invisible. No man on top of the walls could have seen them, and she realized suddenly what Rye and Myles were about.

By the time she and Rachel were taken safely to the top of a distant rise, Brenna could hear the sounds of battle coming from the keep. Surprised by the entry of the enemy through the postern gate, the men defending d'Esteray's keep fought back as best they could, but it was a losing battle.

Though d'Esteray quartered a thousand soldiers, Rye had brought almost two thousand troops with him, gathering them in only a fortnight and riding hard. The men were ready to take back their overlord's wife from the man who had dared steal her, and no quarter was given.

By daylight Hemphill castle was quiet. Only the muffled groans of the wounded and dying drifted on the chill wind, reaching Brenna's ears as she rode slowly back into the keep at her father's side. Dunstan had been unusually silent, keeping his own counsel when he went to retrieve his daughter from the hill, and she wondered at it.

Finally, as their horses clattered over the wooden drawbridge, Brenna ventured to ask, "Father, are you angry with me? You did say Rye was well, and unharmed."

"Aye, he is well," Dunstan replied shortly.

Brenna frowned. "You joined his army to come for me."

"He is my overlord," Dunstan growled, his hefty body shifting slightly in the saddle as he tried to ease the pain of a wound suffered in the battle.

"And that troubles you? That he is your overlord and you must obey?"

Dunstan flashed her a baffled glare that made Brenna think of a bear she'd once seen fighting a pack of dogs. It had had the same agonized expression, as if not knowing how to keep fighting and not daring to stop.

"Nay, not that. I've come to accept William's hand, if not liking it. I answered the call to arms quickly enough for more than your sake, daughter, though little you may credit it."

Brenna's eyes widened. It began to dawn on her what pained her father, and she looked slowly around.

"My brothers—I have not heard."

"Dead."

"All of them?" Brenna's throat constricted.

"Nay, only Rannulf and Myles still live. Whitley, Corbet, Ridgely—dead."

After a moment Brenna leaned from her mount to say softly, "They made their choices, Father, and would never have been content in a land ruled by a man they hate."

"Nay, they would not." Dunstan stared straight ahead, and Brenna saw his mouth set into a taut line.

She lapsed into silence, feeling grief for her brothers, but sorrowing that it could not have ended differently.

She'd come to terms with the conquerors, and indeed, loved one of them.

"I'm sorry, Father," she whispered finally, and when he turned to her, she saw the need in his expression.

"Aye, child, so am I. I've loved all of you and would not have lost a single one willingly. I thank God your poor mother is not here to grieve with me."

"Mother . . ." Brenna felt sudden surprise. Rarely had her father mentioned her mother, as if afraid she would censor him for it, as she often had, to her remembered shame. Impulsively she put out a hand to touch his bloody sleeve. "You miss her, don't you."

"Aye," Dunstan said with a long sigh. "There has been no other woman to touch my heart since my lovely Clarice. If I could have taken her place in death, I swear I would have done so. She was brave, much braver than most men, and when I found that she was again with child, I begged her to see the midwife rather than risk her own life. She would not, saying that a new life was always precious, and worth the pain it might give to bring it into the world."

Brenna's throat constricted. As if knowing the bend of the discussion, the child inside her womb kicked lustily, and she put a protective hand on the rise of her belly. For the first time she fully understood what her mother must have felt.

"I've wronged you," she said simply, and Dunstan shook his shaggy head.

"Nay, child. You just did not understand until you loved someone yourself. I would never have risked my lovely lady, just as your husband would not risk you. 'Tis the way of life, at times, that it costs us that which is dear."

Dear. Yea, Rye de Lyon was dear to her, and so was the child she carried beneath her heart. She regretted all her hasty words in the past and hoped that she could somehow make them up to him.

Turning to look ahead of her, Brenna's heart leapt when she saw Rye. He stood in the middle of the inner bailey, his head bare, blood streaking his mail and sword arm. Suddenly Brenna was nervous. The past fortnight had been spent earnestly praying for this moment, but now that it was here, she feared her own reaction to him.

Reining in her mount as she reached Rye, Brenna looked down at him and tried to think of a gentle welcome to let him know she cared. Unfortunately, she blurted out the first thing that came to mind.

"It's about time you got here!"

Rye looked startled, his blue eyes widening and his brows lifting; then he grinned.

"Yea, *chérie,* I must agree. I missed you, too."

"Good," she said lamely, flushing at his smiling regard and wishing she'd not been so sharp. "I began to think you might have decided you were well rid of me."

Reaching up, Rye pulled her from her mount and into his arms, not seeming to mind that it took both of them to go around her. Brushing her lips with his, he held her close to his heart, and his voice was rough with emotion when he muttered, "Sweet wife, I have gone through hell to get here in time, and I would not part with you now."

"You've missed me?" she dared ask, looking up at him. "You didn't come just to avenge the insult?"

In answer Rye bent his head and kissed her fiercely, ignoring the grinning men around him, the burning buildings and thick smoke. When he set her back on her feet, Brenna found it hard to breathe normally. Her hands clung to his muscled forearms, digging into the mail as she held him.

Sighing, she laid her cheek against his chest. It wasn't a declaration of love, but it was the closest he'd yet come to letting her see the depth of his feelings for her. Some of the tension in him eased as he held her, and Brenna paid little attention to what went on around her as she stood in the protected circle of his arms.

As Rye set about taking over the captured keep and putting his men in the place of those taken prisoner, Brenna saw Rachel clasped tightly in Raoul de Beaumont's arms. She smiled. Her maid was clinging to the knight with loving determination, and Beaumont seemed pleased to keep her there.

Shifting slightly in Rye's embrace as he gave his master-at-arms directions to chain the prisoners below in the dungeons, Brenna saw her brother Myles propped against a wall. Her breath caught.

"Myles . . ."

Looking down at her, Rye followed her gaze. "He is not badly injured. Go to him, see if you can ease his comfort."

He released her, turning back to his master-at-arms as Brenna moved toward her brother. She lifted her skirts over the littered ground, trying not to notice what some of the splotches were as she made her way to Myles. When she reached him, she knelt at his side.

"Myles? Myles, can you speak?"

His eyelids lifted, and he managed a weak grin. "Aye, but not much. If you want to rail at me, please let it wait until I can shout back."

Her hand curved over his shoulder, and she examined his injuries. He had a broken collarbone that pained him, but his wound was a long, bloody scratch that was not mortal. After she tied a strip of cloth torn from her skirt around his cut, she met his quizzical gaze and cleared her throat.

"I owe you an apology."

Shaking his head and wincing at the pain that movement brought, Myles muttered, "Nay. You were supposed to think I was a traitor, else d'Esteray would not have believed me."

Brenna started. She'd not even thought of the man who had taken her, beyond a relief that he had not killed Rye.

"Where is d'Esteray?"

"Dead, I think, the spawn of Satan." Myles groaned a little and shifted position, drawing up one leg. He looked at his sister. "Your sweet-tempered husband gutted him, so I presume d'Esteray is either dead or dying. With a wound like that, 'twould be more merciful if he were dead, but I cannot help but pray that he still suffers. He caused much trouble for all of us."

Brenna shuddered. She smoothed back a damp strand of Myles's hair, noting the tightness of his features.

"And Rannulf? Where is he?"

Myles looked away, his lips thinning to a taut line that warned her of his distress.

"Rannulf is prisoner." Myles glanced back at her, then added gruffly, "I tried to persuade him to give up his mad quest, but he will not. Now he has no choices left. He will swear an oath of fealty, or he will die."

"Myles, I know you suffer because of their actions, but you should not. You tried to convince them differently, and it is not your will if they choose another path. Rannulf must make his own decisions."

A sad smile flickered on his mouth for a moment, and Myles said, "Aye, but 'tis hard to see a brother suffer, no matter the circumstances."

"I agree." Brenna met his glance steadily. "I thought you had broken your oath, and it grieved me."

Leaning his head back against the wall, Myles closed his eyes. "I came to respect Lord Lyon, though it took me some time to come to his banner," he murmured softly. "When I saw that you could love him, I knew that he must be a man who could command affection from those who served him."

"I?" Brenna was startled. "Who told you that I loved him?"

"No one needed to." Myles opened his eyes, chuckling at the irate expression on her face. " 'Twas plain enough to see, Brenna. The only two dolts in the entire castle who could not see it were you and Lyon. I find myself amazed that you haven't slashed each other to ribbons in the process of figuring it out."

Indignant, Brenna made to rise, but her bulk prevented her from doing so, and she glared at Myles as he beckoned for a man to come to her aid.

"You'd better tell him," Myles advised when the soldier had helped Brenna to her feet and she brushed the dirt from her skirts. "Lyon doesn't seem to be very good at guessing what's staring him in the face."

Pivoting on her heel, Brenna stalked away, hearing her brother's soft laughter behind her. She wasn't certain why she should be so irritated, except that it was vaguely embarrassing to conduct one's private affairs in front of an entire keep full of interested spectators. She'd always tried to keep her most personal emotions to herself, and it galled her that everyone had guessed her deepest feelings.

Everyone, it seemed, except Rye.

Moorleah welcomed back its lord and lady with happy arms, and the hall rang with music and laughter as Raissa provided a welcoming feast. Brenna found it difficult to move quickly now, and her sister by law took over the reins of management without a qualm.

Lady Madelon had fled long before Rye's return, wisely guessing his intentions. She'd taken refuge in a nunnery in France, far from her stepson's reach, or that of William. Her plot had gone far deeper than just ridding herself of a stepson she hated; she'd drawn French nobles into her web, making promises of English spoils as well as what lands in Normandy they could grasp.

Father Gutierrez had gone with Lady Madelon, and a new priest conducted morning mass in the chapel. This priest, Father Rémy, announced the banns for Rachel Vernay and Raoul de Beaumont two Sundays after the seige of Hemphill.

For successfully taking the keep, William had granted it to Rye, who had in turn given Hemphill to Beaumont as his vassal. Now a landed knight and baron, Beaumont had promptly asked for Rachel's hand in marriage, which Rye and Brenna had granted gladly.

Just before Christmas, Rye and Brenna attended the wedding mass of the happy couple. It was cold, and the chapel was filled with people.

Leaning on Rye's arm, Brenna felt an odd heaviness

that settled slowly on her. Her back ached, and she shifted with discomfort.

Rye bent over her, his arm around her waist, his voice soft. "Sweeting, are you all right?"

She gave him a troubled glance, whispering so that she would not distract the priest or nuptials. "There is a dull ache that I cannot ease, but 'tis nothing."

The "nothing" quickly became a pressing ache that shot into a surge of pain, making Brenna gasp aloud. Rye's hand tightened on her arm, and ignoring the stares, he swept her into his embrace and carried her from the chapel.

Clasping her arms around his neck, Brenna buried her face in the angle of his neck and shoulder.

"Do not fear, *chérie*," he said softly against her hair as he held her close, "I will not leave you."

Brenna glanced up at him, love surging in her and making her forget her vow not to speak of it until he did.

"I love you," she whispered, then gave a startled gasp as a pain hit. He tightened his grip, his pace quickening.

By the time they reached the hall, servants had come running. Preparations for the wedding feast were still being made, and Raissa came running behind them.

"It's her time, isn't it," she said matter-of-factly, instructing Rye to carry Brenna to their chamber. "Then go back to the chapel. There is no need of you here. You will only be in the way."

Brenna had to laugh at the mixture of irritation and uncertainty on Rye's face, but he bent swiftly and kissed her on the cheek before straightening. He stood by the bed as Raissa threw off her mantle and began making the necessary preparations, shifting from one foot to the other as he gazed down at Brenna.

"My lord?" she murmured, wondering if he wanted to say something, but when he opened his mouth, Raissa came up and gave him a sharp nudge.

"Begone, brother. Men are never good at this sort of thing, and you are in the way."

Releasing her hand, Rye took a step back and away from the bed, and Brenna gave him an encouraging smile. She had to hold tight to her control until he left, then looked up at Raissa.

"I'm frightened," she whispered, unable to stop the words.

Nodding, Raissa said, "You are only human, Brenna. Most women are frightened, the first time or the fifth. Do not worry. I know what helps ease the pain. We'll be here awhile, so let me make you comfortable."

Rye returned to the hall, but he was not in the mood for happy celebrations. He did his best as the wedding party ⸱returned, but his thoughts strayed again and again to the girl upstairs.

When he'd thought her lost to him, it had near driven him mad with anxiety, but at least he'd had some control of the situation. Now there was nothing he could do. It was in the hands of a higher power than his, and he felt more helpless than he'd ever felt in his life.

Rachel was hard-pressed not to stay with her lady, but when she was convinced that there was plenty of help and Brenna would feel better if she remained with her bridegroom, she returned to the hall. Though she had served Brenna long and well, she now had her duty to her husband, and knew it well.

As the noise in the hall grew louder, and toasts were drunk to Rachel and Beaumont, Rye slipped away. He found himself outside, seeking his master-at-arms for company.

"I heard," Beltair said, his breath blowing a frosty cloud in the chill air. " 'Tis what women are made for, to bear children."

"Aye, and 'tis what kills a great many of them," Rye muttered. He pulled his mantle closer around him, taking the proffered skin of wine Beltair held out. He drank deeply, then gave it back. "Why aren't you inside with the others, celebrating Beaumont's marriage?"

Shrugging, the old man gazed up at the night sky. It was a clear night, and the stars twinkled like pinpoints of light against dark velvet.

"I like the quiet. Too much noise and smoke inside. Out here a man can think about things that are important." He slid Rye a crafty glance. "Do you congratulate yourself, my lord, on your success?"

"My success? You mean Hemphill?"

Shaking his head, Beltair said, "Nay. On taming the Saxon shrew. You once said you would, and you have. Keeping a babe in her belly may help."

Rye scowled. "I have not thought of it."

Smiling at his short reply, Beltair said, "You have certainly shown her who's master. I vow, I've not heard her say you nay in months."

"She still says me nay when the mood strikes her. I've not wed a docile wench, by any means. But I did not want a woman who would cringe and leap to my bidding."

"Did you not?" Beltair looked at him curiously. "I once thought I heard you say—"

"Beltair." Rye turned to face him, staring hard at the old man. "Do you think to lesson me?"

"Aye, my lord. You have said often and long that you will not swallow a woman's independence, yet I see you now justifying doing just that. Does this mean that you've decided independence and rebellion are two different things?"

For a moment Rye just stared at him. Then he smiled. "I think you have made your point."

"Then is it so hard to admit that you love her?"

Startled, Rye glanced at the square keep towering above them. A light shone in the room where Brenna lay in labor with his child, and he realized in that instant that the reason he was full of fear for her was because he loved her too much to lose her. It wasn't pride that kept him bound to her, or honor. It was love.

And he'd not told her. He might never have the chance to tell her if she did not survive the birth of her child.

Without responding to Beltair, Rye pivoted on his heel and strode back to the keep, taking the steps to his chamber two at a time.

CHAPTER 21

"BRENNA." RYE KNELT beside the bed, ignoring Raissa's suggestion that he wait. He smoothed back the damp hair from Brenna's forehead. Her eyes were closed, but at his voice she opened them, long lashes lifting to reveal the soft glow of muted gold.

"Rye," she whispered, her voice weak. A faint smile quivered on her lips, and she summoned enough strength to ask, "Did you see them?"

He nodded. "You are not a woman to do things by half measure, 'tis plain to see. But two sons? I shall need more lands, I can tell you."

Shifting slightly in the bed, Brenna glanced up and beyond Rye to Raissa, and her hand reached out.

Raissa, a babe in each arm, bent and laid them beside their mother. The two infants were wrapped in swaddling clothes so that only pink, wrinkled faces showed. Rye looked at them for a moment, then glanced up at Brenna.

"Well, they are not very lovely, but being males, they don't have to be."

Raissa struck him sharply on the shoulder, and he gave her a frowning glance that made her smile. "Idiot! All babies look thus when they are born. The wrinkles will go away, and their faces will not be so red."

Pulling aside the edge of the clothes, Brenna peered at the infants closely. "They look like their father, don't you think, Raissa?"

Appalled, Rye looked uncertainly at the children when Raissa agreed. He put out a finger to touch the dark hair atop the head of the nearest child, then shrugged.

Brenna was cradling them in loving arms, and her eyes glowed with a contentment that warmed him. Before he knew he was going to say it, Rye said softly, "I love you, *chérie*."

Her eyes widened, then began to fill with tears.

Uncomfortable, slightly embarrassed by his admission, Rye cleared his throat. "I would have told you before, but you never seemed to want to hear it."

"Not want—?" She laughed weakly. " 'Tis true what the midwife once told me. Mistress Maisie said that men meant well ofttimes but were usually too thick-pated to know how to convey their feelings. Nay, Rye," she said when his brow snapped down in a scowl, "don't frown at me so. I did not mean you any dishonor, only that we've both been such thick-pated clods we couldn't see what was in front of us. I love you so much—and have, I think, since that day you dared to drag me in front of my father and declare your intention to wed me—that it's all been muddled in my mind. Forgive me for being an idiot." She smiled. "And I will forgive you for being twice an idiot."

For a moment Rye just stared at her, his eyes smoky with irritation, then he began to grin. "Aye, I should know well enough that you would never make such a declaration easy on a man, sweeting."

Rubbing his huge hands over the small dark head of his newborn son, Rye shifted his gaze back to the infants, then up to Brenna again. "Of all the treasures and prizes I could have won from William, you, *chérie*, are the best. And the most valuable."

"You say that now," Brenna returned, her smile weary

but pleased. "I vow, I heard you sing a different melody only a few months past."

"And you will hear me singing many different melodies in the future, I'm certain. But beneath everything, know that you are the prize that I value most."

Catching her breath, Brenna looked deep into his eyes. In the blue depths she saw all her wishes come true, the things she'd longed for and not even realized, and she put her face up for his kiss, thinking that she was the most fortunate woman in all of England.

EPILOGUE

H OLDING HER NEXT to him, Rye reined the black stallion to a halt at the top of a rise. Spring lay softly on the land, and a warm breeze caressed their faces. He held Brenna in front of him, her slender body cradled in the angle of his arm and chest.

"One day," he murmured against the fragrant mass of her fiery hair, "this will all belong to Brandon."

Snuggling closer, Brenna nodded, taking in the roll of hills green with new grass, and the flowers beginning to bud under hedge and tree. "And Barret shall have the lands that belonged to your father in Normandy."

"If we have more sons," Rye said with a laugh, "I shall have to go to battle again. Of course, there is the small keep to the south. . . ."

"Not Marwald!"

"Nay, love, your brother Myles will inherit that when Dunstan is gone. As Rannulf fled to Normandy and cannot return, Myles is next in line. I am pleased. He will be a good man in a fight should I need him."

Rubbing her nose against the velvet sleeve of his tunic, Brenna said, "Nay, no more war. I fear for you."

" 'Tis my duty, *chérie*," he reminded her. "But I am in no hurry, I promise you that."

Turning against him so that her breasts pressed against his chest and she could put her arm around his neck, Brenna teased, "Did I not hear you tell Beltair that you longed for a good fight again?"

"And did you not give me one scarce a half hour later, when I dared suggest you make arrangements to send our sons to Raissa and Geoffroi when they are old enough? You fair scorched my ears with your curses. I only thought to secure them a place well in advance, but you—"

"I am not ready to send them away yet." Brenna raked a fingertip over the stubble of beard on his strong jaw. "My lord, I have something I must confess. . . ."

Rye groaned. "Not another expenditure, I hope, because our coffers have been strained from the king's recent visit as well as the monies I must—"

"Nay, not that. Not yet, at any rate." Brenna took a deep breath and said softly, "I am with child again."

Rye's arm tightened involuntarily around her. "Again? And how do you feel?"

"Excited. I want a daughter. One with my hair and your sweet nature."

"Thank God. I do not think I could bear a daughter with your sweet nature. . . ." Rye ducked the slap she aimed at him, and keeping the stallion under control with his knees, he managed to dismount, dragging her with him.

"Come, sweeting," he cajoled, pulling her across the field to spread his mantle beneath a wide-limbed oak, "let us rest for a time. Your stallion is not accustomed to the weight of both of us."

"Saladin does better than your mount. At least he has not killed his handler." Brenna allowed him to seat her on his scarlet mantle, knowing what he wanted.

It was a beautiful spring day, and the keep was always too crowded with people for much privacy. This day nurses tended the infants so that she could escape for a time, and she looked forward to her time with Rye. Her heart ached as she looked up at his handsome face, tracing the line of his scar with a tender finger.

Rye's mouth found hers in a hungry kiss, and his arms went around her, hands spreading beneath her hips to hold her hard against him. Gently, trying to curb his impatience and failing, he pulled away her garments, revealing the pale, sweet curves beneath.

He sucked in a sharp breath, his eyes smoky with desire and love. *"Jésu,* but you are more lovely than I had ever thought a woman could be."

Brenna was busily tugging at his tunic and chausses, and when she made a sound of frustration, he laughed and reached down to help her untie the tapes that held them.

Sunlight and shadow dappled their bodies as they lay stretched beneath the tree, and when Rye could bear the waiting no longer, he slid between her willing thighs and entered her slowly. Brenna arched to meet him, her arms around his neck, her mouth clinging to his as she met his hard, driving thrusts eagerly.

"I love you," she said over and over, and his reply mingled with hers and drifted on the soft breeze.

"And I love you, sweet wife. Now and always. . . ."

Dear Readers,

I hope you enjoyed Rye and Brenna's story. I certainly did enjoy writing it. The medieval period has always been a fascinating time for me, and I learned a great deal that I would like to explain a bit further.

In the first place, stone castles were not yet built in England when William came over—a fact that escaped me until doing research for *Lyon's Prize*. Most Saxon forts were called donjons, and built of wood and dirt. The first recorded stone keep was built in 1074 by the bishop of Winchester and was rather crude in appearance. I have, you will note, taken a bit of liberty with history here, assuming that a castle complete with inner and outer bailey and drawbridge could have been built by 1077. This is possible, though I did not find actual evidence to confirm it.

I also found out all sorts of interesting tidbits that I tried to weave into the story, such as the fact that no castles—even in Normandy—had fireplaces. Those didn't come until the twelfth century. Heat was provided by a central fire, and at times by a fire in a brazier in the lord's chamber. Another fact was that soap came in liquid form—and we thought we were so modern!—and that cotton did not reach France until the twelfth century. Linen was the chief material for nobles but was rare, as flax did not grow readily.

No nightwear was worn until it became an innovation in the late fourteenth century—hence the portraits we have of the king and queen naked in bed, wearing only their crowns. Underwear was unheard of, except for the undergarments worn by knights to prevent their rough armor from chafing them too badly. Chemises, as well, were not worn until the fourteenth century, truly an age of enlightenment.

As for marriages, most brides did not even meet their bridegroom until the wedding, unless he was a neighbor. The betrothals were usually formed by parents or guardians, to gain more lands or power, or to unite families. Also, in that time, women were more chattel than helpmate. Men ruled, and they were not always fair and just. It was considered very unmanly to allow one's wife to be impertinent, but I imagine many indulgent husbands did their best to live that down. Certainly love did exist between husbands and wives, despite the arranged marriages.

I tried to make my characters true to the times, keeping in mind that women like Brenna were not very common—though they did, indeed, exist. There are even records of women leading their own armies, defying not only husbands, but kings. I like to think that Brenna of Marwald would be such a woman, if the need arose.

If you would like to let me know if you enjoyed *Lyon's Prize,* please write me at the following:

Virginia Lynn
c/o Bantam Books
666 Fifth Avenue
New York, New York 10103

ABOUT THE AUTHOR

VIRGINIA LYNN has over one million copies of her books in print written under the names Virginia Lynn, Virginia Brown, Emma Harrington, and Virginia Bianchi. Shortly after her writing debut, *Affair de Coeur* hailed this author as "a bright new star on the romance horizon." Since then she has more than lived up to her promise as three of her titles have either won or have been finalists for the *Romantic Times* Reviewer's Choice Award, and she has appeared on *Today* in an interview with Jane Pauley. She currently lives in her native Memphis, Tennessee with her husband, writer Chuck Bianchi.

OFFICIAL PRIZE LIST

GRAND PRIZE: *$25,000.00 CASH!*

FIRST PRIZE: FISHER HOME ENTERTAINMENT CENTER

Including complete integrated audio/video system with 130-watt amplifier, AM/FM stereo tuner, dual cassette deck, CD player, Surround Sound speakers and universal remote control unit.

SECOND PRIZE: TOSHIBA VCR *5 winners!*

Featuring full-function, high-quality 4-Head performance, with 8-event/365-day timer, wireless remote control, and more.

THIRD PRIZE: CONCORD 35MM CAMERA OUTFIT *35 winners!*

Featuring focus-free precision lens, built-in automatic film loading, advance and rewind.

FOURTH PRIZE: BOOK LIGHT *1,000 winners!*

A model of convenience, with a flexible neck that bends in any direction, and a steady clip that holds sure on any surface.

OFFICIAL RULES AND REGULATIONS

FANFARE

On Sale in October
WICKED COMPANY

☐ 29518-7 $5.99/6.99 in Canada
by Ciji Ware

From the award-winning author of ISLAND OF THE SWANS, a rich, engrossing tale set in 18th century London's bawdy Drury Lane. Looking to start a new life after her father is unjustly imprisoned and dies, Sophie McGann takes on the glorious and lurid world of the London theatre world—and the only man she loves.

STILL WATERS

☐ 29272-2 $4.99/5.99 in Canada
by Tami Hoag

In the bestselling tradition of Nora Roberts and Sandra Brown, a sizzling novel of romance and suspense by the author of LUCKY'S LADY. Newsaperwoman Elizabeth Stuart and Sherrif Dane Jantzen risk life and love to salve their wounded hearts... and solve a cruel murder .

THE DREAMTIME LEGACY

☐ 29863-1 $4.99/5.99 in Canada
by Norma Martyn

In the captivating tradition of THE THORN BIRDS—a magnificent, epic novel of Australia and an unforgettable woman who builds a business, a homestead, and a life for her children—alone—until she meets the one man who could tempt her more than freedom.

MORE THAN FRIENDS

☐ 29894-1 $4.50/5.50 in Canada
by BJ James

"For sheer emotional intensity, no one surpasses the marvelously gifted BJ James." --Romantic Times